Wanderlust Seasons: Book One

Vagrant Summer

Written By:

David S. McCrae

Vagrant Summer
Book One of the Wanderlust Seasons Saga
2nd Edition

ISBN – 978-1-7348817-0-7

Published by David S. McCrae via IngramSpark

Acknowledgements

The Almighty, God

My Other Half, Juliana McCrae

My Baby Love, Kaylee Quinn McCrae

Chief Editor Extraordinaire, Kayla M. Ware

Newlywed Bookworm, Anna Foxx

Prose Surgeon, Frank Gori

Enchantress of New Visuals, Skye Kelrose

The Endzeitgeist, Thilo Graf

Cyborg Queen, Jenna Moreci

The Alpha Beta, Amy Lynn Lin

The First Red Marker, Brittany Hadden

Roy "Boltar" Camp

And the OG Crew: Matt Cousin, Allen Osborn, Brielle Fonti, Rebecca Bean, Sarah Karpo, Serdar Yegulalp, Benjamin McCrae, and Joseph Ellis.

It has been a long and wild ride for Wanderlust Seasons. I sincerely thank you all for having a hand in this.

Dedicated to the right choice…

…whatever it may be.

Contents

Prologue - An Excerpt from
One Summer

William took great caution in closing his bedroom window. His escape was clean and quiet. The last thing he needed was for his plans with Lauren to be stymied by any sudden carelessness.

The midnight air was crisp and pure, and the waxing moon illuminated the narrow, wooded path to Lauren's house. Three kilometers was a bit of a hike, but it was nothing he could not handle considering everything he had to look forward to.

Dropping his studies was a relief.

A vacation from his responsibilities was long overdue.

Taking the time away for this long, hard look at Eden was the most important, though. Even better, he would not have to navigate this new mindset alone. Neither would Lauren.

But could the two of them really be so bold as to question the authority governing Eden; the ones who have had the power to give orders, make decisions, and enforce obedience for centuries? William's mind wandered through all of the possible scenarios up until the time he was tapping on Lauren's bedroom window.

With a bounce in her dainty step, Lauren slung her loaded, green backpack over her shoulder. Her broad, bright smile welcomed William. "Right on time!"

"I wouldn't leave you hanging," William replied.

He helped her out of the window with care and stealth, respectful of where his hands may have wandered during his assistance. Once she was out and steady on her feet, she asked him, "So, we really *are* doing this? What's the plan? How are we starting off?"

Patting his pack, William answered, "Let's go somewhere we can organize our thoughts. We both have a lot of questions we need to ask the Fifteen, but let's approach them one at a time. The *real* question is: who should we start with?"

She gave him a playful nudge as they started walking back towards the woods. "You *still* haven't figured it out yet?"

He glanced at her. "Is it an obvious answer?"

"Of course!" she chuckled. "I still have to give the Head of Transportation a piece of my mind!"

"Your dad still upset about the Cease and Desist notice?"

"Of course," Lauren huffed. "The battery-powered bicycle my dad invented could revolutionize travel in Eden. But that government goon took his blueprints and threatened to have him arrested if he pursued the invention any further. It's ridiculous!"

William's arms spread wide. "See, this is exactly what I was talking about! What's the point of having these guys in charge if they're not even going to acknowledge things to advance our society? It doesn't make a lick of sense!"

Lauren took his left hand and pulled it to her side, holding it as they walked. "It can't only be the two of us, either. Beyond you, me, and my dad, there has to be more people in Eden thinking these things. Nobody wants to speak up about it, though. Whether it's fear, acceptance, or both, it's holding us back from progress."

"Should we look for more people to join us?"

She shrugged, grinning. "It couldn't hurt. I think we should wait until sunrise, though. We don't want to wake people up."

He pulled her in and gave her a sweet peck on the side of her forehead. "Literally, no; metaphorically…"

Lauren smirked, a visage of purpose and determination overcoming her gentle features as confidence and power grew within. "Absolutely…"

Episode 1: Final Thoughts of a Lonely Cause

Day 63

I

A couple of months can feel like forever. I was huddled near the dying embers of a lonely campfire, poking the coals with hope for a last bit of flame. I thought about home. In the cool, pre-dawn darkness, I wondered if the comfort of a warm bed was worth the welts and bruises it would come with.

A crackling fizzle pulled me from my thoughts. I lifted my head to find only ashes remained of the fire, along with the lingering scent of char and smoke. "Well, crap..." I muttered to no one. I had no more fuel at the ready, and the sun's now-needed warmth was still hiding away beyond the tree-blocked horizon.

Even though it was the twenty-sixth day of the Fifth month, in the middle of summer, the early hours were unseasonably brisk. My outfit was comfortable in the daylight, but did little to help me against the crisp air. My loose tan trousers had a bunch of extra pockets, but were not insulated; my short-sleeved shirt and vest did not protect my arms. I felt it looked good, but a couple of months on my own made fashionability seem hardly important.

With the fire now dead, my best option was to hide in my shelter and wrap up in my blue fleece blanket. Weary, I took time getting up, half-heartedly pitching handfuls of dirt over the ashes.

The isolation of camping in the dense forests of the Gova

Sector was hardening my heart and wearing down my spirit. Though I had been alone since the beginning of the Revolution, the ambience of Gova's dark woods was maddening. The sweet scent of the forest; the wind wafting through fully-bloomed trees was the only reprieve to the assault on my psyche.

The whispers of leaves rattled the silence and echoed off of the surrounding trees. Looking up at the canopy, I realized why it had been so difficult for me to stay asleep. The wind didn't stop at cutting a chill through me, it made a racket too. I knew I had to leave soon. Considering where to go was better than reflecting on how cold and lonely I felt. I started talking to myself. "It's not too late to go back home, right? I'm not exactly part of this whole thing; I'm only trying to get away for a little while. I'm almost eighteen anyway, so I won't be home much longer all the same..."

Home.

The memories hit me harder than my father. Though both parents knocked me around, his blows always hit hardest. The house was a perpetual ground of hostility for me and my siblings. We all coped differently; it made it hard to relate to them. The atmosphere at home was constantly choking; pun sadly intended. So, when the Revolution came, it made for a good excuse to bail.

In those moments by the dead fire, I wondered if I could have truly considered myself to be among the Causes. Although I left my home at the same time as the thousands of us had planned, my motive was escape; not politics. For me, my escape was a small ember in the fire lit in the hearts of my generation at the time.

A man named Devon was the one who started the fire. He published a novel on the Tome Grid; a love story with deep themes and gripping narrative flow: *One Summer*. Not only was it an entertaining read, it made strong and poignant statements which resonated with the young. The work shed a fresh light on the way the land of Eden was being run. Inspired by the book, we started looking more closely at the world around us, and the very nature of authority. Closer scrutiny led to questions—and questions are the best seeds for revolutionary thought.

The Fifteen always governed Eden in a way to keep the people relatively happy. *One Summer,* however, spun our satisfaction and complacency to look like blissful ignorance. Understanding the book and its messages, many felt like we were made subservient to the Fifteen no matter our role in society. The tight stranglehold the Fifteen maintained through their benevolent demeanors was becoming more and more obvious. We were an underclass and everything was built to maintain their power. As such, we saw the best course of action to escape a life of servitude to the Fifteen was to free ourselves from the normality of our society.

This mindset spread through the population of Eden. As it did, it became easier for the younger generation to feel more adamant to do something about it. Most adults, however, lived in comfort, and comfort is the best water to douse the fires of revolutionary thought.

The first facet of the Fifteen's system to be affected was Interactive Studies. The book's underlying attacks on Eden's schooling structure inspired a sharp decline in people even bothering to sign in to their online classes. There was no way to truly grow and achieve our full potential if we were thrust into a job fresh into adulthood based on little more than numbers and statistics in a computer system. We knew in our hearts we could be better than this. Our generation wanted to be the first to break the mold and have true freedom with our paths to adulthood.

Our desire for change didn't stop there. People all over started asking questions no one had seemed to bother to consider before:

Why are there only three channels on the radio? Why not more? Why do they all have to be controlled by one person?

Why can't the Fifteen create a carriage powered by something other than a horse? They probably have the power and the resources to! After all, our trains are powered by the sun; some of our power grids are powered by water and wind. Surely, a cart with its own kind of push could be much more efficient. Better yet, why not try to create a flying vessel?

Why can't *all* of the ISG courses and aptitude tests be unisex? We understand there are good career fits for both men and women. But what if a man wanted to be a tailor or a homemaker? What if a woman wanted to be a carpenter or a blacksmith? What if a wife wanted to work a job while her husband stays at home with the kids? Can't we have more flexibility over the lives we choose to live?

Why is the rest of our arna taken after we have earned a quota each month? Sure, the amount we are allowed to keep is enough for us to live. And we understand the need for the money taken from us to become Income Graces for those who could not earn enough. Why can't we keep the rest of our own earnings, and figure out a different way to satisfy those who fall short?

These were a few examples of the lengthy list of inquiries presented by the citizens of Eden. As more and more people read *One Summer* and word of its message spread, it finally caught the attention of Eliza. She is the Chief Monitor of the schools and content accessed through the Interactive Network.

Not too long after she discovered it, the book was deleted. With it, any and every topic concerning questions to the Fifteen's system were gone. However, censoring the book to oblivion was a questionable decision for Eliza. If reading *One Summer* raised concerns, seeing it destroyed only added to their validity. It wasn't long before you could hear the whispers: "Devon was onto something if the Fifteen needed to silence his work."

Then one day, I received a strange INMail. A single line of text read: *Dear Reader, Discuss the book! Be a Cause!*

"Be a Cause" was a link to the new discussion forum. I was impressed someone would have been so daring as to create a place to continue on topics defying the Fifteen's structure. I registered, joined, and was given a new title along with all of the other members: "Cause."

Many measures were taken to keep the forum hidden from the eyes of the Fifteen. First, the book's title, *One Summer*, could *never* be posted since a future IN search would lead anybody straight to the forum. Second, since "cause" is a common word, singling the forum out in an IN search would be near-impossible. Last, the existence of the forum was to never be discussed in public. Widespread knowledge of the forum could be fatal to the continuing discussions. Threats of being banned from the forum by administrators and other members were a common sight within the topics; even though we all doubted the need to act on them.

On this new forum, a single user put forth the idea to emulate the actions of the characters in the *One Summer*: "Hatcher." His proposal was to have a considerable mass of people walk out from their work or schooling all at the same time. Hatcher became the mastermind of this plan, and a group of users who modified his initial suggestion became known as "Producers."

Hatcher and the Producers organized a list of rules the Causes would abide by during the days following the Great Walk. These rules included staying in groups only with other Causes and minimizing perpetuating the status quo. But the most important rule of all of them; rule number one: *"This is a peaceful protest. No acts of violence, vandalism, or destruction."*

After the date and time for the Great Walk was set, the last stage of preparations involved finding a way for the Causes to stay in contact with each other. The Causes needed to conserve space for the gear they would carry, and toting a laptop around would be too encumbering. To help, one of the creators of the forum—a girl using the nickname "Black"—assigned Contacts to be the Causes' mobile points of access to all of the online discussions.

Finally, the Great Walk occurred at 11:00 pm, on the twenty-third day of the Third month. Thirteen-thousand teens—

coincidentally, fifteen percent of Eden's free population—ran away from their homes and responsibilities all at the same time. The morning after became known as the first day of the Revolution. Through the coordination and teamwork of the Causes, the Fifteen's system was effectively compromised.

This was an attempt at turning Eden around, a revolution to change the way our government would treat us. Most importantly, it would show the Fifteen it was time for a full-on change. Throughout our history, the Fifteen had found countless ways to help those in power stay there, while at the same time blocking out the average man from having any political influence. This left them to shape Eden as they saw fit with no care for the opinions of the lives their decisions actually affected: commoners.

Yes, it was time for a change.

II

Reminiscing about the launch of the Revolution was enough to get my mind off of home, if only for a mere half-hour. All it took was another glancing thought to my personal motives, and my blood warmed me against the cold yet again. There was no real reason to go back. My heart pounded, my fingernails dug into my palms, and I was now on my feet; not cold anymore. "No reason," I said aloud; the words themselves feeling heavy.

I brushed the dirt from my pants and crawled back into my shelter. The mere thought of even going back home sent my brain scrambling to think of something else. I needed a distraction.

My stomach rumbled in response. Living outdoors had made me leaner. I was hungry so often, sometimes it was easy to forget. It was time to eat something.

I broke into the granola I had brought with me. Eating some would tide me over until the sun came up. Then, I would gather more wood to build a new fire and cook some oatmeal. I was also craving some eggs, but the trees around my campsite were too tall to climb and search for nests.

Moving around was warming me up. I rustled around my backpack to gather the breakfast supplies. The way camping gear was optimized for space was weirdly comforting and provided routine. Fitting a pot, pan, plate, and eating utensils for one person to take up as little space as possible was a godsend, as was the malleable shaping of a bag of oats. Dwelling on these thoughts of things having an exact place and structure brought a sensation of order to the front of my mind.

Since the start of the Revolution, Eden had seen its fair share of disorder and chaos. Things were getting a bit muddled back in civilization, which is what drove me out into the Gova Sector to begin with. Again breathing deep the fragrant woodland air, I basked in this sensation of calm only the natural landscapes of Gova could provide. And being by myself meant the only order I was beholden to was my own.

After having everything ready, it was time to wait for sunrise. While reorganizing the items displaced in my searching, I picked up my coin purse and spilled some of it into my hands, feeling the comfort of the coin weight and shape. This was the money for food and emergencies; mostly food.

182 arna in coin—money I spent the better part of a year scrounging, saving, and filching while father's back was turned. Along with my other supplies, the money was meant to last. You can set the date a revolution starts; but not the date it ends.

As dismal as I make it sound, my gear lent comfort. Surviving like this was going to continue to take self-control and keeping my priorities in mind. Remembering home and the violence there was ample motivation. I put the money away, curled back up under my blanket, and dozed off to my thoughts.

The air still had a chill when I woke. I stretched away the stiffness, thinking about getting my breakfast fire going when I heard the telltale rumble of thunder in the distance. "Damn it!" I mumbled, reaching into my bag.

I pulled out my radio headset and tuned in to the Second Channel Airwave Broadcast for a weather report. From the sound of it, I was going to be stuck until the afternoon. To me, though, staying an entire *day* was more appealing to me than hiking around with wet socks on itchy, waterlogged feet. Staying put was best. I put the radio away. In doing so, my cooking kit caught my eye. Oatmeal was out of the question, so I settled for more granola.

As I waited out the rain, the nagging thoughts of going back home kept trying to peck their way through my resolve to stay away. Under other circumstances, I would have listened to it. If my Revolution was built on optimism and hope, it would have crumbled there in the dark with the rain leaking through the single hole in the roof of my crude shelter. A dose of fear overshadowed by anger at my family was my foundation, though. I was going to stick to my agenda on this, until death if it needed to be.

III

As the weather let up, I struck camp and set out. There were times when I would wander in a random direction and find my way back. I called these explorations "being aimless," but really, I was bored. The time had come for me to check back in with civilization, and leave behind the wet, shady vastness of Gova.

Knowing I was returning to the populated areas of Eden, I paced to a stroll in order to enjoy my surroundings for as long as I could. The summer sun penetrated the parting clouds and brightened the canopy. A few sunbeams breached the treetops, streaking from above to litter the forest floor with spotlight rays. The summer heat absent earlier was in full swing; mixing with the fallen rain, and amplifying the mystic scent of dew-dripping flora.

"Now *this...*" I hooted, sending a few birds scattering from the trees, "…is Shalynn at work!" There was no way I was going to finish my time in nature without sending a call of reverence to the Goddess-Spirit of beauty and growth. After all, I knew She cared for me during my stay.

It had been a little over six-and-a-half centuries since the creation of Eden by the divine hands of Paxus and Shalynn. The Gova Sector was a land dedicated to life, creation, and all things pure and natural. In a way, it was sacred ground to be appreciated and experienced; not like the forbidden lands of the Zica Sector.

According to records, when the God-Spirits created Eden, the Master of Beasts, Mammon, was jealous of Their creation. He tried to conquer it, but the God-Spirits and Their children, Delta and Nydia, repelled him.

Later, Mammon seduced Nydia with a promise of undying love, and to propel her to power greater than that of Paxus. Once Paxus found out about this, He and Shalynn built the wall around Eden; shelling it in a perfect circle of protection. They tasked their son, Delta, to guard all inside. Shalynn guards the east from Mammon and his horde of beasts. Likewise, Paxus protects the west, forbidding his daughter, now the Mistress of Nightmares, from ever setting foot into Eden again.

Their protection did not stop there, though. The land known as the Zica Sector—uninhabited by humans—is the ground known as Eden's second defense. If a beast, demon, or nightmare from the Great Beyond were to enter Eden, the spirits of angels residing in Zica would fight it off to protect Eden. As such, Zica is a treacherous and holy landscape. Anybody who had ever ventured into the Zica Sector never returned. It was common knowledge in Eden to stay out of Zica.

After another reverent nod to the east, I continued forward. Every breath I took was deep and cleansing. The crisp, natural atmosphere energized my spirit. It all took me back to more pleasant memories of my quaint, Doma Sector neighborhood, and the times I would retreat to the nearby woods. This last hike through Gova gave me the push to face civilization again.

Although running into *anybody* out in Gova would have been sufficient to quell what loneliness was left, I was hoping to see a Contact more than another fellow Cause. It had been a whole week since I last posted with one, as well as check any Revolution news. It would at least be a courtesy for me to post and tell everyone I was still alive.

As I gathered and organized my thoughts for my next post, the distant roar of a charging train filled my ears and snapped my attention. I sighed with relief and focused my hearing. For as long as I could remember, I was good at pinning down at least the direction of sound. Anytime I wondered where my father was in the house, I had but to listen for the creaks in the house he would set off with his large frame. Though the sound of the train seemed to echo from all directions at once, I managed to pin it down from my three o'clock. I turned to the right and made haste.

Half an hour later, I was approaching the Southern Gova Station. I doubted the presence of a Contact since Gova was rugged country and not a popular location. Regardless, the station would be a good place to refill my water bag and leave the area.

After filling up, I stepped onto the weather-worn platform for the westbound line. Strands of vines and ivy wrapped around the supports to the structure, and even climbed all the way up the beams and along the roof over the benches. Leaves and acorns littered the wooden floorboards enough to prompt me to scan the area to see if a broom was nearby.

In doing so, I saw a young man sitting on one of the benches. He had the look of a fellow Cause. Heavy gear-laden backpack at his feet and the extra pockets sewn into his pants were practical markers. The contrast of hope in his eyes against a scruffy, rough-looking appearance all but sealed it. He was near my age, not a kid but not fully a man yet either.

The Cause obliviously stripped off his plain red shirt in a fashion lacking modesty; flashing a lean and muscular physique it was clear he took pride in. He gave the dirty shirt a quick smell before wrinkling his nose and shoving it into his backpack. Without urgency, he pulled out a neatly-folded olive green shirt and donned it. The shirt looked fresh as the day it was purchased.

I took a seat on the bench and waited for him to finish. After straightening his clothes and closing his bag, he took notice of me. The two of us nodded to each other. He visually appraised my belongings, then conspicuously caught my eye and said, "The book?" His voice had a cheerful, near-infectious tone.

I addressed him with a smile. "The book." Using this phrase was a way to make sure we were talking to another Cause. The phrase was a code for peace of mind when speaking to strangers.

At last, after a whole week alone, it lifted my heart to hear the sound of another person's voice. The alone time was okay and all, but encountering this young man allowed a chance to get my mind off of the plaguing thoughts of home. We were strangers, ignorant to each-others' situations, aside from our stand as Causes. I was ready to talk about news and events instead of crying siblings and my best hiding places.

He reached his hand to me. "I'm Jonathan. My name is 'Skipstone' on the forums."

I replied in kind, shaking hands. "I'm Dartmouth. 'Brigg' is my username."

"Ah, so you're Brigg, eh?" It was a delighted reaction, as though the forums gave him a good window into seeing the person I was—at least online. "What brings you to Gova?"

"What else other than camping out?"

His lip curled. "More like 'hiding out', right? It's a shame you're not a Contact, no offense."

"None taken; I was thinking the same thing," I smiled. "When you changed shirts I was really hoping it was going to be to white, but I guess we're both out of luck."

"Looks like it." He removed his shirt again and turned it around after noticing he had put it on backwards.

I asked, "Any trouble out there in civilization? Are the police stepping up patrols? What about the Fifteen?"

His face scrunched. "The police and the Fifteen are starting to make this feel like a stalemate. I think people aren't threatened by us since everything's been non-violent."

I leaned deep into the backrest enough to arch my back, giving me a great view of the treetops. "Well, that's how it's been since the beginning."

"Watch out, though. It's been two months since we all walked. The Fifteen may get tired of us soon enough. Vade and her police could make a move any day now," he warned. "Cenia is already preying on our fear of upsetting Paxus and Shalynn."

I remembered a discussion from the Forum, causing a grumble in my throat. "'Defying our creators.' *That* was a fun thread to argue through." I sat up straight to address him, catching the hint of caution through his sharp brown eyes. "Speaking of which, I'm surprised the Fifteen haven't found the Forum yet."

Implications played out on his face as his eyes widened. "Funny it hasn't. Eliza must be losing her touch."

I uncorked my water bag for a drink. "Well, we're still keeping all the right secrets. Keeping the name 'Cause' out of their ears is helping a great deal, too." The water from the station's well was crisp and refreshing.

He nodded in agreement, responding, "I'm sure if they ever hear it, they would dig in and find the forums, giving them a huge advantage."

"Let's pray everything stays calm and easy until the Fifteen know the real demands."

His expression flickered uncertain. "You think they'll listen?"

I took another swig before answering. "I think those are

questions on every Cause's mind: will the Fifteen listen if things get bad enough? How out-of-control do things have to get first?"

"Well, it's not like any 'Causes are suffering badly'," he quoted from the forums.

After a brief pause, I asked him, "When was the last time you saw a Contact?"

"Yesterday, before packing up to come here," he smiled. "Interesting stuff going on."

"Curious. What's up?" I asked.

He quickly leaned toward me, excited to share the news. "Some guy dressed in blue has been running around and playing hero. He's been acting like a guardian angel to the Causes. I heard he ran a distraction to divert police away from a group about to get pinched. Another time, he reminded a crew of Causes to keep it together when an argument got hot. But strangely, he tipped the police to *arrest* another Cause, but only because she was stealing from a convenience store."

My eyes narrowed. "That *is* odd; getting a Cause arrested. But he's also helping us out. I'm not sure how I feel about it, but I guess I'll look out for him."

He nodded. "You're better off with the heads up, yeah."

Before I got a chance to continue, the train pulled in and was ready to take passengers. "Are you getting on?" I asked.

"Oh, no. I got off the last train. I was resting here a bit more before I go 'camping' myself. Gonna go straight to the falls at Shalynn's Canvas."

"Great choice!" I stood to board. "Make sure you bathe before sunset, though. The nights have been cool out here. Take good care and be safe out there."

"Drop me a message next time you see a Contact!"

"You too. Take it easy and travel safe." I said from the still-open door. Since trains exiting the Gova Sector were free of charge, all I had to do was hop on and find a seat.

IV

I eyed an empty booth at the end of the car. Making my way over, I passed a few potential fellow Causes with nods of acknowledgement. When I made it over to the seat, I noticed a young girl sitting across from it. She had the look of a Cause, but she seemed a bit younger than the rest of us.

It was a curious situation and it sparked some kind of protective instinct; perhaps because she was about my youngest sister's age. The girl looked no older than twelve, and was taking a stand in the Revolution by herself. I took the empty seat, as I was intrigued, and intended to find out the girl's story.

The first thing I noticed was how familiar her outfit seemed. She was wearing knee-length denim shorts, a plain white shirt covered by a thin denim jacket, a pink visor, and white sneakers. The combination evoked Lauren, the female love interest from *One Summer.* She was a bit young for the sensual tones of the character, though.

The look on her face was the last thing to catch my eye. I realized in the time I had been sitting across from her, her facial expression remained unchanged. There was a gentle sweetness to her features, but it was being masked by a cold and stoic stare with empty, lifeless blue eyes.

Observing further, I related well to the sullen, troubled expression. I wondered if I would make the same face while dodging my parents or listening to the thumps and cries from the other room. Even though my siblings and I had long since taken our own paths in coping, I could sense in this girl the need for a brother at her side. It made it all the more puzzling for her to be on the train alone. Of course, I was not going to know what she really needed until I got her talking.

I decided to go with the foolproof introduction. "The book?"

The young stranger blinked and twitched, as if my question

yanked her out of a hypnotic trance. She looked up to me and promptly turned her gaze aside with a nod.

"Are you okay?" I asked.

She repeated her motions. This time, though, she did not nod.

There was a long and awkward pause before trying again for a substantial response. "I see you're dressed like Lauren from the book." She did not respond at all.

Now, it was beginning to worry me. A younger girl like her was not safe if she failed to be attentive to her surroundings. Anyone ill-intended could snatch her up and she would never be heard from again. Things were not piecing together. I at least wanted to know what she was doing all by herself. She appeared to be a Cause, which made her an ally—a sister even.

Getting creative, I sat back and with the straightest face and asked her, "What do you do when you're riding your oven down the street and all the wheels fall off your fireplace and you don't have enough scrambled eggs to paint the front porch?"

The girl's eyes narrowed and her eyebrows slowly rose. She then cracked a smile, looked at me, and laughed.

"Much better!" I said with a wide grin.

She apologized, stifling the rest of her giggles. The young girl looked over me and my possessions. "The book, right?"

"Yes, the book." I was glad to finally get a response. "So what was with the long face?"

She was timid. "Well…I have a lot to think about."

"Well," I said, reclining across my seat, "don't go thinking so much you can't see what's going on around you. A cute young girl out on her own needs to watch herself to be safe; especially if she runs into less-reputable people. Not every Cause joined for the Mission."

Through a sweet smile, she asked, "How do I know you're not one of them?"

"Me?" I was unprepared to answer. "Actually, the reason I

wanted to talk to you was because I was wondering if you're alright. You're all by yourself."

She folded her arms with a cocked eye—more playful than it was accusing. "I don't even know your name!"

"You do now. I'm Dartmouth." I extended my hand.

"I'm Mika." Mika gave a dainty handshake.

"'Mika'...it's unique. I like it."

She grinned, taking her hand back. "Yeah, I get that a lot."

My eyes focused out the window, enjoying the sight of the scenery whizzing by as I continued to ask Mika for information. "So, you're a fellow Cause, right?"

"Well, sorta…"

I turned to her again, spotting the uncertain teetering on her face. "How 'sorta'?"

"I'm not really in this for the Mission; not on the forums or anything either." She paused, folding her hands in her lap. I'm out here looking for my father…"

Both my head and shoulders recoiled back. Her reply was far off the mark from what I was expecting. "Your father? He step out on you, or is he missing?"

Mika's lips pursed. "I haven't seen him for a few months. I went home one day and he wasn't there. He left a note, but it didn't say where he was going. It also said he couldn't return home." Her tone was of a story she had repeated one-too-many times. She fought a sob, reaching to her bag for a handkerchief.

I leaned in a bit closer. "You and your father must've been pretty close when he was around, right?"

Her face contorted as though I had asked a stupid question. "I'm his daughter. Of course we were close."

I winced. "I'm sorry. Family togetherness isn't really my thing right now; hasn't been for a while."

She caught me square in the eye. "Your family fights a lot?"

Dismissively swiping my hand, I spared her the harshest of the details. "So to speak; we certainly never get along."

"So you're a Cause to get away from them for a little while?" she asked.

"Actually," I rolled up the left leg of my pants and adjusted my seating to show her the huge scar on the back of my leg. "When you've got things like this to remind you how violent your family can get, staying away comes natural."

Mika gasped at the sight of the mark running from the back of my knee to my ankle. "That looks horrible. What happened?"

I caved; regaling her with some of the softer tales of may various scars.

V

"I see," Mika whispered, blinking away a forming tear.

"That's only the half of it, but you've heard enough." It felt good to say some of it out loud; to share my truth and have a listening ear provide validation. "So you see, I'm not only here for the Mission either. It's like you said: to get away, if only for a little while. Truth is, if I can find a place to settle in all this, I'll never have to go back at all!"

"You're going to abandon your family?"

I closed my eyes and absently traced another scar under my lowest left rib. "I already have." My voice was a touch hoarse.

Mika shied from eye contact, looking out the window. "That's really sad. Won't you get lonely? My Dad always told me even people who want to be alone; they still need somebody. People need each other, or bad things happen..."

I leaned forward enough to where it coaxed her to turn and look to me again. "*Me* being lonely isn't too big of an issue. I've gone the last two months alone, anyway." I sat up again. "For you, however, I'm still curious as to how you're on this train by yourself. Are you with the Causes? Do you have a group?"

She shuffled her feet, looking down to them. "I'm using the Revolution so I can ask for help from Causes. It hasn't helped as much as I thought it would, though."

Mika's forlorn tone felt genuine in its frustration. "What happened? Is it anything I should post on the forum?" I asked.

Her mouth curled down into a noticeable pout. "The people who tried to help me before always wound up feeling like I was holding them back, or I would slow them down if they were trying to avoid police. Then they would give up on me." She let out a sharp grunt. "The last group I was with got me the ticket for this train. Since then, I've been sitting here, thinking about it all."

I could feel my face wrinkling in disgust as my shoulders peaked up in a wide, angry shrug. "Well, that's not fair. What are *they* doing that's so important they can't help you out?"

A thought blitzed through my mind: *Come to think of it, what am I doing right now? Not anything too important, for sure.*

Now understanding Mika's situation, I felt I had the time and capacity to step in. But I could not bring myself to blurt it out yet. It wasn't going to stop me from probing for further details, though. "I have a couple of questions, if I may."

Her eyes and ears perked as she sat up straight. "Yeah?"

I took to my bag, looking for a spare piece of parchment in case I needed to write anything down. "Your father's name?"

Mika's mouth crept open. She then went into pause and shrugged, shaking her head. "I always call him Dad; Daddy."

The answer furrowed my brow in equal confusion and intrigue. "No name? You *never* heard anyone call him by name?"

Her mouth buttoned with her deep thought. "I'm sorry, no. But if I remember, I'll tell you."

It felt unusual, to say the least. Most kids her age would know their father's actual name. Since she was seeking help, though, I believed she would have told me if she knew. I let it go and went to my next question. "Your mother, is she looking for him, too?"

She drew in a breath and huffed. "She died when I was born."

I grimaced, both in apology and disgust with myself. Even with my heart withered towards my own parents, it was not fair to see Mika unable to see her parents at all. "Sorry."

"It's all right. You needed to know, I guess." Mika smiled through the sad thought, sweeping her blonde locks away from her eyes. She adjusted her visor and reclined in her seat as I was. She seemed casual, with an innocent charm shining from her now-relaxed face and lilted speech.

"All right, next question: Do you have anything on hand to help us look for him?"

Mika reached into the front pocket of her dirty pink backpack and pulled out a piece of canvas. She looked at it herself before handing it over to me. "This is him; my dad."

On the canvas was a hand-drawn, black and white picture of a stern-looking man. It was well-drawn, with a definable level of detail. This was a worthwhile piece of help for the search. I could not help but ask her, "Did you draw this yourself?"

Mika smirked and bounced in place as if the illustration was a source of pride. "Yeah, he posed for it the whole time! It took me a week! What do you think?"

Impressed, I chuckled. "I think you're pretty good at drawing people. This will help a lot." I took a deeper look. Though the picture had been drawn with care, there were distinct erasure marks around the ears and the eyes. It seemed she had striven for perfection out of love for him.

In my time observing the picture, it all came together for me. No mother, a missing father, and few trustworthy enough to dedicate to helping her. It sounded like a twisted recipe for disaster if Mika was to go on like this much longer. I felt the need to step in; I had to. If I could not be a good brother at home, at the very least, I could try to be a good brother on the road.

I sat up straight in my seat and met her eyes with mine. "Mika, if you're still up for help finding him, I'd be glad to join you."

"Really?" she peeped. "Do you really mean it?"

I eased forward and lowered my voice. Mika leaned in as well, all ears. "Look, I understand if you decline. It sounds like you've dealt with enough from other Causes. I want to help you find your dad and I can only promise I'll do my best. It's up to you to decide if you want to trust me." I took a beat. "I'm asking because I don't think it's a good idea to leave you to this by yourself."

Mika let the silence hang for a moment. "You know what? I have another way we can look at this."

I chuckled, curious. "What's?"

"You can come with me to help find my dad...This way you won't be lonely and I'll have help. It's a win-win." Her beaming smile punctuated her statement through a screen of naïveté. She relaxed a bit once she stated her almost-transactional proposal. I felt she needed somebody to protect her, she felt I needed company. With such a darling perspective, how could I decline?

"Makes sense," I agreed with a nod.

She let out a giggle. "I knew you'd see it my way."

With another handshake, Mika and I became a team. It was the first time since the beginning of the Revolution I found the need to travel with somebody. I truly felt this girl needed help, protection, and a brother. Maybe there was something to what her father said; maybe I needed to be needed.

I was not alone anymore, I had purpose. It was exciting despite the baggage that comes with looking out for another. I had some doubts, but knew they would be put to rest in due time. I was used to solitude—there was a safety in it. But with this new mission in front of me, it was time to get used to having company.

VI

The train's next stop was the most densely populated sector in all of Eden—the Pata Sector. Pata was an ideal hideout for Causes, as its many hangouts, lounges, inns, and chapels were great places to blend in to avoid the attention of police.

Winding up in Pata was beneficial to our search. It would be easier to find a Contact and any possible information concerning Mika's father. This was a great place to start, and I was excited. Everything about helping Mika felt *right*, and Pata's evening bustle was an encouraging sight.

We arrived in the Pata Sector's Station East. Looking to the sky and seeing how late it was becoming, I asked Mika if it was all right to hold off from hard searching until the next day. Although the train ride had been comfortable, we had spent most of it wide awake in conversation. I also did not want to stay on my feet much longer; feeling like I had walked enough for the day. She seemed understanding of the decision and chose to follow along.

I protectively held her hand as we navigated through Station East. It was best to keep her close and move quickly, since station security was on a vigilant patrol. Glancing around, I took notice of the train station being uncommonly tidy. The musk of dirt tread in from the roads was noticeably absent, and the trash bins were freshly emptied. "Riley must be in town," I commented. "Station staff isn't slacking tonight."

The two of us cut through the crowd and to the station entrance. A carriage being pulled by a burly brown horse crossed right in front of us. I had to tug Mika back a bit to keep her safe. But the distance between was not enough to shield us from the animal's odor.

The usually-firm dirt roads of the Pata Sector's eastern districts were still loamy from the earlier rainfall. Mika and I kept an eye out for soft spots in the road as we navigated. I was once again overcome with the desire to avoid walking in wet socks.

Once we were about fifty meters away from the station, getting into the business district, a sudden firm hand on my shoulder stopped us cold. Before I had the opportunity to react, I heard a woman's voice ask me, "The book?"

I released my breath in relief as I turned to see who had stopped me. "Yes, the book."

A trim, athletic redhead who stood about ten centimeters shorter than me was the source of the sudden halt. The girl appeared to have been injured. Her left wrist was bandaged up, as well as her right ankle, which had dressings up her calf, halfway to the knee.

The young woman looked at Mika with a curious point and raised eyebrow. "She's with the Causes?"

I corrected her. "She's with me, and I'm a Cause. You can take that for what it is. Now if you'll excuse us…" I turned away and made an attempt to continue along, barely giving the girl a second look or any more attention.

"Uh, wait, wait!" she persisted, snatching Mika's other hand.

I felt the tug. "Hey, what's the big idea!?" I contested.

"The big idea is," she scowled, stepping up to me, "You were alone when you got on the train. Now you're taking this young girl with you. Doesn't that seem strange to you; to *either* of you?"

I rolled my eyes, "Not really; people in on the Revolution pair up in groups all the time. How is this any different?"

The girl stammered, twirling her finger in the untucked tail of her red T-shirt. While she stalled, my brain answered the question for me. In my due acceptance of this new mission and purpose, I failed to even consider how we would appear in public. Mika and I knew why we chose to travel together, but our pairing was going to make it easy for a few Causes to get the wrong idea.

I recalled the arguments during the Revolution's planning stages. The women among the Causes were split on as to whether or not they should have participated in the walkout. I, for one, did not see the harm in it since both men and women had roles that contributed to the way the Fifteen's system worked. If the Causes wanted to properly compromise the system, the women had to be involved, too.

Some girls, however, were not buying into the idea at first. They felt it was a better idea to stay safe at home and have the guys handle the campaign. Some others believed putting a bunch of unsupervised teenage boys together with a bunch of unsupervised teenage girls was, in almost every capacity, a terrible idea. This "Slippery Slope" logic—as it was called—was a much more compelling argument in my eyes.

The debates on these topics raged for pages and pages and pages. In the end, the Producers had to step in and remind us: if the Causes were going to emulate the questions fielded and inspired by *One Summer*, then it was vital to have to women alongside us in the walkout. This also encouraged quite a few women on our side to become Contacts, rather than be fully-active in the Revolution.

I recalled those times, and some of the debates I threw myself into. While the names of some of my online opponents escaped me, I could not help but remember the name of one girl who word-fought with everything she could type at me.

Everything came together, but I needed to test my theory first. Squinting a curious eye to this young woman, I said, "We're two months into the Revolution and there are *still* some girls concerned about the whole 'slippery slope' thing?"

Her face shifted to bewilderment, easing into an entertained smile. "I'm surprised anyone still cares enough to mention it. That was the best argument I could come up with."

"*Your* best argument? As in…" Her reply had thrown me for a loop. It was easy to get back on track, though, as I recalled more of the names involved in the online debate. Even though many argued over the slippery slope logic, the name of the one who started it all could not be so easily forgotten. "I thought you may have been someone else, but you're 'Kay', aren't you?"

She blinked, staring at me with mild disbelief through her limpid green eyes. It was as if my guessing her identity pulled the next sentence out of her mouth and sucked it down the small storm drain at her feet. "E-excuse me?"

Quieter, to avoid citizens overhearing, I repeated, "You're Kay, from the forums." As she stared at me, now off-guard, I jogged her memory by rattling off some of our heated online run-ins. Although the logic was sound to me, I still rallied for the women to participate in the Revolution; slope be damned.

After I recited a few short episodes, she cut me off, "Okay! I get the idea." She paused for a moment, exhaling with a grunt as she set down her loaded duffel bag. After a mighty sigh, she said, "You must be Brigg. At least, I'm pretty sure. You aren't the only one who gave me a hard time on the forum."

"Looks like we both win at the guessing game," I replied, trying to lighten the air between us. I then gestured toward the young girl. "This is Mika."

She introduced herself formally as we gestured our way into a handshake. "You were right; call me 'Kay'." After a pause, she asked, "So, okay. You're paired up. Where are you going now? Diner? Inn?"

I felt my mouth creak open as my gaze toward her narrowed. *Is this for real? What does she care?* I thought.

Mika answered, her face flickering to hold back a scowl, "Well, we *were* going to look for a place to stay for the night."

Before I could assist Mika's answer, Kay shot in, keeping the growl in her eyes out of her tone. "Actually, last time I saw a Contact, I read about a nice inn around here owned by an old man named Roy. It's cheap, and it's clued. So there's got to be another Contact stationed there."

"Clued, eh?" It sounded a bit too convenient, but it was not a time to be skeptical or picky. Also, since the news of this clued location was posted via Contact, then it was at least worth our time to look into it.

Mika took my hand again and readied herself to go. "Thanks!" she said to Kay as she walked with me. "See you around."

"Uh, hold up!" she called to us. "I'm coming with you!" She slung her bag back over her shoulder and ran to catch up.

Her insisting to come along had me stop short after only a few paces. "What's this all of a sudden?" I asked, turning back to her. "Why do you have to be following us around?"

"Well," she replied, shuffling her feet in place, "if we're all going to go to Roy's anyway, what's the point in having us split up? Don't Causes pair up all the time, like you said? Also, I at least have a rough idea of where the place is. I can help lead you there."

I growled low to myself and shook my head as I saw right through her explanation. To spare Mika any discomfort, I kept my reply to, "I get the feeling there's a more honest answer hidden in there somewhere."

"We'll save my confirming or denying that for later." Her lip lifted in a smug curl.

"Whatever," I scoffed in annoyance.

Mika tugged on my hand. "Don't worry about her. Let's go."

I grunted in discontent as I gave Kay a signal to lead the way. "Ladies first."

Her flowing, red ponytail whipped as she turned and haughtily stepped ahead of us. Reluctant, we followed her.

VII

The busy streets of the eastern business district were a delight to observe as night fell and the street torches were lit. With it being a Saturday night, the cafes and bakeries were staying open a bit later. The aromas of various dishes and desserts were making it pretty difficult to want to keep all 187 of my arna in its place.

I caved soon enough and bought some sweet buns for the

three of us. Although Kay's introduction to our group felt as sudden as it was unwanted, I could not find it in myself to exclude her from enjoying a soft, buttery roll.

After another thirty minutes, though, my patience wore thin. My withered inclination to continue being nice sounded loud in my voice with a high, sneering, sarcastic tone. *"I at least have a rough idea of where the place is. I can help lead you there."*

Kay rewarded my mimicry with a glare, to which I flashed a sardonic grin.

We had been searching for Roy's for over an hour, growing more annoyed with each passing minute. We had a growing sensation this all could have been avoided if Kay had minded her own business.

Some of the blame was on me though; I should have been more persistent in pushing her away from us. "Honestly, I have no idea why I let you lead us into this. Face it; we're lost."

"Oh, come on," she defended. "Would you have even heard of Roy's if I hadn't said anything?"

"Probably," I countered. "We may've even found it by now!"

Mika murmured. "I knew we shoulda left her…" she yawned, "…back at the station."

I released Mika's hand to fetch my water bag as I responded with a grunt. "Not a chance; she was going to follow us anyway. You might not have seen her posts on the forums, but she crashed into things uninvited all the time."

Kay huffed and looked to be on the verge of replying when I continued. "To her credit though, she *does* have a point—we'd be stuck for a safe place to stay if she hadn't told us about Roy's."

A young man with long black hair stopped and turned around after hearing us mention Roy's. "The book?" he asked.

Startled by the sudden change of pace, I answered the gruff youth. "The book."

The Cause wore a baggy pair of dark green pants and a gray

pull-over shirt, a fairly generic Cause outfit. The pocket on his left leg was bulging with small tools. His pack was unique: a brown cloth ring which hung off of his left shoulder and came across his body to rest on the right side of his waist; almost like a sash. I could only think it good for riding a horse or bike.

He took a look at the girls and stroked his thin goatee. His lazy brown eyes casually exchanged gazes between himself and the three of us as he filled us in on his reason for stopping. "You mentioned Roy's, right?"

I nodded. "Right."

An inviting grin glowed. "I'm going back there right now. I'll be getting a room there for the night. Are you lost looking for it?"

I glared at Kay. "Very much so."

The stranger was able to conclude the facts. "I see."

Feeling spiteful, I added, "This woman doesn't know where she's going."

He laughed. "Well, who is 'this woman' and who are you?"

"I'm Brigg from the forums."

His face lit up. "You're Brigg!?" His arms and smile spread wide. "Bro, it's me, Doctrine!"

This was a delightful surprise. I was face to face with an ally from the forums. "Doctrine, wow! Great to meet you in person!"

Doctrine shook my hand as he looked over Kay and Mika again. He curled a sly grin. "Nice there, Brigg. Cute company!"

"Excuse me?" Kay protested.

"Uh," I corrected, pointing to her, "*this* one isn't really with me. She's just following us around. It's our good friend Kay!" I made sure to use a twitch of sarcasm.

His head turned to the side while keeping his eyes fixed on Kay. "Odd. I didn't think I'd see Miss 'Slippery Slope' traveling with a *guy* in her party."

Kay raised a finger and opened her mouth, but was cut off my Mika yawning wide and loud. We saw it as more of a signal than anything else. "Can we go now and talk later? It's getting late..."

"Fair enough," he agreed. "Follow me. I'll take you there."

VIII

Although it was another five blocks, we were fortunate to have somebody with us who actually knew where he was going.

We arrived at Roy's inn in what seemed like no time. The place was a two-story brick structure muttering "squalor" over "hospitable." It was not exactly what you would look at for a comfortable night's rest. The dark, narrow alleyways to both sides of the building did not help much either.

Doctrine explained in a toned-down voice, though loud enough for us to hear over the buzz of the crowded street. "What we have here is a guy looking to capitalize on the Revolution. He opened this inn, and his business hasn't been the best. This is the Pata Sector, though; not Lucra or Fanda. Going 'clued' has helped him boost his sales."

As I glazed over the exterior, Mika drew closer to me as Kay took her other hand.

Doctrine ushered us with his hand as he walked towards the front door. "Trust me; it looks better on the inside. It's only fifteen arna for one night, too."

I sighed as my expectations fell past my comfort zone. "Anything's fine as long as we aren't at risk of being turned in to the authorities. At least it's cheap."

We entered the inn and saw why Doctrine was vague about how much better it looked on the inside. The lobby was dimly lit and the furniture looked a little too close together. It was as if we walked into a stuffy antique shop rather than an inn. The scent of dust was lingering in the air as well, all but sealing the feel. I could see, though, how one would get the "simple and cozy" impression of the place. And it most certainly beat building a shelter in any of the Pata Sector's less-than-fragrant alleyways.

An older man with graying hair stepped up to the counter. "You're back."

Doctrine led in. "Hey, Roy. I hope you still have 'Summer Special' vacancies, because I brought some friends back."

Kay whispered to me, "We barely know this guy."

I needed to calm her before she could say anything to stifle our luck. "I know him well enough from online, so don't complain. It's a cheap, clued room, and we were headed here all the same. I don't know about you, but I feel like getting a shower sometime soon."

Kay smelled her clothes in response then turned a conceding glance to me. Doctrine gave twenty-five arna to Roy. We were given two room keys and pointed to the stairs.

After Roy went back to his office, I said to Doctrine, "I thought you said rooms were only fifteen arna."

Laid-back and proud, he replied, "Fifteen for one person; four more arna for each additional. Roy cut us a break and only charged us twenty-five. We can split it evenly later."

"So you're saying you *used* us for a discount?" Kay grumbled.

"You're just oozing complaints!" I said. "I'm sure you can pay fifteen arna for your *own* room if you like. I'll pay a measly six arna over fifteen any day, or eight if you want to get your own room. Be grateful. Doctrine is even covering the last arna, paying seven."

"It's my way of saying 'thanks'," Doctrine chuckled.

Mika let out another obvious yawn as Doctrine opened to door to the room. Without preamble, Mika dropped her things in a trail and collapsed into the only bed. "Thank you...very much, Mister Doctrine," she mumbled as she nestled under the light brown blanket and decorative throw.

Kay, Doctrine, and I placed our things down and took to situating the room. While we were smiling at how cute Mika was in taking to the bed, we realized there was only enough room on it to fit two people. It would be easier on the second person with Mika's petite frame occupying the other side.

The rest of the room was not exactly spacious, but it had enough room to fit all of us and our property, and for two to sleep on the floor once we got situated. At least it had a nice, clean bathroom with a working shower. The room itself looked like the lobby below—antique and dimly lit. It seemed a lot less stuffy and a little more welcoming though. A small bowl of potpourri on a short, narrow stand did its job of dispelling the scent of dust.

As I took a seat in the leather chair in the corner, Kay threw a set of blankets in my lap. "I found these stashed in the closet."

I unfolded the thick, tan comforter as I caught what Kay was saying to me. "Um."

"Um, nothing!" she sneered. "Mika's already in the bed. So you're out of it."

The two of us went into a stare-down of sorts. In her eyes, I could see she was aiming to gauge my response to her pushy insistence. Knowing the idea of Mika sharing a bed with either me or Doctrine would have played right into her slope logic, I caught myself in time to deflect the bite in her tone. "Sounds like a plan. Looks like you and I were on the same page when Mika beelined it for the bed."

Kay's face hiccupped; her mouth curled. "Glad we have an understanding."

As Kay stepped to her bag, I picked the comforter up and set it aside. In those moments of silence, something in me did not want to let her easily get away with her sassiness. "So Kay, is this how you've been spending your time as a Cause; following other Causes around telling them what to do?"

She paused and turned a shoulder to me. "Yeah, what of it?"

Are you really going to say it? Yeah!

I caught her eye. "No wonder you were by yourself."

Kay piped up, "Oh come on! What's *that* supposed to mean?"

Doctrine stepped out of the bathroom. "Children, children!" he interrupted. We stopped so he could have his say. "Damn, if I had known it was going to be like this, I'd have paid the whole fifteen arna and stayed alone."

I held up my hands in defense. "Hey, I told you she wasn't with me when we met."

"While you do have a point there, I'd like to get a good night's rest regardless." Doctrine turned to Kay. "It's your turn to use the bathroom. Brigg and I will discuss this."

Kay huffed and stormed into the bathroom.

Doctrine turned to me and looked me in the eye. "Honestly, it is what it is. Mika's already in the bed, so I don't mind the floor, either. We're all tired; let Kay do her thing." He stroked his goatee as he recalled the question he had previously asked me. "Oh right, how did you get paired up with her?"

I felt free to go on a red anger tangent speckled with harsh, opinionated commentary. While I managed to fit all of the facts in, it felt good to vent my frustrations of Kay's presence.

"Whoa," Doctrine remarked. "That all happened today?"

"Yeah, all within the last six hours. I picked up Mika, and Kay has been following me since." I turned to Mika, expecting her to say something. But she was already fast asleep under the covers of the bed. All I got from her was a solid, slumbering expression.

A knock sounded on the door. Doctrine walked over and took a look through the peephole. "The book?" he called to the visitor.

"Contact," a female voice answered.

"Ah, yes," Doctrine said as he opened the door, "I had Roy tell the Contact we were here."

My heart lifted with relief. I was prepared to finally post on the Cause Forum.

The Contact let herself in. She was a fair-looking woman, clad in mostly white, as most Contacts were. She swiped her long dark hair away from her face and introduced herself. "Yes, I will be your Contact this evening."

Doctrine called on me. "When was the last time you posted?"

"About a week ago," I answered.

He grabbed his bag, pointing to me. "In that case, you're going first. Some people are probably worried about you."

"Well, I *was* camping out in the Gova Sector all week. It's not exactly easy to find Contacts out there."

"Ugh, or a good IN signal," the Contact added. The demure girl appeared to have a fixation for organization as she began situating herself at the small, wooden table in front of the leather chair. Instead of simply pushing the lamp and clock aside, she picked them up and placed them back on the table, making the corner of the room look like a comfortable workstation. By the time she was ready to have us make our posts, she had made the chair the most inviting spot in the room.

The endearing stranger relinquished the seat in front of the computer and instructed me to take my time posting on the forum. She was in no hurry.

I first sent a private message to Skipstone, as promised. Then, I checked for any new topics of discussion. I spotted the topic Skipstone had told me about: "Blue-Clad Glory Seeker."

"What do you have there, Brigg?" Doctrine asked.

After reading a few of the posts made by other Causes, I replied, "A Cause I met in the Gova Sector told me about this. According to the topic here, there's some guy who dresses all in blue. He's been going around and helping Causes at random."

He sounded surprised. "You don't say. I knew I should've read about it when I first saw the topic."

Kay came out of the bathroom as I continued reading posts. I resumed speaking. "When a group of Causes asked who he was, all he said was 'Blue' and ran off."

Impressed, Doctrine hummed. "So it's a mysterious hero persona? Like a vigilante? Sounds like *someone's* spent a little too much time in the Tome grid's 'Adventure' section."

Through the slightly-open bathroom door, Kay spoke with a high mark in her voice, "You're talking about Blue?"

We turned to her. Glimpsing through the crack, I found it strange Kay would even utter a word to us while wearing nothing but a towel. My curiosity of what she might have known stilled any incoming comments, keeping me on the subject. "Do you know something about him?"

"I don't know anything *specific* about him. I saw him once, though. He foiled a thief who had swiped another Cause's backpack. That's all I can really say."

I went back to the screen. "I guess we'll keep an eye on it. For now, I need to make my post in 'It's Okay; I'm Still Alive!'" The topic was reserved for people who were absent from the forums for a period of more than three days. It was a method of reassuring every Cause of each-others' health and safety.

Kay was displeased with the lack of news I could provide to the community. "You've been gone from the forums for a week and there's nothing to report? There has got to be *something* interesting you could tell the Ca—" Kay slowed her speech to a stop, realizing if she had finished the sentence, I would oblige her by posting the day's happenings. Instead, she veered off. "Never mind; do your thing." The bathroom door shut and locked.

I thought for a moment as I was making my post. Once I was done with it, I clicked on "New Topic." With a sinister grin on my face, I stroked the keys.

The Contact knew what I was up to. "No malicious or filler topics!" she reminded me.

"Oh, yeah," I sighed, turning to face Doctrine. I stood from the chair and presented the laptop to him. "You're up."

He paused, pointing his thumb behind him toward Mika. "What about her? Should we wake her up so she can post too?"

I stopped to think before answering. Remembering Mika was

never a Cause to begin with; answering Doctrine's question in front of a Contact was going to take some care. Even though Contacts were not directly affiliated with the Causes, I was still uncertain of how one would react to knowing we were breaking the rule to stay in groups only with other Causes.

The Cause Forum was reserved for those who were registered at the time the Revolution began. Since Mika was never a Cause, nor registered with the forum, she could not post. I could not let her get found out; especially due to her age and situation. If this Contact were to find out twelve-year-old Mika was not with the Causes, it could have presented a problem I was not sure we could handle so soon into the mission to find her dad.

After a suspicious pause of thought, I answered Doctrine. "Remember? Mika told us she posted yesterday. She said she'd be fine earlier."

"She did?" Doctrine replied. "I don't remember."

I had to try again. He was not catching on. "Oh, I remember now. She told me before you ran into us on the street. It's all right. Mika will be fine."

I was not sure if he understood the truth or simply accepted my story for what it was. Instead of pressing, he let it go and approached me to take over the chair.

I made no obvious signs of relief, but inside, I quivered. While I committed to helping Mika search for her father, it was going to make things difficult if certain people discovered her position in relation to the Revolution. To ward off any outward indication something could be wrong, I put those thoughts in the back of my mind to stay focused on the activity in the room.

Kay emerged from the bathroom in sky blue cotton pajamas. "Yeah, Brigg: no malicious or filler topics." She turned to the Contact expecting a supporting comment.

Instead, the Contact stood vigilant, watching Doctrine post.

Kay folded her arms and raised an eyebrow at the focused

young woman. "You Contacts don't say much, do you?"

I reminded Kay, "They're not supposed to. Remember, they are not like Causes. Associating with us too much would likely get them more involved."

"Brigg is right," the Contact agreed.

"Think about this, too," Doctrine added. "When has a Contact ever given you his or her name?"

"Hopefully never," the Contact said with a witty lilt. "We're here to help you, not *be* you. Black made rules for us, too."

Affirming the Contact's position, I strode over and sat at the foot of the bed. Kay turned a glare to me, her clear mistrust of my motives still prominent.

With seething disinterest in her inaudible assumptions, I rolled my eyes and moved over to the corner opposite of Mika. I left plenty of room for Kay to sit between me and the sleeping girl. All I wanted out of it was to preemptively shut her up.

All we could hear was clicking and typing as Doctrine continued to make posts on the bulletin board. It was as if he had not seen a Contact in weeks.

After wrapping up his posts, he announced, "Hey guys, we've got a newsflash here. It's straight from Aeon!"

Excited to hear it, Kay and I stood and made our way over to the screen. One of the Producers was making an announcement for all Causes to see and discuss. The two of us read the post word for word as we loomed over Doctrine's shoulders.

He spoke as we were still reading. "It looks like eight of the nine Producers have finally arrived at their meeting place."

I nodded as I skimmed over the rest of the post. "Sure took them long enough!"

This was a key piece of news every Cause was to know. The Producers were gathered at a special meeting place, prepared to approach the Exta Sector to speak with the Fifteen about the details of the Causes' questions and demands. However, there was still one who was not with them.

We read through the list: Bogen, Lily, Aeon, Ki, Rosa, Moll, Matthias, and Cecilia.

There was a noticeable problem with the list of attendees. "The only one still missing…is Hatcher," Kay muttered.

I stood back straight and folded my arms. "Why would the creator of the entire plan be the last one to show up?"

He sat back in the chair with a slight grunt. "Distance?"

"Makes sense," mumbled Kay, sitting on the bed.

"When was the last time Hatcher even made a post?" I asked.

Answering with action, Doctrine sat forward again; hands to the keyboard.

Kay gave an iota of praise. "Good idea, Brigg."

I tilted my head to her in thanks.

A moment later, Doctrine had an answer. "Five weeks ago," he muttered with a sense of dread.

There was a brief, uncertain silence.

He followed with additional facts, spoken with a reprise of similar anxiety. "Making matters worse is what he posted."

I dared to ask. "Which is?"

Doctrine quoted in a deep, different voice as if he assumed it was how Hatcher sounded in person. "Don't confront the Fifteen without me. The success of the Revolution rides on my presence at the time of the Meeting."

Kay raised her voice. "So you're saying the Causes are stuck until Hatcher meets with the rest of the Producers?"

"Essentially, yes," Doctrine sighed in clear frustration.

I turned to once again gaze at Mika, who was still fast asleep. Mika's mission gave me something productive to pass the time. To me, the feeling of being "stuck" waiting for Hatcher to arrive was a bit lost. The squinting, scrunched expression on Kay's face told me she was nowhere near feeling the same way.

Doctrine addressed Kay. "You need to post?"

She thought, making her way over to the bed. "Nah, I've got nothing relevant. If you wouldn't mind editing your post to tell everyone I'm fine, I'd appreciate it."

As irritating as Kay had been, Doctrine saw no harm in such a small favor. "Sure thing," he said, returning to the keys.

Soon after, we dismissed the Contact with our sincerest thanks. Doctrine, Kay and I chipped in two arna apiece to give her a generous tip for her time and service.

Kay commandeered the other half of the bed next to Mika. Doctrine and I assumed our sleeping arrangements. I let Kay's continued wariness of my presence slide for the night in light of simply being too tired to care anymore.

I took the tan comforter, my pillow from my bag, and set up between the door, the bed, and the bathroom. If anyone started moving around in the morning, it would be sure to wake me up.

Taking position on the floor was not as bad as I had thought it would be. The comforter was fluffy enough to act as a thin mattress, and the temperature was a few degrees cooler at floor level. It was good enough for me to not even need a blanket. Once I was comfortable on my back, I knew I would fall asleep as soon as I could empty my mind.

There was a different feeling in my heart as I closed my eyes. Not only was I no longer alone, but I now had a solid and purposeful mission to press forward with. And even though Kay had muscled her way into it, I needed to try and at least tolerate her as somebody who could help us locate Mika's father.

I knew there would be a lot more to look forward to in the days ahead. But for the time being, I had to get some much-needed rest. I drifted, wondering what tomorrow would bring. Not only for me—but for Mika, Doctrine, and even Kay.

Episode 2: The Ordeal of Pata

Day 64

I

As I had expected, the first person to move around was the one to wake me up. However, I was not expecting to be tripped over and fallen upon. Mika's light frame tumbled onto my legs as her foot got caught under my comforter-mattress.

"Good morning to you, too, Mika." I laughed, groggy.

Mika rolled to the left with a stammering apology peeping from her mouth. She stopped and sat, curling into a sitting ball with her arms around her legs. "Good morning, Dartmouth!"

I needed to correct her, just in case. "Remember, Mika: we only go by our real names if there are authority figures around. Call me 'Brigg' as long as it's our group."

"Sure thing…Brigg." Mika then stood, grabbed her things and proceeded to the bathroom.

The sun was beginning to peek through the window as the first beams of the morning light spread themselves across Kay's face. She squinted and grumbled, rolling away from them to face toward me. I sighed and shook my head. I found it a shame Kay's softer, more innocent features would go back into hiding once she was wide awake with her attitude on full display.

Doctrine slept well, also. His mouth was agape and his body was sprawled across the floor with a blanket rumpled over him. The sun glinted off the drool crawling from his mouth, eliciting from me a quiet chuckle.

Still not quite awake, I sat up and waited for my body to conjure the energy to stand. I rubbed my palms over my eyes before using my fingers to flick away the crust of a good night's sleep. As I did, I heard the shower turn on and the rustling of clothes coming from behind the bathroom door. *I hope we can take care of her and get her back to her dad,* I thought. I was thinking "we" at the time because I knew Kay was going to follow us once we left Roy's anyway. I groaned low at the thought and hoped Doctrine would follow along to help maintain order.

One more detail whispered concern. With no real idea where to start and only a hand-drawn picture to go on, I felt the search for Mika's dad was going to require patience and care. The best thing to do was to ask other Causes first. The Pata Sector was crawling with Causes in its crowded city streets. It was not going to be hard to pick some and ask them. This was, however, an operation to be done with caution. There was no telling where and when police would be around.

The Fifteen had made no direct attempt to confront us since a lone incident in the beginning. Since then, it had been the police in each individual sector carrying out captures of any unruly or disorderly Causes.

As the threat of sector police kept Causes on their toes, many were anticipating the Fifteen to make a move of their own. Everybody knew the power and influence of the Fifteen was still far greater than that of the Causes. Regardless, morale remained high. Hopefully, Hatcher would show up before anything catastrophic happened. In the meantime, for us at least, Mika's father was the goal.

II

After everybody was awake and showered, we prepared to

embark. Before beginning the search, however, our first destination was the lobby for a free breakfast.

I led the march down the staircase to find four other people, two boys and two girls, outside of Roy's office. The stuffy atmosphere of the lobby felt even more cramped with so many people now scrunching into it. Thankfully, everybody was bearing the floral scents of the inn's bath soaps.

A dainty redhead in a yellow shirt had her ear to the door, gently knocking on it. The other young woman, a tall beauty in a long, dark blue skirt and hooded shawl, crossed in front of the two males and took a seat on one of the chairs. "It's been ten minutes now!"

At first glance of the two young men, I became curious about the strange white rectangles sewn into the backs of their black shirts. As I whispered my thoughts on it to the others, the one on the right stated, "If he wants us to go away, he could at least poke his head out and say it."

I tapped one of the boys on the shoulder. "The book?"

He was a bit alarmed at first as he turned his head to answer, "The book."

The other boy turned to us as well. I glanced to him before addressing both of them with my next question. "All of you?"

He nodded; his light brown eyes easing with his relaxed smile. "Yeah, all of us."

I brought my voice back to speaking volume and addressed the girl at the office door. "What's the problem?"

The redhead said, "Roy locked himself in his office and won't come out. We have to return our keys, and the free breakfast hasn't been set up yet."

The young man on my right took his room key out of the right-front pocket of his brown cargo pants and held it up next to his face. "Obviously, talking to Roy is more about the breakfast than it is the keys," he smiled, toothy.

Doctrine wiggled past us to approach the door. "How do you know he's in there?"

She backed up and pointed to the bottom of the door. "If you peek under, you see his feet."

He did as instructed, getting on his hands and knees to take a look. "Yeah, I see them."

The male on my left joined the girl in blue by sitting in the chair across from hers. As he flopped, he grunted impatiently. "We've done everything short of breaking down the door."

"Not necessary," Kay smiled, stepping up with her bag open. The gleam in her eye and the confident push in her voice put all of the attention in the room to her.

The young lady in blue did not seem convinced. "We've been trying for long enough. If you have a plan, go for it."

Kay produced two small hairpins from her bag. "I'm going to pick the lock."

Doctrine backed away and gestured, presenting the task at hand to Kay.

"Give me a minute," she boldly boasted; kneeling in front of the doorknob.

As Kay worked the lock, the redhead in the yellow shirt broke the ice. "I'm Chloe, by the way. What about you all?"

I shifted a polite point to her. "Is that your real name, or your forum name?"

Chloe leaned against the wall next to the office door, almost knocking down a landscape painting with her narrow shoulders. "I'm using my real name. 'Chloe' rolls out of the mouth easier than 'AvidReader_388,'" she replied with a laugh. The memo about creating simple names wasn't posted until after I already signed up on the forum."

"Glad I'm not alone," the girl in blue chuckled. Flicking her dark bangs underneath her hood, she added, "I went with my Tome grid name, too. 'Twilight Needles'. Call me Twilight."

The boy in the brown pants threw his room key onto the front counter, then used both hands to scratch at his scalp through his short, dirty-blond hair. Stepping over to sit on the stairs he spoke. "I'm Bark. I joined the forum only a week before the walk. My buddy over there talked me into it, and I'm glad he did. It's been a blast so far."

Standing, he approached me. "Call me 'Pitch.'"

"Ah, Pitch!" I said with delight. "The spearhead of 'Team All Unisex' himself! I loved reading your input on the forums!"

With exaggerated thumbs up, he replied, "You're damn right!"

With a wide grin and a handshake, "I've gotta ask: Those rectangles sewn into your shirts; your work?"

He tugged at this shirt, nodding with pride. "It is, yes. It took me a bit longer than it would have if an *actual* seamstress had done it. But I can always get faster and better at it."

Getting a closer look at the material, I asked, "Velcro?"

"It is, yes." Pitch reached into his small green duffel bag and brought out another rectangular piece of cloth. "Art shirts!" he triumphantly announced.

Bark puffed up in response, "It was my idea. Pitch liked it so much; he read seamstress tutorials over his sister's shoulders. I never understood why those are only in the girls' curriculum."

Pitch added, "Yeah, Shalynn forbid a man wants to learn how to mend his own clothes."

Bark took the canvas from his friend and handed it to me. "See, this cloth is art canvas with hook-end velcro sewn into it. Now, you can illustrate on it and stick it to the back of the shirt for everyone to see! When you have to wash the shirt, you peel the art off of it so it doesn't get ruined."

Nods of impressed approval crossed about the lobby.

Chloe was the first to ask them, "Are you selling those?"

Pitch answered, "We will; once the Revolution is over." He then shuffled through his bag again and pulled out another art canvas backing.

Bark was smiling. "Oh, you guys are gonna love this."

Pitch cut off his partner. "Let's not be rude. We haven't even asked for *their* names yet." He turned to Doctrine. "Who are you four? Are you all in the same group?"

My friend took his frown away from busy Kay and swapped to a smile towards Pitch. "Yeah, we all grouped together last night. I'm Doctrine."

I reached to Bark to shake his hand. "I'm Brigg." Bark looked at both of his hands with a sense of confusion; feeling he had dirtied his hands to itch through his scalp. With a lazy, indifferent shrug, I relaxed him, and we shared a shake.

Our youngest teammate nodded to Twilight. "I'm Mika."

Chloe smiled wide to her. "You're an early user, too? I don't recall a 'Mika' on the forums."

Mika caught on quick and rolled with it, knowing she could not let her status as a civilian be known to too many people. "Yup, that's it!" she agreed, keeping from details.

I pointed toward the office door. "And our apprentice locksmith over there is Kay."

Kay responded by heading off everyone's comments. "Yes, *that* Kay. And yes, I'm traveling with two men in my group. It kinda fell together this way."

"Well, technically, you…"

Doctrine gestured sharply to me. It was enough to communicate the point to keep from sharing too many details about our situation. It was the right thing to do, after all. There was no need to bog down the conversation with errant issues.

Twilight was observing Kay. Biting her bottom lip matched well with the look in her faded gray eyes. It was a mischievous glance with fresh desire to heckle someone who had been so outspoken against girls being involved in the walkout.

Pitch caught onto it as well, shifting the conversation back before any forum drama could spill out into the lobby. "Well, it's very nice to meet you all!" He was waving the canvas in his hands as his way to draw our attention back to it.

"You as well," I replied with a smile, pointing to his hands. "So, like you were saying: what'cha got there?"

Pitch unrolled his piece of canvas to show all of us a design he had created himself. It was a picture of an analog alarm clock with fifteen hours on it instead of twelve. A small box overflowing with tools was illustrated next to it. At the bottom, below the symbolic artwork, "Time for a change!" was written.

Doctrine folded his arms, nodding slowly with a grin. "Fixing the Fifteen's clock. I like it!"

Pitch waved the canvas. "When the Revolution ends, we're going to market this particular backing to Causes. I don't know what we'll charge though."

I cracked a natural smile. "Very awesome! You two will do well selling these."

"You see," Pitch replied, "this is why we're in on the Revolution. We don't want to be *assigned* our occupations. Bark and I want to stay a team and market these shirts. And me, I'm content tailoring and designing clothes."

Twilight nodded, smiling at the duo. "I like your style! I also want to market clothes. My grades and aptitudes are on track to steer me away from it, though. I'm going to wind up working in a botanical lab or some nonsense if I stick to the Fifteen's ways."

Mika responded to Twilight with a sense of anticipation in her voice. "I want to see more of the clothes you made. If they look as pretty as what you have on right now, I would be at your store all the time!"

Twilight's face grew bright with the first smile anybody had seen on her. "Why, thank you!" she beamed. "You're sweet!"

Mika then asked, "Are the three of you together in a group?"

"No, she's not with us," Bark replied.

Mika followed up with a bold claim. "She should be."

Their faces flickered in delight as they all shared a glance to each other. Kay, not quite feeling the same way, called to her from the office door. "Mika, what are you doing?"

The joyous expression on Twilight's face suddenly fell off at the sound of Kay's unnecessary question. The curl of mischief came back to her lips as she engaged Kay. "We were all about to ask you the same thing. You still don't have the door open?"

Kay had failed to open the door. "You're now two-for-two on failure to deliver after opening your mouth, Kay!" I taunted.

Chloe cut off her side conversation with Doctrine to add her share of words. "Does this girl really know what she's doing?"

Doctrine took his cloth ring backpack and opened one of the pockets. As he rummaged through it, he growled, "I knew she couldn't get us in there."

"Give me a break!" she defended. "I'm trying *something!*"

Doctrine, frowning hard, pulled a large knife out of his bag and walked over to Kay with an intimidating posture. He stood to her side and pushed the blade of the knife to block her view. He ordered her with a deep, grinding tone, "Move."

Kay froze as she stared into her own eyes through the reflection of the blade. Seconds later, she backed away. Doctrine inserted the blade of the knife between the door and doorway. After jostling it and jiggling the doorknob for a few seconds, the door popped open. He then placed the knife on the front counter. Kay relaxed and stood.

Everyone filed into the office while Doctrine peered at Kay with a silent, scolding stare. It was clear enough Doctrine's patience with the pushy woman was wearing thin.

Chloe was the first to speak on the state of things. "I don't like the looks of this."

"That makes two of us," Pitch agreed.

The four of us turned our focus to the alert from inside Roy's office. Mika and I continued ahead, leaving Doctrine and Kay to themselves. It seemed he wanted to have a word with her.

I stepped into the office with Mika close behind. "What's up? What happened?"

Bark and Twilight were examining objects strewn about Roy's office. Roy was slumped forward with his head on the desk. He bore a happy and relaxed sleeping expression.

Pitch surprised the room by stating what should have been obvious from the start. "This guy's dead."

Mika gasped and hid behind me.

In a soft, calm tone, I gave her instructions. "Mika, go to the lobby with Doctrine and Kay. We'll take care of this."

"Okay," she quivered.

"Actually," I thought again, "send them in here too. Also, lock the front door to the building and make sure nobody sees you do it." I took a deep breath in an attempt to calm myself.

Mika nodded, scampering out of the office. Doctrine and Kay came in shortly after.

Kay approached the desk and scrutinized the layout of objects. She picked up a small pouch and stirred its contents with her finger. Her head slightly jerked as her eyes spread to alarm. She pulled her finger out, which was now stained with an odd green fluid. A moment later, she interrupted what little chatter there was by saying, "That's pretty screwed up! Food coloring on bad jayda."

"Jayda!? Let me see," Doctrine requested.

Silent, she closed the pouch and threw it to him.

While Doctrine observed the pouch, I examined Roy's hands. His fingertips also had traces of the food coloring. My insides shuddered and throat lumped up.

"Yes, definitely," Kay said. "You wipe the coloring away, and I can guarantee you those bulbs are gray."

Pitch shared, "Yeah, man. Gray jayda is no joke. I won't even touch the stuff unless I pick it right off the plant."

Kay delivered an odd look toward Pitch as she spoke. "I'm not a fan of this stuff at all, to be honest. But I think the more pressing issue here is: Who gave this stuff to Roy? Clearly, nobody in their right mind would suckle on gray jayda."

I nodded, speaking, "Maybe someone had it out for this old man, and went so far as to dye this stuff and pass it off as good."

Doctrine then asked openly, "Anybody see the Contact?"

Everyone in the office went wide-eyed, turning their stares to Doctrine. I cocked my head and said, "You don't think—"

Kay dropped the pouch back onto the desk and dashed to the door. "Where's Mika!?"

Mika popped her head in. "I'm right here. What's happening?"

Pitch and Bark scurried towards the door. Bark tipped his head to Mika. "Some bullshit is what's happening!" His face twitched upon realizing the use of such a strong word to the child.

Doctrine snatched Bark's hand. "Yeah, I don't think so." His voice oozed suspicion, but I could not pin out exactly what Doctrine was thinking.

Struggling to be released, Bark shouted, his eyes swelling with fear and frustration. "Let go! What are you doing?"

Doctrine smoothed his voice. "Oh, nothing much. I just wanted to ask the *artist* if he happens to have any *green dye* with him." Doctrine cocked his head and narrowed his eyes, as though his stare could flush guilt out.

The drastic implication had Bark draw a deep breath and holler in Doctrine's face. "You're out of your damn mind! Art dye isn't edible! He'd've spit that shit right out!"

Mika cowered in closer to me and Kay. I felt her clutching the back of my vest and could see her reach for Kay's hand. Kay and I caught each other's' eyes with a silent agreement to shield the girl if this shouting match came to blows.

The next minute was a silence palpable with discomfort. Frowning, Doctrine hesitantly released Bark's arm and shifted to his side, brushing his hand through his messy hair. "Ok," he sighed. "Alright, yeah. I guess you're right. I just really don't like the idea of this being done by someone involved in the Revolution. This isn't how we're supposed to do things."

Kay moved over to lean up against the doorway, speaking as she crossed. "Who's to say it wasn't someone who knew Roy was *assisting* Causes. Let's think a bit beyond this; beyond what's in this room. There's definitely more, but we're in no capacity to investigate it ourselves."

Nobody would admit it aloud, but what Kay said made sense. It was now difficult to point the accusing finger at anybody in the office. Looking at Roy again, I felt a man of his age could have had a share of close enemies. Us Causes could not relate, as our *real* enemies sat in the government seats.

Doctrine awkwardly lifted his hand to pat Bark on the shoulder. "Again, sorry."

"I'll get over it." Bark sighed, returning a pat on the shoulder to Doctrine; offering a smirk of acceptance and forgiveness.

Doctrine approached the desk one more time, stroking his goatee in contemplation. "So...I don't know about you all, but I don't feel like getting shipped home—or to the Labor Fields— because of this."

Everyone saw the point Doctrine had, and most of us agreed with him. Kay, however, had a look on her face telling me she still had something to say.

"So, what do we do about it?" I asked, nervous of what the answer may be.

Our four new acquaintances shifted their ways out of the office. "You should all do the same," Twilight advised as she made a subtle nod toward the exit.

"Take care and travel safe. Maybe we'll see you around," Chloe peeped, not even stopping as she slipped out.

In the next minute, they were all gone; leaving us alone with the body.

Doctrine crossed past me and over to the desk. Using his untucked shirt as a glove, he opened one of the desk drawers. "A refund for the room, anyone?"

Kay vehemently objected, "What in the name of Paxus are you doing!?"

Even *I* felt Kay's tone to be warranted this time. I groaned as well, surprised and disappointed. "Doctrine, you can't be serious!"

"Hey, *my* coin purse is starting to feel a bit hollow. We don't know how long it's going to take for Hatcher to step forward either." He untied his purse and started removing coins from the drawer. "Think of it this way," he nonchalantly pointed his thumb at the body, "he doesn't need it anymore and we never got our breakfast."

My gut roiled about this, but there was some level of truth to be worried about arna. With Mika to look after and a search to conduct, a little extra coin would not hurt. Roy did not have a wedding ring on his finger and there were no keepsakes or items indicating this man had any close family.

"I don't like it, but he's right. I'll take some if you don't mind. We should see if there's any granola or anything in the kitchen that travels well, too."

Kay crossed her arms. "This isn't right."

I looked away, "I know it's not Kay, but we might need the money to look for Mika's dad, and she needs to eat too." My stomach twisted more, but I held myself back from getting sick.

"*Whoa!*" exclaimed Doctrine. I was so busy with Kay's criticism; I had not noticed him still searching. "We've got a whole different level of jackpot in *this* drawer!"

I crossed toward him. "Is there a lot of arna in there?"

Doctrine glanced to Mika, casually censoring his next statement. "We can say old Roy here was—or knew someone who *is*—a talented illustrator of the female frame, and probably isn't a fan of drawing clothing." His eyes were completely transfixed to the contents of the drawer, and his expression grew somewhat conflicted. He stroked his goatee, hot under the collar.

The lusty look on Doctrine's face fueled my curiosity, "Seriously, a stash of por—"

"—Illicit artistic contraband," Kay interrupted, keeping the conversation kid-friendly.

I took the interruption in stride, nodding in approval to Kay. "Yeah, what you said," I agreed politely. Kay moved Mika closer to her as I engaged Doctrine. "So, Roy probably had a few more issues than we thought. What's this doing here? We can see it belonged to him, but was he making it himself; maybe had plans to sell it?"

"Don't know, man," he answered, picking up the picture.

Kay spoke up. "You're not really taking that picture are you?"

"I am," he answered. He then pulled more from the drawer. "This one, too. And this one; and this one…"

I had to throw my hands up. "Look Doctrine, the arna is fine. But I've gotta draw the line there. I didn't join the Revolution to engage in Level-3 crimes. The Assembly Lines aren't for me."

"Don't sweat it, man. I'm not going to drag you down with me over this." He finished putting the pictures in his cloth-ring bag and approached me with some arna in his hand.

"You can give the money to Brigg; I'm not taking any of it," Kay said, still empathetic to the situation as a whole.

"More for us then," Doctrine handed me sixteen arna, tucking an equal amount in his own purse.

Mika asked us, "Did those other Causes go to get help?"

Doctrine answered bluntly. "I doubt it."

She pouted. "How come?" Though she seemed mature for her age, there were a lot of things going on I felt were hard for someone so young to understand.

He eased over to her and knelt down, placing a hand on her

shoulder. He looked into her eyes to emphasize the seriousness of the situation. "There's something you need to understand, Mika— we can't afford to be accused of this."

"Coming from the guy who looted the desk?" Kay sniffled.

Hearing Kay's logic, Mika scowled at Doctrine with clear disgust in her eyes.

I was a bit torn by Kay's point. Not only did I feel it was not fair to leave Roy behind, but taking the coins, too; and the pornography as well? It was disrespecting the dead, plain and simple. But sixteen arna, although ill-gotten, could spell the difference between fuel for the road and starvation.

Doctrine stood back up and turned to the rest of us. "We'll leave the doors open. Make sure it will be easy for anyone to walk right in and find him. As for us, we're raiding the kitchen then escaping out the back."

Kay objected. "Shouldn't we at least contact Morie to come collect the body?"

I was interested to hear Kay mention one of the members of the Fifteen: Morie, Chief Mortician and operator of the Spirit Furnace. Kay was right: it was appropriate to summon her.

Doctrine jostled in place, stuck halfway between walking to the kitchen and leaving the inn. I saw in his eyes he would leave us behind if he felt he had to. "If calling Morie is your idea of a good plan, you can stay behind all you want. I know Roy needs to hit the Furnace and go see Paxus, but if you're bringing Morie here right now, I'm out of here!"

I stepped close to Kay and made an attempt to hurry her along. "This isn't exactly easy for me, either. But Doctrine does have a point. You know if you call on Morie, you have to wait for her to arrive on the scene before you leave. What do you think is going to happen then?"

Kay sighed and nodded as an understanding. Mika left to follow Doctrine. It seemed Kay had a lot more to say about this, but was keeping it to herself. She bowed her head to pray over the body, then turned back to me, shaking her head in fiery discontent. "Don't take the food; let's just go," she muttered.

Inside, I got the gut feeling there were some aspects of the Revolution that were only going to last for so long. If other Causes had to make choices the likes of what we had done, it would be easy for personal beliefs to overtax the rules put in place by the Producers. Finding Roy dead was an automatic lose-lose situation for all of us—a fact well-indicated when the other Causes left us in haste.

Hopefully, Kay would realize leaving was our best option.

I knew I did.

III

It took a couple of minutes to catch up to Doctrine and Mika. Once we were regrouped, we took our time and paced ourselves to a stroll. Everyone was quiet; still trying to absorb what had happened. For all of us, it was our first time ever seeing a dead body up close. And for me, specifically, the looted arna weighed a little heavy in my purse.

Suddenly, Kay spoke up, "Today is Sunday, isn't it?"

I answered her before I knew for sure. "I believe it is."

She clapped once with a relieved grin. "Good! I want to go to the nearest chapel. Please!"

I gestured, knowing what she was getting at. She wanted to go to a chapel so she could ask Paxus for forgiveness. It sounded like a good idea since I also felt tainted by our actions.

Doctrine was the only one to push off the idea. "Let me level with you guys. I'm more inclined to get out of the Pata Sector altogether. I've spent way too much time here, and that Roy issue was the last straw. Also, I'm now packing…" he glanced to Kay, "…illicit artistic contraband. Like I said, I'm not going to drag you guys to the assembly lines with me. So let's split here."

"You sure; just a little longer? A Repentance Rite might do you some good," Kay offered, stopping to turn to him.

Doctrine turned and paced a bit as he spoke. "I'm not really a chapel person. I'll pray or do a rite wherever I want. I don't need a chapel to do it in."

"Come on, it's Sunday!" Kay insisted once more. "Come with us to the chapel. Afterwards, you can do whatever you want. It's not like we're asking for much beyond you joining us."

Doctrine took a few deep breaths and visibly calmed. "I'd much rather get out of here before the next train departs. I know what you're looking for in there, but Roy's death isn't on us. I'm trying to survive; and frankly, I know bringing contraband into the chapel won't help forgiveness come to me any easier."

Mika asked him, "You're really leaving?" There was an apparent sense of disappointment in Mika's voice as she asked. She hadn't said much since we left the scene at the inn. Maybe she still didn't understand the situation we are in, but she understood she didn't want us to split up.

Doctrine smiled to her the way a brother would. "Don't take it personally, Mika. If there is one person in your group bothering me..." He smirked coyly as he nodded his head toward Kay.

"Say no more," I interrupted him.

Kay caught on to the subtle snub and objected. "Hey!"

Mika presented her hand to Doctrine. "It was nice meeting you, Mister Doctrine! Thanks for helping us out."

He shook her hand and ruffled her hair a bit. "You take care, Mika. These two have their history and their quirks, but you've got good help. They'll find your father in no time. Try to keep them from butting heads too much, okay?"

Mika smiled back at him. "Don't worry; I will!"

Doctrine turned and addressed me again. "I've got to hand it to you, though; you guys are a lot better than some of the other

Causes I've been meeting lately. Sometimes I want to choke some of these guys. Or at least smack 'em around a little."

"I know what you mean!" Kay chimed, glaring at me with the faintest hint of a grin hidden behind her playful scowl.

"Yeah." Doctrine's eyes narrowed as he scrunched his nose and pinched his fingers tightly together in front of his face. "You came really close." As Kay's brow furrowed, he offered a gentle chuckle of reassurance. "Kidding, kidding!"

"Violence is forbidden for Causes anyway. Remember?" Child-like, I stuck my tongue out. My addition brought out light laughs from the team. It felt good to have a little fun after the gravity of what had happened. It's hard to explain, but sometimes you need to feel something other than the heaviness that accompanies being near the dead.

I saw no possibility of Doctrine changing his mind and accepted it for what it was. "Travel safe, alright? And don't get caught with those pictures."

He replied in kind. "You be safe, too. Be careful."

In a brisk jog, Doctrine left us. It was a bit hard to see him go; especially since we always got along so well on the forums. Even though my view of him was marred by his actions at Roy's, I was hoping I would see him again.

As I watched him disappear into the crowd, Mika tugged my shirt. "Are we still going to the chapel?"

"Yeah." My voice croaked as I tried to pull myself away from the thought of the stolen coins.

IV

Remembering our escapades from the previous night, we managed to backtrack to a nearby chapel without much trouble.

Chapels throughout Eden also made for good sanctuaries from the outside. We would temporarily be free from the view of the public eye. Even though many of Eden's citizens were indifferent to the actions of the Causes, there were still quite a few who strictly opposed us. Seeking solace in the chapel was a good way to keep away from those types, if only for thirty minutes.

The floor of the chapel was a dark wood; almost black. Tasseled cushions of various sizes and colors rested on shelves along the left and right walls. Stained-glass windows bearing images of angels illuminated the room with help from the morning sun. The only thing interrupting the scene of serenity was the sight of the chapel attendant lighting chandelier candles as he squirmed to keep his balance on a decrepit, aged ladder.

The three of us proceeded at our leisure toward the altar. My head turned repeatedly as I soaked up the calming, righteous atmosphere the chapel was giving off.

We kneeled at the altar and readied ourselves to perform a Repentance Rite. The altar consisted of ten candles in a semicircle with a kneeling stand in front of each. At the center of the altar was a black candle representing all of the sins of the people of Eden. Effigies of the God-Spirits, Paxus and Shalynn, were turned away from it; facing to the west and to the east respectively.

Serenely sighing, I muttered to the statuettes, "When was the last time I came to talk to you two?" My eyes lowered, glimpsing the inscribed placard at Paxus's feet:

One of Eden's Almighty Creators
The God-Spirit Paxus | Guardian of the West

The Hand of Justice and Good Judgment
Pinnacle of Strength and Generosity
He Who Displays Unmatched Bravery, Chivalry, and Respect
All who practice His seven principles do so
to the pleasure and favor of Paxus.

With a smile, my eyes naturally veered to the other placard.

One of Eden's Almighty Creators
The Goddess-Spirit Shalynn | Guardian of the East

Goddess of Wisdom and Growth
Ultimate Example of Beauty and Purity
She Who Encourages All Trust, Enjoyment, and Prudence
All who practice Her seven principles do so
to the pleasure and favor of Shalynn.

The seven tenets of each God-Spirit served as both attributes to live by, and focal points for prayer and repentance. Everything about the situation at Roy's reeked of displeasure in the eyes of Paxus and Shalynn; especially our unauthorized refund. It was our responsibility as children of Eden, their creation, to reflect, repent, and seek their favor again.

I was the first to reach forward and grab the black candle, using the flame to light the white candle at my stand. This was my sin, and it was time to ask for repentance.

While praying intently over what had transpired at the inn, those four measly coins in my purse felt to be increasing in weight. There was a clear tug-of-war in my heart and soul over what was right and what was right for me; for us. By the time I was lifting my head and snuffing the candle, I knew I needed to take action to balance these wrongs. Thankfully, I was not also under the burden of having porn and stolen food, as well.

I was done with the rite, but it left me with frayed relief. Glancing over to Kay, I felt a twinge of jealousy toward the serenity pouring from her relaxed features and silent, puttering lips. How I wished my heart had been equally at ease.

Looking past her, I saw the basket for the chapel's upkeep

donations. My breath pushed out as this beacon of opportunity presented itself. Without even putting a second thought to it, I took my purse off of my belt and walked to the basket.

Sixteen arna. I took the four coins out and looked them over. This—*this* was the right thing to do. And yet, it still weighed against our necessities. "I'll donate half…yeah, half works."

With a relieved smile, I placed two of the 5-arna pieces into the basket, and fished around to look for two 1-arna pieces. As I fingered through the coins, Kay groaned at me. "Really, Brigg; in front of Mika, no less!? What kind of example are you setting?"

My hands shot out of the basket, leaving all of the coins, including the ten arna I had placed in. "It's not what it looks like!"

"Puh-lease! After what happened back there, try to convince me otherwise!"

The heart-piercing pout in Mika's lips traveled up to her eyes and furrowed brows. Trying to keep the full-picture out of the ears of the chapel attendant, I tiptoed around the words. "I put ten of *that* arna in the basket; I was trying to get change so we could keep half of what we got."

Kay took pause before replying. "Let it be. I have arna, too. Two arna isn't going to break us."

I drew a breath and sighed. Mika eased in close to Kay, still giving me a hard look of disappointment. I seldom make apologies for my actions. Although having arna meant maintaining independence, we all have a sense of what is right and what is not. Looking at Kay's eyes and Mika's, I knew sixteen arna was not worth the weight on my heart.

There was a sudden swelling of spirit within me; graceful and calm. She was absolutely right. I was being needlessly stingy over some ill-gotten arna. My chest relaxed and a light breath escaped my nose. "If that's the case, then..." With a smile, I took the other two hot coins from my pouch and tossed them into the basket. "…six less won't kill us either."

Kay's brow lifted, engaging me with a gentle stare. In a flash, she broke into a sheepish smile, chuckling and turning her gaze aside. "You're something, Brigg."

Mika approached me and wrapped her arms around my waist. "Thank you." Her praise was muffled as she nuzzled her face into my shirt. With all of the tragedies and hardships she had been through, she needed to see a little goodness still existed.

I felt a stab of longing. I had not had something as clean and kind as a hug since the last one my mother ever gave me. Make no mistake; I never wanted to go back. But between the beatings and the screaming, hugs from mother were warm and welcome; before puberty made a mess of things.

I patted Mika on the head and released a deep sigh. "It's nothing, Mika."

Sincerity poured from Kay's eyes as a smirk curled up. "Nothing except the right thing to do."

I thanked her with a nod.

Mika's embrace was sweet and soft. I longed to savor that moment of genuine affection. The affirmation in Kay's eyes and the gentle squeeze from the young one was the right combination of sensations to bring my heavy heart to an airy bubbling.

With a single pat to Mika's back, I offered a simple "Thank you," prompting her to back away.

As she broke the hug, she dug into her pockets and took out two 1-arna coins. "See, look! Like Kay said: two arna won't break us! Here, take it!" The joy of her innocent and selfless gesture brought an irresistible smile to my face.

I took the coins and slipped them into the left pocket of my vest. "I'll make sure to use these for something special!" Mika grinned back and nodded with pleasure.

The three of us glanced to our extinguished candles. A steady, pleasant warmth swirled in my gut as the curling smoke carried the sin of mine away. I knew, though, true repentance only came by letting loose the stolen money.

As we stepped off the altar, a voice spoke to us from halfway down the chapel. "You guys, too, huh?"

It was the four Causes we met at the inn. They had felt the same call as we did and come to the chapel as well. "Oh! Hello, again!" I casually greeted.

"Feel better?" asked Bark. His demeanor was significantly lighter than it had been when I last saw him.

"Oh, you have *no* idea!" I exhaled.

Chloe swayed with her steps; her hands in her pockets. "We're here for the Rite, too."

Pitch looked us over again. "But it looks like not all four of you felt the same. Where's Doctrine?"

Kay answered, "He split after we left the inn."

His arms shrugged wide. "Even after all that? No Rite?"

"Nope; he was pretty stiff about it, too," I replied. "He insisted on getting as far away as possible."

Mika spoke up, changing the subject. "The four of you are a group now?"

Twilight dignified the little girl's question with a mature, sisterly countenance. "Yes, we are, Mika. It's all thanks to what you said to us back at the inn."

"Yeah," Bark agreed. "It made perfect sense to have Eden's up-and-coming male tailor, a seamstress, and an artist on the same team. Chloe having good medical aptitudes is a great plus, too! We can learn a lot from each other while we wait for Hatcher."

His words caught my attention. "Ah, so you all heard?"

Chloe clarified, "Read about it last night, too."

Kay, Chloe, and Twilight swept themselves into a conversation about the Producers and Hatcher. While listening, I saw Pitch mumbling in close to Mika.

The look on Mika's face slowly grew more cheerful. She covered her mouth and giggled. "You're welcome."

I gestured for her to come to me. "What did he say to you?" I whispered.

Mika smiled in pure delight, cupped her hand over my ear and whispered. "'Thanks for telling the pretty girls to travel with us.'"

I chuckled. "Did you do that on purpose?"

Her wide smile was contagious. "No... It surprised me."

I had a sudden thought, causing me to speak up. "Oh, Mika! I have an idea. Can you hand me your picture? We can at least ask these guys if they have seen your father."

Kay overheard. "Yes! Do it; it's a good start!"

Mika took the canvas from her bag and handed it to Twilight. The other three peered over her shoulder as I asked them, "Have you seen this man before?"

They examined the drawing closely, occasionally looking to each other with shaking heads and puzzled looks. They all answered negative.

Bark asked Mika, "Did you draw this?"

Mika bobbed her head. "Yes. It's my dad."

Hearing the news, the four were now focusing deeply on the picture. The desire to help us was broadcast well through their faces and subtle gestures. Bark was the first to say anything concerning the picture. "These erase marks around his face don't help much. Would you be able to redraw this?"

"Daddy posed when I worked on it. I don't think I can..."

Bark clenched his teeth and curled his lip. "I mean, *I'd* be able to *maybe* copy this if I had the time to do it. But I don't have a steady workstation, and I don't want to hold you all up."

Chloe groaned, nodding to the rest of them. "I don't think we'll be able to help you, sorry."

"That's all right..." Mika sighed, taking the picture back.

Bark extended his hand one last time. "I'd hate to cut this short. If you'll excuse us, we have a Repentance Rite to perform. We wanna get out of Pata soon, too."

Pitch patted Mika's head. "Good luck in your search!"

"Alright," she peeped, grinning to him.

Kay, Mika, and I took turns shaking their hands and declaring a pleasure in re-meeting them all under less stressful circumstances. While it was a bummer not starting the search with a lead, I took into account they were the first people we had asked. Hopefully, there would be more Causes who would have information for us to work with.

After leaving the chapel, the search for Mika's father was on.

V

Several hours of searching efforts passed quickly. The activity occupied us until well into the evening. Despite finding and asking about forty other Causes, nobody had seen Mika's father, nor had any clues for us to follow. Many of them left us with heartfelt apologies and an assurance we would be contacted if they saw anything. Some even made comments about finding me and Kay as an unlikely team based off of our forum spats.

Though a fruitless day for our purpose, it was a good time to grow accustomed to traveling in a group. Throughout the day, Kay worked well alongside us without a single shred of the entitlement she had exhibited before. She was cooperative, actively invested in the search, and almost even pleasant. I did not even want to question this shift, but I could sense our time at the chapel may have played into this brighter, more cohesive attitude. We all followed each other's requests and instructions with true Cause-style teamwork.

Once the sun fully set, we felt it was time to begin looking for another inn to stay at. I regretted not having asked any Causes where they were taking up shelter. It soon got to a point where we were all getting tired. Thus, any inn would do, whether or not it was clued or had a Contact nearby.

Quite a way into our search for a place to rest, Kay pointed to somebody who appeared to be a Cause. He was walking into a nearby inn with a content, relaxed expression emanating from his drowsy eyes. Though the unusually high collar of his sleeveless green shirt covered his mouth and nose, we could feel his merriment without having to see a smile. "Somebody's looking forward to a good sleep," Mika said with a snicker.

Kay made a humorous observation. "The bird's nest on his head says he just woke up. He needs a hat; not a visor."

We ambled toward the billowing white awning sheltering the front of the building. As we stepped onto the property, the same young man came running out of the entrance, dashing in our direction. A worried and frantic look overtook his previously cheerful disposition.

We could hear a man shouting from inside the inn. "Go back home if you want to sleep somewhere!"

The youth looked back as he continued running; not realizing he was going to run into us. I pushed myself a bit forward and braced for an impact, lining my hands up to catch his shoulders as he ran into me. As his body met my hands, Kay braced me from behind. The young man spun into the impact and around, muttering a quick apology.

I managed to grab him and ask, "The book?"

He nodded impatiently, trying to leave. "Yes, the book."

I probed, leading the girls into following us. "I'm to understand they don't want us in there?"

He stopped, adjusted his glasses, and turned to me to say, "All of the inns are being like this."

"All of them?" Kay asked, leaning her head forward.

"Yes, all of them." He signaled to us to keep moving. "Yesterday, clued inns were all over Pata. But now, rumor has it a group of Causes poisoned an innkeeper with bad jayda bulbs."

The shock swept over the three of us. I tried to remain stone-faced. "Really?"

"Yes, come," he instructed, swooping his arm, leading. "I know a cafe we can sit at. I'll tell you what I know."

Even though we had the best idea of what really happened, we couldn't blurt it out and risk looking suspicious. Any Cause would be jumping at the chance to have the real story. We chose to play it safe and follow him to the cafe.

As he led us along, I initiated the usual string of introductions. "I'm Brigg, by the way."

"And I'm Kay."

"I'm Mika."

The young stranger stopped in his tracks; following a short beat with an unexpectedly haughty scoff. "So, you're Brigg? Huh; paired up with Kay, of all people?"

I sighed, grinning. "Yeah, we've been getting that a lot today."

Still facing forward, he threw his hands up in a wide, exaggerated shrug. "Perhaps you'll recognize _my_ name." He turned to meet my eyes with a cold gaze. "Call me 'Dice'."

The name punched me square in the front of my brain. I did not have to say a word back to him. The two of us were acquainted enough from our interactions on the forums.

I was now truly engrossed in the misfortune of encountering yet another Cause I did not get along with online. Dice and I had multiple back-and-forth spats. Most of them were results of my stepping in to defend those he would bully and harass with his reasoning; especially newer members who hadn't quite figured everything out yet. His posts and replies evoked a superior smirk; a bad vibe for the Cause community.

Kay eased in, commenting on the silent stare Dice and I shared. "See, if the two of you could have kept your cool on the forums, we'd already be sitting down and ordering drinks!"

"You're one to talk!" Dice and I replied simultaneously. We then looked to each other, slightly surprised though undeniably entertained by our mutual ire.

I could tell Dice was now much less inclined to fill us in on what he knew. Although we were there when the incident occurred, there may have been some inkling of information we had not heard. I decided I was going to try and gain his trust to get info. However, if he wasn't going to cooperate, I wasn't going to sweat it.

After a long and awkward pause, Kay pressed, "So...what *do* you know?"

He turned to get a good look at Mika, lifting his brow with intrigue. He then reached into the lower left pocket of his black cargo shorts. He produced three black dice with white dots. They were crudely crafted; clearly hand-painted. "I don't call myself 'Dice' for nothing." His remark was accompanied by a twinge of cocky arrogance.

What the…? Is this for real?

He rattled the dice a bit before throwing them to the side of the building next to us. "Odd," he called, predicting the outcome.

Mika tapped me and whispered in my ear. "Weird…"

"You're telling me."

We followed and examined the dice. The results were one, four, and five.

Dice huffed, nodding his head. Seeming bothered by it, he picked up his dice and put them back in his pocket, seeming annoyed at his self-inflicted defeat. "Total came up even, so I'll be good for now. Let's just go."

VI

It was a short two blocks to a welcoming table at a nearby café. We slid into the bench seats, keeping Mika in the middle. Dice sat at the opposite end of the table from us. His interest still appeared to be fixated on Mika. I, for one, was curious as to why he appeared so intrigued by her.

After placing an order for beverages, Dice got down to business. "As I was saying: police found an innkeeper dead in his office around eleven o'clock this morning. The news got to Naro in time for him to make it the top story on *This Week in Eden*."

Kay reacted. "*This Week!?* Oh man, that's the worst!" She then turned to me. "We didn't hear about this throughout the day."

"Yeah, we didn't even tune in for the show. We were too focused on—" I cut myself off. Not only was the waitress arriving with our drinks, but the *last* thing I wanted to do was blab our business to Dice.

Dice treated my pause as an opening for his antics. "Too focused on...what? Dawdling? Napping?" He shifted focus to Kay. "Or are the three of you now teamed up to preach Kay's stupid 'slippery slope' nonsense?"

I replied quickly. "You have your business, I'm sure. We have ours. Let's stick to what affects all four of us: *This Week in Eden*."

"We can," he said. A smirk displayed satisfaction at his jabs. "Friendly reminder: we're 'revolutionaries' in public."

Mika, Kay, and I all gave a subtle reaction. Sitting at a cafe with so many other ears around, we needed to refrain from using the name "Cause" to refer to ourselves.

Dice let a few more seconds pass before continuing. "As far as the broadcast goes: I tuned in for the whole thing. Naro directly blamed a group of 'unidentified revolutionaries.'" He made quotation marks with his fingers. "I don't think it's so simple, though. We're up past two months since the Revolution started this *could* be an incident unrelated to us as a whole—"

Kay chimed in, "But it's perfect to get citizens and clued businesses to think twice about us."

Dice slapped the table. "It would have been *nice* without the interruption. At least on the forums, I can finish my own sentences. But I guess I should've expected as much from you."

Mika jolted at the loud bang before she snuggled, cowering, pulling me and Kay closer into her. She was clearly uncomfortable; unwilling to engage in the conversation.

I replied through clenched teeth, "Watch the volume, Dice. We're still in public."

Dice now fixed on me, rolled with an exaggerated motion calling, "Even." The dice clattered to a halt on six, two, and two. His eyes narrowed at the result.

"Are those dice really necessary?" I asked, puzzled. "We're trying to share information here."

Scooping them up, he replied, "Sharing regardless, there's only so much I put up with from other revolutionaries."

I sipped my drink. "Guess there's no mystery behind your traveling alone."

His lip curled high. "You're begging me to roll again?"

"Let's get back on topic, guys." Kay's voice strained a bit as she spoke. I could sense she had more to say to the surly boy, but was holding it back for the sake of figuring out the situation.

Dice chuckled, tilting his head forward to his straw. "For once, I actually agree with you, Kay." He sipped, "We sat here as revolutionaries to hash out business. Dwelling on our online 'relationships' isn't productive to the here and now."

I folded my arms, reclining into the backrest with the same indignant posture I would model for my siblings. "I'm listening."

"Good. It's hard to absorb information when you're flapping your own jaw anyway." My lips buttoned at the sneer, to which he added, "What? You're making it too easy!"

I quietly pictured myself punching him in the throat for a moment. I knew from personal experience it was impossible to speak through the choking sensation, and it hurt a lot. My fist had clenched with the impulse and desire to silence our new *friend,* but I kept my composure and pushed the thought down.

"Actually," he trailed off, pulling his dice out of his pocket.

I sighed, "This again."

He shook the dice as a glazed expression of thought came to his eyes. "We'll go with eight or less to continue," he stated with a deliberate growl, throwing the three dice onto the table.

The results were five, four, and two.

"You failed again," I announced.

He raised his voice in a vicious sneer as he picked up his dice. "Why don't you try listening next time? In case you didn't understand, this conversation is over." He stood and dropped two arna on the table for his drink.

His wager repeated in my head, helping me notice he was right. The anger swelled again. "What? You're leaving so quickly?"

Kay leaned forward in protest. "You can't!"

"The dice say I sure can," he jeered.

I didn't want him to leave yet. If Dice tuned into the whole broadcast, he *had to* have known more details on Naro's slanderous attacks. More importantly, we needed to know of what evidence was being used to point the finger at these alleged "unidentified revolutionaries". With the inns being wary of Causes, we couldn't guarantee being able to find a Contact. Dice was our best bet for any factual news.

In haste, I spit out the first thing I could reason to try getting him to stay. "The odds of rolling eight or less on three dice are uneven anyway."

Dice flashed a toothy smile. "I suppose that should tell you how much I was inclined to continue." He picked up his backpack and started walking away.

Still reeling from the revelation Dice was going to withhold what he knew, I had not noticed how quiet the cafe had gotten. A Pata Police officer stopped Dice before he made five steps.

It felt like time had stopped as my heart raced, and my situational awareness confirmed my immediate fears. Two more Pata Officers to our left and another two were past Dice covering the door. We were surrounded.

My heart sank into my stomach to meet what little of my beverage I had imbibed. As the first officer backed Dice onto the bench, I could picture the four of us being taken away in restraints. Even worse, I wondered what would happen to Mika if the police found out she was not actually with the Causes.

My first instinct was to shout for everyone to split up and run. However, seeing how casually the officers approached us, I figured it best to hesitate and listen before acting.

The officer who stopped Dice addressed the four of us as a group. "We presume the four of you are revolutionaries, yes?"

Kay, Mika, and even Dice looked at me as if they wanted me to suddenly be the group representative. I felt uplifted to see the panicked expression on Dice's face once again. Before I could bust his chops about it, though, answering the officer's questions had to come first.

My thoughts trailed to the point where the officer lost patience. He asked me directly, "Are you the leader of this group, young man?"

I took a deep breath and exhaled to calm myself. "Yes, we are revolutionaries." I answered with a quiver. "What do you need?"

I looked to the other three, trying to muster a confident façade. I signaled with my hands for everyone to stay put for the time being. Our group had to come off as orderly and mature as possible. Maybe we would have a chance to escape if the time seemed appropriate.

The officer looked to his partners and nodded, then said, "Before we continue, we'd like to fill you in on what's going on." His voice was stern but calm. He emitted a sense of confidence and authority, but did not seem to be trying to intimidate us.

Much more at ease with the officer, I proceeded with only a hint of reluctance. "We heard about the broadcast and some rumors. Is this about the poisoned innkeeper?"

"Yes, it is," he replied, "We'd like to ask for your cooperation. We've been instructed by Vade to round up revolutionaries and bring them to the Gateway Inn for questioning."

"Vade," I nervously repeated, "Head of Justice."

Ryan made an attempt to calm us. "We can understand how her name can scare you kids."

Dice cracked another comment. "We're not fond of the term 'Labor Fields,' either!"

Ryan laughed before concluding the announcement of his mission. "Trust me; we're only trying to get to the bottom of this. Once we find the murderer among your allies, you're free to go. We're not here for anything else but the culprit."

"Why do you think it was revolutionaries?" I asked.

"Were you listening to anything I said?" Dice bitterly interrupted. "I told you: Naro placed the blame on us. Thus, the police are going to seek *us* out for questioning."

"The young man is right," the officer affirmed. "The fact it was likely to have been done by a revolutionary is the only reason we're bringing you in. You'll be assigned a room for the night and will be questioned. Once we're done with you, you'll be free to go in the morning."

"So," Kay mumbled, "you only need us to cooperate and answer some questions?"

He nodded. "Correct, miss."

Fretfully gritting my teeth, I reasoned. "Well, a man's dead. While the police are being polite about it, we should cooperate. We are sort of cornered here, after all."

Dice shook his head. "Say it out loud, why don't you!"

"Well," the officer spoke, "we've gotten similar reactions all night from the ones we already have at the Gateway."

There was justified hesitation in our decision to assist the police. It appeared Naro's influence on the public had taken effect toward the Causes. We were being rounded up like Terra Sector livestock and confined to the Gateway Inn.

Not a single thing about this situation seemed proper. Vade had the power here and it felt like a setup. My mind busied itself forming conspiracies of Vade and the Fifteen using this roundup to squeeze the Revolution; to force us into silence. But I did not see a way out; it was uncomfortably familiar.

VII

Our arrival at the Gateway Inn was greeted with nervous smiles and desperate gazes from other Causes involved in the police search. In their eyes, I saw my own worries mirrored. We were all trapped in this together. It's difficult to compare the sensation of having your fears validated by peers.

Including the four of us, the police had managed to wrangle in a sizeable audience of Causes—although comparing it to the thirteen-thousand of us made me wonder if this was the amount somebody like Naro or Vade would have had in mind.

Focusing on the cluster of swirling, unspoken questions eased my face to a gentle scowl. Were they going to try and make us go home or herd us to the Labor Fields? Had my choices endangered two of my fellow Causes and an innocent young girl caught in the tide of our movement? I felt responsible since I was the one the others let speak. Guilt mixed itself into my cocktail of emotions.

Kay whispered to me, breaking my concentration. "Remember, we use our real names here. Got it, Dartmouth?"

"Sure thing, Susan," I whispered back.

Since we knew Mika was not using an alias, the two of us turned to Dice. He gave us a cold, uninterested gaze as he declared his name, "Charles." He then turned away from us to separate from the group.

"Where are you going?" I asked.

"I'm gonna eavesdrop on the officers to see what they know

about this whole thing. I'll keep my ears open for any other names of the Fifteen."

"You think this is...a trap?" Mika asked him.

He turned back to look her in the eye, pushing his glasses up the bridge of his nose as he sharply spoke. "You would have to be stupid to not think this is a trap."

Kay added, "The names 'Haz' and 'Dallas' come to mind in a situation like this."

Dice agreed. "Haz, Dallas, Vade—it doesn't matter. Any one of them can slap you in the Labor Fields and move on with their day. However, it wouldn't surprise me if Naro showed up. He was the one who started this whole thing with his damn broadcast."

"We should leave here the moment the police are finished with us," I said.

"Definitely," Dice agreed. "I'll see what I can find out."

"Go for it." We dismissed him.

It was oddly satisfying to see the hostile first meeting with Dice had become a strange, frayed faith in each other to get through this danger. Regardless of our malice towards each other, I was willing to cooperate with him as long as it kept us out of the Labor Fields. Seeing him going forward was a good first step.

An officer took position in front of the crowded foyer and announced the layout of the questioning procedure. They were going to have three Causes to a room. Once settled in, the police would fingerprint and question the Causes in each room as a group as well as individually.

This procedure created immediate complications for our group of *four*. Also, three of the four of us had a much better picture of what went on concerning the murder of the innkeeper. Despite the newfound hint of fragile trust, I made the executive decision to keep Dice separate from the rest of us.

Before I could explain my plan to the girls, the police began creating the groups of three for us. They were deliberately choosing Causes at random and pairing them all up. Anybody who was traveling in a party appeared to go into a low-key panic.

Kay nudged me with urgency. "What do we do?"

I made a split-second decision to hopefully keep us out of trouble in case we were to get separated. "Tell them the truth about everything. Well, maybe except the 'refund' we took."

She shook her head with a sense of disbelief. "What? You want me to cover for you now?"

"Look, I got rid of the coins. Seriously, tell them the truth about Roy; we were in our room together the whole time. They only care about who gave him the jayda."

I turned to Mika. "You understand?" Mika nodded.

I looked at Kay, "With your bright red hair and bandages, you stand out. People probably saw us go in or come out from around the back."

Her eyes widened upon her realization. "They're probably going to question us hard if the police have hints about us."

"You," an officer called, addressing Mika, "little girl!"

Mika looked at him and pointed to herself. "Me?"

The officer sounded hurried; like he wanted to get the groups formed quickly in order to quiet the mounting ruckus in the foyer. "Yes, come over here."

Kay and I fearfully watched Mika make her way over to the officer. We saw her get paired up with Dice. And although we couldn't put any solid degree of reliance in the boy, we could at least breathe easy knowing Mika would be with somebody who was at least not a *complete* stranger.

I exhaled and relaxed. "I guess they thought Dice was alone."

"We got lucky, yeah," Kay replied.

Within moments, the two were out of sight. "I guess this leaves you and me with someone else here." I was filled with nervous energy thinking about the events again.

Kay groaned as she looked over the crowd in the lobby. "I

wouldn't be too sure."

A tall, bulky officer called to me. "You, sir!"

A second later, a female officer called for Kay. "You, ma'am!"

My chest pulsed, and a lump blocked my throat. With gritted teeth, the two of us split from each other and over to the officers. I hesitated for a moment, looking only once to see Kay's desperate, frightened eyes gazing back into mine before the two of us slipped out of each other's sight.

VIII

The policeman gave a stern order to me as he led the way to room 3-12. "Wait here. We'll return later when we're ready to question you." I agreed nervously, still feeling off about the situation.

Even after the officer left, I continued to stare at the door, concerned about the others. The feeling of things spiraling out of my control made me cringe. Who knew what Kay was going to say to the police; or Mika, if the police pressured her too much? Moreover, Dice's way of making decisions made what could come out of his mouth next an absolute crapshoot.

Imagining how Mika might be handled by the police put my insides in a twist. Her father was still missing and her mother was dead. The poor girl was one false move away from a one-way ticket into the arms of Exta's Orphan Matrons; to be brought to adulthood alongside other orphans and children of Labor Field prisoners. It was a fate nobody would desire, nor wish on anyone.

As the other two Causes made small talk with each other, I was considering my options. I was still under the suspicion this was all a setup staged by Vade and Naro. It would only be a matter of time before a form of retreat would be necessary.

Even though it would serve to complicate escape, I knew in my heart I was not leaving without Mika. Getting her roped into this crisis was my responsibility, and I refused to let her wind up in anyone else's hands before reuniting her with her father.

Suddenly, the other young man in the room broke my train of thought. "Thinking about Kay and Mika, right?"

I could only exhale in frustration.

It took me a few seconds to understand what had been said to me. I turned around, asking, "How did you—?" Getting a glance at the gentleman, I realized I had been roomed together with Doctrine. It was a much-needed pleasant surprise. "Doctrine! How are you still in the Pata Sector?"

He approached me with a reminder, extending his hand for a shake. "For the sake of protecting the Producers and the other Causes, call me Sydney. Don't let the police catch wind of our usernames. Too much inside information could crash everything for us." I nodded in understanding and revealed my name to him in turn. He continued, "I got sidetracked on my way out when I ran into a couple more Causes I know from the forums. I wound up joining them for a meal. Before I knew it, hours passed on me. I split from them, went to get onto the train, and the police were right there. They told me what was going on and I agreed to cooperate."

I folded my arms and gave him a wry grin. "This is coming from the guy who said, 'We can't afford to be accused of this'."

He protested my remark. "Lay off it, bro. I know as much about this as you do."

"Pretty much." He had a point.

Overhearing us, another voice spoke with a deep, invested curiosity. "Wait a minute. Are you saying you know something?"

I glanced over to the corner where the voice had come from. There sat a young woman, looking directly at me with an intently sharp gaze of curiosity and concern. With my sudden halt and instant, wordy well of nerves at the question, one might think I was guilty. "Hi there; sorry, miss. You know, with all of this going on, it's easy to forget about manners and…introductions." I was trying to keep my eyes to hers, but the deep green of her irises looked as easy to get lost in as the thick forests of Gova. Her blue top had a low V-neck which displayed a bare, sleek collarbone, and her shorts showed off her noticeably muscular legs; legs that had probably been on the move for some time now. This unexpected beauty caught me off-guard, putting an awkward swirl in my gut and a subconscious inclination to deepen my already-shifting voice. I hoped desperately no one else in the room had noticed these clear heralds to my lack of experience with women. Thankfully, her long brown hair was attractive enough to keep my switched-to-simple brain from sending my words or eyes towards the realms of typical teen-boy idiocy.

Doctrine chuckled at my awkward stumbling. "Smooth recovery there, Dartmouth." Okay, obviously *he* noticed. My heart sank as I silently hoped he was the only one.

Right after, her voice cut through the awkward silence. "So, it's Dartmouth and Sydney, eh? I'm Zoe." She lowered to a whisper, "'Month of May' is my name on the forums. 'May' for short." She smiled briefly to both of us and offered a nod of kindness and acknowledgment. After the introductions, her topics of priority went right back on track. We explained to her what we knew about the whole situation. Most importantly, we let her know we had nothing to do with the plot. We happened to be at Roy's when the whole thing went down.

The conversation teetered into discussing recent goings-on. The three of us soon touched on the subject of Hatcher. May shared all of the information she was able to discern from her Contact visit from earlier. There had still been no sign of him. The Producers declared they could only wait for him for so long. Regardless of this extended absence, many Causes still felt confident Hatcher would show up.

Our whispers were cut short by a knock at our door. It was

now time for the police to focus their interrogation on us.

They asked to see Zoe first. She cooperated and obediently followed the officer. After they were out of sight, I said to Doctrine, "Looks like we're next, huh?"

He nodded, not saying a word.

The air in the room suddenly felt heavy and weighted. Doctrine's mix of slight actions and awkward silence caused my heart to shudder. Something had begun to feel off-kilter. I thought for a moment as I tried to relax myself by sitting on the bed. "What do you plan on saying to them?" I asked.

He did not look at me as he gave his answer in a dark and serious tone. "Do you plan on telling them the truth?"

My eyes darted to the right as I spit out a quick reply. "Yes. I mean, we didn't do it. And nothing has been mentioned about missing money." I gasped into my next thought; whispering. "Oh man! What about you; what about the porn?"

He laughed, patting his belongings. "I should probably tell them I was there, too. I'll hand over the porn to be destroyed. The assembly lines aren't looking appealing, either." Doctrine appeared anxious; as though the porn was the last thing on his mind.

His change in demeanor unsettled and disturbed me. I was silently starting to question what kind of account he was going to present to the police. "You all right, man?"

He breathed a few deep breaths. "Look, Dartmouth, Brigg, buddy…" He turned and rigidly ambled over to me; putting his hands on my shoulders.

The ensuing silence was long and disturbing. I stammered a bit before telling him, "If you're going to say something, you'd better say it now before the police come back."

His hands released their grip, now simply resting on my shoulders. "You need to run."

"What did you say?"

He gave my shoulders a squeeze; head still down. "You, Kay,

and Mika need to run." After a beat, he elaborated. "Let's be real, man. This whole thing is a trap. I know it; you know it; and I'm sure a bunch of the others get the feeling, too. Trust me and get out of here once the police come to take me."

I swiped his hands away and backed up a step. "What about the investigation? We were both there to find Roy dead."

"Forget about Roy; understand. Once I leave this room, there's a good chance I'm not coming back."

What he was implying drew my face into a scowl. "Is there something you're not telling me? What have you gotten yourself into to make you say a thing like that?"

Doctrine's hands eased downward in a gesture asking me to calm down. "I've gotten around during the Revolution and—"

The door opened, cutting him off. Standing in the doorway, a Pata officer read from a scroll. "I need to see Sydney."

Doctrine breathed deep and patted me on the shoulder. "That's your cue, man. Do as I say, and shoot me a message soon, if you get a chance."

I did not want to clue in the officer on anything Doctrine had said to me, so I replied with an affirming nod. Although he was so on-edge when he was speaking to me, Doctrine followed the officer with little sense of hesitation.

I was now alone; left to consider Doctrine's warning. He sounded so certain of my need to escape, I was inclined to go into the hall and find out what room Mika and Dice were assigned to, just in case. However, I had no idea what the situation in the hallways was, and did not want to arouse any suspicion from the police. In the end, I decided to stay still and at least prepare to give my testimony to the police before making moves to escape. While considering other details, May returned to the room.

I took the next few minutes to explain to May the information relayed to me by Doctrine. It had turned out May, too, had plans to escape before the Fifteen were to get too close to the Gateway.

She was planning on skipping out soon, seeing as her role in the interrogation was done anyway. "Hopefully, I'll be able to get out of here without being seen. Or, I'll tell them I'm going out for a bite to eat."

Her suggestion lightened the mood a little. "Sounds like a good plan. Go out for dinner and don't come back."

Her responding smile was genuine, which was a refreshing sight amongst how disastrous everything around us felt.

"Actually, I'd also like to tell the police what I know. Sydney isn't looking for us to wait up for him. So once I come back from my questioning, we'll go for it."

"Well, didn't he mention you having two other people?"

She was right. Before I did anything, it was imperative I found Mika. I had to take extra consideration to figure if it would have been worth it to seek out Kay or Dice.

With Dice having been assigned to the same room as Mika, leaving him behind would be difficult if a roll of his *stupid* dice put in him the need to tag along. The memory of his brow rising at the sight of her replayed in my head, fueling the idea he wanted to know more about her, or why she was with me.

And Kay? Although we had spent the day getting along and helping search, I still felt uneasy around her. Throughout the day, Causes had supplied us with frequent reminders of our forum bickering. Coupled with the fact she was still, technically, never *invited* to travel with us, it all felt like good enough reasons to leave her behind.

After dwelling on it, I answered May. "You're right, but it's three people now," I confirmed before changing my attitude. "If anything, I need to find one of them and ditch the other two."

"Interesting." She sauntered over and sat next to me on the bed. "What's up? Forum drama spilling over?"

My brow fell flat as my eyes cast an apathetic glance into hers. "Are the names 'Kay' and 'Dice' familiar to you?" I kept my voice at a whisper, careful to make sure no passing officers could hear.

She pondered it for a few seconds before her look of thought was replaced with one of confusion. "Forum drama it is! What are you doing traveling with *them*?"

I threw my hands up. "I've been getting that all day with Kay. And to tell you the truth, I don't even know! She decided to start following me. Dice is fresh, though. We bumped into him on the street shortly before winding up here."

Zoe stood and took one long, striding step toward her backpack as she reached her arm out to grab it. She sat back down and placed her bag between us. Her questions continued. "Who is it you want to keep with you? I heard Sydney say the name, but it slipped my mind."

"Someone who I can *actually* get along with." I decided to spare her the finer details of Mika since we needed to stay focused on our situation. Beautiful and charming as May was, I still didn't really know her. How could I be sure how much information I could trust her with? For the time being, the fewer strangers who knew, the better.

The two of us continued with tales of our Revolution exploits. She was impressed by the fact I had spent an entire week in the Gova Sector. The curious young woman had been wondering if hiding out there was worth the risk of being distanced from society. I assured her as long as she did not wander too far from the train tracks as I had, she would manage fine.

We carried on about nothing in particular as we waited for Doctrine to come back.

After fifteen minutes had passed, I started pacing in anticipation.

Another ten minutes passed, during which Zoe and I took turns poking our heads out the door.

Another ten minutes passed, and Zoe's breaths became shallow and frequent. Her eyes darted to the direction of every minor and insignificant noise she heard. I was beginning to think something had gone wrong when Doctrine tried to surrender the pornography. *I'd hate to think they arrested him,* I thought to myself anxiously.

The blaring sound of trumpets broke our worried reverie. The sound was followed by rhythmic thumping, seemingly pounding from all around.

Zoe jumped at the sudden percussive explosion and screamed in an up-octave pitch. "What was that?" Her eyes were wild and zipped in every direction, and her body language spoke of someone on the verge of a blind, panicked run.

I was unnaturally calm. The sound of the thumping continued to reverberate as I walked to the door to peek out and assess what was going on. Inside, it was almost comforting to find the crisis I had been anticipating since Doctrine left. We knew something was coming. Now; no more waiting.

To the left I caught a glimpse of a crowd of Causes forming. The air was palpable with tension, and I had an apprehensive feeling about what was coming next from them. I was about to look to the right when Zoe pushed herself past me and managed to blurt out an apology, alongside something about taking her chances in Gova, and being quick to escape.

She was not alone in running for the side exit; several Causes tried the same. The blue-uniformed Pata Sector police seemed to be conspicuously absent. Then I heard the first screams.

"They have clubs!" someone shouted.

"She's bleeding!" another shrieking voice called out. The halls echoed in a chorus of wailing and screaming. People ran in every direction, though the noise was occasionally punctuated with rhythmic thumping sound. The frantic Causes bumping and banging into walls and slamming doors chopped through the rhythm; muddying it to a cacophony not far from the sounds of an armchair tumbling down a tall flight of stairs.

I stepped out. Within seconds, my eyes were drawn to the sight of Mika running in the opposite direction. Cupping my hands over my mouth, I called to her as loud as I could.

"Mika!"

Mika managed to hear me over all of the deafening commotion. She changed her direction without hesitation and turned to run toward me. "Brigg! They're here!"

I reached out and took her by the hand. "Where were you going?" I asked her, following the flow of people to the exit.

Mika scrambled in place, then tugged my arm as an insistence to follow her. "I was going back for Dice."

I had no interest in risking anything to help the pretentious bully. I tried to lead Mika toward the exit. "Don't worry about him. He can take care of himself."

The determined girl objected, "That's not what *he* told me!"

The instant confusion brought on by her reply almost overpowered the chaos in the hall. I stopped and turned to face her. "What do you mean?"

Mika's logic was consistent. "I think Dice needs company."

I was still in a hurry to get us to safety. "Explain it later. We need to move! If he finds us, he can follow if he wants."

Looking into Mika's sullen eyes, it was obvious my reply was not what she had had in mind. "Okay..." she whimpered.

I led her by the hand and sped our pace as a few more Causes passed us. Stopping in the hall had cost us precious seconds— seconds splitting the difference between escape and capture.

Suddenly, a large crowd started to spew back from the exit to the stairs. A deep, grainy voice called out, "They're guarding the emergency exit! We've lost a few! They're clubbin' 'em."

Uproar ensued. "We're stuck!"

"What are we going to do!?"

"See? I told you this was a trap!"

Mika's grip on my hand loosened.

The clamoring crowd of Causes now cluttering the hallway had become frenzied. A voice from the end of the hall interrupted the havoc. "We've got two of them coming up the stairs. We have to turn back around."

I shouted over the echoes and roars within the hall, trying to get more details. "Two of what?"

The youth's voice rang back as the group began to double back down the hall. "I don't know what they are, but they're definitely *not* Pata Police—WHOA!" With an echoing burst, the door at the end of the hallway slammed shut. "They're here! Someone help me hold this shut!"

"Not Pata Sector police?" This didn't make sense to me.

"What are we going to do?" Mika asked, pulling on my hand.

Turning back to look down the hall, I could see a blockade of gray. Three policemen with caps and shields were advancing towards us. "Yeah, those are definitely *not* Pata police."

A couple of Causes broke from the mass and dashed shouting toward the oncoming officers. The police lifted their clubs high but kept the rest of their bodies stone still, not moving their shields or breaking their hall-blocking formation. One of the brave youths shoulder-checked the shield on the left, only to bounce off, shout, then get knocked in the head. The other Cause scrambled away, tripping over his own feet in an attempt to escape before lamentably falling victim to a heinous and morbid bludgeoning. After the tide of Causes broke against the gray-clad formation, The police took a single step forward and banged their clubs against their shields with a unified *thump*.

Taking it in and realizing the magnitude of it all, I boomed out what felt to be our only chance. "Window exits!"

An unsure young lady called back to me. "We can't jump out the windows; we're on the *third floor*!"

As more banging and shouting filled the hallway, the notion to lead the panicked mass to safety suddenly overtook me. I contested their panicked uncertainties with a rigid disposition and certain conviction in my attitude. "I don't think there are any other choices right now! Follow me, quick, and let's all figure it out behind a locked door!"

With my choice of the last word made clear, I ran with Mika into the nearest room. I hadn't noticed at first, but several other Causes had decided to follow me. Many of the others dispersed into nearby rooms. As for the brave souls who guarded the exit or blocked the shields to buy us time, they were last seen being pulled away by those mysterious officers who were, we could only assume, taking direct orders from the Fifteen.

I let as many into the room as I could until it felt dangerous to leave the door open any longer. I secured both locks on the door to try to buy us as many extra seconds as we could get.

As I finished fastening the door, a hand gripped my shoulder from behind. As I jerked, I nearly elbowed my assailant in the nose before I recognized the bandaged hand. Kay jumped back a half step, surprised and clearly distraught. "Brigg! *Where* are you going? Did you even *try* to find me? Were you planning on ditching me?"

We were all in shock; every one of us. Whatever our differences, we had one common need: to escape. I grunted dismissively at her. My adrenaline was high and I did not have time to argue. Mika spoke up. "Not now, Kay!"

Before the group of Causes could mutter any comments through their entertained smirks, I cut off the chance in order to speed up our escape. "Yes, Brigg is with Kay! It's been funny all day!" I turned to Kay. "Escaping now; explaining later. We need to get moving because we *all*..." I pointed to the group, "...don't have time to argue." In haste, I reached into my bag. "Who else has rope?"

A few raised their hands and shuffled through their bags.

"Pull it out and tie some knots in it! Big knots; a few inches apart!" I took my length of rope and tied it to the base of the bed. "When you escape from here, the only things you need to do are run fast, run far, and run like you stole something!"

They all agreed; springing into action.

Within moments, we had constructed a length of rope with which we could safely drop into the alley below. One by one, the Causes filed out of the window.

Kay grabbed onto Mika and held her worriedly. "Are you going to be alright going down by yourself?"

Before Mika could answer, there was a loud bang outside of the room. The door shook violently and the room itself rattled with the blow. The tallest, strongest-looking young man in the room ran to the door and held it back. "Everyone, *get going!*"

The other Causes were now going faster and faster. Amongst all of the rush and panic, the thought of a weight limit must not have registered for everyone. The bottom leg of the bed broke under the weight, sending several Causes on it tumbling to the alley below.

"Oh no!" Kay exclaimed as she gripped onto the ledge and leaned out of the window. "Is everyone okay!?"

We were running out of time. I pushed Kay out of the way and onto the bed. "Throw the rope back up here!"

It was taking the Causes in the alley below a moment to recover from the fall. From what I could discern, though, everyone seemed to be fine; relatively speaking. One of them pitched the leg of the bed back up to me, but I missed catching it. After two more tries, I got hold of it, and tied the rope to another leg of the bed.

The locks on the door were beginning to rattle loose. "Hurry up!" the burly Cause shouted over the sounds of splintering wood and bending metal.

"Kay, go!"

"Well, you know I'm going to wai—"

I cut her off. "Yes, yes, I know! Wait for us, then! Go! The door isn't going to last!"

Mika jumped and shouted at the sound of another impact on the door. She threw herself into me and clutched the side of my shirt. I felt her shaking as she wept.

I leaned in to console her. "Mika, don't be scared. Think of your father and how you'll be able to see him again if you escape from here."

A tear rolled down her cheek as she forced a thankful smile.

Kay was now out of sight. The only people left in the room were Mika, the young man holding the door, and myself. I asked him, "Are you going to be alright?"

He grunted, holding back another blow to the door. "Well, let's be honest. This is probably the end of the Revolution for me. Don't worry about it though. It's going to end for all of us eventually, right? You guys get out, and keep it going for as long as you can."

"Right." I agreed as I patted Mika on the head. "Mika, it's your turn. Go ahead and wait for me with Kay."

She nodded, sniffling one last time before taking herself slowly out the window.

I turned back to the strong youth one last time. "What's your forum name? I'll want to thank you personally on the forums next time I see a Contact."

"Pibs," he said with a grin. "Thanks, Brigg."

"No; thank *you*. I'll make sure you get the credit you deserve."

With the next hit to the door, the doorknob shot off and hit the floor. "You have to go, now!" Pibs said.

I backpedaled upon seeing the doorknob at my feet. I swiftly turned toward the window and made my escape, leaving Pibs behind to complete his sacrifice for the near-twenty he helped make it out of the Gateway.

During my descent into the alley, I looked to my right to see another group of Causes escaping using the same method we did. Getting a closer look at the bottom of their rope, I could see the unmistakable high collar of Dice's green shirt. He seemed to be preoccupied with himself and not taking notice of me.

I then looked to my left and noticed Kay was leading Mika down the alley by the hand. Was she trying to leave me behind? "Oh, that stupid bitch!" I shouted. I was low enough on the rope to simply let go and drop.

Upon hitting the ground, I stumbled; accidentally tripping somebody. "Hey, watch where you're going!"

"Sorry!"

"Brigg?" It was Dice. "Brigg, Kay is taking Mika away!"

I stood and looked down the alley. "I know! Follow them!"

He took his dice out of his pocket and started to roll them.

I hollered, "Does it look like we have time for your nonsense!?" I grabbed him by the front of his shirt and thrust him in the direction Kay was running before dashing ahead of him.

Everything was still a rush, and I knew I was not thinking clearly through this festival of adrenaline. Escaping the police and catching up to Mika were the two thoughts pushing every other want and need aside. So although it was appealing to a calmer me to lose Dice in the confusion, I *did* tell Mika he could follow if he wanted. With a brief glance back, I could see Dice picking up his pace to try and keep up.

X

A mixture of fear and rage powered my run. Kay's suspicion and pestering made her company unpleasant, but now I had to race to catch her. *She is not going to take Mika.* Every step thus far, I had been nothing but kind to the kid, and all I wanted for her was for her to be safe. This crazy woman was not going to take her. For the first time in my life, I felt like I had a purpose and a family, and Kay was *not* taking it away.

Fortunately, I had caught sight of Mika in enough time to see which way Kay was leading her. They turned right through another alleyway. I made the turn and saw Mika again. The way her legs were moving made it look like Kay was dragging her. It only served to further enrage me; she was hurting Mika. I continued pursuit as Kay went for a left turn.

Shortly after they were out of sight around the corner, I heard Mika give out a cry of pain. I gave a quick thought to the worst.

Before my negative thoughts got too out of control, I turned the corner and saw the two of them. They had stopped. Mika was collapsed on the ground, holding her left ankle as Kay kneeled down to help her.

We were well into the last straw with this. Without hesitation, I stomped over to Kay; fully conscious of the seething scowl occupying my appearance. She scrambled to her feet and turned away; knowing full-well I was not going to let this slide.

Without really thinking about it, I grabbed her by the shirt and pinned her back up against the outside of the nearest building. The top of her ponytail was the only thing to cushion her head as it bounced off of the brick structure.

"How DARE you!?" I shouted. *"WHAT gives you the RIGHT? WHY?"* I was shaking, feeling her pulse quicken in my grip. I was barely holding back.

Her eyes widened as she gripped my arm with desperate, shaking hands.

"Answer me!" I demanded, pushing and shaking my fist into her collarbones. "We've been getting along all day! I *thought* we had an understanding! Were you playing nice until you had an opening to *kidnap* her!?"

Mika called out. "Brigg, don't hurt her! She only wanted to protect me!"

"Yeah, well she *HURT YOU!*" Still gripping Kay's shirt, I

pulled her away from the wall to give her a look at the injured girl. "Is this your idea of *protection*, Kay? Look at her!"

Dice showed up, took one look at Mika, and attended to her. Mika hugged him and started to cry. It was like a bucket of ice water to my burning rage.

Before I let the calm sink in, I pulled Kay close to me and said through clenched teeth, "The *only* reason I'm not laying you out on the ground right now and ditching your ass here in this alley is because we're all Causes, and we're all trying to avoid capture! The next time you pull a stunt like that, you had best be thinking about protecting *yourself* before anyone else! Do you *understand?*"

Her quivering bottom lip and the tear rolling down her cheek complemented her meek nod.

I let her go. A brief, awkward silence was about us; the kind where everyone seems afraid to be the next one to speak.

"I don't think she expected you to throw her to the wall there," Dice chuckled.

"You didn't have to do that," Mika murmured.

I countered, "*She* didn't have to drag you through the alleys. You twisted your ankle."

"He does have a point there, Mika," Dice offered. "This entire stunt was unnecessary, and got you hurt. It won't bode well for you trying to find your dad with broken ankles."

His reply took me aback. "Oh! So she told you?"

With a laugh, Dice answered, "Only after I apologized for earlier at the cafe."

Mika glanced up to me with a strained smile; still fighting the pain. "Yeah, I told him about my dad and how you two are helping me. And I think we can help Dice with his—"

Dice sliced through, sharp, with a slew of incoherent non-words before correcting her. "Hey-hey! Agreement; agreement!"

She stopped with sweetly-acceptant compliance. "Right."

It appeared Mika and Dice being separated from us earlier had proven beneficial. Dice was not acting as disagreeable as he was before the incident. Perhaps it would not have been a bad idea to invite him to follow us. He obviously cared about Mika, and having an extra pair of eyes on Kay seemed like a good plan. After all, we still were not far from the Gateway Inn and still at risk of being found by the Fifteen.

I decided to put aside my online history with Dice, at least for the moment. Putting these thoughts to the test I asked, "Dice, can you carry her?"

"Can you carry her things?" he grinned. "Does this mean you're inviting me in?"

"Well, you and Mika seem to be getting along now and—"

He interrupted, "That doesn't mean I think any more of you."

"Great; just great." Kay murmured.

I turned around to her, raising my voice again with the deliberate intention of keeping her on edge. "*You* have said quite enough tonight! We're on the run now. So you had better take all your mumble-grumble thoughts about your damn 'slippery slope,' shove them, and accept things for what they are. We don't have the luxury of being able to care about each other's opinions and reservations right now. Am I making sense, Kay!?"

Through gritted teeth and another tear, she croaked, "Yes. I understand."

Dice stood, lifting Mika onto his back. "Is Kay still coming with us?"

I picked up Mika's bag and slung it over my shoulder; cutting into Kay's eyes with my irate stare. "Are you still *following* us?"

Kay picked her bag back up and nodded. "I have nowhere else to go…"

I added. "Do you understand? You *pushed* yourself into our company. I chose to give credence to your arguments from the forums; I understand your inhibitions. I did the best I could to respect you and put you at ease throughout the day. But this stunt;

this *damn* stunt! You pissed me off. You get no more leeway. So for now, you wanted to follow, so you're going *follow*. You had *better not* try that again!"

Her lips pursed, and she refused to speak or look to anyone.

I nodded to Dice. "We're going now."

Over the course of the next hour, we navigated the streets and alleyways of Pata. With every corner we approached, I had to shift my head to look in all directions. Every single person we saw looked like a police officer at first glance. The sight of any human figure gave my heart a jump. Even the simple act of walking out to cross a street was done so with staggering reluctance.

After another thirty minutes, Dice eased us with an uncanny realization. Even though the Fifteen had stormed the hotel with those gray-uniformed officers, there were no police outside or surrounding the building. Even after escaping and running, we had not seen any police since; not even a Pata Sector officer. None of the police even bothered to shift outside after I had blasted "Window exits" at the top of my voice.

While we would have liked to simply chalk it up to a lucky break, there was no way it could have been so simple. Once Dice presented this odd detail, I recalled having had seen a building surrounded by police in the past. With such a significant corral of defiant "revolutionaries" sitting like fish in a barrel, surely Vade should have had the whole *block* on lockdown so not a single one was missed.

Something was strange about the way this trap was sprung. And all Dice and I could do was flop a bunch of half-baked theories around until we finally felt it was safe to stop walking.

The well-shrouded alley had a firm soil. I asked Dice to get my blanket from my bag and place it onto the ground. After he set it up, I placed Mika down onto it. She was exhausted and was struggling to stay awake.

"We'll have to stop here for the night." I looked over at Kay, expecting her to object.

Dice was looking around. "This will have to do since I doubt any inn is going to take us."

"Sure…" Kay muttered, her head still hanging down, and her eyes to the alley's dirt floor.

I couldn't understand why, but I saw myself through her behavior. It was all there: stare to the ground; an anxious twitch at voices; the buttoned frown; low on words due to fear. This was a terrible mirror to be looking at as the sound of my father's voice from all of my own memories was punching through to accompany the saddening visual.

Naturally, the question surfaced only to myself: *Are you really going to be like your father?*

Regardless of the reasons behind my violent outburst, I felt sorry about what had done earlier. I cleared my mind to soften my voice as I addressed her, "Kay."

She slowly looked up to me. "Hmm?"

I folded my arms, calm and apologetic. "Even though I'm not happy with you right now, I shouldn't have put my hands on you so harshly."

She stammered, shaking. "I...I don't know what to say."

I pocketed my hands. "You don't need to say anything. I only need to tell you I'm sorry. A lot happened back there, and everything was a rush. But the least I could have done was take an extra five seconds to think twice."

Kay leaned against the left-hand wall of the alley, then slid down to sit on the dirt; wordless.

Looking to at least get her talking, I tried another approach. "Look, we both want the same thing: Mika back to her father safely. Am I right?"

"Three of us, actually!" Dice corrected, inadvertently preventing Kay from answering. "If you all don't mind, I'm going to stick with you for a little while. Like Brigg alluded to earlier: it's probably best for us to stick together. On the bright side for you guys, you probably won't have to deal with me rolling my dice until we're out of danger. I don't mess with arrest or bodily injury. I have my ways of dealing with people, but I'm not stupid enough for huge risks."

Acknowledging Dice's stance, I approached Kay, trying not to intimidate as I stood over her crouched position. "Look Kay, our discussions from the forums can only tell me so much. I don't know what your issues are. But for now, they're going to have to take a back seat."

"My issues are *not* your business!" she cautiously snipped.

My teeth gritted on impulse as I responded, trying *so* hard to keep a calm demeanor. "They are when you make them *my* problem; and Mika's. So, from here on, let's try to ease up on forum drama. Let's all work together through this, and start making our way out of Pata. Can you do that for us?"

Dice spoke to support. "Yeah, come on, Kay. Even *I'm* on board with this chuckle-head for the sake of survival. Let's drop the bullshit, get over here, and let's get some damn sleep."

Kay looked up to me, sighed hard, then stood on her own. With a soft fire in her eyes, she nodded and walked past me. She then retrieved a brown blanket from her bag, put it up against the left wall, and laid down facing the building. "I'm not expecting it, but please be here in the morning."

Dice offered a glance, interpreting Kay's request as a subtle invitation to leave her. I replied with a struggled smile and a dismissive wave. Though it was tempting in every sense of the word, it still did not feel right to strand a fellow Cause during this new and extreme circumstance.

Mika, Dice, and I situated ourselves to sleep close to where Kay has set herself down. With mistrust still peeking through my remorse, I tied some string around my hand, tying the other end to Mika's leg. It was the only way I would allow her to sleep next to Kay. After making sure Mika wouldn't be going anywhere, I laid myself on the alley's turf. The smell of waste-crates and dirt accompanied the discomforts of both the ground and my worry.

Though I was exhausted, questions plagued my thoughts as I slipped to sleep. I was wondering why the Pata Police were not there when the raid occurred. I was also wondering if May made it out to safety. Yet, there were two questions I remember most distinctly:

Where was Doctrine?

How did he know enough to warn me?

Day 65

I

Sustaining comfort in the dark alley eventually proved impossible. I awoke for the fourth time that night with numbness in my left arm. I exhaled with a grunt, seamlessly sweeping into a wide yawn. My eyes opened, letting in what faint light the stars in the sky provided. It was still not enough, though; I could hardly see a thing in the shadows.

The pale gray luminescence slowly overtook the darkness. My eyes gradually adapted to the poor visibility brought on by the dead of night. Every movement I made was carefully dictated only by what little I was able to see.

I untied the string from my wrist and stood, looking down at the rest of my group. Dice was lying flat on his stomach, sleeping silently. Mika was snuggled against Kay; resting her head on her shoulder as Kay curved her arm around her. It looked as if the two of them were keeping each other warm. A brief gust of wind burst past us, on cue to make my presumption a fact.

My eyes soon became focused on Kay, and my harsh handling of her replayed in my mind. I clutched my hands together as I reminisced remorsefully about pinning Kay against the building. I remembered shouting; the look on her face. I remembered the sound of my voice and the burning in my throat: *"How dare you?!"*

As I tried to focus, a memory caught me off guard. I could remember the times where it was the front of *my* shirt being grabbed; *my* back to a wall. The familiarity of it was too real to me. I gave it barely a thought before my father's voice emerged from my memory and shot through the silence of the alley.

"How dare you?!"

My teeth clenched and body shuddered as I scrambled to think of something else. However, my mind was set back, once again reminding me of my original purpose behind taking my stand as a Cause: to escape the things fogging my mind with fear and poisoning my heart with anger.

I realized through my earlier actions, I was not doing an acceptable job of distancing myself from the violent nature I sought so desperately to leave behind. I knew I was going to have to watch myself in the coming days. Keeping any fit of anger in check was not going to be an easy task considering the people who I regrettably allowed to accompany me. But for my sake, and Mika's to an extent; no—*especially* Mika's; I had to put myself up to the challenge.

I dropped to my knees, lowering myself next to Dice on the blanket. I tried to get at least somewhat comfortable. My eyes shut tightly and a loud breath pushed itself from my lungs. Before slipping back into slumber, I muttered to myself, *"How dare you...?"*

II

It was going into the early hours of the afternoon, and Kay and I had barely said a word to each other. As a matter of fact, most anything said among any of us was by me, instructing everyone where to go to keep us on as low a profile as possible. Everyone was calm and cooperative.

As opposed to the night before, which had been suspiciously quiet, there was now a significant police presence in the streets. There were intermittent sightings of both Pata Sector police and those gray-clad police from the Gateway. During our careful travels, we passed by a district bulletin board. On it, there was a new posting; a large notice slightly resembled a "warning" label, headed by bold red letters.

CAUTION, CITIZENS OF THE PATA SECTOR

Last night, an attempt to capture the revolutionary responsible for an innkeeper's poisoning death resulted in the potential escape of the perpetrator. Police will be patrolling the streets in search of the culprit. Until he or she is caught, we may continue resorting to actions which could inconvenience you in the coming days. Please be patient as we seek to arrest the culprit. We appreciate your understanding during these difficult times. If you have any tips or questions, feel free to approach me or any of my officers.

-Vade

With the bulletin causing a stir to the public, sticking to the alleyways of the Pata Sector proved increasingly difficult as the day rolled on. As Pata's everyday hustle and bustle grew busier, more and more people were beginning to notice us. Clearly, people slipping in and out of alleys with backpacks and a young girl looked suspicious. Considering the events of the night before, and the new threat of increased police presence, all of us were tense, fearfully anticipating the Fifteen on our trail.

Once we were in an area with enough cover, Dice spoke up. "Hey guys, do you think we should stop for a bit?"

Kay exhaled as though she had been holding her breath for an hour. Sitting, she glanced at him. "You think so, too, huh?"

Dice nodded. "Yeah, it's getting too crowded out there. The

damn bulletin has everyone on edge..."

Despite my desire to keep moving, even I was in agreement. "So what do we want to do from here?" I asked.

Without hesitation, Dice replied, "We should wait here until evening; or at least until things calm down out there."

Mika stopped advancing down the alley and turned around. "Is it a good idea to stay still? Aren't we still trying to hide?"

Kay squirmed with indifferent gestures, staying silent. But this was not the time to be keeping ideas and suggestions to ourselves. I addressed the group. "Look, guys. Reservations about each other aside, we're a group of Causes trying to stay in the Mission, and trying to stay alive. If you feel you have to say something, go ahead and say it. In a situation like this, we can't afford to be silent to one another. We need to be open."

"For us, communication is the best way to keep ourselves away from the Fifteen." Dice was right, and we all knew it.

I looked to Mika and saw a face rife with innocence and worry. "Is something wrong, Mika?"

She hesitated, not giving me an answer right away. She hemmed and hawed, unable to find the right way of expressing her thoughts. Something was clearly bothering her, and it was obvious, despite her apparent reluctance, she wanted to tell us. "What's this going to do to looking for my father?"

I let out a sheepish groan, disappointed our situation turned into "escape now; dad search later." Now seeing a new level of opposition, it was all the more reason to keep the purpose of the Causes in the forefront of our minds. "We have to get out of this and into the clear before we can go back out there to look for him. If we get captured by the Fifteen, the search is over for all of us. You understand, right?"

Her pout edged into a forced, tight-lipped smile under furrowed brows. She didn't like my answer, and none of us could blame her, but at least she understood.

Dice was rearranging some of the objects in the alley for cover as he said, "By the way, it all makes sense now."

I assisted Dice in setting up shelter. "What?"

After setting a small crate down, he shrugged wide. "Come on. Building not surrounded; the whole place filled with guards, but *none* came after us outside; no one searching the streets for the rest of the night after we got out; and now the bulletin." He paused briefly, cocking his eye to me before he continued. "The Fifteen let a bunch of us escape on purpose. There's no reason they couldn't have caught us last night if they really wanted to."

No one said a word. Although farfetched, something about the idea worked. I took a breath before adding my thoughts. "They let us escape to make an excuse to spread out across this area of Pata. They needed a reason to guard the streets this heavily." It then occurred to me. "What if the Fifteen have already found the person who did it, and are making this up at this point? What if this is all a game?"

Kay actively nodded, adding to the idea. "To have a good reason to put more police on our tail. No killer on the loose; just an opportunity to call on more guards to hunt more of us down."

I pointed to her. "Sure sounds like an 'inconvenience' to the citizens of Pata to me."

Kay leaned against the wall, folding her arms; head tilted down. "The Gateway not being guarded from the *outside* made it much easier for us to escape—too easy for it to have been an accident. Vade *had to* have known this!" She paused for a moment as we all looked to one another. "There's no way she wouldn't have had the outside covered if she wanted to make sure none of us escaped."

Dice shifted worried eyes to all of us; his voice increasing in its intensity. "We need to get out of Pata...*yesterday!* Vade's patrols are probably going to continue spreading out."

Catching each of their eyes, I said, "As soon as night falls, let's run as far as we can towards Pata's border. Until then, let's stay hidden. If anyone has to go anywhere in the meantime, leave your gear here so you don't stand out. We cannot draw attention to ourselves right now."

As a way to express their agreement, everyone pitched in to build our cover in the alley. A few well-placed waste-crates and draping blankets tucked into a small alcove out of view of the street made up our cozy—if slightly smelly—afternoon hideaway. Even being crammed close together in such a small space was tolerable compared to feeling like we had to look over our shoulders for police every five seconds.

One thing was for sure, we needed to keep our eyes open for a Contact. It was likely news of the raid had reached the forums. This wasn't exactly the kind of thing Causes would want to keep to themselves. Someone *had* to have gotten it back to the forums by now. All we needed to do was add what we knew about the incident to any related information posted by other Causes. Hopefully then, the big picture would come into view.

Waiting around for the right time was as stressful as it was boring. However, it gave us time to further reconcile, as well as share our opinions on what appeared to be the Fifteen's decision to finally make an offensive act against the Causes. It brought to light our concern for the Producers' position and the ever-present question of Hatcher's situation.

Dice and Kay did not beat around the bush when it came to expressing their concerns for the Causes as a whole. There was an equal concern for Mika. If the Revolution were to end so abruptly, there was no telling where she was going to end up, or even worse, if she would ever see her father again.

III

The cover of darkness we had waited for was finally upon us.

All one could hear were the light gusts of wind softly howling through the Pata Sector's torch-lit streets.

It was time to move out. However, even with the dark of the night in full effect, we had to stay vigilant and had to watch our backs. We were still unsure if the Fifteen's special officers were any different from ordinary police.

We boldly set foot into the open street. Upon looking around the vicinity, wide grins spread across our faces despite the tension. Apparently, we were not the only ones who had been waiting for night to fall. From out of the shadows, more Causes swept into the dimly-lit street. Each one was carefully making their way toward a safer area. The familiar sight of Causes scampering down the street in low profile lifted our confidence. It easily reminded us of the day the Revolution began.

We stuck to the side of the street as we jogged in the direction the rest of the Causes were headed. Dice made mention of Station East being back in the other direction. To me, that was the point. Expecting to get out of the Pata Sector by train would be way too obvious. Vade's officers were probably guarding the stations, ready to take in any unsuspecting Causes.

There was an unspoken consensus to get out of the Pata Sector on foot. The sector had become hostile ground after the events of the previous night. Getting out of there altogether in the quietest fashion seemed like the safest option.

Now came the time to make a critical decision: what sector we would escape towards? We had some decent options since the three closest sector borders were those of the Gova, Terra, and Fanda Sectors. But I was far from willing to return to the Gova Sector after having spent the previous week there.

The Terra Sector was a welcoming option. Although Terra was one of the four divisions of the Labor Fields, it was not as guarded as one would think. It was mostly farmland and greenhouses. The population was all farmers, livestock herders, and botanists. The lay of the land was wide open, with most of the population spread out in small farm houses. It was a viable option to hide out and lay low for a while.

Last, the Fanda Sector presented a much better opportunity to find Mika's father before she got dragged farther into danger. Fanda was a sector more about business and entertainment than homes and neighborhoods. It was home to the acting stages, one of Eden's two Gaming Coliseums, and Eden's Grand Station. At times, it could be as crowded as the Pata Sector since people from all over Eden would go there to unwind and have fun.

As the four of us continued following the other Causes, Dice, Kay, and I weighed the options carefully. Mika, on the other hand, was focused solely on finding her father. Her vote was for Fanda.

I sided with Fanda as well, as helping Mika was still my main concern, and it would still get us away from this mess. I had every intention of sticking to my word. Likewise, it would have given the girl a shock if I were to suddenly renege and separate from her, leaving her with Kay. Recalling the incident the night before, I knew I wanted to leave Mika alone with Kay as much as Kay wanted to leave Mika alone with me.

Kay felt it safer to go to the Terra Sector and distance ourselves from as many people as possible. But I had trouble trusting her judgment and credibility. She clearly had motivations she kept secret, and she was making them Mika's problem. I decided to mention aloud.

"What?" she grumbled, though restrained in tone, "You were fine with my input earlier today, right? Does my opinion not matter here?"

I defended. "I didn't say that."

She took a stride to me. "Then why even bring it up?"

"Because you still haven't apologized, nor explained yourself for the way you've been acting towards us. How are we supposed to trust you? How are we supposed to feel like we can rely on you at all? How do you expect for everything to be fine-and-dandy with no consequence to anything you've done or said? Why are you so convinced you don't deserve to be held responsible for your own actions?"

"Didn't you say a while ago, 'everybody's input is important'?" Dice shot me a crooked smile—an expression stating clear pleasure in seeing my own words turned against me. It appeared he was game to team up with Kay to antagonize me.

I answered in an attempt to stave off confrontation. "Yes, and it's still true: everyone's opinion *is* important."

"Well then, what's the problem with Terra?" Kay pressed.

"You mean *besides* being part of the Labor Fields?"

"Seriously, Brigg?" Dice challenged, folding his arms. "Terra's got the security of a public playground in broad daylight. The fact it's one of the Fields means jack shit!"

His counterpoint gave me no sense of pause. "Well, despite the lack of security, still, if we distance ourselves, we also single ourselves out. If we're found out there in Terra, we have nowhere to hide. Whoever finds us will be exclusively focused on our party. It's different from last night, when there were so many other Causes to be taken besides us."

"Okay," Dice hummed. "That makes for a much better argument." Removing his visor and fiddling with it, he then said, "What I'm now wondering is *who* would be out there to find us. Estyr has better things to do than send patrols over countless square-kilometers of open plains, and Vade would stick to residential and business areas to find Causes."

"Good point, but I still think it is best we try to blend in with other people. Mika wants to go to Fanda. I want to go to Fanda. So we're going to Fanda whether you two like it or not. But it doesn't mean you two *have* to come along."

Dice reached his left hand into his pocket. He then hesitated for a bit. "I can't help but have the sinking sensation you're going to get us all captured."

I threw my hands up and paced in a small circle. "Well then walk straight east through Gova until you hit Zica! Nobody'll ever look for you there. Better yet, climb the wall, leave Eden. Say hi to Mammon while you're out there!"

Kay pushed her hands down, raising her brow to me. "All right, we don't need to go that far. Let's cool it."

Conceding that the Master of Beasts and the Zica Sector were not things to mention casually, I took a breath and engaged Dice, calmer. "I figured you'd want to stay with Mika as well, right?"

He took a breath, turning his gaze to the ground. "Honestly," he exhaled, "if helping the kid constitutes dealing with *you*, I think I'd be better off going with Kay to Terra."

Mika stopped walking upon hearing Dice's words. "I thought you said you'd help!" Her face fell as her bottom lip jutted out with a slight quiver.

Dice coldly dismissed whatever previous conversation he had had with her. "Look, kiddo, I told you why I'm out here doing this in the first place. I can't take care of my business if I'm toiling in the Labor Fields."

Relating to the realness of Dice's argument, I shrugged toward Mika, "I'm not really sure what else we can say to him. He seems pretty set on this."

Persistent, Mika tried once more. "I know you guys don't get along. But don't go; it's not safe."

"Nobody's safe anywhere right now anyway. So you two take care of each other, and don't get caught." Dice broke to cross the street and take an upcoming left turn—a path leading toward the Terra Sector. On his way across, he called out, "Come on, Kay. We don't need this guy!"

Kay followed him for only a few steps before calling back to him. "In case you forgot, Dice, I'm not leaving Mika. I don't want to go to Fanda, but Mika's safety comes first."

"Looks like you're on your own!" I sneered. Although this situation was swing-and-miss on getting Kay off my back, shrugging Dice off felt like a good step towards easing some of the unnecessary tension within our group. Having one less in our group would also help decrease our chances of getting seen or captured.

Dice stopped in the middle of the street and turned back to us. With surprise in his voice, he asked, "Are you serious, Kay?"

Other Causes passing by watched as our group appeared to fall apart in the middle of the street. Their whispers crept through the sounds of their hurried footsteps as if every one of them had something to say about the scene we were creating. The fact we were speaking louder than any Cause in the street was more than enough to have anybody focus their attention to us.

Dice continued to stand in the street, deeply pondering his new situation. He was all for leaving us behind if Kay had gone with him, but with Kay's position set in stone, he appeared hesitant to go through with it alone. He reached into his left pocket again as he took a few steps toward us. Letting out a disgruntled sigh, he pulled his dice out. His hand dropped to his side with each die gripped between each finger. Dice looked to Mika with apologetic concern. Whatever he and Mika talked about back at the Gateway Inn, it certainly was giving him food for thought concerning his roll.

After a few more seconds, he announced, "All dice: odd." He turned his palm forward; and with a flick of the wrist, sent his dice tumbling to the ground between us. I heard Mika peep a brief, sad groan as the results presented themselves. The dice came up one, five, and four.

Mika whimpered in disappointment.

Smirking, I helped Dice pick them up. "Looks like you're going to Ter—"

He quickly interjected, grumbling, "Fanda with you guys."

Befuddled, I tilted my head up and handed him his third die. "But you said—"

He interrupted again, "Did I say what I'd *do* on all odd?"

Mika cheered; glad to have Dice still along. Without saying much else, we followed the road toward the Fanda Sector. As we continued on, shouts and screams echoed through the streets; coming from the roads leading towards the Terra Sector. I couldn't help but feel, though; being right this time was a useless victory. With those Gray Police on our tail, there was no victory to be claimed until we actually set foot in Fanda.

IV

The next two days of the Revolution seemed to go by slower as we continued avoiding Vade by day, and skulking through the shadows at night. Tensions continued to run high as news continued to spread about the Fifteen's actions. Naro even went to the trouble of making a broadcast to boast the supposed futility of our attempts to escape.

Another member of the Fifteen also stepped in to make matters worse for the Causes. Cenia, the Head of Community and Social Relations, placed a strict curfew on the citizens of the Pata Sector. Now, *any* person seen on the streets after the torches were lit would be approached by the Fifteen's special police. If it was a Cause, they were taken away. Anybody else would be given a warning and sent back to their home.

Since it was so easy to distinguish a Cause from an ordinary person, this made the chances of being captured much higher. In many cases, Cenia's curfew made the Pata Sector much more difficult to get out of.

Many Causes were unsure as to what this sudden spurt of captures meant. Some felt the Fifteen were trying to restore some of the balance lost when the Causes all simultaneously shirked their duties to society. Others felt the more uncouth youths out there were painting a bad picture of the Causes as a whole, like the few bad apples spoiling the bunch.

Whatever the case was, morale remained unshaken. The Causes were making progress. If the Fifteen were going through so much trouble to bring us to a halt, there had to be something more to the captures than what could be seen by the naked eye.

Day 68

I

Stressed, exhausted, and more than a little irritable, I felt as if the moonlight of the midnight hour was demanding I go to sleep. I had to stay awake, though. Kay and I were the ones keeping watch in the alley as Dice and Mika slept. She and I paced left and right, sharing what was left of my bag of granola.

We had taken to the idea of sleeping in shifts. Of course, it was a wonderful idea if you were the one on the blanket. Keeping my eyes open on pure adrenaline and willpower was taking its toll on this fourth night as lookout.

Gray Police officers were a common sight now. With the curfew in place, all it would take was for us to be seen and that would be it for us. I was too tired to assure myself of a chance of getting away. Moving from one place to the next was a great risk every time. With all things considered, the four of us had done a fine job in staying out of Vade's clutches.

I peeked out of the alley, focusing my gaze through a small crack between two crates. Our next objective was only a few hundred meters away: a bridge. The border to the Fanda Sector was only a few kilometers past the other end of the bridge. The main problem was the three Gray Police officers on the lookout for anybody violating the curfew. Of course, ignoring the bridge and attempting to ford the river was an option. But a four-meter drop into water of unknown depth would have made quite the splash; enough to alert anybody. Getting our gear soaked sounded unappealing as well.

"How does it look over there?" Kay's voice was hushed to a whisper, her body shuddering at the bite of the cool midnight air.

I told her the situation, adding my gut feeling it was not going to change any time soon. Kay rose to her feet, mustering the courage to step further out into the alley to look into the street. She was able to see much more than I could have out of the tiny crevice I had been hiding behind.

After a minute or two, she reported back to me as well. "It looks like we're not the only ones waiting to get across the bridge. I see a couple of other groups hiding out there, too."

I rested my eyes, leaning my head into my lap. "Think we should move soon?"

She sat back down next to a soundly sleeping Mika, leaning back against the crates. "Not sure." She buried her head in her hands and grunted. "Ugh, how can something be so exciting and so *boring* at the same time?"

I felt her pain. "I don't know. Something had better happen soon, before any more Gray Police come to stand guard."

An hour passed…slow and boring. The streets were so quiet, I could almost hear my own heartbeat; like the ticking of a clock.

The rhythmic thumping of footsteps wiped away the boredom as quickly as it did the silence. Hearing those taps making their way down the middle of the open street possessed me to spring to my feet. Kay and I gathered our things while waking up Mika and Dice. Within seconds, I stepped from behind the crates to get a clear view of the street and the bridge.

I was not the only one curious about the source of the sounds. As Kay had said, several other Causes had apparently been hiding, and heads poked out of other hiding spaces throughout the vicinity. Kay, Dice, and Mika soon joined me to catch a glimpse of the sudden commotion.

Three figures stood in plain view of the officers guarding the bridge. A discussion between them began, but we were too far away to hear anything. As the guards took careful steps toward them, it seemed as if these three other people were taunting them away from their positions.

"They're bird-shit crazy!" Dice whispered.

Two of the Gray Police ordered the third to continue standing guard. The third guard took both of his weapons off of his belt and wielded them with a defensive yet menacing posture, looking almost spider-like, sitting still until its prey was to fly into its web. Anybody trying to cross the bridge would find themselves on the receiving end of a brutal attack.

The three youths backpedaled. It appeared their attempt to distract all three of them didn't pan out so perfectly. The officers did not appear to feel so outnumbered at three to two. They drew their rods, one of them saying the first thing to become coherent to me: "We're taking you three in!"

In a split second, one of the men on our side pointed behind the officer and shouted, "*Now!*"

The two officers looked behind themselves to see nothing but the bridge they stepped away from. With their guard down, the three brave distractors jumped the Gray Police, grabbing their weapons and trying to wrest them from their grip. One of the three, a young woman, shouted into the open night, "*Everyone, make a run for it!*"

We were briefly scrambling in place. My body was twitching and my foot lurched repeatedly, wanting to take the first step forward. All it looked like was an awkward, jerky dance. Kay pushed us forward. "Let's go, this is our chance!"

I shook the rest of the cobwebs out. "Yes, steer clear!"

Causes filed out of the alleys and into the street, all advancing to stampede the bridge. A number of Causes, including us, slowed down a bit as we approached the confrontations in the street. Many were still afraid of the weapons the Gray Police carried.

The lone third guard scampered in place, overwhelmed by the number of people suddenly charging forward. As the officer's guard was down and focused on the mob, one last figure showed up on the bridge. In a flash, the boy effortlessly yanked the rod from his hands and swung it at him. Every Cause in the street ran full speed to get across the bridge before the advantage changed.

The officer on the bridge took his nightstick and readied himself to engage the mysterious youth. The four of us kept as far away from the scuffle as possible as we blew past it.

Once we were almost to the other side, Kay stopped for a moment, forcing the rest of us to follow suit. She looked back to the last man to appear and called to him. "Blue?"

Without turning around to look at her, he called back, "Not the time to distract me, go! Make sure everyone knows good ol' Blue took care of you all."

I pulled Kay by the wrist. "You heard the man, go!" The four of us sped off into the night.

It seemed Blue, the fabled glory-seeker, was not working solo in his efforts to help the Causes. However, Blue's actions, as well as those of his entourage, were in direct contradiction to the rules set by the Producers.

The events at the bridge presented the question as to whether or not Blue was actually a Cause, or if he was helping in his own fashion to make a name for himself as the rumors surrounding him suggested. Whatever the case, his actions led us all to safety for the time being. The whole ordeal spanning those past few days had been exhausting and frustrating. Thankfully, that chapter of the Revolution was over for us. We were finally able to stand down, relax, and take our time.

Our next stop was the Fanda Sector. Now out of hostile territory, the search for Mika's father would continue once we recuperated from the Ordeal of Pata.

Episode 3: Choosing Sides

The situation in the Pata Sector grew increasingly worse. With Naro, Vade, and Cenia in command of the Gray Police, more and more Causes were winding up in the hands of the Fifteen. Any Cause who managed to escape the Pata Sector was considered lucky.

Vade continued to keep the pressure on. Soon, she announced a fourth member of the Fifteen—Riley—putting his hand into cutting off the Causes.

Riley is the man in charge of the train systems running all throughout Eden. Thus, as a way to contribute to Vade's plan, Riley cut off train services in the partitioned section of Pata. People could enter, but leaving was out of the question.

The Causes in the Pata Sector were now forced to fend for themselves. The rest of our forces spread throughout Eden extended moral support. Though it would not prevent them from being captured, the principle of the gesture was still felt.

The Fifteen had the advantage at this time, but the tables were set to turn in an unexpected way. With the countless words of encouragement from our side to our peers, who would have thought so soon after the Ordeal of Pata, two Causes would stand out to bring true physical opposition to the Fifteen?

We did not see it coming until…

Day 69

I

It was a humid and overcast morning. The heat of summer made the outdoors all the more miserable. Luckily for us, we were seated comfortably in a bistro in the eastern section of the Fanda Sector. We took our time to wait for the weather to break as we ate breakfast in the pleasant and colorful atmosphere the street-side eatery provided. We didn't mind. The cushioned seats and the smell of cleanliness were a pleasant change from the hard alleyway ground and the stench of musty waste bins.

Dice's sharp eyes spotted our motive for entering this little hole in the wall, and we were thankful for it. As we were passing by while looking for other Causes, Dice had spotted a Contact sitting all by his lonesome through the window.

It was clear this business was clued. It was subtle, but little touches like the 'one' arna 'summer' specials board with travel-friendly foods like jerky and granola hinted the business was sympathetic to, or at least willing to profit off of, the Causes. The hostess placed a white towel over her arm when she grabbed the menus before seating us. She took us over to a corner booth near the back of the restaurant so close to the kitchen we could smell the bread baking.

"We'd like to join the boy by the window," Kay implored.

The hostess smiled and said, "He'll join you shortly." She hung the white towel on a coat-hook next to the booth, and walked away. As she said, the Contact made his way over to our booth within a matter of minutes.

Having not seen a Contact in several days, we decided to hold off our search for an hour or so to make our posts. Looking over the menu, it seemed like a good spot to grab a bite while we were at it. Mika did not mind since she was well aware of everything we had to say. There was also the lure of fresh food, and our mouths were already watering from the aroma.

My first order of business was to honor my word to Pibs. I began a new topic with an opening post detailing his heroic actions back at the Gateway. I asked for anybody who escaped because of Pibs' stall tactic should reply to thank him as well.

Kay, Dice, and I took turns passing the Contact's laptop between us. There was as much to be said about the Ordeal of Pata as there was to learn. The thread on the Cause Forum took a quick two days to reach nearly seventy pages of posts.

The most important information was a particular observation made by two members who shared one forum name: "Al & Jal." They compared the Ordeal of Pata to a similar series of actions carried out by the Fifteen at the start of the Revolution. The only difference was the location of the attack.

Specifically, on the night of the Great Walk, The district of South 7 in the Lucra Sector was partitioned off and heavily patrolled. Anyone who was found roaming the streets at the time of the Great Walk was tracked down and captured. Within the first two hours of the Revolution, three-hundred Causes were already in custody. What had happened in the Pata Sector was the exact same type of attack: partition, patrol, and capture.

"It sounds like Al and Jal know what they're talking about," Dice mumbled, concentrating on his typing.

"Maybe a little too much. Suspicious?" I asked.

"No," Kay huffed, protesting my tone. "I've heard too many promising things about Al. I'm not sure who Jal is, but I'm sure he or she is helping him put all this information together."

Kay's words sparked another question. "Speaking of hearing

promising things, what was with you and Blue yesterday?"

"What do you mean?"

"Well, you stopped and called to him as if you know him."

Her hand wiggled in an absent-minded wave. "I was making sure it was really him. You remember the post you read right? It was like the thread said: guy dressed in blue sweeps in to save the day. I wanted to see if it was actually him."

Mika took her fork from halfway to her mouth and placed it on her plate to speak. "Who were those other guys?"

Dice replied, reading, "They were random volunteers."

We all looked at him. Kay asked, "How do you know?"

"Blue actually posted in this thread. He says right here: *'I walked around through the groups waiting to cross the bridge and asked them to help. It took me an hour and a half to find three people with enough guts to step out there with me.'*" He stopped talking and continued examining the other posts.

"Wait, Blue is actually a Cause and is on the forums?"

"Obviously," Dice replied sardonically.

"I don't think I've ever seen a post from him, and there were topics openly questioning if he was even a Cause. Doesn't it seem weird he would only be lurking, yet be so active now with the Revolution is kicking up?"

Kay interjected. "Not everyone is as outspoken as you Brigg."

"Or you," Dice replied. "Or me, for that matter."

I nodded in approval and self-awareness. "Did Blue give any names?"

"Memento, Al, and Tricky were his helpers."

"So, Al was there, but no Jal?"

Dice gave another newsflash, reading the screen with his finger. "After this wave of 'thank you' posts here, Blue goes on to say it was thanks to Al they all made it out of there."

I probed. "Did they stay together afterwards?"

We all looked to Dice, anticipating a response. "I've got

nothing," he sighed. "Looks like Blue posted, mentioning Al's role in the whole thing. He's made no other posts since then. However, I see here, Al & Jal made a late-night post yesterday. At the start, they say Blue 'left to do his own thing'."

"They? If Jal was there, why didn't she help, too?" Mika's tone oozed puzzlement.

Such a surprising angle got all of us thinking as we turned to look to the perceptive preteen. Two people sharing the same forum name would surely stay together. The name evoked the image of a young couple, posting together and running off. It was practically what the protagonists did in *One Summer*. While contemplating the possibilities, I chuckled. "You're getting more observant, Mika," I ruffled her hair and endured a side glance from Kay for the affectionate gesture.

"I'm saying what I'm thinking. Guess it comes with hanging out with you guys."

Kay jabbed. "It's like you said; any input is important."

Her remark elicited a clean smirk from Mika and Dice. I rolled with the punch, though. "Glad to see my words have impact." I continued eating; still trying to cling to the good reasons I let Dice tag along in the first place. Although he still rubbed me the wrong way at times, having another face Mika could trust, as well as having someone who could help keep Kay from acting out, was worth his abrasive nature.

I observed him as he tapped away, concentrating on his thoughts and keyboard strokes. After a few minutes, he exhaled with clear discontent. He rolled his eyes and leaned his head into his hands, shaking it in disapproval.

"What's wrong?" Mika asked.

Dice kept his volume low as he made the announcement. "New hot topic: 'Getting back at Naro'; posted by none other than the heroes of the moment, Al & Jal."

The title grabbed our attention!

Dice moved the laptop to the center of the table to where all of us could get a clear view of the topic. Besides the Contact, who had so far remained quiet and kept to himself, the rest of us crowded around the screen to read the first post.

Posted by: Al & Jal
Topic: Getting Back at Naro

After what they started in Pata, it's clear the Fifteen aren't going to stop until we capitulate and betray our Cause. They've arrested, and even beat down, innocent people in a peaceful protest. The two of us are confident no Cause murdered an Innkeeper; they're using death as a pretense to raise pressure on us and maybe turn off the Clued.

If we're going to keep the Revolution alive we HAVE to respond. Naro broadcast their lying accusation. Naro is turning public opinion; he has made himself a priority.

We'd all like to get up and push his face in, but it's not going to solve anything. Naro might be the voice, but he can simply be substituted with another. As long as they can make broadcasts, they can keep putting the pressure on us.

So, here's our idea: We need to take out the Radio Tower in the Fanda Sector. Without broadcasts, the Fifteen won't be able to control public opinion. We can't do this alone; we need the people on our side.

We're calling as many Causes together as we can to ransack and destroy the tower. All we're wondering is how many people we can get and when the best time to do it is.

Anybody have suggestions?

-Al & Jal

"Are they serious!?" Kay exclaimed.

Dice turned the laptop to face him again. After scanning the topic, he said, "Well, there're already 400-plus replies to this topic—"

Mika interrupted, muttering, "more than four hundred..."

I squeezed next to Dice so I could read for myself. After reading a few of the posts, it looked like a plot was forming.

"May I?" I asked Dice, looking to usurp control of the laptop.

"By all means," he sighed, passing the laptop to me.

I ran a search for all posts made by Al & Jal. All the while, I was trying to think of a way I could respond to this topic. My gut instinct told me what they were planning to do would open a door we could not close. If we attacked, we were escalating. Sure, Al & Jal made a few good points, but attacking the Radio Tower did not feel like the right answer.

I found the post I was looking for:

Posted by: Al & Jal
Topic: Getting Back at Naro

*It's settled then! This Sunday during the broadcast of **This Week in Eden** is when we'll take care of this once and for all. That way, Naro will be right there to regret his choice to paint us as villains. After all, we'd hate to disappoint his expectations!*

Al & Jal

Dice rattled his namesake in his fist, a familiar tic when he was nervous or intrigued. "Well, this is an interesting development."

"When are they doing it?" Mika anxiously wondered.

Worried, I exhaled through my nose before answering. "It's happening Sunday. During *This Week*."

Kay's eyes widened; her voice pitched with surprise. "The day after tomorrow!"

I nodded, "Something about this seems wrong to you, too?"

Her face winced. "It does, a little. But the Causes are losing patience, and now Gray Police and the Fifteen are closing in. We *should* let this go. We have more important matters to attend to. After all, we're still a ways away from the Radio Tower."

Mika spoke up. "Should the Causes really do it…?"

"What?" Kay challenged.

Her head tilted back. It was a gesture I was starting to recognize as her thinking pose. "Will busting up the Radio Tower really do anything to the Fifteen? Won't it make them mad?"

"Who cares if it makes them angry?" Dice jeered, brushing off Mika's question. "Look, kid. They can get angry all they want. But if they can't make broadcasts, then they have no way of slinging mud at us to the public."

I was quick to interject. "Wouldn't they take more drastic measures, though?"

"Like what?" Dice scoffed.

"Well, if they'd go out of their way to close off a large area of one sector like they did the other day, who's to say they won't—I don't know—close *all* sector borders."

"Or maybe even shut down *all* the trains…" Kay added.

I nodded in approval of her input.

"Broadcasts will be one less thing to worry about." He started sounding unsure.

I spread my hands out in a giving gesture. "I don't think you're seeing the big picture here."

Kay chuckled. "This feels like a forum spat."

"Alright, let's treat it like the forum. What's your opinion, Kay?" I asked.

"I'm still not sure if this is even our fight; we have other priorities. I, for one, want to get Mika safely out of the Revolution and back with her dad, or have you forgotten? Besides, if you want to stop it, you've got over four-hundred Causes to convince." She leaned forward in a conspiratorial manner, "And you only have two days to do so."

The others continued eating as I attempted to put my thoughts into words. Within moments, I began typing my post of protest:

Posted by: Brigg
Topic: Getting Back at Naro

Am I the only one in this thread who thinks this is a bad idea? I don't know about you all, but I've noticed the Fifteen step up their methods to stop us. Yes, I'm aware there have only been two major capture attempts. But still, if we push harder what will they do back?

If we all storm the Radio Tower, what stops them from unleashing their Gray Police with more violent methods? Really think about it.

My group and I have been talking about this. The Fifteen have the power to close off sectors and shut down the trains. They could even have the citizens of Eden hunt us down for rewards.

So please, for the sake of every Cause's neck, I must discourage this attack on the Radio Tower. Just continue going about your business.

-Brigg

My hands were shaking. I wondered how the other Causes on the forum would respond. "The thread is still busy; I'll check it again in a few minutes."

Mika mumbled with a mouthful of fluffy scrambled egg. "Think they'll listen to you?"

I could only shake my head and hope.

Kay spoke, pushing her plate aside. "Do I agree with their idea? No. But having over four-hundred people suddenly change their minds seems like a pretty tall order."

Kay and Dice did a good job of making the task sound hopeless, which I already knew it was. The more they spoke, the greater the feeling of imminent failure became. Sure, ignoring it and letting it happen anyway was an option to take into consideration, but deep down, I knew the consequences would far outweigh whatever message Al & Jal were hoping to send by ransacking the Radio Tower.

As expected, when I refreshed the forum looking for replies to my post, I was bombarded by negative responses. In some cases, questions of my allegiance came forth from some of the more outspoken Causes. It was a thoroughly disheartening sight.

"The look on your face says it all, Brigg." Dice remarked, his voice emanating a mild sympathy behind his usual cockiness.

I buried my face in my hands, trying to calm down. I had realized now by participating in the Revolution, I was committing myself to a lot more than what I bargained for. Apparently, I had associated myself with a bunch of overzealous youths who sought to uncover the truths about Eden at any cost. Yes, *any* cost. It did not surprise me it now included arrest or self-sacrifice.

I felt in my gut these machinations would not achieve any beneficial results for the Causes. It would only serve to anger the Fifteen and lay the foundation for them to act more severely toward our side. Something had to be done. However, through the posts, it became painfully obvious words alone were not going to do it. We had to take action.

However, with two days to go and no time to plan properly, I stood up and the words spilled out. "We have to go there…"

"I see," Kay smiled, "So we are going to join in?"

Dice readied himself for a roll, kneading his wooden dice in his left hand. "I know what he's going to say," he groaned.

I took a deep breath before finishing my statement. "We had better get there in time if we intend to warn Naro about what's going to happen."

"*What?!*" Kay shouted.

"Interesting," Dice muttered, casting his dice to the table.

Even Mika seemed shocked at my idea. "Are we really?"

"It's the only way we can buy the Causes more time until Hatcher shows up."

Kay recoiled. "Hatcher, you say? What's your idea, now? Why didn't you mention him sooner? Or bring it up in your post?"

"In all honesty," I took a beat, breaking eye contact with her, "I *just* got the idea."

"Even more interesting…" Dice whispered under his breath. He picked up his dice again and rattled them some more.

Kay rolled her eyes and tried to ignore him. "Well, while his dice decide whether or not he should follow with us, I'd like to take this time to ask if you are out of your da—darn mind. Well?"

I gestured in a way demanding an answer. "What other options are there?"

"We could ignore it, you know—"

"And let the consequences of *their* actions come to us? If the Causes raid the Radio Tower and the Fifteen retaliate, it's safe to say *all* Causes, whether they helped or not, will be sought after."

Kay considered it. "All of them?" Her tone had changed.

"Yes, all of them. Including…" I let Kay piece together the end of the sentence for herself as I slowly turned to look to Mika.

Mika was briefly puzzled, staring right back at me. Kay, too, looked to the sweet youngster, whose mind was in a fleeting moment of disarray. Reluctantly, Mika pointed to herself and questioned with a distinct quiver in her voice. "…Me?"

Kay scowled. "What would the Fifteen want with Mika?"

I turned the floor over to Mika to answer Kay's question. "Mika, would you be so kind as to state for us, once again, why you're here with us in the first place?"

"Well," she shyly lowered herself back into her chair. It was apparent my presumptions concerning the Fifteen had Mika in a fit of nerves. "I said before, I'm only hanging around with the Causes so they can help me find my father."

Kay objected. "Wh-what does that have to do with anything?"

"That's exactly my point!" I countered with conviction. "Mika has never expressed interest in the Revolution."

"Wow," Dice interrupted. "Right. Mika has nothing to do with the Revolution. But the Fifteen won't care if they retaliate; all they'll care about is revenge. Unfortunately, Mika will be innocent, being found guilty only by association."

"Thank you!" I sighed. "I'm glad somebody understands."

"I do," he nodded, zipping his collar up the rest of the way to cover his mouth. "Now, since you've brought up enough points to make it obvious you're not going to change your mind, this is where we part."

Dice's declaration caught me off guard. "Are you serious?! After all—"

"All the mutual back-scratching," he cut me off. "Sure, it was nice hanging out and all, but I'm not going to rush head-first into *that* level of trouble. We *just* escaped Pata, after all." He picked his dice up off of the table and left a tip for Contact. "Maybe I'll run into you again. Try to stay the way you are—all three of you."

He had one foot out the door of the restaurant by the time I thought to ask him. "What do you mean?"

Dice did not answer and kept walking, soon out of sight.

One thing became certain to me: Dice was no ordinary Cause. There was a lot he never bothered to say about himself. To top it off, his method of "decision-making" was unlike anything I had ever seen. He was a strange guy and always kept me guessing. I was glad, at the very least, he grew civil towards us.

Personally, it did not matter to me at the time whether or not we would see him again. I wished he had left us saying more than he did. There was an empty feeling of something missing in his sudden change of direction. Kay, Mika, and I felt the hole he left, and all we could do about it was let it creep around in the back of our minds until the day we would meet again.

II

My heart was set, Mika was willing to cooperate, and Kay was still focused on following the two of us around. I think she didn't want to have to be alone and needed a reason to cling to a group. Looking back on it, it was an odd mix for a Cause group.

Nevertheless, my point concerning Mika's peril had an impact. Although anxious, she agreed to help us stop the raid on the Radio Tower instead of simply waiting for the worst to happen.

Kay, on the other hand, was more interested in keeping Mika in sight. Of course, since her other options were to be unwanted or abandoned by us anyway, she felt it necessary to do what she could to help out with our new mission.

Although Kay had done a fine job of making things more difficult, it seemed I was becoming more tolerant of her the more she followed me. It was as simple as accepting the fact she was only being herself. From my perspective: she was an overly cautious woman who was too quick to suspect wrongdoing.

I wanted to spend time over the next couple of days to try and make Kay feel more like part of the group. It would have been a welcome change from walking on eggshells and fearing any move I made could be misconstrued. A change in my own attitude felt like a good start.

All throughout our hasty journey to the heart of the Fanda Sector, we heard many Causes make mention of the raid taking place on Sunday. However, not once did I hear anything about any naysayers on the topic. It was clear my words not only fell onto criticism, but were soon washed away from the news altogether. The more I heard about it, the more difficult the task of stopping the raid seemed.

I warned Mika and Kay it would not be a good idea to tell anybody of our intention to warn Naro. There was no telling of the consequences if news of our mission was revealed to the rest of the Causes. We decided to keep low and act as if we were going to mind our own business throughout the ordeal. Hopefully, if I ever found the need to introduce myself, nobody would remember the post I had made in Al & Jal's thread.

The three of us had a lot of ground to cover in order to make it to the Radio Tower. Fortunately, it was by no means impossible. Something would have had to severely sidetrack us in order for us to fail in making it there in time. But with no Gray Police in sight, we were clear to take the most direct route there.

The only thing holding us up was our decision to fulfill Mika's wishes. We would spend some time showing off Mika's picture and asking about her father. I felt Kay and I owed it to her since we had not really been spending a lot of time helping her to begin with. Mika was delighted we finally had the opportunity to take time-outs to help her as I had intended to from the start.

The last thing on my mind was how we were going to go about warning Naro of the incoming throngs. Everything ranging from how we would approach and enter the Radio Tower to the words we would say to Naro had to be carefully planned. Our words and actions at the tower all had to come off flawlessly in order to make it look like a warning instead of a threat. Through the tension, we had the confidence to get it done.

This was for the wellbeing of every Cause. It was also for the Producers, who still patiently awaited the arrival of Hatcher. Most of all, it was for Mika, along with anyone else who was merely mingling with the Causes for reasons unrelated to the Revolution.

Day 70 – Evening

I

Gathered around a small table in a musty chapel basement, Kay, Mika, and I focused on a blank cloth parchment. The suspense brought on by our plans to speak with Naro only served to add weight to the atmosphere.

I prepared a black marking stylus, taking the tip to the cloth's corner and scribbling on it. There was an odd sense of relaxation in the smooth, sliding sound of every back-and-forth stroke. Although the canvas was otherwise blank, our hopes were high to have it marked with the bearings of our plan for the next day.

After testing the stylus, I reached over to the upper left corner of the cloth and wrote "12 Noon," saying it softly as I marked it.

"Naro's broadcast goes on the air at noon, tomorrow," Kay reiterated in a nervous exhalation.

The next image passing through my mind was of me getting tackled by a Gray Police officer. It caused me to wince and lightly shake. Trying to maintain a façade of bravery, I brought my fists to my face. The back end of the stylus rested gently on the middle of my forehead as it seemed to disappear from sight down the bridge of my nose. "What time do you think it would be best to approach the Radio Tower?" I asked.

Kay replied, "'Half past *never*' sounds promising!"

Her unexpected comment put the first smile on my face since the start of our planning. My hands dropped, falling to dangle between my knees. I smirked and shook my head to let her know her comment was acknowledged, yet unlikely.

Mika found it amusing as well. However, her eyes looked hopeful Kay's reply would be taken into consideration. It was apparent she was the most anxious out of the three of us to find a way to back out.

I asked Kay with a stare, "Seriously?"

"Yeah," she groaned. Kay threw her hands into her lap and leaned far back into her wooden chair. She let her head and neck hang off of the back to give her a view of the ceiling.

I turned back to Mika to see her head hung and hands folded. "It doesn't make sense," she mumbled.

"What?" I wondered.

"You've been saying you wanna keep me out of trouble. But we're going to the Radio Tower tomorrow and…" She stopped and sighed heavily, giving off the feeling her words and thoughts were tangled together.

Kay growled. "I'm still not sure how you talked us into this."

I felt no inclination to dig for answers. With haste, I said, "I'm not sure either." Then, to change the subject back, I took the stylus to the parchment again and wrote "11:00 am".

Mika objected. "We'll only have an hour to do something!"

Kay scoffed. "Knowing Brigg, that's exactly the point!"

"You're a step ahead of me, you two," I said with a grin. "We want to warn Naro with enough time to act."

Kay stopped me. "What are you saying? You want them to send the Gray Police after the Causes?"

"No, no, no!" I defended. "If we warn Naro too early, he'll have a troupe of Grays on the mob. But if we wait too long to warn him, we may not have enough time to create a solid plan."

As I reached to mark on the parchment, Kay stamped her foot in protest. "What kind of plan could we possibly come up with in an hour?"

I stopped, leveling my eyes to meet hers; responding with the utmost honesty. "I have no idea."

Kay threw her hands up in frustration. "Fan-freaking-tastic!" She stood and paced about the room. "You mean to tell us the only thing we can *actually* plan is approaching Naro—**NARO**—and everything else will have to be improvised," Kay paused to raise her voice. "*If* he doesn't have us arrested on the spot."

Her comment on imprisonment put a jolt in my chest. Once again, I tried to remain calm. "Pretty much." I could hear in my own tone how unsure of myself I sounded. I gritted my teeth as the specter of second thoughts invaded my mind.

With droopy eyes, I reviewed the parchment. "12 Noon" and "11:00 am" remained the only things written. In retrospect, it was a waste of canvas since it was not hard to remember.

"I'm going out to get some air!" Kay huffed as she took hold of the railing on the staircase.

Mika and I watched her amble up the creaky stairs. "Don't be too long," said the young one.

Hearing Mika, Kay stopped before the top of the steps. All we could see of her was feet. She said nothing as she appeared to turn around and take one step down. She stopped again, turned back, and continued upward, leaving the basement.

To avoid a scene, Mika and I chose to keep to our opposite ends of the table. Surely, if Kay saw the two of us any closer when she got back, I would never hear the end of it.

"She needs to start trusting you more," Mika remarked.

I exhaled, still looking to the stairs. "Tell me about it."

Mika reached over and turned the parchment so my writing appeared right-side up to her. She looked it over with an unsure expression dominating her face. Despite her focus there, she stayed on topic. "Kay told me it's hard to know who to trust."

I felt the need to carefully steer my words to avoid vilifying Kay. "In many ways, she's right. Matter of fact..." I paused and reclined against the stiff backrest. "There's a question I've been meaning to ask you."

An innocent look of curiosity overtook her doubtful disposition. "What?"

"Think back to when we first met on the train. Did you think, even for a second, you couldn't trust me?"

She sat back in her chair with her arms folded and her head tucked down to her chest. After thinking, she answered. "Yeah. When you first sat down, and I didn't know you."

I pointed at her. "Right there is what Kay was talking about. I had to gain your trust, right?"

"Yeah," she hummed before turning the question in another direction. "So why doesn't Kay trust you? You've shown her you're not a bad guy."

Lowering my tone, I looked back to the stairs and said, "I'm get a vibe from Kay like she thinks my kindness is all an act. To her, I'm looking to…get something out of this; for my own gain."

As I spoke my mind, Mika tried to get my attention. "Um…"

I was still focused on ranting about Kay. "She is *really* stuck on her arguments from the forums. Man, back at the Gateway—"

Mika spoke louder. "Brigg!"

I acknowledged her. "What's up?"

Mika rotated her head to look around the basement. "Kay left us alone…right now."

"Yeah, she went out for air." I chuckled, failing to realize why she brought it up specifically.

"Don't you get it?" Mika pressed.

The way she said it got me to think about the detail a little harder. "Kay left us…"

"Alone."

It hit me. By leaving the basement, Kay now appeared to have some inkling of trust in my intentions towards Mika.

"I'm not out of the woods yet with her, though," I grumbled.

"It's a start." Mika shrugged; the sensation of the forming bond bringing a smile to her once-worried face.

I gestured toward her. "*You* still trusting me to help find your father is what really matters to me. I'm sticking to my word."

Mika smiled, breaking eye contact. "You really mean it?"

"Definitely!" I assured her. "Again, I'm really sorry we have to make this little detour. But this has to get done."

She shook her head. "It's okay. You're right; we can't get the Fifteen madder than they already are."

I rephrased it. "I'm mainly doing this for our long-term protection. This will stall both sides, give us time to find your father, and even buy time for Hatcher to show up."

Mika had a request. "And we can say we're doing this for Dice too; wherever he is, right?"

"Sure," I said, seeing no harm in it. Feeling nosey, I finally asked her, "What exactly did the two of you talk about, anyway?"

Her eyes relaxed and her answer came quick and succinct. "He told me not to tell you."

I sounded off with a defeated laugh, "I should have known." It was admirable for her to be so determined to keep his secret. I let the subject go, and we moved on.

It felt relaxing to be able to talk to Mika without any interruptions. The two of us kept swapping random questions and answers about ourselves and others. At one point, we had almost completely forgotten about our plans for the next day. It was like nothing else mattered to us other than the words we exchanged and the bond we shared.

During this time, Mika leaned forward and took the parchment and stylus. Pulling the table a bit closer to her, she gave herself room to start marking up the cloth. "What are you up to?"

Glancing to me, then to her hands, she answered with a smile. "I'm going to draw you! Or at least…*start* drawing you. It'll take time, like it did with my dad."

I felt I could come clean to a nagging thought. "To be honest, I wondered if you had help with your dad's picture because it's so good. Seeing your talent would be great."

Her gaze flashed a curious disappointment. "You didn't think I drew it? Really?"

I grabbed the picture of her father. "You don't run into a lot of twelve-year-olds this talented. Then again, I'm seventeen, and haven't moved beyond stick figures."

"Well, now you'll get to see what I can do! So if anyone asks, you can support me." She started marking out a faint oval.

"Speaking of things other Causes would be curious about: What's with the outfit? I said you look like Lauren from *One Summer*. But you never really gave me a clear response."

Mika was shy to the question at first. She was under the impression I would laugh if she told me the real reason for her outfit. Of course, I promised I would not. Mika's face was turning red as she spoke softly. "I like the character so much; I want to grow up to be like her. I figured this was a start."

I thought back to reading *One Summer*. The character Lauren was a smart, carefree, ambitious teenager who had an equal amount of respect for herself as she had for others. As the author, Devon, described her, she was a *"sharp and quick-witted young woman whose beauty and intelligence was the envy of boys and girls alike."*

"I see." I nodded encouragingly, assuring her I, in no way, found her explanation to be foolish.

Mika clarified her motives. "I want to grow up smart and pretty. It's sort of the other reason I like having Kay around."

I recoiled. "Say what?"

She giggled, knowing she surprised me. "I want Kay to teach me how to be a woman. She looks like she can show me the right ways of things."

I suddenly felt uncomfortable, like we were on the doorstep of that special talk parents have with their maturing children. I cut the subject short, somewhat regretting asking the question in the first place. "Maybe when Kay gets back, I'll excuse myself and you two can talk."

"That would be nice." She cracked a nervous grin.

On cue, Kay returned to the basement. She spoke on her way down the stairs. "I've come to the conclusion you are insane."

"Maybe a little bit!" I wittily responded as I stood. "But you should've already had at least a few hints."

Kay squinted at me as I patted Mika on the head, passing her. "Where are you going?"

"Air sounds good to me, too."

"Go for it!" she invited. "There's plenty of it out there."

I promptly exited the basement, leaving Mika to talk with Kay.

As I stepped outside, the cool air of the late hours rested upon my skin like a soothing caress. The air in the basement had been damp and heavy, and the outside air felt so crisp in comparison. The refreshing feel of it caused me to close my eyes and indulge in the sensation, and the fresh smell of nearby flowers relieved me of the musty odor of old basement.

Upon opening my eyes, the first thing to grab my attention was the Radio Tower. The target was only one kilometer down the street. The building was only two stories tall and was constructed of strong, gray-colored stone. The actual tower was the large, thin, steel spire protruding several decameters into the sky from the top of the building. It stood as the tallest structure in all of Eden.

I rejoiced briefly at the thought of how fortunate we were to find a place to spend the night so close to our destination. I stood erect and stared at the tower for several minutes. As my thoughts cycled, I felt my heart react in numerous ways: shudders, chills, and that gut feeling you get when you are afraid—really, really afraid. In the end, though, I breathed in deep and blew it all out through my nose. I saw us succeeding tomorrow. It was all I needed to think of to bring my spirits back up.

One last chill shot down my spine as the thought of the Gray

Police pushed my focus aside. It was a testament to how incredibly risky the operation was. I could not help but think of how low I would feel if I were to lead us all to our capture.

I shook the thought out. There was no more room for uncertainty. Our hearts and minds had to be in the mission.

Confident, I raised my finger and pointed to the tower in the distance. "I can't believe I'm going to save your ass tomorrow. Please, hear us out and let us work together to stop this. It's for the good of everyone…you'll know it, too."

Even though I knew nobody heard me, it felt better to get it out in words. If anything, it served to solidify my confidence in my motives. I'm sure if the tower were a sentient being, it would have thanked me for my comments.

Reentering the chapel, I looked down the center aisle. With my eyes fixed on the effigies of Paxus and Shalynn, I walked halfway toward the altar. Slipping my hands into my pockets, I pushed a big breath out of my nose. "Are you two watching this?" My gaze shifted to Paxus. "Tomorrow, encourage us in respect and bravery." Then, I looked to Shalynn. "Bring to us prudence, trust, and wisdom. We're covering a lot of bases tomorrow. We'll make you proud; I'm sure of it."

With my hope restored, at least slightly, I returned to the girls and reviewed the plan. We were to enter the Radio Tower at 11:00 a.m. sharp. This way, Naro would not have enough time to retaliate drastically against the Causes. However, from there, it would have to be played by ear based on Naro's reactions to our news and advice.

With only slight hesitation, we settled on our plan to stop the raid. Soon after, we executed the first part of our plot: A good night's rest.

Day 71

I

The three of us woke up at about 9:30. This gave us plenty of time to gather the courage to make our final preparations for approaching Naro. Having planned our one-hour window the previous night, timing was everything.

After some time praying at the altar, it was about time to finally execute our plan. "How do you two feel?" I asked calmly.

"I'm nervous," Mika quickly answered.

Kay looked down to her. "You're lucky. You're only nervous. I feel like I'm gonna throw up."

I took a deep breath and held it briefly, almost as using it to steady myself, then exhaled slowly through curled lips. "What are you two so nervous about? This was my idea in the first place. If anything happens to us, it's entirely my fault."

Kay growled, "Oh, thanks! I feel *so* much better now! I'll make sure to remind myself with every swing of my pickaxe how it's all okay because it's Brigg's fault!"

They both went silent. I was afraid to say anything else beyond a signal to move forward. It's not like there was much left to discuss, anyway. All we knew was our goal and our means of achieving it. Everything else, the outcome included, was not for us to decide. Our own words and actions were the only things we were in control of. The reactions of our enemies remained yet to be seen.

II

By the time 11 o'clock rolled around, the three of us were making our final approach to the Radio Tower. The three of us were about a hundred meters away from the tower when we noticed an older man approaching the building from around the corner. This man was being escorted to the tower by one Fanda Sector policeman and one Gray Police officer. With such an entourage, and the fact he was carrying an iron briefcase, presuming it was Naro seemed like an obvious guess.

I jogged a bit closer and crouched behind a bush to get a better look as he entered the tower. His beige short-pants and short-sleeved collared shirt did not really emanate an intimidating essence of authority. The only thing making him look remotely important was the case he carried on his right side with a grip so tight, you could see the muscles in his forearm hard at work. Those who had seen Naro in the past could verify he always had the iron case near his person at all times.

Kay exhaled as she stopped walking for a moment. A small chuckle got caught in her throat for a moment. She was clearly ripe with discomfort. Once she got out her awkward huff of a laugh, she focused her attention on Naro. "I always pictured the Fifteen as the type to dress in a way a bit more imposing. I know Vade does; she's scary."

Mika and I agreed silently as we watched.

This development lifted some of the stress we were feeling. However, we knew the Fifteen were an unpredictable party, and Naro could easily have us tossed to the Labor Fields in time to go on the air for his broadcast without missing a beat. I was questioning my sanity one last time before taking the next few steps forward. I could feel my stomach tossing and turning, doing somersaults inside my gut, in combination with Mika's hand shaking in mine as her fingers squeezed tightly around mine. I could even feel her fingernails starting to dig into my skin.

Kay's voice trembled. "In case you needed a reminder, I *still* can't believe you talked me into this, and I *still* don't agree with it."

In a sudden burst of confidence, I broke free of the quiver within my soul, taking the lead with a solid stride. "Let's get this done. We all know the worst that can happen. If anything goes wrong, I'm sure there's a way we can prove we came to help."

"How can you be so sure?"

"We have to make sure we steer the conversation in ways to convince him we came to help. If anything, making it look like we're siding with the Fifteen through this could work in our favor to get this done."

Mika sided with Kay, seemingly out of last-second desperation to back out. "What if they don't listen?"

I threw my hands up in an unknowing gesture. My shoulders shrugged and my head cocked slightly to the side. Did they really want me to answer? It was time to go forward. After all of the hesitation, this was now our chance to change what could have been the beginning of the end of the Revolution for every Cause.

We stepped into an empty lobby. Flat, firm, tan carpet covered the floor to all four corners. The large window above the door gave a glowing beam of light to the barren, rectangular foyer. A lone metal folding chair with a green pillow on the seat was the only piece of furniture. It was up against the wall opposite the front door with two other doors to each side of it. The door on the right had a large gate covering it from top to bottom.

After the front door closed behind us, we were able to notice another eerie property of the unsettling, vacant foyer. There was no sound. It was as if we had all gone deaf. Even the sound of our own breathing had become muffled.

Kay and Mika took hurried steps toward the more inviting of the two doors. I, however, decided to examine the other. Indeed, it was tightly secured with no chance of budging without a key. I ran one of the bars between my fingers before joining the girls.

As Kay reached for the handle, the door flew open to reveal the tall, menacing figure of a Gray Police officer.

Mika shrieked in a way I had never heard her before. In trying to back away, she stumbled to the floor. Kay backed up several steps as well, pulling my hand to follow her. "I knew this was a bad idea!" she declared.

The officer spoke before we had a chance to move any great distance. "What are you doing here?"

I thought quickly. If we ran, we would be chased. Since the officer did not make any sudden moves, it felt best to simply answer his question. "W-we're here to see Naro."

Kay released my hand and calmed down a bit. Mika scrambled to her feet and hid behind us. We prepared ourselves for anything the officer could do. It took us a moment to get our bearings straight as the officer stepped from the doorway and looked us over. "Are you Revolutionaries?" he asked.

"The million arna question," I thought to myself. The consequences of answering truthfully would set the pace for the upcoming hour. I swallowed hard and reluctantly nodded.

The officer circled around us with his massive hands stroking the gruff stubble on his broad, chiseled chin. We kept our eyes on him as he continued to scrutinize us with a scornful glare. Once he was in a position between us and the door, he withdrew his nightstick from the holster and held it to his side. "Naro was expecting this."

The three of us cowered back. "He was?" I asked. "Does he know about what's going to happen?"

The officer raised a bushy eyebrow, intrigued by my question. "What do you mean? What's going to happen?"

Stammering at first, Kay chimed in. "W-w-wait; we asked you first. Why was Naro expecting us?"

The officer stepped up. "Not so much expecting you

specifically, but Naro expected revolutionaries showing up one day to try getting on the air during his broadcast." He put his nightstick away. "But only the three of you; no more? It's not what he expected. State your purpose here."

Things were starting to calm, but we had to remain on our guard. The truth got us on the good side of the intimidating officer, so I found no harm in telling the man what was going on. "You see, we're not really looking to wind up on the air."

Kay cut me off, "We need to talk to Naro before he goes on."

"Concerning…?" the officer pressed.

I chose to let loose and spit it out. "This goes back to you asking us about what was going to happen. We came here to warn Naro: as soon as he goes on the air, this Radio Tower is going to get run over by a mob of revolutionaries."

His face crunched. "A mob?!"

His authoritative roar shot fear into all three of us. I felt Mika jump and clench the back of my vest. I continued to explain through the tension. "Yeah, a mob! We tried to talk them down, but they wouldn't listen!"

The officer exuded clear unease. "And you're telling me you came here to give us a heads up about it?"

We gestured positively, preparing ourselves for the results of our delivery of the big news. Sure enough, the officer ordered us, "Wait right here." He scurried through the door and up the stairs.

Shaken, we waited. The silent foyer became a lot less stuffy as our hearts lifted. We had done the right thing. Now all we needed to do was figure out a way to keep the Radio Tower safe. I was sure if we pulled together with Naro and the Gray Police, everything would turn out for the better in the long run.

III

The officer retrieved us from the lobby and led us to an office on the second floor. Inside, Naro was preparing the last of the news items for *This Week in Eden*. We were told to enter without knocking since we were now expected guests.

Our confidence had a sturdy foundation. Together, Kay and I pushed open the large double-doors to take us into Naro's office. Mika cautiously crept in behind us, staying close to my side. I heard Kay inhale deeply as her pace slowed. I kept to her speed while Mika decided to stop.

We stayed centered on the wide, red carpet crafting a path down the middle of the office. Past a small, comfortable sitting area to the right of the entrance, Naro's office stretched far back. The room itself exuded an ambiance of power and mystery. The wall behind his wide, dark, mahogany desk was painted with a massive landscape mural of the Fanda Sector. A series of painted canvases along the left and right walls depicted landscapes of Eden's other ten sectors.

Two other desks were to the left—smaller, but similar in build to Naro's. A woman was seated at each one, focused on whatever they were doing at the computers. One of them wore a gray cloak with a collar so high in the back; it arched well over her head, hiding her profile. The other had a circlet adorning her forehead, and wore a shawl with a white "+" on the front. I knew who she was: Sandra, the Head of Hospitals and Medicine.

"It doesn't even feel like we're at the Radio Tower anymore," Kay whispered.

"I know, right?"

"Scared?" I could hear a slight quiver in her breath.

"Yeah, a little," I agreed. "Sandra's sitting right over there. Who's the other one?"

"Not sure. I bet we'll find out, though."

Mika whimpered, stunned by the sight and size of the office. She had fallen behind slightly, and jogged to catch up with the two of us and took our hands into hers. We proceeded to the desks.

As we continued toward the back, the silence in the office was interrupted by the sound of a shifting chair and a drawer shutting. Naro emerged from behind and bellowed with arms stretched out. "Welcome, Revolutionaries!"

I locked up. Naro's voice was strong and well-projected. The way they were spoken, those two words sounded like he said so much more. It was as if his foremost priority was boasting his authority in an attempt to send us cowering into a corner. It was not the time for fear after getting this far. This was the man we had come for.

Kay nodded, bowing to him. "Hello." Her voice was meek, but there was a twinge of assuredness.

Naro's disposition remained unchanged as he continued to speak with flair in his booming, authoritative voice. "The bowing isn't necessary, my dear! I'm certain it means nothing coming from the likes of you youngsters, anyhow! Please, step forward here to my desk." He motioned to the space at the edge of his personal workspace. "I've been expecting you."

I tried to act casual to ease my nerves, as well as those of the girls. "Yeah, the officer told us."

Naro's hands came together in a single, thunderous clap. His eyes narrowed as his voice remained unwavering. "Then let us cut right to the demands here. What is it you want to say during the show? Please tell me it has something to do with you all giving up and going home. My show could use less of this 'Revolution-related filler.'"

Throwing off his need to push the conversation along quickly, I stopped it short by replying, "Well, nothing actually. We're not here to be on the air."

My answer elicited a scoff from the women and a dark chuckle from Naro. "Surely, you can't be serious. You're not out to clear your names, or declare innocence on the innkeeper?"

"No, I'm serious." My back straightened as I briskly defended our reason for this visit. "We had no intention of coming here to interrupt your show. We kind of have something more important to deal with right now, if you care to listen."

Naro ambled around the desk to approach us. The three of us backpedaled, keeping our eyes fixed on him. "This…" he began, easing his booming tone, "…is not going as we had predicted."

"Predicted?" I repeated.

He slid his rectangle-frame glasses down away from his narrow, gray eyes and proceeded to wipe them with a white cloth he produced from his pocket. "Yes. We even had ten of our Gray Patrol on standby—"

I interrupted him with a scoffing laughter. Kay and Mika reacted as well, affirming my reaction toward him.

"What's so funny?" Naro shouted the question at us as his confusion grew into frustration.

I shook my head confidently as I looked up and caught Naro square in the eye. "You're going to need more than ten of them."

"A *lot* more than ten," Kay added.

Sandra stood from her chair. "What are they talking about?"

Our confident attitudes and cryptic ambiguity snatched their full attention. Now they were taking us seriously, it was time to redirect them to the actual issue at hand.

Over the next few minutes, we explained the plot to them, as well as stated our true intentions for being at the Radio Tower. I made sure to dig into Naro on the outset; letting him know his slanderous broadcasts were the first thing to light the fire. Naro stood straight, arms folded, with a perpetual, derisive smirk. He didn't hide his refusal to take any blame for simply doing his job. Sandra, however, appeared flustered and annoyed. I wanted to believe she agreed with me, but felt it was a stretch.

As we spoke to him, Naro's crooked grin and sure posture wavered. His first question came out with a crack; one as much in his voice as it was in his previously-intimidating stance. "What is it they plan on doing when they get here?"

Kay answered with clear threat in her tone, "Oh, they're going to trash the place and bring it down! They were saying four-hundred people are more than enough to make the Challenge Tower the tallest structure by the end of the day."

I played along with it. "Ooh, ouch! I didn't hear *that* one! I guess the neighborhood needs to watch out for what direction the spire's going to fall in."

The threat to the spire brought all three of the Fifteen members to a desperate alert. Naro looked drained and on edge. "Four-hundred of them—and my tower!?"

We had complete control of the conversation at this point. We were the ones with the information; the ones with the answers. My heart raced as a sensation of invincibility coursed through me. "Yes, four-hundred Causes are marching their way here to bust up your tower! Your broadcast and accusations did a good job of ticking off a lot more Causes than the Radio Tower can handle. This mob consists of hundreds of us young men and women who are taking everything way too far. We came to warn you—"

I was cut short by the jarring sensation of a hand being brought across the back of my head. "You idiot!" Kay screamed.

The jolt startled me. I shouted back, sidetracking the conversation, "What?!"

Kay's eyes were distressed as she leaned in closer to me, softly hissing. "Do you realize what you said?"

I tried to repeat myself, unable to immediately pinpoint my alleged error. "I said he did a good job of angering the Causes, and we came… here…"

Kay, with her voice still stern, condescendingly held her hand to her ear. "One more time."

I slowed down my speech and examined my words as I spoke them. "He angered…the Cau—"

That was it. Realizing my mistake stunned me into silence.

Every word I had spoken before Kay slapped me replayed in my mind. My head, still stinging in the back, swayed slowly from side to side. There was no way to recover from this. We could only hope the Fifteen did not catch on to what a "Cause" really was.

Such hope was rightly squashed when Naro chuckled, sweeping into a solid laugh. He was on to my slip-up and had already begun to ponder the possibilities open to him with this critical piece of information. "All this time…" Once again, Naro's tone and demeanor changed back to stiff and authoritative.

My heart quaked and my head dropped down to meet the top of my chest. Mika tried to comfort me by giving my hand a gentle squeeze. I smirked, only to reassure her. There was no comforting myself, though. Both Kay and I knew the seriousness of this blunder. All I could do was prepare myself for the consequences.

"Eliza!" Naro called.

The woman with the high collar stood, stone-faced. "Yes, Naro?"

My chest felt to have shattered. Eliza was now at the ready to make use of my leaked information.

Kay cut in, stomping around. "Right in front of the Monitor of the IN! Absolute freaking genius! You *bonehead*!" She stormed over to the sofa. "I need to sit down and wait for the Gray Police to come arrest us!"

Naro had waited patiently for the tangent to end before he addressed Eliza again. "Yes, Eliza. Please, run a search for any sites related to 'Cause,' 'Revolution,' and 'Radio Tower.' That should take us to what we've been looking for. Also, see if you can get a hold of Biktor and ask him how *this* wasn't—" Naro cut himself off. He was not set to make the same mistake I had by haphazardly spouting intelligence.

Eliza cocked a chilling eye at me as she responded, "I'm on it!" She took a great pause before sitting back down; her odd stare boring into me. Pursing her lips, she hung her head and shook it.

Her expressions were relating well to what I was feeling in my gut.

Naro approached me up close. Although he was a few centimeters shorter, he still stood strong and dignified in front of me. "You, boy, have saved us a *lot* of trouble."

My head was still hanging low with my thoughts racing. I was at a loss for ideas and all I could think about is how such a colossal blunder didn't have to happen. Now, the Fifteen were practically at the forum's doorstep, and it was all my fault.

I could hear Naro talking to me, but his words were going in one ear and out the other as his voice began to sound muffled. It was difficult for me to understand anything beyond my sudden feeling of worthlessness. Within moments, though, my trance was broken by a loud bang and a strong, mature voice. "Hold it!"

Mika and I spun around. Kay sprang up from her seat, interested. "Who is this now?"

I looked up to see the perpetrator of the interruption. A tall, youthful man with a slender build, shaggy blonde hair, and a long stride was marching up the red carpet.

At first glance, I was grateful to see a fellow Cause. His dark brown pants seemed to hold many items in the six zippered pockets sewn into them. His belt held two small pouches to each side which jingled with the sound of arna coins as they bobbed about his waist. A simple, collared blue shirt waved around, not tucked in. Over his shirt, he wore a dark red robe with black trim in an odd, yet efficient fashion. The back of the robe was folded up to his shoulders and held in place by a second belt hugging his chest. The way he wore his robe gave him more storage for his personal items. His belongings clattered along with his wide stride and confident swagger.

"And who do you think you are barging into my office like this!?" Naro roared.

"Quick intro: My name is Bogen. And on behalf of—" He stopped short in his introduction and took a look around. After a moment to think about it, he addressed me. "Br—" His mouth sputtered. In pause, his glance turned sideways. "I'm pretty sure I know who you are."

My posture tightened as I gasped. One of the Producers, Bogen, had arrived on the scene. I pointed to him. "How do you know who I am?"

As Bogen stepped past me to talk with Naro, he placed his hand on my shoulder and moved in close to my ear. If he had gotten any closer, the tuft of blonde goatee in the middle of his chin would have tickled the side of my cheek. "You're not the only one who objected to the upcoming raid. But I certainly didn't expect you to show up in Naro's office."

"Yeah…" I groaned. "About that—"

"So, if I understand correctly," Naro interrupted, "you're all here to stop your own kind from destroying your own enemy."

"It doesn't make sense to me either," Kay replied from across the room. "Personally, I didn't care one way or the other at first!"

Eliza called to Naro. "I've found it, Naro. They have an entire forum on the Interactive Network. The code-word 'Cause' is what kept it hidden for so long. It seems they're led by a group called 'The Producers.'"

"What?!" Bogen hollered out in disbelief. "How did they—?"

Before he finished his sentence, I raised my hand, guilty.

"You told them!?"

I raised my head, though my posture remained slumped and resigned. "It was an accident."

Bogen gestured to stay on the topic of the raid. "We'll talk about this later. There isn't much time left before the rest of the Rev—" he stopped speaking, shooting me a frustrated look to further accentuate his furor, and corrected his statement. "There's not much time left before the other *Causes* get here."

Naro called everyone to his attention after hearing a brief report from Eliza. "I can't believe I'm doing this, but I will be willing to bargain with you if you can stop your Causes today."

Bogen stepped forward. "I'm one of the leaders of the Revolution for the side of the Causes. I have more than enough influence to take care of this myself, but I'm glad the three of you are here as well. It will help." He held out his hand toward me. "I'm sure a lot of people have read your post based on how many negative replies it got. I felt your point deep down, though. I agree this raid is not the right answer." He patted me on the shoulder. "Mistake or not, you're still on my side in this as long as you still want to stop it." He extended his hand to mine, and I obliged. His grip was tight and sure.

Kay and Mika came walking back to join the talks again. Kay appeared relieved since one of the Producers was on our side. Mika, however, was on edge. "We're running out of time!"

Bogen knelt down; bending his tall legs at the knees and arching is long back to meet her face to face. "You're right, young lady." Bogen pleasantly chortled and ruffled her hair. "Cute kid!" He kissed her on the forehead.

Kay gave him a protective shove. "All due respect, Bogen: Really; at a time like this?"

Bogen caught his balance as he responded with grit in his voice. "And you are…?"

She hesitated. "I'm...Susan."

His brow dropped. "I don't recall a 'Susan' on the forum."

"No forum names, remember?" Her voice was hushed as she jerked her head slightly toward the members of the Fifteen.

Bogen pointed his right hand towards Eliza and his left toward me. "Behold! The reasons why that is no longer relevant! So forum name—"

Bogen's taunt was cut short by Naro's impatience. "Can we get on with this!?"

Once again, Naro's shouting sent all of us into a shiver. Shattered with nerves, Bogen took the conversation while Kay,

Mika, and I gathered our things. "Right…bargain. I heard you say bargain. What kind of bargain were we talking?"

"What do you want from us in exchange for your help?"

"Well," Bogen exhaled, calming down, "There's a list of things the Causes on the whole are looking to ask the Fifteen."

"Like what?" Naro emitted an odd mix of dismissiveness and eagerness that manifested in the form of a condescending scoff caught in his throat.

Bogen lazily shrugged, "The answer, in its entirety, will come in due time, Naro." He followed up with a deep breath and a solid demand. "What we really want right now is for you to call off the Gray Police from the Pata Sector, have Cenia lift the curfew, and get Riley to restore the train service, unobstructed. If you promise those things, we will promise to stop the raid."

Naro looked to Eliza and Sandra, appearing to seek their opinion on the matter. "I don't see a problem," Eliza said as Sandra agreed with a brief nod.

Naro blew a long breath before continuing. "For how long?"

Bogen was on top of keeping his haggling in our favor. "You and I will discuss the details after we stop the raid. There's a special announcement I've come to give you on behalf of the Producers. We don't have the time right now. Trust me, it won't obligate you to do anything more than I've already asked."

Naro thought a moment before taking a key out of his pocket. "Sandra!" he called.

Sandra stood, adjusting the folds in her shawl. "Yes?"

Naro tossed the key over to her. "I need the yellow case from the gated storage room."

Sandra nearly missed catching the key. "Sure thing."

Naro turned back to us as Sandra made her hasty exit. "All right. I'll leave it be for now. However, if you fail to stop the raid, Pata will stay as is."

I blurted out, trying to contribute. "Also—"

Bogen whispered in my direction. "Hey, dude. You're killing my whole vibe here."

"We still need an apology."

Naro pushed out a breath. "An apology for what?"

Trying to tie up all the loose ends, I said, "An apology for accusing Causes of the murder of the innkeeper."

Bogen snapped his fingers. "You know what, he's right!"

Naro regretfully shook his head. "I'm afraid I can't."

"Why not?"

"You see," he explained, "one of your Causes was *indeed* the murderer. Vade has already caught the perpetrator."

"She has? Really?" Bogen nodded. "Well, at least whoever it was is no longer associated with us. They sure caused us a lot of unnecessary trouble."

"It seems we have reached our agreement," Naro concluded. "As long as you keep this tower safe, I will counsel with Vade, Cenia, and Riley to cease their actions in Pata."

"It's agreed," Bogen announced.

Naro shook each of our hands to seal the deal. "Yes, agreed."

As we looked to the clock to see only seven minutes remained, Sandra returned with the yellow case. "Ah, good! Bring it here," Naro requested before turning back to us. "Give us a few moments will you?"

Bogen pulled Kay, Mika, and me aside. "I want to thank you all for being here. It made things a lot easier." He then addressed me specifically with a tone of regret. "However, Brigg, by your slip up, they found the forums."

"What's going to happen to me?"

He lightly squeezed my shoulder and got close to whisper. "Spilled milk. Let's worry about it later. We have the Fifteen in a position to negotiate. So I'm sure this will end well anyway."

Kay added, "Forum regardless, the Causes still have leverage. Hatcher still has the trump card for our side."

"But his last post was almost six weeks ago—"

Naro interrupted us. "Young people, I have something you can use to help you."

The four of us drew closer to him as he took the yellow case from Sandra and prepared to present us with its contents. I inhaled slowly as my nerves calmed. I was beginning to feel a lot more relaxed with this feeling of unity. As odd as it sounds, I was glad the Fifteen had accepted us during this uncharacteristic rebellion against an act orchestrated by our own kind.

Naro opened the case to reveal a strange device I had never seen before. It was a small gray box with a handle sticking from the bottom, and a wide red cone popping out from the side. It looked as if the tip of the cone had been driven into the box. There was a button on the handle. The device was surrounded by a protective material to keep it from damage while in its case.

We stood there, bedazzled by the mysterious tool. "This is a voice amplifier. Feel free to take it by the handle."

I was the closest, so I reached in and grabbed it. It was a little weighty, but easy to wield with one hand. Looking closer, I saw a circular screen on the back of the box part. "How does it work; how will it help?"

Naro continued, "You can use this so you can speak louder than the entire gang of Causes headed our way. The fact you'll even have a device like this should stop their advance."

"They'll have no choice but to listen to us, then," Mika added.

I continued to rotate it in my hand to examine it from every angle. "What do I do to use this?"

With a laugh at my quizzical curiosity, he taught me. "You simply press the button on the handle and speak into the screen."

As instructed, I pushed the button on the handle and spoke: "***Like this?***"

Everyone in the room jumped and covered their ears at the sudden burst of noise. "Yes. Like that," Naro replied, amused.

Kay wondered, "Why would you give us control of something like this? You had it hidden away for a good reason, right?"

"I will explain everything later. Let's get through this and we'll have a chat after my show."

The time was 11:57 am. Naro was to go on the air and we were going to stop the raid.

Bogen took the voice amplifier and the lead. "He's right. Let's get out there and stop this madness." The four of us, now led by Bogen, rushed back to the entrance of the Radio Tower.

Naro bid us good luck.

IV

We burst through the front door of the tower to see the legion of Causes drawing close. Mika backed away behind the rest of us, suddenly overtaken by the sheer size of the assembly. The rest of us gaped in amazement at the result of Al & Jal's planning. The sight of the crowd put us under the impression this was the start of a full-on rebellion rather than a simple protest.

Since the congregation of chaos and determination made their way up the middle of many of the Fanda Sector's streets, the citizens had all cowered indoors. Even if we stopped them from taking over the tower, I was afraid they had already dealt damage to the title "Cause". It felt as though the non-violent creed the Producers had put in place was coming to a crashing halt.

Bogen's brow furrowed. The front line of the whole rabble slowed at the sight of us standing at the Radio Tower entrance. He found the brief hesitation as his chance to stop their advance. "I refuse to let this happen while I'm in charge here!" He lifted the voice amplifier to his mouth, pushed the button, and belted out as loud as he could. "***My fellow Causes, stop!***"

The mob's marching slowed a little more, but they still seemed determined to complete their mission.

"They aren't listening!" Mika cried out.

Bogen let Mika's comment slide as he lifted the amplifier to his lips again. ***"As a member of the producers, I, Bogen, order you all to stop! Right now!"***

With the right words spoken, the flock of Causes reacted. Soon, the front line came to a stop, turning around to halt the rest of the crowd. The chain reaction took several moments to bring the Causes to a complete and attentive stop.

There was clamoring and excessive chatter from the once-hostile mass. We allowed them a few minutes to talk amongst themselves as we caught our breath. We could hear our forum names being mentioned by the crowds.

Kay leaned to me. "It seems word of your post got out."

Rickety, I nodded, still shaken by how close we were to failure.

"Now, if this gang doesn't run us over anyway, we'll consider ourselves lucky."

I shared my own perspective of luck with her. "We were already lucky to have Bogen show up like this. They probably wouldn't have listened to us otherwise."

Bogen continued speaking to the horde, leaving a dramatic pause between each sentence. ***"Causes, this plot was brought to my attention by our contact, Black. I've read every last post up to last night. It was then I realized things have gone too far. We should not be resorting to acts of destruction and terrorism like the one planned for today."***

Many of the Causes could be heard referencing Naro's hostile broadcasts toward our side.

"Please, allow me to finish!" Bogen ordered, bringing the bickering to a stop.

"Definitely lucky," Kay whispered. "They're listening. There *is* some order to this."

"I don't know if Al & Jal are here. Frankly, I don't care. But if the two of you are in the audience, and can hear me,

know I will not accept behavior like this among our kind here. Myself, as well as the other Producers, worked long and hard on assembling the rules the Causes should be abiding by during the Revolution. What Al & Jal suggested was going completely against everything we've organized."

We could see the Causes nodding as light murmuring resonated through the mass.

I stepped forward, trying to take the voice amplifier from Bogen. He jerked his hand away and gave me a smile. "Don't worry. You'll have your chance to speak."

Kay muttered something I could not quite hear. When I turned to ask what she had said, she refused to repeat it. She and Mika began snickering to each other while Bogen was piecing together his next statement.

I let it go and walked past the two girls, re-entering the Radio Tower lobby. I grabbed the lone chair, brought it outside, and offered it to Bogen to stand on.

Bogen took position standing on the chair and released another announcement into the ears of the Causes. *"As of right now, the producers are still waiting for Hatcher to arrive. Once he does, we will meet and discuss our demands as planned. Until then, we have negotiated with Naro. The Fifteen will lift Pata's curfew, restore train services, and scale back on those gray-suited police. They caught the innkeeper's killer, and acknowledge there is no more reason to have Pata locked down the way it is."*

The multitude threw itself into a mild uproar at this news. It was apparent many of these Causes were looking for some more action to pass the time and cripple the Fifteen. They pressed forward a few steps, forcing Bogen to shout into the voice amplifier until they came back to order.

Bogen then handed the amplifier to me. Nervous, I took it and lifted up into position on the chair. Looking out at the mob, I froze, knowing I was face to face with everybody who shunned me on the forums. The thought of every set of eyes piercing me sent a quiver down my spine.

I tried to shake it off, breathing slowly. I swallowed hard and gave my speech to the awaiting audience. **"Um, hi everyone. Yes, it's me, Brigg."**

A lone "Boo-o-o!" sounded out and echoed through the crowd. Some turned to scowl at the heckler.

I shrugged it off. **"As of a few days ago, I appeared to be the only one who opposed this. Up until ten minutes ago, I thought I was alone."**

"Uh…Hello!" Kay called out.

"I thought _we_ were alone in this. I wasn't sure if we were doing the right thing by coming here to warn them of you all coming. When Bogen arrived, however, that confirmed this siege was a bad idea. Everything about it was wrong and Al & Jal should be ashamed! I think it would be best if we continue to go about our business and wait for Hatcher to arrive. We've done a good job of sticking to the itinerary of the producers. Let's try to keep it up. I'm confident all of our questions will be answered in due time once the Fifteen hear what we want."

The Causes cried out various responses while some in the back of the crowd seemed to listen and leave. Nevertheless, many did not seem so convinced. Their main argument was the fact Hatcher had still not been heard from. Without solid proof of Hatcher showing up soon, any attempt to diffuse such an argument would fail.

Bogen thought of a quick enough response to the audience's newfound lack of confidence. He whisked the voice amplifier back into his possession and took my spot on the chair. **"I didn't want to resort to this, but I'm left with little choice."** His dramatic tone hushed the crowd once again.

Kay muttered, "I don't like the sound of this."

Reluctant, Bogen continued. ***"If it so happens something has gone wrong with Hatcher, the Producers are going to have to proceed without him."***

There was an awed and delicate silence. For the first time since the legion arrived, there was absolute silence among every one of them who had stayed long enough to listen. Bogen's words even had Kay and Mika intrigued.

Bold, Kay was the first to speak. "I thought Hatcher said—"

Bogen cut her off with the amplifier still active. ***"I am aware of Hatcher's announcement of crucial information and his request for us to wait. We will give him one more week to show himself or post on the forums. If we do not hear from him by then, the Producers and I are going to proceed in our talks with the Fifteen without him."***

The announcement itself produced an unsettling air. This came from the same mouth that, moments ago, criticized actions going against the Producers' rules. Kay was quick to blurt out, "We're going to defy Hatcher!?"

Bogen defended himself. "I'm just as much a Producer as Hatcher. I am able to override his word at a time like this."

The horde clamored as Kay, Mika, and I tried to understand his stance. "Look, Bogen," Kay pressed. "I'm not trying to undermine your authority or anything; but are you sure this is a good idea?"

Bogen addressed her with confidence. "Who's to say this won't happen again? Who's to say Al & Jal may not plot another get-together like this?"

I added to Bogen's side. "We don't know what every individual Cause is thinking. Maybe this raid attempt would give other Causes the idea to try this elsewhere."

Bogen nodded. "I'm certain the rest of the Producers are not up for cleaning up any huge messes the likes of which we could've seen here today."

Kay was willing to accept Bogen's announcement. "I hope you know what you're doing."

Without another word to her, Bogen turned back to the crowd and readied his voice one last time. **_"Please continue to go about your business. We will see to it Naro carries out his part in our negotiations. There is nothing else for Causes here today. Please return to whatever it was you were doing before this."_**

Grumbles and mixed reactions could be heard from the multitude of Causes as they started spreading out to leave. Our mission of stopping the siege on the Radio Tower was a success. An invigorating feeling of great accomplishment washed over me as I sat in the chair to catch my breath. Mika approached and placed her hand on my shoulder. "We did good, huh?"

Bogen answered for me. "We're not done yet. We need to wrap things up here with Naro. Then, I have to get back together with the rest of the Producers and tell them what happened here."

I stood, grabbed the chair, and led everyone back inside. As I reached for the door, there was a loud bang. We all looked around to see a small object had been thrown in our direction from what was left of the grouping of Causes.

Mika picked it up and gasped in surprise. We gazed at the object: an unmistakable black die with white dots. Mika giggled as she snatched the voice amplifier and turned toward the streets. **_"It came up as a five, Dice!"_**

We heard his voice over the rest of them. "Damn it!"

My smile came natural. I took the amplifier from Mika and called out to him. **_"Get your butt over here, you bum!"_**

It seemed to me Dice's decision to leave may have been thrown to the wayside by a later roll of his dice. Mika was excited to see him again, so I chose to push back my reservations about the grouchy gambler. Having him with us through the Ordeal of

Pata gave us a chance to know him better. Despite his deep-cutting attitude, it felt right to have him back.

V

It took us most of the afternoon to bring the whole episode to a close. Most of it was spent in Naro's office, being specific about the terms of our negotiations. Naro assigned Eliza to send a message out to all of the Gray Police and order them to return to the Exta Sector and the Labor Fields. This would keep them out of the public eye and out of the Causes' hair.

The resuming of train service was a problem, though. After the trains were ordered to stop, the crews began maintenance on them or simply went home. It was going to take some time to bring the trains back to running order with full crews.

Naro assured us he would not drag in carrying out his end of the negotiations. He had Eliza send a message to Riley to get the trains back up as soon as possible.

Although Naro had told us he would give us details about the voice amplifier, he was pained to have to renege on it. While he enjoyed teaching people about media and communications, the information on the amplifier and its origins was not fit for Causes to hear, as long as they still opposed the system. We accepted it for what it was, but I was looking forward to coming back to it once things calmed down.

During these talks, we saw a side of Naro a lot more into his authoritative role than the Naro we saw at first. He told us the Radio Tower was his home. His life and its mission all rested within the tower's walls. Communications, media, entertainment, and everything we heard from the radio were the focus of Naro's existence. By the time he got done explaining how important the tower was to him, we felt as if he would drop dead on sight if anything were to happen to it.

Throughout the conversation, I felt the growing sensation of there being more to holding authority as a member of the Fifteen than any of us could ever understand. To hear Naro being overly passionate about his role as a key person in Eden's structure left a chill behind at the thought of the mysteries surrounding it.

The whole discussion tempted me to throw some questions at Eliza and Sandra. However, it was best to keep from trying to find out too much. We already had Naro pour himself out to us. We were not about to try and bleed them dry.

Bogen also informed them of the Producers being prepared to discuss bringing an end to the Revolution. This, of course, meant our demands for the truths about Eden would have to be met. Bogen left that detail out, though. He only wanted to persuade them with the aspect of putting Eden's state of turmoil to a close.

Naro, Eliza, and Sandra responded cooperatively. They viewed the outcome of the raid as a ray of hope for the Causes and the Fifteen. This was our opportunity to work together and restore peace to Eden once again.

Bogen had them fooled. By omitting our specific demands from the conversation for the time being, he lured them into a sense we were ready to surrender. The sly man's tongue was slick and his words were carefully chosen.

By the time the negotiations were over, Bogen had their attention. They were willing to listen to anything we had to say if it meant the end of the Revolution. They chose a meeting place not too far from the location where the Producers originally gathered. Once there, the terms would be discussed.

Mika, Kay, Dice, and I kept our mouths shut most of the time. When prompted to speak, we simply agreed. I had said enough throughout the day to mess things up. The last thing we needed was for me to muck up the negotiations.

It was well into the evening by the time we said goodbye to the three members. Bogen set out to rejoin the rest of the

Producers to wait for Hatcher. He kept to his word and was going to announce to the public of Hatcher having one week to arrive at the meeting location.

Everything looked to be in place. But whatever key piece of information Hatcher had would then be factored out of our leverage against the Fifteen. All we could do was hope Hatcher's presence at the meeting would not be as important as he declared.

Finally, with the raid prevented and peace restored for the time being, we could continue with what brought the four of us together in the first place:

We had one week to search for Mika's father.

Episode 4: Hatcher's Response

Six days passed, and there was still no sign of Hatcher. By this time, the forum became flooded with countless opinions on where he was and what he was doing.

Al & Jal still remained the most outspoken duo among the entire population of Causes. Unfortunately, instead of adding input to the subject of our missing leader, they chose to set their sights directly on me and my party. With their influence established, they openly questioned our allegiance and managed to squeeze in a cowardly jab at Bogen's ability to lead as a Producer. Bogen rightly responded with a lengthy post to justify our actions in going to Naro. It was enough to put Al & Jal in their place for the time being.

With Pata restored and Naro's end of the bargain upheld, many Causes found it difficult to judge us too harshly. Still, my slip in revealing our name to the Fifteen was brought to light when Naro publicly called us "Causes" during *This Week in Eden.* Our group had to endure another storm of negative comments. Thankfully, the Producers stuck by our side, chalking it up to an unfortunate-but-necessary sacrifice to get things moving forward.

On the topic of the day of the raid, it became known Al & Jal *were* in attendance. The reason they did not step forward when we were holding the mob off was a mystery. Fortunately for us, Al & Jal's lack of action turned some criticism toward them. If they were so adamant about the siege of the Radio Tower, why did they let us stop it so easily?

We were delighted to have Dice back as part of our team. Despite his disagreeable nature, he still did his part to keep things civil. Through spending the week together, we learned Dice's Interactive Study Grade was noticeably higher than mine or Kay's. This was a fact he knew we would commit to memory for any event in which he would offer his own brand of advice.

Dice also explained in better detail why he left us in the first place. He was merely looking out for his own skin. At the same time, he did it to see from a distance I was not just blowing hot air when I chose to step forward and stop the raid.

His words, not mine.

What he did not expect to do was find himself roped into the mob by nothing else but a roll of his dice. To my credit, though, he told me he factored the possibility of meeting up with us again into his odds for the roll.

Kay was warming up to me and Dice. I could feel from her a new and welcome sense of ease, but she still felt a bit off and reserved when we would have conversations about personal things. When winding down at the end of each day, she was usually the first one asleep. I could sense there was a lot on her mind, but she was not quite ready to share it. Still, she pulled her weight; contributing well to the search for Mika's father.

As the week rolled on, though, we were all getting anxious. The end of Bogen's deadline was at hand, and our search efforts were unsuccessful. We were not sure what we would do with Mika if the meeting came out in our favor and the Causes were called to disperse. In the end, we were forced to wait and see.

Day 77

I

The search for Mika's father took us farther west through the Fanda Sector. In due time, we arrived at the border of the Binda Sector.

Binda is a large, residential sector dotted with small business districts. Its landscape and layout are similar to two of its neighboring sectors: Archa to the northeast and Doma to the south. Binda also shares its northern border with the Exta Sector, where all of Eden's products are assembled and shipped from. Being so close to both Exta and Fanda make the sector the most beneficial to live in; and the most populated one in Eden.

Our first order of business was to locate the Delta Business District—the exact point where the borders of Doma, Binda, and Fanda connect. In the center of the district, there is a decorative landmark outlining the borders. Citizens of the area oftentimes find themselves playing around like children, acting like it's a big deal to go from sector to sector in an instant—or to stand in three sectors at the same time.

We were given information from a lone Cause concerning our search for Mika's father. He happened to see a man who looked like the one in Mika's drawing. According to the Cause, her dad was assisting a business in the sector's lower eastern side. Though it was a bit unlikely her father would be in such a plain-sight place, any lead was better than coming up dry.

Mika was ecstatic at how close we seemed to be. It was the best clue we had received since we started the search. The jumpy young girl's attitude shifted from timid yet cheerful to excitable and talkative. She was no longer keeping herself in the distant meekness we were all used to. Mika felt like she belonged with us rather than following a group of protectors. This was her time to shine and we were there to smile with her.

Dice spoke with spread arms upon our crossing the sector's border. "Welcome to my place. I hope you enjoy your stay."

"You're from Binda?" Mika asked.

"Yes. My home is quite a ways west from here, though," he added. "And no, we're not going to pay my house a visit. It's *too* far west from here."

Mika smiled, pushing the sharp tone aside. "Fair enough."

Dice turned the subject on the rest of us, asking where we all came from. Within our answers, Kay and I discovered we were both from the Doma Sector and Mika was from Archa. Dice chuckled at the coincidence in the findings. "Well, maybe after the Revolution, it'll be easy for the two of you to keep in touch."

Kay shot me a playful, sideways glance. "Not sure why."

"Personally; realistically," he said, smirking, "I couldn't care less what *you guys* decide to do after the Revolution. I'm going home and back to my studies. But at least this past week has us respecting each other a bit better. And I'm still getting kicks out of how people react to us all being in a group."

My grin came naturally. "No lie, I'm right on board with you. But I think Kay is getting the short end of the stick."

Kay nodded to me with sincerity. "And I appreciate you and Dice stepping in to defend me on the forums. I'm getting sick of being called a hypocrite."

I shot both thumbs up. "Forget the slope, and screw what others have to say about it. We have our mission here. So we'll keep backing you up."

Mika came giggling over, skipping right past us. "Kinda like a boyfriend, right?"

My body came to a sudden halt, brows furrowed in confusion

and shock as Dice erupted in a fit of laughter. "I'm not touching *that* comment with a ten-meter pole."

Kay deflected, casual. "I don't think I'm a good fit for Brigg."

I was intrigued and interested by her response. She would have reacted to Mika's comment differently a week ago, and I was sure we all knew it. This was a surprise to me with few other ways to describe it. My mind quickly righted itself as I stopped to engage Kay. "Why is that?" I made sure to sound teasing enough to hide my actual curiosity.

As soon as my eyes met hers, I locked up. The expression on her face made me feel like I had said something wrong. Her eyes were open wide and her pupils were like specks, as if she had thought of a thousand answers at once. It sent a chill to my heart. Backtracking to examine what I had said, I got a sinking feeling Kay may have thought I was trying to *flirt* with her.

I nudged her shoulder. "Kay?"

She shook briefly, blinked a few times, then looked at me. She opened her mouth for a moment as if she were about to say something, then stopped herself and softly bit her bottom lip. "Never mind."

I pressed. "What?"

"I said never mind!"

I took the message loud and clear. Without another word, she ran to catch up with Mika and Dice. I followed with slight unease.

II

Once we arrived in the Delta District, Mika handed me the picture of her father. She felt it was necessary for us to refresh our memories as to what he looked like.

Everything seemed to be going smoothly, but the erasure marks in Mika's drawing continued to bother me. In my eyes, they left a lot of room for a potential error if it were to be left up to

Kay, Dice, or myself to spot him. Mika was the only one among us who could reliably identify him without help from the picture.

Dice was the most wary of this detail. He went so far as to question the accuracy of the drawing. Mika defended, feeling she made no mistake in doing the best she could. We even showed Dice the picture of me Mika had begun drawing a few days back. It was enough to ease his doubt, if only a little.

He knew he was being harsh, but played it off as being realistic. He declared our chances of finding him to be less than ideal since the illustration was not completely accurate. Regardless, we kept our eyes open for Mika's father as we made our way to the Delta Landmark.

Each business we passed on our way to the landmark was met with our eyes peering through the windows and scanning any outdoor kiosks. Every café, inn, and shop was invaded by our four-person search party as we methodically picked the path to the Delta apart. This was one lead we were not going to take lightly. By the afternoon, we felt the whole district knew this fact.

At one point, the proprietor of a fabric shop reinforced our previous lead. His information led us to believe Mika's father was assisting businesses at random to earn arna and food. Mika agreed it may have been true given their circumstances before he went missing.

However, the fabric store owner told us the man was last seen in the Doma area of the district. This was good news since we were headed in the direction of the borders at the Delta.

All the way there, Mika was bubbling in a way I had never seen her before. Her excessive energy was keeping us positive and motivated. Gathering leads had us so anxious and occupied, before we knew it, the Delta Landmark was within sight.

The four of us walked towards the center of the cobblestone circle, approaching the feet of the tall, stone statue in the middle. The sculpture was of Delta, the Son of Paxus and Shalynn. Seeing the sure and steadfast look on the Son's face, I felt a swell of warmth and assurance. Out of the corner of my eye, I caught a glimpse of Kay bowing her head.

I stepped forward and touched the feet of the statue. Below, on the pedestal, there was an engraving.

As Paxus guards Eden's west, and Shalynn guards its east,
so does this God-Spirit protect all within their divine wall.

He is Delta, the Son and Guardian
Avatar of Obedience
Beacon of Humility
Guide to Preservation
Example of Appreciation

Those who practice these four principles do so to the
pleasure and favor of the God-Spirits.

"Obedience…" I repeated with a huff from my nose.

"Yeah, Delta's probably not our biggest fan right now," Dice said with a laugh.

Kay opened her eyes and lifted her head. "Don't even *start*, you guys. I was busy enough in the 'Defying Our Creators' thread. I don't need a reprise of it."

Dice rolled his eyes before resting them to a relaxed glance towards her. "In our defense, that was probably the *only* thread where Brigg and I *both* took your side."

"And believe me," she said, touching Delta's feet, "I really appreciated the backup. It's hard feeling like we're losing favor with Paxus and Shalynn in order to pull off this Revolution."

I broke from the statue and paced toward one of the empty benches encircling the outer area of the landmark. "Once we get what we want from the Fifteen, we can all go for a nice, long,

Repentance Rite. In the meanwhile, I'm sure the God-Spirits can look on us with at least *some* understanding."

Mika followed me, with Kay and Dice close behind. As I sat, I took my bag of granola out and passed it to Mika. The four of us relaxed and snacked, happy to be off our feet for the first time in hours. In quiet contemplation, I couldn't help but dwell on the conversation we had had by the statue. Even though I knew it wasn't time to be worrying about the God-Spirits, my conscience was making it difficult to be at complete ease.

Glancing around to take my mind off it, I could see a girl watching us from another bench. I briefly looked at her and tried to tune into the conversation Mika and Kay were having. Soon, though, the other girl was too distracting to ignore. She kept looking at us, then looking into her things in an off-rhythmic pattern. I brought it to everyone's attention.

All of us looked to her. The next time she turned her two eyes to us, she was met with all eight of ours. She shuffled her belongings around and put them all away. Within moments, she stood, turned to us and walked in our direction. Her gray cape flapped behind her.

"What's with her?" Dice wondered.

"I don't know, but we should be prepared for—" I stopped in mid-sentence. My memory gave itself a kick-start as the woman's gentle face became much clearer as she drew closer. Though her clothes were different, her face was unmistakable. "Zoe? Month of May, is that you!?"

"Zoe? Month of May?" Kay asked.

"Yes, it's her, from the forums!" I stood from the bench, ready to greet her. "We met back at the Gateway. She was in my room when all of us got separated."

"I see," Kay nodded.

Zoe stood erect and mature. "Brigg, it's nice to see you again. And don't worry about the forum name for me anymore."

"Oh, alright, Zoe. It's great to see you, too!" I smiled, stepping to her to give her a friendly hug. "I'm honestly glad to see you again. I thought maybe Vade captured you back in Pata."

Zoe daintily scoffed. "Don't worry about it. It's in the past. But the Ordeal of Pata *did* prompt me to forfeit being a Cause."

Kay smiled, friendly. "Still, Zoe, it's nice to meet you. I'm Kay, and this is Dice and Mika."

Seeing I didn't ditch them at the Gateway, Zoe cocked an eye at me. "I thought you said you were going to try an—"

My face warped with wide eyes and a buttoned lip. It was enough to communicate my thought: *Please, please, please don't finish that sentence!*

"No," Zoe recovered, shooting me a discreet wink. "It wasn't you, it was someone else."

I shifted to get away from the subject quickly. "So what's up? Got something to fill us in on?"

"Actually," she replied, politely pointing "I came over here to see you, Kay."

Kay's brow rose. "Me? What for?"

Dice whispered to me. "Those two never met, right?"

Zoe approached Mika, who was seated next to Kay on the bench. "May I?"

Mika relinquished her seat to Zoe, who cut right to the chase. "From over there, I noticed you're injured." Zoe was, of course, referring to Kay's bandages.

Kay took a sharp breath in and broke her eye contact with Zoe; glancing to her left hand. "Oh, these?" She wiggled her fingers to display full functionality. "It's nothing."

Zoe opened her bag to display a well-equipped first aid kit. "Whatever hurts, I'm sure there's something in here to help ease the pain."

Kay replied in steadfast defense, tapping on her left wrist. "There is no pain here for you to relieve. See?"

I tried to get the stubborn girl to cooperate. "Please, Kay, she's only trying to help."

She continued to stand her ground. "I don't need any help here. I can take care of my own wounds."

Zoe persisted again. "If I could see the injury, I can recommend a treatment."

Dice took a shot at calming the projected storm. "She's right, you know. You should know what treatment options—"

"That's enough!" Kay belted out.

Her outburst silenced all of us.

Remaining stoic, Zoe took her refusal graciously. She stood and accepted Kay's position on the matter. She brought her open bag over to me. Out of it, she handed me three vials and explained them one by one. "This green one is an antibiotic gel for cuts to prevent infection. This greenish-yellow one is a salve for burns and rashes. And, this red one slowly develops scar tissue into regular skin."

I was intrigued by the effects of the red gel she presented. I leaned in close to her. "Can I get some of those? I've got this big scar on the back of my leg I'm kind of embarrassed about."

"Certainly!" She smiled, presenting me with two more.

Mika ventured to ask her, "What else do you have in there?"

"Why, I have all sorts of medicines and…oh yeah…" Zoe dug through her bag and pulled out a roll of dressing. "…bandages." She turned to Kay and handed them to her. "The ones you have on look worn and old. Replace them when you get a chance."

Kay gazed at her for a moment then reached her hand out. "Thank you." She sounded ashamed of her previous rudeness.

Zoe took her hand into both of Kay's, delivering the bandage with a caring grip. "I'm glad I was able to help you in some way."

"This is a big help," I assured her, examining the red gel.

She bowed to all of us before turning to depart. "Well, it seems the four of you are in good shape then. I'll be on my way."

As Zoe was leaving, Dice nudged me on the shoulder with my granola bag. "You're just gonna let her leave?"

I took the bag and scooped out a handful. "Why shouldn't I?"

"Having someone with good medical aptitudes in our group would be good," he reasoned. "And even though Kay refused her care, it doesn't mean she can't help us if we get injured on the road. We still don't know how much longer the Revolution is going to stretch on for if Hatcher doesn't pull through."

"Leave my injuries out of this," Kay grumbled. "I'm not opposed to the idea, though. Dice makes some good points. She's not a Cause anymore, though. So I'm doubtful she'll accept."

I thought so as well, but started feeling like it would be worth a try. I looked to Mika, who also appeared to be fine with the idea. I turned away to look into the Delta's crowds and managed to see Zoe through the bustle. "Be right back." I broke into a dash to catch up with her.

Zoe stopped and turned to me when she heard me calling her name over the crowd. But instead of greeting me with another smile, her face was somewhat fallen. Seeing it caused me to stop in place, then pace more carefully towards her. As I approached, she sighed and said, "I was *really* hoping you weren't going to follow me. Because this isn't the first time this has happened, and I'm confident it won't be the last."

I pocketed my hands, casual. "I'm guessing other groups you've helped asked you to join them?"

"And I'm sorry, Brigg," she groaned, slowly shaking her head. "My answer has to stay the same. I can't return to the Revolution as a Cause. Using my medical aptitudes this way is the best I can do, but I can't stay in a group. I hope you understand."

"Well, I do; but I kinda don't. What's really stopping you?"

Her mouth twitched a quick frown as she took great pause before answering. "I can't really get into too much detail. But the

Ordeal of Pata was a much bigger deal than everyone thinks. The Causes are going to have a lot on their plate if the meeting with the Fifteen goes south."

Her vocal quiver and darting eyes screamed of dodging something within her answers. "What makes you think so?"

Zoe hesitated again; annoyance pulsing in her eyes. "What I think in that regard isn't up to me. Please, leave me to my duties, and don't worry too much. Tomorrow's meeting with the Fifteen is the only thing you need to focus on. Pray tonight for the Producers' success. Trust me: you *want* them to succeed." Her tone towards the end cried *Please stop asking questions.*

I wanted to keep pressing, but was not looking to upset her more than she already clearly was. Zoe's words, however, rang loud in my concerned mind. Whether this was a well-wishing or a warning was up to anyone's guess. It all weighed heavily as I decided to respect her stance and allow her to go on her way.

Walking back to the others, I had to consider how I would relay this information. If Zoe's parting words *were* some sort of warning, it was my responsibility to share it with the party.

Kay smiled at me as I returned. "I guess it was worth a try."

"It was," I agreed, sitting, "but something is up with her. I'm not sure what it is."

Her face shifted to mild alert. "Did she say something we should be concerned about?"

I gave the three of them a quick rundown of my conversation with Zoe. As they considered what could be implied by her words and behavior, Dice spoke up. "You know, I had a feeling something was up, but I didn't think to say it until you had already chased after her."

I wanted to hear some explanation to quell my curiosity. "What did you think it was?"

Dice made sure he had everyone's attention before continuing.

"Where would a Cause obtain an array of medical supplies?"

I answered to the obvious. "A hospital, of course."

"It's not so simple, Brigg," he continued, shaking his head in disapproval. "I managed to catch the comment where you *thought* she got captured back in Pata."

"Yes…"

He turned to face me, giving off a sure stare. "Those captured in Pata wound up in the hands of the Fifteen, correct?" The girls and I gasped during his brief pause. We caught on, but Dice still clarified. "Call me crazy, but I think she *was* captured before she could escape, and Sandra *may* be having her as an on-foot medic in lieu of the Strip Mines or Assembly Lines."

Kay added, "She *did* shed her Cause name."

Dice pointed to her, nodding in approval. "And since the Fifteen now know about the forum, Eliza can help Sandra keep tabs on Zoe. If Zoe were to post input for the Causes on the forum, she would be in for a world of trouble."

My eyes swayed to and fro while considering all of these points. "Can anyone think of *anything* that could possibly disprove this theory?"

Silence; a blank and disquieting silence.

This was an unfortunate realization since we had already met Sandra in person, but didn't speak with her too much. We could only go by this theory to see a link between her and Zoe.

One thing became clear to us: we needed to make sure the gels and salves provided by Zoe were truly what she said they were. Since this medicine was likely provided by Sandra, we had lingering doubts to trust it first-hand. Although Sandra was routinely famed and praised for her kind benevolence while performing her duties, as a member of the Fifteen she was still an enemy to the Causes. We could not discount the idea of Sandra sending medics to aid Causes, biding on an ulterior motive to spring out and benefit the Fifteen.

The only thing we knew we could trust were the bandages given to Kay. I decided to wait before applying the red gel to my scar. Until we could go to a hospital to ensure the gel was safe, it was not going anywhere outside of its vial.

We prepared to continue our journey into the Doma Sector. As we embarked, Dice matched his pace with Kay. "So Kay, what is the big deal with—"

I sensed Dice's curiosity in Kay's bandages. To keep the peace, I jabbed Dice in the ribs with my elbow. "Don't."

"Ow! What was that for!?"

"Our own good," I muttered.

III

We targeted a line of shops near the Delta Landmark. It was not long before we were presented with the best news we had yet to come by: a glass sculptor identified the man in Mika's picture. He did not catch his name, but told us he was last seen at a café three streets away. Mika took off running, almost leaving the rest of us behind.

Excited by this lead, all four of us started running through the streets in the direction of the café. Mika led the way, dashing far enough ahead to almost be lost in the crowd."

Kay called to her, "Don't leave us behind!" Her worked breathing sounded more like a huff of delight toward Mika's excitement.

Mika cut her dash down to a jog for us to catch up. She fidgeted in place with a bright, beaming smile across her face. "I don't want to miss him."

I slowed down while approaching her. "Trust me," I said, catching my breath. "I don't either. We don't know what's going to happen with the Producers tomorrow. Finding your dad tonight would be perfect."

Dice and Kay signaled their agreement as we all regrouped and paced to a brisk stroll. We were at the right street within the next minute.

As we rounded the corner, Mika had stopped short. Her attention was fixed on two male waiters who were attending to the café's patrons. I took Mika's picture out of my pocket and alternated between looking at it and examining the faces of the waiters. We were still too far away to make a positive match.

"What's wrong?" Kay asked, placing a hand on Mika.

"I…" she hesitated.

Dice adjusted his glasses, joining me in the visual comparison. "I'm seeing a resemblance to the one on the left."

Mika spoke up with a shake in her voice. "I think we need to get closer."

Kay stopped her. "Hold on a second. Are you all right?"

The little one sighed. "Yeah, I'm okay. I can't believe it's almost over. Just in time, too, right?"

I patted her on the head. "Hey, we can stick around for a little while. We still have time before the Producers do their thing."

We walked the rest of the way to the café. By the time we got there, the two waiters had gone back in to retrieve orders. Waiting for them to return, we took seats at one of the tables next to the door. Mika turned her chair, wanting to greet her father on sight. She fidgeted anxiously, wobbling back and forth while peering through the doorway.

I rested my head in my hands, eagerly anticipating the reunion.

"I bet you feel satisfied," Kay said as she leaned back.

"I am, yes," I replied. "Fanda is a big sector, and the four of us can only cover so much ground in a day. Coming up dry all week has been pretty frustrating."

She exhaled with a mild growl, rolling her eyes. "I'm sure that goes double for Mika, right?" Kay said it in such a way as to reach for Mika's attention.

Mika, however, was too focused looking into the café. Her smile erased in an instant; she sniffled and started to cry. Three words were uttered to crush all of our hearts: "It's not him." Her bottom lip quaked, her eyes flooded and her face was soon buried in her hands. The sight of it sank us.

My head shook, desperately trying to hold back tears of my own. It killed me to see Mika in such a state. Kay, on the other hand, while shedding a tear of her own, took a sisterly approach to Mika's dismay. She opened her arms and invited her to come close. Mika became wrapped in Kay's embrace.

The waiter approached us. He *did* bear a close resemblance to the man in Mika's picture. He had the same narrow chin and dark, crew-cut hair. The erase marks in the picture, unfortunately, were the deciding factor in directing us to the wrong man.

The busy gentleman noticed Mika. "Is she alright?"

Mika continued crying into Kay's chest as the rest of us tried to find a way to answer the man's question. We dismissed him, insisting we had the situation under control. Dice, Kay, and I remained silent, simply waiting for Mika to finish letting it all out.

This incident opened my eyes to the true magnitude of the situation. It made me realize finding Mika's father would be much more difficult than we had thought. Who was to say a future lead would take us right back to the same guy? With only the hand-drawn picture as our best clue, this event made the entire search seem impossible to succeed.

IV

Mika's attitude flipped back to the timid girl we knew her as at first. Having her biggest dream ripped from her hands was a heavy blow to her heart. She did not say much to us and was actually keeping herself more shut in than I had ever seen her.

For the night, we found shelter in a three-room inn near the

Delta landmark. Thankfully, with two beds in the room, a comfy chair, and plenty of space, sleeping arrangements didn't even need to be discussed. Everyone would be capable of getting a good night's rest.

Mika showered as Kay, Dice, and I discussed where to go from there. Dice recommended it would be best to take our minds off of Mika's father for a little while. To him, our unfortunate failure called for a change of direction. Finding a way to distract Mika from the sudden heartbreak was a sound solution to bringing her spirits back up.

I took this time to declare the need to focus more on the events of the Revolution. Tomorrow, the meeting between the Fifteen and the Producers was to take place. I felt it best for us to stay around the Delta throughout the next day. The events of the meeting were going to be broadcast live over the radio, as it would be the week's edition of *This Week in Eden*. It was in many Causes' best interests to be listening in as the meeting was taking place.

After we set the plan for the next day, Dice excused himself from the room. He was going to run out to grab some snacks, also looking for some time alone to himself to gather his thoughts and ideas. His tone sounded inquisitive and analytical, like he was coming up with another plan.

Before he stepped out, he hesitated, turning around in the doorway. "You two want anything while I'm out?"

I was indifferent. "Not really..."

Kay, however, took him up on it. "If you happen to pass by a bakery, see if you can grab some cupcakes or something."

"Of all things," He muttered with a smile. Dice closed the door with a subtle nod and left.

I took the opportunity to empty my backpack onto one of the beds to reorganize it. Upon evaluating my supplies, I realized all of my granola was gone. "I should've asked him to fill this..." I thought aloud, expecting Kay to respond.

Kay was distracted in her own bag. I watched her sift through her things as she remained oblivious to my observing her. I ignored any intentions of grabbing her attention and finished emptying my backpack.

Among the items strewn about the bed was the picture of me Mika had been working on. I took the piece of canvas and looked it over with focus. I was thinking of all the times I had ever looked at myself in the mirror, trying to get a feel for how close Mika was to capturing what I really looked like.

I turned the picture towards Kay. "What do you think?"

"About?" She was still looking at her things.

"This picture."

She turned her head up and then cocked it to the side. With peering eyes she replied, "I think it erases any doubt I may have had of Mika drawing the picture of her father."

I glanced over the picture again. "You doubted it?"

"At first impression, absolutely. I have two younger sisters, so I'm used to seeing kids her age produce art at only half of Mika's level of quality."

I savored a longing glance at the picture. "Come to think of it, my siblings and I weren't even *encouraged* to spend our time on artistic things. Our parents saw it as a waste of time. So you're not getting anything beyond stick figures with my family. I'm kinda jealous, actually."

She snorted. "Of all things to be jealous about…"

Her comment slid to the side as I turned to call towards the bathroom. "Hey, Mika. This picture of me is looking great!"

"Huh?" Her voice was muffled through the closed door.

"Bah." I cupped my hands over my mouth and spoke up. "Don't worry about it; never mind." Setting the picture on the pillow behind me, I said quieter, "It can wait until she's out."

Kay upturned her bag, emptying her gear into a heap on the floor. "She's been in there for a little while."

Having caught a flash glimpse of some of her more private garments, I respectfully snapped my gaze back to my own items. "Doesn't take much thought to see why."

"Of course; she needs the space."

I was counting my money. The last two weeks had taken my funds down to 105 arna. I would have included the two arna in my vest pocket, but I was still saving Mika's well-intended gift for something special.

After I heard a bit of rustling followed by the sharp zip of a swiftly-fastened zipper, Kay said, "Thanks for not staring. I put them away."

I grinned, still facing my gear. "You noticed?"

"Your head moved so fast, it was hard not to. You're a gentleman." She sighed, smiling, sifting through more of her things. "I'll admit; the past week has me feeling kinda silly about making a big fuss on the forums about the slope."

"You were being true to yourself, that's all. This is the situation now, though, and I'm glad to see you being so graceful about it." The coins slid off my hand and back into the pouch. "You've even grown on Dice a little bit."

"Mika's been encouraging me." She started folding her extra clothes. "I don't know how she softened up that hard-ass. She's tougher than she looks; clever, too."

"You think she'll bounce back from what happened tonight?"

Her lip curled. "By morning; guaranteed."

"Come to think of it," I reached behind me to grab the picture. "We probably shouldn't talk about pictures of people for the rest of the night."

Kay nodded with a thinking pout. "Good call."

After putting the picture away, I took my vest and shirt off to fold them. "I'll shower after Mika unless you want to go next."

"Nah, it's all yours. I need to get this done."

I retrieved a pair of loose-fitting shorts and a thin cotton A-shirt from my gear, along with my soap bar, toothbrush and paste. Thinking about getting clean was making me feel sweatier, causing me to sneak my nose towards my armpit. *Yeah, I need it.*

Ready for my shower, I picked up the pace to put all of my gear away in order to clear the bed. As I was setting the backpack on the floor by the nightstand, Mika shut the water off.

Right on time. I seated myself in the leather chair by the bathroom door, toiletries and clothes in hand.

Kay peeked over the bed to catch my eye. "I'll talk to her when she comes out; see how she's holding up."

I confirmed with a thumb up.

Mika came into the room in a pastel purple nightgown. Her tone was much brighter than I expected; musical in its inflection. "Who's next?"

I mimicked her notes, "That's me." Standing with a smile towards Kay, I caught the positivity in her expression. It put my heart at ease, allowing me to see a smile on my own face as I turned toward the bathroom mirror.

The shower was spacious, but it took too long for me to get the water to a good temperature; not "dead of winter" or "liquid sun." I spent the first ten minutes of my shower barely moving; standing relaxed and limp, allowing the showerhead to spray directly into my face. I occasionally tilted my head down to massage my scalp with the jets.

In my private time, I was able to take notice to how well I was putting on a front for the others. What had happened at the café kept pounding at my brain. Not finding Mika's father was turning into a frustration far-too-often visited throughout the last week; a frustration spilling sand from my hourglass of ever-dwindling patience.

Where was he?

Why did he skip out on his daughter?

What's not adding up?

Fists tightening, I fought to refrain from pounding on the wall. Although it would have only been a light tap at most, I didn't want a vibration or echo to alert the girls to my ire.

I had to keep it in, but I knew I needed to find an outlet for the churning in my chest. The tight twist of the week's repeated failures was one of the many ingredients to cook up a poorly-timed outburst. There was still lingering guilt from the way I handled Kay back in the alleys of Pata. I could not afford to have anything needling me.

Too familiar was this throbbing of aggravation; the desire to lash out; shout, throw objects—something; anything. It was the anger of father, through and through. Getting it under control was more important than ever considering the trust and new camaraderie that my group had been enjoying. I could not risk having it all ripped away by my own careless hands.

The water cascading down my body calmed me well. To further dispel the knot in my gut, I utilized the ample space in the shower to punch at the air. My arms flung forward and from the side, sending droplets of water flying every which way.

I had to break this spell of anger; to leave the bathroom with a smile on my face and pep in my voice. The therapeutic cleansing was proving effective, and the wild punching was helping me to pace my breathing to a calming rhythm. By the time I was turning the water off, I felt better than I had all day.

With one last, big, deep breath of the hot, post-shower air, I turned to the mirror with a confident smile. The thoroughly-fogged mirror wasn't having any of it, though. It pushed a laugh out of me as I grabbed a cloth to wipe it clear.

Once I was dressed and back in the room, seeing the sweet wide-eyed expression on Mika's face helped assure me that everything was going to be all right. Her smile was genuine and contagious. She still had hope and faith in the three of us who were by her side to help.

Shifting our search efforts aside, the events of the Revolution were back in our focus. Our next few steps depended on the results of the Producers' meeting. We decided to stay put in the Delta Business District; making our only mission for the next day to sit back, relax, and tune in for *This Week in Eden.*

There was an itching feeling in the back of my head about Hatcher, though. There was still no sign of him, not even a forum post. I continued to hope Hatcher's information would prove irrelevant in the end. The only other thing we could have hoped for was for him to arrive at the last minute.

Day 78

I

I opened my eyes during the early hours. Although I had fallen fast asleep earlier in the night, the events of the day were back to nag at my mind once again. Zoe's words were proving hard to shake from the stack of worries among my thoughts.

Easing out of bed, I crept over to the window and peered out of it, but I was not able to see through to the other side. The window appeared to enter into a dark, midnight void with my lone reflection standing within it. I took a long look at myself— minutes. Saggy-eyed relaxation contorted into a visage of concern. "What do you know that we don't, Zoe?"

"My thoughts exactly."

The sudden sound of another person's voice gave me a start. I turned to see Dice. His crooked grin and derisive huff made it appear it was his intention to spook me.

Dice took his left hand and swept it through the scraggly, black mop on his head. He was not wearing his glasses or his visor, let alone a shirt. His body stood wiry with barely a sense of masculinity to it. Still, he carried himself with the high-minded haughtiness I learned to know him for.

I whispered to him with a lift of my shoulders. "What do you think? Any new ideas?"

"Still nothing. We definitely need more information."

I exhaled, looking into the window again. The sincerity in his tone and his active gesture of helping navigate the Revolution's more confusing scenarios were beginning to feel more like an honor. Such a statement was saying a lot considering our online past, and the dozens of times I had had to grit my teeth through some of his wayward, to-my-face insults. "You know, Dice, I appreciate you sticking with us. You've helped a lot."

He folded his arms, staring at the window with me. "Frankly, you two don't make it easy sometimes. The fact we've failed to find Mika's dad isn't helping either. But Mika needs all the help she can get, and she needs people she can trust. I can endure you guys a little longer."

"If we're that much of a bother to you, why did you even consider coming back to us?"

"I already told you, I rolled—"

Even though I still didn't understand how Dice measured his rolling habit, I still had the sense he may have been leaving something out. I cut him off. "Not buying it, man. I refuse to believe you came back purely on a roll."

"Since when did I tell you to believe me?"

I paused, acknowledging the annoying merit of this question.

Before too long, he answered for me. "I tell you what I tell you because it's fact. What don't tell you, you don't need to know in the first place. I have absolutely no reason to lie to you."

I tried to argue. "Isn't omitting information also lying?"

Dice grinned with a wide shrug. During a small pause, he ambled to the window; almost pressing his face to the glass. "It isn't lying if nothing comes out of my mouth."

It looked like the one tiny hole in his argument. "So what did you leave out?" I asked.

Still facing the window, He flashed his dice for a moment before putting them back in this pocket. He rolled his neck, which sang a few gentle pops. "See, this is where you lose, Brigg."

My face fell into a scowl. "Enlighten me; how's that?"

Dice kept his hands in his pockets and turned to face back to me. "The true answer ties into the deal I made with Mika, and it stays between her and me. So do me and the kid a favor and don't be so nosy about it. Keep this in mind: I will always tell you everything I feel you need to know. I'm not going to fill your head with shit irrelevant to you. Take heart in the fact that even though I'm not particularly fond of you, you do have my trust and I wouldn't lie to you."

This was the most drastic contrast I had seen from Dice all week. There was not even a shred of his attitude or persona from the forum. This new face of trust and honesty was the last thing I expected from him. I was appreciative, but taken aback. My response came out stunned. "Th-Thank you." I turned my head, catching my reflection in the window one last time. "Come on, man; let's get back to bed."

He poked my shoulder. "This time, stay in it. Okay?"

II

The morning was beautiful and the Delta was buzzing with excitement. From end to end and all around the statue, Causes gathered in a public mass. Sector police were assigned to the scene. As they observed the activity in the Delta, it did not take them long to notice all who gathered were talking, laughing, swapping stories, and even picnicking. They stood guard, provided crowd control, and conversed with us as well.

This gathering was planned upon the announcement of Naro replacing the week's edition of *This Week in Eden* with a live broadcast of the meeting. There was no news more important than the potential end to the Revolution.

A few hundred Causes were in attendance and anxiously awaiting noontime. At noon, everyone would turn on their radios and crank up the volume. The meeting would be heard throughout the Delta, leaving nobody in the dark about it.

The four of us spent the time until noon socializing with the masses. My name had become quite famous, and many Causes seemed pleased to meet me. Kay and Dice had become popular as well since they were in my company. To many Causes, there were still no diminishing returns on the irony of me traveling alongside the two of them.

Mika, however, was still a mystery to many. Since she was not originally a Cause, she was not a member of the forum. We took this time to relax about handling Mika's story and introduce her and her situation to others. Many were receptive to Mika and offered to stay in contact if they were to come across her father.

Spirits were high and anticipation resonated throughout the Delta. Soon, the ending stages of the Revolution would be within reach. With it, we would know the truth about Eden we were certain the Fifteen were keeping hidden. This would be the day it would all come to light.

The days of the Fifteen's absolute control would soon be over so a new era of Eden could begin.

III

Noon struck. The Causes all sat around the Delta Landmark, fidgeting with excitement. One after the other, radios were presented and propped up high. Switches were flicked on and volumes were increased until the sounds from them echoed through the streets as planned.

The time had come when the first words of the broadcast came forth from every speaker. "Good afternoon, Eden. I'm Naro and this is a historic edition of *This Week in Eden.*"

The Causes cheered, but remained mindful of the need to stay focused on the radios. None of us could afford to miss a word of the meeting with the Fifteen.

Naro made his full introduction to the show. "With us here today are eight youths from all around Eden who claim to be the leaders of this rebellion Eden has been dealing with. We'll start with you, Bogen, and work our way down the table."

"And what a table we have here, folks!" He chuckled half-heartedly and continued. "Yes, my name is Bogen and for all of the Causes listening in who would know what this means: He did not arrive."

There was muttering and mumbling among the assembly. In the time it took the Causes to calm down, the rest of the Producers had finished introducing themselves.

Next, the members of the Fifteen introduced themselves.

They started with the men: Naro, Haz, Dallas, Syre, Riley, Biktor, and Joseph.

Then the women: Eliza, Sandra, Estyr, Rayna, Morie, Vade, and Cenia.

Naro finished the segment by stating Aegis, the last member, could not make it to the meeting. After the formalities, the Producers and the Fifteen officially started the long-awaited event.

Joseph of the Fifteen was the first person to speak. "We want to make the citizens of Eden aware of the damage your actions have inflicted since the start of this whole mess." Joseph passed the microphone to the other members.

Vade was first. "Police resources are stretched to their limit; especially our Gray Unit."

Eliza came next. "Research on Interactive Studies has halted. We will not issue occupations to anyone participating in the rebellion. This is affecting Cenia's plans for you all as well!"

Cenia then lamented. "The land to build the new district in Binda is ready. But none of you young people seem willing to prepare to develop it. That is supposed to be the district for your age group, and you're going to squander the time you should be spending building it up to take a stand in this revolution of yours. Come now, it's time to grow up and become adults!"

Sandra spoke. "Injuries among your numbers are staggering. I am struggling to keep up with medical procedures. I can't keep having my doctors leaving their posts to venture into the woods. And hospitals only have so many kits for on-foot medics."

Having immediately thought of Zoe, the four of us all shared a glance to each other. Dice accompanied his look with a vaguely triumphant smirk.

Last, Naro shared a complaint of his own. "I keep on having to interrupt people's entertainment programming with news of your shenanigans. The citizens are growing weary of it all."

The microphone was handed back to Joseph. "These are only a fraction of the problems we are facing in order to keep Eden in the balanced state we once had it in. I want every one of you revolutionaries out there listening to understand the trouble we are having and end this nonsense."

One of the other Producers huffed loud enough to be heard through the mike.

Joseph addressed him, "Do you have something to say, boy?"

The sound of the microphone being passed was now familiar. "Yes, I do," the Producer replied with confidence. "You want us to understand you and give up when you haven't taken the time or effort to understand us."

A female chimed in. "Matthias, an attitude won't help."

"Come on, Ki. You know I'm right."

"Yes, but you can be professional about it."

Although it was an amusing tangent, we all knew they were right. Eden's leaders only saw us as a menace and wanted nothing more than to put an end to our protest.

Bogen had called the two to order and took the mike from them. "What Matthias is saying is a reflection of how all of us feel. We feel our wants, needs, and feelings are being tossed aside for the sake of keeping the balance you speak of tipped in your favor."

Applause rang through the streets.

"You've got us all wrong!" a Fifteen member replied; his voice pushing with stiff assuredness.

Bogen acknowledged him. "Um, 'Haz', was it?"

Haz was given the floor. "You say your *needs* are neglected? Clearly, your feelings appear more important than your needs. You fail to understand the system; you are not yet mature enough. To maximize your potential within our system, you need to forego things like wants and feelings to achieve what you really need." His voice had heart and sincerity pouring out of every word.

There was silence in the streets and in the meeting as well. The next one to speak was Matthias again. "What makes you think you know what we need?"

"I've got this one…" Joseph growled.

"All yours," Haz confirmed, passing the mike back.

Joseph uttered with a sneer in his tone. "It isn't so much we know what each *individual* person needs. We know exactly what *all* of Eden *doesn't* need." He took a beat, giving everyone a moment to dwell on his answer. "You need to trust us in this. The Fifteen know what the Revolution will ultimately result in."

"Interesting choice of words," Dice remarked on the side.

Joseph followed up by saying, "Eden does not need your Revolution. Now, stop. Return to your homes and help Eden clean up the mess you've all made. It would be in every Cause's best interest to do this while we are still being nice about it."

A Producer spoke up off-mike. "Is that a threat?"

"A very strong recommendation," replied Joseph

The Causes in the Delta were expressing mixed emotions. Some were grinning in anticipation. Others seemed to be concentrating, staring into nothing while awaiting the next statement. Every emotion in between could be felt as the chatter across the airwaves came to a stop.

Loud announcements for silence filled the Delta as every Cause eagerly awaited the Producers' response. Bogen was handed the microphone. "We will not back down until we're satisfied."

"What will satisfy you?" Joseph asked off-mike.

"At the least, we, the Producers, and the Causes scattered across the landscape, demand you answer our questions."

"Well of course, our answers depend on the nature of those questions. Is it the same rigmarole we all had to deal with before Eliza got rid of *One Summer*?"

Bogen took a deep breath and spoke. "Six-hundred and fifty-four years ago, Paxus and Shalynn created us; put us here in Eden. They gave us life and they gave us order. With it, they blessed and assigned the first Fifteen. Everyone knows and understands this.

"Shalynn encourages growth, prudence and wisdom. Paxus leads us with strength and bravery. So we ask you: why are we being held back from growing when we know we can do so with wisdom and prudence? Why can't we display strength and bravery to try things differently?

"Why, since our creation, have the leaders of Eden kept things in this constrictive grip you call 'balance'? What purpose is it serving? What is it preventing that Eden 'doesn't need'?" His voice was gradually getting louder and more dramatic. "Why must the citizens of Eden be subject to your view of the way things should be with no consideration of what the people you serve want?" Bogen finished up with two final, bursting questions. He went all out and quoted two questions from the last paragraphs of *One Summer*. "Why are we kept from making our own life decisions and forced to have them made for us? Do you realize those decisions we are kept from making could be the ones to push Eden forward to a new age of prosperity?"

The reaction from the throng at the Delta was deafening. Even the police seemed impressed. Citizens along the streets and in the nearby shops were applauding as well. Since our demands were now out in the open, people finally understood the position of the Causes. They even appeared curious as to how the Fifteen would respond. Once the multitude calmed, the familiar sound of off-mike huddling could be heard. The Fifteen were talking amongst themselves.

Joseph spoke again. "The answers to these questions will satisfy the Revolutionaries?"

A female Producer answered, "With action, of course, yes."

Several of the Fifteen's members reacted. "Action?"

Bogen answered. "You know, change, perhaps?"

"Change…"

The Fifteen continued their private discussion. Within a minute, the mumbling stopped short. Joseph spoke to the Producers as a whole. "This is something our side must decide on elsewhere. If you will excuse us, we will return as soon as we have chosen what to do."

"Take all the time you need."

The romp of footsteps filtered into the sound of a shutting door. Within an instant of the door closing, Bogen took the mike and made an announcement to the Causes. "We, the Producers, would like to thank you all for being a part of the Revolution. While the Fifteen discuss their response, I want to say I am truly pleased the Causes held strong. Brigg, if you're listening—and I know you are—thank you for helping the Causes down this path."

Calls and hoots were directed at me by those who knew I was in the Delta. Mika hugged me while Dice patted me on the shoulder. Kay made no physical contact, but gave me a special look. Her eyes resonated with a glint of appreciation and her smirk displayed contented approval.

I smiled back and nodded once, enough to be a reply.

The Causes in the streets and the Producers at the meeting continued to wait for the return of the Fifteen. To keep the show going, the Producers continued to ham it up on the radio as they waited. Bogen kicked it off by asking, "What changes are you looking forward to once this is over?"

Rosa answered right away, expressing the desire to see options for travel improved. Bicycles and carriages propelled by batteries and motors. Like trains, except not confined to tracks. I tuned in to the excited chatter in the Delta. The wide-eyed stares of minds slipping to imaginary visions accompanied their vivid descriptions of anticipation.

Ki then added her answer. "What we've got right here and right now: we're on the radio, saying and doing whatever we want. I know I want to hear a few new channels. Anyone who wants to do some dramatic reading on the radio can hit me up when this is all over. We'll start a channel."

The announcement fired up some of the crowd. One group sitting near us started packing their things so they could venture back towards the Radio Tower once the broadcast was over.

Matthias was ready for more flexibility with content portrayed in stage plays. Since he was one of the writers for a performing troupe, he would constantly have to run his scripts past Naro in order to gauge the "appropriateness" of the work.

Bogen took the microphone. "Citizens of Eden: This is only a fraction of the things we Causes wanted. We're certain every person here in Eden has *something* they wish was different. Or you have *something* you would like to do, or make, or accomplish. Unfortunately, our laws and the statutes the Fifteen have us under keep us from these things.

"We really, truly hope these changes aren't only for our generation, but for all of them. If there is anyone we should be thanking more than anyone, it's Devon. You inspired this movement, sir. I hope you are listening, because every Cause from Lucra to Binda offers their most sincere thanks."

The Delta resonated with loud, uproarious applause. As it wound down, some Causes broke into a chant. "Devon, Devon, Devon!" With wide smiles, the gang and I joined in the chant.

"Oh, I almost forgot!" Bogen continued, prompting the Delta to quickly quiet down. "We definitely want to send thanks out to

Hatcher as well, for encouraging us to take these steps towards a new and more prosperous Eden. Hatcher, if you're out there, we managed fine without you."

Another round of applause started escalating. However, many of us soon wished Bogen could have anticipated the level of irony in his remark. For as soon as he finished speaking, the Fifteen returned from their deliberation. Unfortunately, they were not filing back into the meeting in the professional manner we had anticipated. Loud bursts rang across the airwaves as the doors were kicked open. "*Nobody move!*" a voice shouted.

"What's going on?" I asked the crowd, though knowing no one would actually have an answer.

"Gray Police!" One of the Producers shouted loud and clear.

Screams and shouts were heard over the radio mixed in with sounds of chairs knocking around, scampering, tumbling, and banging. Chaos had erupted at the scene of the meeting. The response to the commotion became contagious through the airwaves. Causes panicked as they awaited any coherent sentences to be spoken from the meeting.

My mind was focused solely on the sounds emitted from the broadcast. Once the noise cleared up, a few discernable sentences rang clear throughout the landmark.

"One of them got away."

"Find him!"

In the background, somebody hollered before her voice seemed to fade into nothingness. "Causes! Stay strong! They're hiding something!"

Haz hollered almost in a cheer, "It's the Strip Mines for them until the Causes stand down!"

"No!" I shouted.

"This is terrible," Mika agreed.

A voice rang out. "The Producers are captured!"

"Which one got away?" a girl called back.

I mumbled, low enough to where only the others could hear me, "The fact even one got away could be important."

The sudden sound of a hand bumping the microphone brought the Causes in the Delta to full attention. The sounds of shuffling, shouting, and havoc had subsided. Radios were almost silent where only a light muttering peeped over the airwaves. After a moment, the deep, angry voice of a woman spoke the final words of the broadcast of the meeting:

"Causes, this game is over. Return to your homes and we will set your Producers free. As of right now, you have no leaders. You are merely nuisances with futile questions. This is your only warning. I swear, as the Head of Justice in Eden, I will make it my duty to put an end to this by any means necessary."

"On behalf of the Fifteen, this is Vade, signing off this edition of *This Week in Eden*. Good day and good luck."

The broadcast was cut.

IV

A heavy and disrupted air circulated throughout the Delta as the radios were shut off and put away. Fear set in quick and some Causes had already begun to behave as though this truly was the end. The Producers had been arrested and there was nothing anybody could do about it.

The mass in the Delta gathered the strength to converse with their peers and partners, questioning where to go from there. Those who managed to hear of one of the Producers escaping seemed to think there was still a shred of hope. Others felt intimidated by Vade and considered giving up a good option.

Some of the Causes seated about the Delta decided to blame me for not allowing the Radio Tower raid to be carried out. Whatever could be said about the situation was brought into the mesh of speech flooding the area.

My mind wandered, focused on the series of questions Bogen had asked the Fifteen. I recalled how thorough Bogen was with his words. He left no detail out in his attempt to pressure the Fifteen for the truth.

They took drastic action to silence the questions we needed the answers to. I realized this was not too dissimilar from Eliza deleting *One Summer* from the tome Grid, sending it and all of its discussions into oblivion. Last, the sound of that woman's voice on the radio repeated in my head:

"Causes! Stay strong! They're hiding something!"

It clicked, all seeming to be true. "For the Fifteen, this was no better for them than deleting *One Summer* in the first place. This is only gonna make the Causes more aggressive."

"I was thinking the same thing!" Kay replied. "And from the sound of it, this crowd is far from wanting to back down." She paused for a moment then stood, cupping her hands over her mouth. She shouted over the Causes to gather as much attention as possible. "Hey, everybody!"

She got a few of them to look at her. "What the heck are you doing!?" I asked.

Kay turned back to me with a positive grin. "Let's get everyone to calm down and think before we have another mob charging the Radio Tower."

Dice reached into his pocket and prepared his dice. "I'm not quite feeling you there, Kay. Think we can settle this crowd?"

I understood. "We should try; I think she has a point. It reminds me of something Hatcher once said during the planning stages. 'Even though there are several thousand of us and we're all taking our own path in this, remember: we are still a team.'"

"Now that you mention it…" He put his dice away.

Mika stood, joining Kay in trying to quiet down the crowd. The two of them working together grabbed a lot of attention. Once Dice and I added our efforts in silencing the audience, everyone settled and waited for what we had to say. The others felt with my name among the most popular, influencing the panicked horde would be easiest if they let me do the talking.

I wanted to approach this to get my point across as well as try to calm everyone down. Once I had myself together, I spoke out to the awaiting multitude. "Everyone, suffice it to say, there is no need for me to repeat what just happened." I took a long beat to make sure I had as much of the audience's attention as possible. "Now, let me ask you all a question. I know there was a lot of chaos coming out of the radio, but how many of you managed to hear one of the Producers escaped the meeting?"

A few arms went into the air as people turned their heads about to see the results.

I confirmed the outcome and continued. "Yes, one of them escaped, and it's only a matter of time before we hear from them. Be aware: the Fifteen have not threatened the Producers' lives in any way. I'm sure the Fifteen feel they have won. How many of you here feel like the Causes have lost?"

More hands went up. Clearly there were more people who had lost hope than we thought. I felt intimidated and almost hesitant to tell these people the Revolution was a step in the right direction. Some of the Causes even stood and began to leave. Regardless, I tried to stay focused. There were a lot of people left to reassure.

I took a deep breath and went for it. "Contrary to what Vade said, we're still strong. The results of the Meeting are a perfect example as to why we were right to question the Fifteen. We were headed in the right direction, but stumbled along the way. Our advantage has changed because the Fifteen continue to hide the truth from us and the citizens of Eden.

"Hatcher once said we're all a team. I'm standing up here to tell you: what our team has done to Eden is the right thing to do. The Fifteen are holding Eden back from progress and they are hiding what we have the right to know as citizens of Eden!"

Dice leaned into me and whispered, "This group is looking a little more convinced."

I nodded to Dice as I decided to go for a finishing touch to my speech. "We have the Fifteen up against a wall. They know what we want and have sought desperation to keep it from us. We must press forward and keep the pressure on them!"

A roaring, masculine voice thundered over the audience and echoed off of the buildings surrounding the Delta. "I totally agree with you this time, Brigg!"

The voice had come from my left. Turning, I saw a slender young man, dressed in black, with lengthy blonde hair rise up from among those who stayed seated. "Who is he?" Mika asked.

I called out to the youth. "What is your name?"

The stranger began maneuvering through the audience to get within a reasonable speaking distance. While making his way over, he introduced himself. "My name is Albion, but everyone calls me…" He paused in mid-sentence until he stood face to face with me to finish it. "…Al!"

Though he was a little shorter than me, his all-black clothing and the way he carried himself had me think twice about being overly confrontational. His deep, green eyes glared into mine, telling me he had something to say.

Slighted, I shoved him to give myself some space, getting my fingers caught in his right sleeve, which was deliberately torn and tattered in absurd impracticality. "What brings you to finally show your face?" I asked him.

His attitude was cocky as he whipped his blonde locks and ran his long fingers through them. "Hey, easy! Didn't you say we're all a team? Do teammates shove each other?" He brushed his shoulders as if I had gotten them dirty.

I turned his question back. "Speaking of teammates—Jal?"

"Jalako? She's doing her own thing right now."

Kay charged in. "You had to have come up here to interrupt Brigg because you have something to contribute, right? If you're going to add to this, then say something!"

"Right, right!" he gestured, composing himself. He turned outward and said his part. "As I said a moment ago, I agree with Brigg. We have to keep the pressure on."

Kay distracted me from Al's speech. "Watch out, Brigg. This guy has been ripping into you all week because of the Radio Tower. I'm not sure if he's being sincere."

Mika seconded the motion. "He's stuck up and creepy…"

"I wouldn't trust him either," Dice advised. "His tone is a little too facetious for my taste."

I kept my team's advice in the front of my brain and readied myself for anything Al would try to pull on us. My attention shifted back to Al, who was concluding his thoughts. "It's time to show the Fifteen what we're made of. We need to step up our game and show them what real 'rebellion' is!"

I was praying I misunderstood Al's proposal. "What!?"

Al turned to me while still speaking audibly enough for the Delta. "You heard what the Fifteen said, right? They called our actions a 'rebellion.' Now, correct me if I'm wrong, but aren't 'rebellions' supposed to be a little more…*action*-oriented?"

Dice filled his question. "Something like that…"

"So as far as I'm concerned…" he resumed, "we haven't been 'rebelling.' All we have been doing is merely 'objecting.'"

I pushed at Al's shoulder again, spinning him to look at me. "What are you getting at?"

"My point is: if we want to keep the pressure on the Fifteen, we need to show them less of this diplomatic objecting…" He threw in a long, dramatic pause. "…and take the magnitude of our stand against them to a whole new level!"

With those words, Al seemed to have gained control of the multitude. We could see them nodding, grinning, talking amongst themselves, and rummaging through their bags and items. Once again, I felt the sting of Al's inherent need to lead the masses. It all seemed to be set in stone once the Causes in the Delta started applauding Al's speech.

"Wait a minute!" I hollered, reaching for Al's shoulder. "Do you realize what you are saying!?"

Kay scolded him, sharing my thoughts as well. "You're telling Causes to break the Producers' rules again!"

Al lifted his face smugly. "The Producers are no longer in the picture. Therefore, there *are* no rules now! We'll make the Fifteen talk, even if it means turning Eden upside-down to do it!"

The situation in the Delta had become much worse than we could have expected. If the Causes started exhibiting violence, there was no telling what the future would hold for us. I tried one last time to reason with Al. "You forget: there's still one more Producer out there. Hatcher, too."

Al had grown tired of me; becoming cross, and unleashing passionate fury in a concise, conclusive eruption. "The last Producer doesn't matter! The Gray Police will catch up with him eventually. And do *not* get me started on Hatcher!"

There was substantial approval from the Causes in response to Al's final words. I watched in heart-stopping despair as Cause after Cause rose from where they sat to follow Al out of the Delta.

My head shook. "No," I whispered, knowing protesting Al with aggression could escalate the problem. "This is wrong."

Kay spoke to me softly, "Brigg, I'm sorry. I don't think there is a way to change this. The circumstances are too extreme."

How I wished there *was* something I could do; wished there *was* a way. Unfortunately, I felt all of my luck had been drained back at the Radio Tower. Kay was right. Al had the upper hand on influence and there was nothing I could do to reverse its impact.

The lowest part of my gut was tumbling; my shoulders and chest rattled. Inhaling deep through the shudders, my glance

turned to the base of Delta's statue. I read the engraving again:
Avatar of Obedience…

   …practice these principles…

   With a grumbling sigh, I muttered, "Sorry, Delta. You're gonna have to wait a little longer…"

   Mika tried to comfort me with a hug, but it was to no avail. As I witnessed each Cause disappearing into the distance behind Al, I could feel the tiny shreds of hope for a peaceful solution slowly fading out of existence.

   Regardless of the direction the Revolution was looking to take, one fact remained clear: the Fifteen had our answers and it was up to us to get them.

The Producers had been captured.

The Causes became divided.

The outlook for the Revolution was now lost in a
fog of conflict.

And still, there was no response from Hatcher.

Episode 5: Separate Paths

The four of us decided to double back into the Fanda Sector to hide out for a couple of days after the incident at the Delta.

As it turned out, Bogen's public announcement of the Causes' demands made many of Eden's average citizens a lot more understanding of the role we had given ourselves. The impact of the meeting inspired an increase in the number of clued businesses cropping up, making it easier to get assistance. Any time we went into town on the following day for supplies, we were engaged with excitement and praise. Many shopkeepers looked forward to the changes looming ahead for the future of their businesses.

The surge of support for the Revolution in the first twenty-four hours was felt all throughout Eden. More young people were reported to have left their homes to be among the Causes. Even some adults with established lives and occupations managed to encourage their families to close up shop and take the stand with us. Although *One Summer* had long since been sent into oblivion, the undying ideals it had presented were now stronger than ever before. It was as the book said: waking everybody up.

There was a problem with this, though. With no reasonable way to crack down on clued businesses, the Fifteen appointed Gray Police to every residential and business sector in Eden. This meant six of Eden's eleven Sectors were now being patrolled by Gray Police.

The only fortune in this was the Gray Police force's limited amount of officers. Due to their numbers, their patrolling areas were spread far apart. Therefore, the Causes never saw more than two of them in one place. The only thing they had to be wary of was encountering them as they patrolled the streets.

Our time in the Fanda Sector was spent laying low and surveying the situation through Contacts. As we waited for any news, we found no sign of Hatcher, the missing Producer, or any action by the Fifteen other than the deployment of the Gray Police and a massive overhaul on security around the Radio Tower.

Al & Jal regrouped soon after the Delta incident and took to the forums to turn more Causes to their rebellion. There was no news of any actions perpetrated by them or their followers as of yet. However, their time spent in recruitment for their overzealous vision had us worried their activity would escalate soon. We were thinking Al & Jal were going to plan more events like the Radio Tower siege. The two of them had the advantage now since they would no longer need the Cause forums to organize their plots. Thus, getting a heads up about any plans was out of the question.

On a lighter note, we realized both of the times our party saw Albion in person, Jalako was not with him. Dice presented two possibilities: Either Albion had some on-and-off relationship with her, or Jalako was instructing Albion from the sidelines. Either way, it was beginning to feel as though Jalako was the one to watch out for; not so much Albion.

The 80th day of the Revolution was dawning. But the brilliant summer sun on a warm, breezy morning was not going to expel the dark cloud hanging over the heads of the Causes. It was indeed a new day for the Revolution as a whole.

Day 80

I

I greeted the morning with my first smile since Sunday. Hiding away and analyzing everything had not been our idea of fun throughout the previous day. It was good to see a pleasant morning at the same time we scheduled ourselves to move out.

With everything going on between the Causes, it was best to get Mika out of the thick of it. Mika had become sorely afraid of what would happen to her; especially if she were to wind up in the hands of the Fifteen before finding her father.

The newfound understanding by Eden's citizens would serve to favor our search efforts. This opened up a wide range of opportunities. We made our next order of business to find a way to get Mika's picture into more hands. Dice knew who could help us out: his father; a gallery painter. Taking a proactive foot forward to help, Dice volunteered to lead us to his home in West Binda, and ask his father to handcraft a few copies of the picture.

Before we set out for Binda, I summoned one of the Contacts and checked the forums one last time. I was hoping to find any news we would find useful. Nothing relevant to our interests turned up, but I noticed I had an unread private message from, of all people, Blue.

When I announced it aloud, Mika, Kay, and Dice were hovering over my shoulders within seconds. Since Blue's exploits in the hero department were still commonplace, it felt like a privilege to get a message from him.

Hey Brigg,

I've been paying attention to what's been going on with you. Looks like you've got your hands full with Al & Jal. I know it's kind of weird getting a message from me out of nowhere like this, but there are a few things I need to know. I'm trying to get some info from people who seem to know what's going on. Since the Producers are indisposed right now, I'm going for the next best thing.

First, I was wondering, with everything going on with them and all, did you get a chance to find out who Jal is? Back in the Pata Sector, Al helped all of those Causes cross that bridge, but Jal was not with him. I don't even know if he is a she or not. Kinda funny, huh?

Second, you wouldn't happen to know which Producer escaped the meeting, would you? Also, do you know if Black, the Producers' personal Contact, was with them?

Last but not least, I'm wondering if you are planning to oppose Al & Jal. It seems to be the question on everybody's mind since the meeting. The hot news is about how Al upstaged you at the Delta.

As for me, I'm going to keep doing what I do best. Since the Gray Police are now all over the place, my job is going to get a lot more fun! Once I find out what I need to, I'll see what I can do to support the remaining Causes. You and your friends take care of yourselves. Good luck in whatever you choose to do. I'll be rooting for you.

-Blue

I opened a blank message to reply. "Well, it's good to know some things haven't changed."

Dice had something to say about it, though. "Remember, people have had questions about Blue since he first started playing hero. It seems to me he wants to work alone, but still use others for information. I would be careful of your wording before you decide to type anything."

"Duly noted," I mumbled as I began stroking the keys.

Hello Blue,

It's good to hear from you, even though we never formally met. We saw you, by the way. One of my partners, Kay, called out to you while you distracted the Gray Police. I'm glad to see you're still the same Blue we've heard about, and the recent events haven't changed what you feel is your role in the Revolution.

In response to your questions, though, I'm afraid we don't have all of the answers. But I will tell you what we do know.

The only things we managed to find out about Jal: she is a woman and her full name is Jalako.

We still haven't found out who the missing Producer is. However, your question about it actually made me remember about Black. Before you asked about her, I had completely forgotten she was with them.

Last, we don't intend to stage any retaliation to Al & Jal. We've decided the best thing to do is to continue to set the Producers' example and let the Gray Police handle the rebels Al has rounded up. I have a feeling Al & Jal will bring themselves down in due time.

We have quite an agenda in front of us. We have a young girl in our group who is searching for her father. Our goals right now involve getting her back to him before she winds up caught on the bad end of the Revolution. So we have our hands full as it is.

We want to know what the Fifteen are hiding as much as the next person. But for now, we have to focus on this. We'll keep in touch and let you know if we find out anything new. Be careful out there, OK?

-Brigg

I let everyone read my reply before I sent it out. "I guess we *are* cozy now." Kay said, pushed out by a lighthearted huff.

I didn't turn to look as I scanned to find what could have made her say such a thing. While catching and correcting a few small typos, my head swayed. "I don't follow."

She pointed at various spots on the screen. "We, we, we, we, we. There's an 'us.' Look there; I'm even 'one of your partners.'"

"Partners," Dice scoffed.

Making one last click to send the message, I turned around to face the others. "Hey, don't say it like *that*, Dice. We're all pitching in; all involved in this." My gaze shifted to Kay and Mika as well. "Is there anything we should call ourselves besides 'partners'?"

Kay put her arm around Mika, who leaned into her. "I've got nothing."

"Don't thank me yet...partner." Dice laughed, politely pointing at me. "We have to see if my dad will even help first. Chances are, though, the moment you guys follow me through the front door, he's gonna be excited. Big surprise: I never made it friendly with the kids in my neighborhood. He'll be glad I actually have company, and will *probably* do anything you ask him."

I closed the laptop and handed it back to the Contact, along with a five-arna coin. "It's still a clear step forward. The best thing we can ask for right now considering the state of the Revolution."

Mika stood eagerly to gather her things. "All right! Let's get moving, partners!"

Dice handed two arna to the Contact as well, then walked to his backpack. "You all heard the girl: Let's get moving."

II

We returned to the Delta, arriving around ten o'clock. From here, Dice recommended we hop on the train via the small station cutting through the south side of the district. It was only a few blocks south of the landmark.

Even though the events of the past few days were fresh in everybody's minds, people were surprised to see train services running as normal. On the surface, it appeared the Fifteen were not going to disrupt the lives of the average citizens in the same way they did in Pata. Instead, they were going to bide their time, let the Gray Police do their job to pinch Causes one by one, and hope the arrests and threats would demoralize the rest into giving up and returning home. Of course, this was all speculation stemming from the fact we were not ambushed and tackled by police on the way to the Delta's train station.

Other groups of Causes were waiting for the next outgoing train. As we waited and conversed, many of them asked me the same question Blue did concerning Al & Jal. I gave them the same answer: We will wait and see.

It was not even noon yet, and I had already grown tired of talking with other Causes about the state of the Revolution. After we boarded and claimed a booth for our group, I slung my gear to the floor and flopped up against the window. Before realizing how thirsty I was from all the talking, I had already put my water bag out of my arm's reach. I simply flailed my hand in the direction of my gear with deliberate futility, closing my eyes and mumbling whiny non-words.

With a clear laugh in her breath, Kay assisted. "I guess you didn't think things would blow up like this when you spoke up, huh?" She reached over and handed my water bag to me.

"Please," I implored, sitting straight to drink. "Let's talk West Binda and getting this picture copied. If I have to talk about the meeting, Albion, or the Delta *one* more time…" I drank instead of finishing the sentence, deliberately cutting myself off.

Dice had taken the seat next to me. "Well, I hope it won't bother you to hear me mention that guy, because Al & Jal's actions in the coming days are going to be what gauges how long we should stay at my house." He waited for Kay and Mika to be seated, then continued on in a more hushed tone once we were huddled together. "If Albion and Jalako are going to start tearing things up, and the Fifteen get more aggressive with Causes, it will affect how much time we have to look for Mika's father before the risk becomes too much to travel."

Kay nodded, passing her canteen to Mika. "What do you suggest?"

Dice kept his eyes locked with Mika's throughout his entire explanation. "If things get hairy, our best course of action is to scale back our role in the Revolution for a little while and approach the police with a copy of the picture. If we come across as average citizens, or kids who forfeit the Revolution due to Vade's threats, we could get professional police and detectives to search for her dad."

The instant Dice mentioned the police; Mika broke eye contact and started shaking her head. By the time he was done speaking, Mika's hair was fluffed up and thrown about by her wilder, more desperate movements. "No!" she pled, trying to keep her volume down. "We can't."

Dice's unrelenting stare bored into the frazzled girl, as though it was exactly the reaction he was expecting from her. "Is there a reason we cannot involve the police to help locate your father, Mika?" It came out biting and specific, like an indirect accusation being asked of somebody on a witness stand.

Kay swept in, stern, to defend Mika. "Dice, what are you—?"

His finger shot up, cutting her off. "I asked..." Their eyes lingered in a stretched pause. As if it were timed with the clattering of the train, Dice punctuated, "...Mika; not you."

Kay and I shared a long glance of concern and confusion. While I disapproved of his voice and attitude towards Mika, I could not blame Dice for finding this avenue of thought we had previously failed to tread down. Mika had always told us she chose to ask Causes due to our vagrant nature and the fact there was little to distract us while the Revolution was hovering in the soft stalemate before the Ordeal of Pata.

My words; not hers, of course.

I, too, was going over in my mind why I had never thought to ask about this. Although I had asked for his name to no clear answer, I had not considered asking into the man's life or the kind of person he was.

Mika heaved a few quick breaths before engaging Dice with a pout and eyes of rattled confidence. "This wasn't part of our agreement."

Dice's chest puffed and nostrils flared. The train's clatters and whirs were the only things keeping us from falling into absolute silence as his stare held unwavering. Mika's pout turned to a lip buttoned with frustration as she tried to muster the same ire into her own eyes.

"All right, you two. Let's ease up. We can all talk about this later when we've calmed down. Mika?"

She turned her attention to me. "Yes?"

I made myself firm. "You should know all three of us want the answer. It may not be part of your agreement with Dice, but it *is* part of the agreement between you and me. When we get out of public and over to Dice's house, you need to tell us. Am I clear?"

My mention of our deal took her from alarmed defense to courteous acceptance. With a struggled smile, she nodded. "You're right. I'm sorry." She looked left, right, then all around; leaned us into a huddle, and spoke low. "I think my dad is trying to avoid the police or the Fifteen." My mind flashed with sharp concern in the moment between her sentences. "Remember Brigg, my dad's note told me not to look for him. When you're looking for someone who's missing, you go to the police, right?"

My heart eased. Even Dice and Kay, also surprised, were nodding in understanding.

A smile peeked on Mika's face. "My daddy probably didn't want me to go to the *police* to look for him. The idea to ask other people seemed like the way to go. Later, after the first group of Causes helped me, I chose to stick to asking Causes."

Although Dice appeared to accept her answer, he dug deeper. "Was your father doing anything unusual before he disappeared? Was he being secretive; maybe doing something illegal?"

There wasn't a hint of hesitation in Mika's shaking head and falling eyes. "I don't know." She pointed to me, her expression brightening slightly. "But if I remember anything, I'll tell you."

"That-a girl." The smile I spoke with hid the nagging in the back of my mind. Dice, Kay, and I couldn't hide our feelings about this new possibility. For me, being the first of our group to agree to the search, this new facet of the task was tough for me to consider. In a way, I was glad Dice brought it up. However, deep in my gut, I was trying not to doubt Mika's integrity towards us.

I had to step away for a few moments and try to clear my head. While up and about, I figured it was a good idea to see if I could get any information on the train. It would be a few hours and a number of stops before we reached West Binda, so taking the time to ask around seemed harmless enough. I excused myself from the others, taking Mika's picture with me.

III

Navigating straight toward the refreshment car, I stopped to ask people aboard the train about the man in the picture. The only person who knew anything was trying to direct me back to the Delta. He had seen the same guy we mistook the other day. Our group needing more than a hand-drawn picture to get anywhere further in the search now felt like a definite fact.

Time passed. After asking around, I relaxed alone in the refreshment car, nibbling on complimentary cookies, pondering thoughts I had yet to share with the others.

While looking at the picture of me Mika had been working on, I was beginning to feel the burden of my good intentions. Ever since Mika walked into my life, everything had changed. I thought back to those first sixty-two days of the Revolution and how I managed them alone. Sleeping in the woods; being concerned with only my own food and money; the lack of criticisms and opinions from my peers; no hostilities; no drama; complete self-reliance and freedom.

Riding the rails from time to time was fun, too. The swaying and rocking made it easy to fall asleep, and the clean, hospitable environment of the lounge car made it easy to relax. The aroma of free cookies and lemon tea held the faint scent of vital money left unspent. It always made me wonder if any other Causes had considered camping out in the trains. Of course, the ever-present threat of getting snatched up by Riley or his crews was always there, so I never overstayed my welcome.

There was a lot to miss about being alone, but the thought of selfishly backing out on my word to help Mika didn't sit well with me. I knew if I had not met Mika, I would still be alone and probably with nothing to do except hide indefinitely or await my capture by the Fifteen. I had her to thank for helping give me a purpose, and yet a part of me was wishing she had never come along. It was a difficult emotion to fight with.

"Is this seat taken?"

The sudden question coupled with a blaring horn from the train snapped me away from my personal time. I turned to look up and saw Kay, standing with a distraught expression. "Hey, what's the matter?" I asked her.

"I've been watching you for the past few minutes. You've been staring at that picture all spaced out. I've never seen you so deep in thought." She picked up my bag and placed it on the opposite end of the booth. Keeping her legs in the aisle, she occupied the seat next to me where the bag once sat. "Look, if you want to be alone, tell me now. I don't want to bother you."

"No, you're fine," I assured, smiling. "I was about to grab some cookies and head back."

There was a distinct softness in her tone I had never heard her use before. She scooted a little closer to me. "Your face tells me otherwise. If I'm being nosy, you can stop me, but is there something you wanna talk about?"

I folded the picture back up and put it in my left-front vest pocket. Turning away from the window to face her, I broke a cookie in half to share. "I'm not sure what I would do if anything were to happen to her."

She shifted her legs out of the aisle and under the table, taking the treat. "Mika? What do you mean?"

A shallow sigh escaped. "At first, when Mika and I met, I didn't have to go with her and she didn't have to come with me. I chose to help; you chose to follow us; Dice was doing his own thing, but now he's helping. Everything about where we are right now all stems from something I had the option to disregard in the first place."

Kay took a small bite. "Perhaps. But it's all good, right?"

"Well, it's not *bad*." I started massaging my head; running my fingers through my hair. "We're all-in on this now, and I don't want to have any doubts of doing the right thing—in regards to both the Revolution and helping Mika."

She nodded with a pensive stare at her cookie. "You might be thinking too hard about this. As long as we're not doing anything to put ourselves in danger, we can take things one day at a time. There was nothing wrong with your decision to help Mika."

I took out the picture of Mika's father. "Ha! You weren't saying *that* two weeks ago."

She swayed into me with a playful nudge. "I know I went with my snap judgments at first, but I can see what you're doing for

Mika is genuine." Kay gently took the picture from me, looking at it with hope in her expression.

Nestling my back into the corner of the booth, I grabbed another cookie and broke it. "I guess I can't focus because I feel like I'm having so much expected of me now. Even the other Causes are waiting for me to do something about Al & Jal."

Kay's hand swiped the air in bold dismissal. "Forget about them! We need to do what's best for us, and for Mika. I don't want anything to happen to her either. So let's get this done, and soon; before things get worse. If anything, with going to Binda, Dice has taken the burden of the search away from the two of us for a little while." She gave the picture back to me, sliding it into my other vest pocket.

I knew she was right. I had been putting a weight on my heart which only felt heavier the more I made it my sole responsibility to find Mika's father. To hear I didn't have to bear the weight alone brought me a great sense of calm.

Kay and Dice were not mere followers or hangers-on, and I felt a bit ashamed to have thought of them in such a way despite how things were at first meetings. We were no longer just a group of teenagers with an anti-government stance and rickety online relationships. We were a team. Kay helped me see it for the first time. The weight was lifted, or at least lightened, offering me much-needed relief. I grinned, stretching out. "Who would've thought Dice would actually *relieve* people of a hard time?"

"I'm sure he's only doing it for Mika and whatever agreement the two of them have. He probably plans on leaving our group once she's safe at home." She peeped half of the first word of whatever she was going to say next, then stopped. This brought us to an odd silence; one only cut off by the crunching of cookies and the howling echo of the train going through a short tunnel.

Twice more, Kay turned her head and cracked her mouth open, but still hesitated to speak. "What is it?" I asked her.

Her eyes shifted to the left and the right. In full-tilt evasion of my pressing, Kay stuffed the rest of a cookie in her mouth. She growled with silly scarfing noises, catching my eyes with a wide, goofy stare.

There was nothing to stop her sudden assault against the cloud of seriousness surrounding us. It all dissipated as I burst into laughter loud enough to interrupt the other conversations in the lounge car.

Through her own laughter, Kay quickly covered her mouth to avoid spitting out the cookie. She paused, took a careful breath, and swallowed. "See, that's more like it! Let's cheer up, mellow out, and move forward. Okay?"

"This coming from Miss Uptight herself."

Kay was on top of my shot. "Being with you and Mika has taught me I need to calm down and look at things more carefully. It doesn't make sense for me to calm down only to have *you* suddenly be antsy about everything. We need to chill out and take things as they come."

"Unless it's the Fifteen. *Then* we panic and run."

Kay clearly wanted nothing of such a scenario. "'Like we stole something,' right?"

My lifted spirit filled me with joyous energy. "Like you stole that turn-of-phrase from me."

She gripped my shoulder, jostling me. "There you go. Now you're getting it. Dice's house first; we figure out the rest later."

A tone of gratitude towards Kay wove seamlessly into my words. "You're right; thank you. The Revolution, the Fifteen, Al, Jal—they can all wait until after we take care of Mika."

She stood and placed my bag back next to me. "There's that 'we' again," she replied through a wide grin. "I'm gonna go grab some more cookies and take them back."

I smiled to her with a thankful expression. "Well, since I don't need any more *thinking* time, I guess I'll go back too."

Kay and I walked over to the cookie trays and started picking out the biggest ones. My mind was focused on stocking up on anything edible, while Kay appeared to have enjoyed the half of cookie I gave her. She did not waste any time putting the first one she picked up into her mouth.

Our hands bumped while reaching for the same treat. She withdrew her hand and took the cookie out of her mouth. We stood silent for a moment. I looked to her, but her face was turned toward the end of the car. "Kay?"

She stayed facing away from me. "I'm going back. Are you right behind me?"

I was hesitant, not sure about this sudden change of face. "Yeah."

Kay marched forward; I followed at my own pace.

As we were about to exit the refreshment car, a voice from another table distracted us. "What happened?"

Another one. "I don't think that's good, man!"

We both stopped and turned around. A single group of Causes had their eyes transfixed to the windows. Noticing the looks of puzzlement across all of their faces, a warm shudder rocked my shoulders and chest. "Is everything all right?" My voice quaked; a part of my mind darkened into no real desire to know the truthful answer.

All of them looked to us as the only one of them standing spoke. "We blew right through the train stop."

I planted myself against the nearest window, looking out to notice the train was still going at full speed. The station we were supposed to stop at was vanishing in the distance. The other group left the refreshment car to alert other Causes.

No sooner did the strangers exit, a loud clank sounded once from both ends of the car. I felt a jolt as my heart felt to stop; the sound echoing in my mind.

After a pause of unsure panic, Kay ran over to the door.

"Don't tell me it's locked!" she growled, yanking aggressively on the handle. She jerked, almost shrieking, "It's *not* locked...no..."

The thought of Mika and Dice being two cars away gripped my heart. My chest pulsed as I desperately shouted with intense vigor. "For the love of Paxus, don't tell me that door is locked!"

Kay's arms slumped to her sides as her voice cracked, "Okay, I won't tell you."

I sprinted to the door and tried to open it myself, dropping all of the cookies. I gripped the handle, pushing and pulling in a futile attempt. "No!" I slammed on the door with my palms. "This can't be!" I slammed again. "No! Just...*NO!*"

"What's going on?"

In answer to our confusion, a lazy, deliberate voice came from the PA. "Hello, Causes."

A chill ran down my spine at the tone filling my ears.

The voice continued. "We've passed the North Doma station on this non-stop trip to the Exta Sector. Your conductor today is Riley and I am your co-conductor, Sydney."

My teeth clenched in anger and dread. "Doctrine!"

"The Exta Sector?" Kay screamed. "Did we get captured!?"

I could barely get the words out of my mouth through the daze swirling through my head, "By Sydney; 'Doctrine' Sydn—"

Kay grabbed my shirt. "Snap out of it and pay attention!"

Sydney continued the announcement. "Don't panic, folks. We're going to give you options to consider during our trip, so when we arrive at Exta, you will know what to expect. For those of you who are *not* Causes aboard this train, we will reimburse you for your time spent with us and take you back to the Delta. You can blame the Causes for this inconvenience."

The air in the car had become cold and heavy. Kay shuddered and shook her head. "I'm scared. What are they going to do?" Her head lifted and eyes spread, panicked. "Mika! What about Mika?" She turned right back around to struggle with the door again.

I commanded her to move aside so I could try to kick the door in. Ten kicks with all of my strength had no effect on the sideways-sliding door. I tired myself out, bending forward with loud breaths. Kay examined the door closer for the lock, perhaps in an attempt to pick it. The locking mechanism, unfortunately, was not visible on the door's exterior. She, too, gave up. We could only stand in front of the door, desperate and dumbstruck.

Doctrine's announcement continued. "You will have three options once we arrive. One, we can book you into the Labor Fields. Two, we can set you up a private meeting with some of the members of the Fifteen—this option could either work for you or against you. Third, if you really don't like Eden the way it is, we can arrange for you to be sent to the other side of Eden's wall, where you will die out in the Great Beyond."

Kay shook as her knees grew weak. "What's going on?"

Although feeling nauseated, I caught Kay by the shoulders before she completely lost her balance. I kept my grip loose and caring. Her expression was glazed and out-of-focus; a perfect mirror to the fear blanketing across all of my ability to look at this situation rationally. Not the least bit convincing, I spoke soft, ushering her back to the booth. "Come on, Kay. Let's try to think. Let's sit down."

She wriggled from my grip, crashing onto the seat. "You *did* hear that, right—the wall? What *psycho* speaks about the Great Beyond so casually!?"

Glaring to the ceiling's speaker holes, I replied through gritted teeth. "Somebody with a *lot* to gain. Even for him, he's being *way* too confident." The mere act of talking about him made me want to punch something; anything. Seeing Kay in such a drained and frantic state, I could not bring myself to lash out. I had to keep it in and try to focus until Sydney's cocky voice would put closure to this horrible announcement.

"The Fifteen and I have been preparing for this for a while.

Thanks to the events of the past few days, it's time for us to step in and to put you Causes in your place. You can call us the 'Deserters,' and you can think of me as the one in charge. We are those who've lost hope for the Causes' victory. But most importantly, we have been offered truth. We are on the path to knowing what you cannot. Let it be acknowledged: our side is capable of things you would not understand in this lifetime.

"The Causes will be stopped; the Revolution will end. You, my friends, are the first batch to go. Have a pleasant trip and get plenty of rest. Good day."

A tear rolled down my face as I eased back into the booth. "'Friends' my ass, Doctrine! No—*Sydney*." I pounded on the table. "Sydney, how could you do this to us?"

"We are so dead!" Kay wailed before collapsing back into the booth and bursting into tears. "It can't end like this, right? Please tell me it won't! I don't care if it's a lie!" She punched the seat hard enough to rattle the table.

For her, I had to. "Kay, it's not going to end like this." Pausing, I had to reach deep for the motivation to repeat it. "It's *not* going to end like this!"

Kay's crying receded into weak sniffles. Seeing her sit up and wipe her tears gave me comfort and a shred of belief it was possible to do something about our situation. Whatever "something" was, though, I couldn't fathom how to look for it.

IV

There was no calm; only despair and anxiety. The moment Kay and I had enjoyed mere minutes before was unceremoniously shattered; replaced with Sydney's last words to me repeating in my head: *"Once they take me out of this room, I'm probably not coming back."* My fists clenched tight each time my mind echoed the warning.

He was the one calling the shots now, even declaring himself as the leader of this new group: the Deserters. I knew this turn of events would only serve to make the Revolution even uglier than it had already become.

Kay and I sat in our booth, facing each other and pondering the options given to us over the announcement. Thinking more closely into them, the most appealing was meeting with a Fifteen member. By making the other two options Labor Fields or something essentially equivalent to death, it would take the average person no time at all to decide which was the easiest.

Sydney called himself the leader of the Deserters, and we were the "first batch to go." There was an abyss of missing information preventing me from understanding how he could have gone from such an active Cause to...this; this Fifteen-cozy, ex-Cause traitor. I tried to pick apart anything from his announcement, but a lot of it was coming back to me as an unfocused mesh of noise and cockiness. It was difficult to keep my mind in one place as the guilty thoughts of Mika and Dice kept blocking out my ability to analyze anything.

It was hard—if not impossible—to think the four of us would be able to regroup on our arrival in Exta. Mika and Dice were two cars away, and we had no chance of reaching them. My heart was heavy at the thought of Mika ending up as I had feared she would. Now, it would only be a matter of time before she was in the custody of the Fifteen. The God-Spirits only knew what would happen to her afterwards.

Nothing was fitting together. Not a semblance of a plan was forming. Every bit of strength I had was trying to hold me back from lashing out and completely trashing the refreshment car in utter frustration. I had to stay calm for both my sake and for Kay's. It pained me to see her shift from being so gentle and caring to a crying, sobbing, hopeless mess. I felt it was the best I could do in consideration of the situation as a whole.

There we sat, alone, questioning our fate. Occasionally, Kay would say, "There has to be a way out of this," but she was unconvincing; almost saddening. Each time she repeated it, it only added to the grip of helplessness around my panicked heart. I didn't have it in me to tell her to stop saying it, though. It could have been the only thing giving her any shred of hope.

After the first thirty minutes, I stood and meandered aimlessly around the car, looking for anything to help us. Kay watched as I paced and prodded, waiting for an idea to come to me.

She soon joined me. We were more or less trying to kill time before our inevitable demise.

Giving up, I sat back down and leaned my head against the window. Kay sat next to me soon after. "Where's your crazy idea this time?"

I glanced at her. "What are you talking about?" I almost didn't want to hear it as I shut my eyes and slumped against the window.

She gave me a soft nudge on the arm. "Come on, you know. Escaping out of a third-story hotel window and deciding to stop a mob aren't exactly everyday ideas." Kay slipped back to the other side of the booth and sprawled across the whole seat.

While I appreciated her faith in my tendency to think quickly, this situation was a lot more complex than anything else we had faced. A lot of my motivation to do anything had been draining from my body since first hearing the still-echoing heavy clank of the car's locks.

Is this even possible? Come on, Dartmouth; think of something!

I opened my eyes and took a look outside. The landscape of the Doma Sector looked like a blur—caused as much by the train's speed as it was my utter inability to focus. It was much easier to make everything out in the distance. Ahead of the curve in the tracks, I could see a bridge over the river.

A flash of desperate impulse shot me up with a surge of adrenaline. My body jumped to attention so suddenly and dramatically, my knees banged into the bottom of the table.

Through wincing, I burst with great energy. "That's something!"

Kay sprang up; her left shoulder also bashing into the table. Her shout of pain swept into, "Wha-a~a~at is it!? What's 'something?'"

I shifted out of the booth and hobbled over behind the cookie counter. "We're approaching a river. And if we can get a window open in time, you and I are going to jump!"

Kay, standing and approaching the counter, stared at me wide-eyed with her mouth fully agape. Wordless, pained breaths peeped from her throat and her head swayed with a light shake. It was my first time seeing her at an absolute loss for words—as though she were wishing I had thought of *anything* but that.

I grabbed a cookie off the tray and aimed for Kay's hanging mouth. She turned her head aside and swatted my hand; snatching the cookie from it. "Please...say I heard you *wrong*."

Pulling a stool from behind the counter, I replied, "No can do. This train is going nonstop, and this could be our last chance. Now come on, help me look for a way to loosen a window."

Kay appeared hesitant about the idea as she held the stool in place for me. After a minute, Kay asked, "What about Mika and Dice? Are we really going to try to escape here without them?"

Keeping my balance on the stool was too difficult through the jostling of the train, and hearing of Mika and Dice put a shake in my heart and knees. I needed space to think, so I dropped down, grabbed the stool, and swung it into the resilient window.

For Kay's question, there was no soft answer. "Yes, staying with Mika and Dice is important, but hear me out." I swung again, leaving the first crack in the thick glass. "There's no way we can guarantee any of us will see each other once we get to Exta." A deep breath; another swing. "We would be gambling our freedom for a *chance* to stay near Mika." I reared back even farther for my next swing. "The kid isn't even a Cause, and without her dad in the picture, we can kiss goodbye any idea the Fifteen will let her stay near us. The police will end up searching for her dad whether she likes it or not, while you, me, and Dice get to swing pickaxes in the Strip Mines."

The mere thought of everything falling apart caused me to erupt in a broad and wild swing. It left a wide, solid crack streaking all the way from one side of the window to the other. I set the stool down for a short break.

Kay gritted her teeth and hung her head. "So we really are?"

"I'm sorry; we *have* to." I pointed to the booth where we sat. "Can you grab my things, please?"

She did so, but with little haste and crippling reluctance. Placing my gear next to the window, she grumbled. "We can't see what bargaining with the Fifteen will do?"

"Kay!" I hollered, "Stop it; stop putting second thoughts into my head! We both wanted a way out of this, right?"

She flinched at my volume but replied with understanding and respect. "I did, yes. I still do. And you're probably right. This could be our only chance." After a few weak, stuttering breaths, she nodded. "Come on; let's crack this window. We'll figure out everything else later." She took the stool in hand, waiting for me to clear away so she could take a few shots. Kay gave everything she had in powerful strikes.

I took my vest off and started stuffing it into my backpack. Knowing I had the picture of Mika's father brought a lump to my throat, swirling nausea, and deep pain I had never felt before. Movement and sound within the train blurred and faded as I could not help but get sucked into the vacuum of guilty thoughts. "Mika, please understand." I choked on the words, erupting into coughing sobs. "Dice, stick with her, please!"

I hated absolutely everything about this. Staying free and in the fight was now at the cost of both the party and my heart being torn in half. Regardless of whether it was seen as an act of necessity or cowardice, the bottom line was I was breaking my promise to Mika to save our own skin.

"Brigg!"

My head snapped to the side. Winded, Kay was leaning forward onto the stool. "I think we're almost there. Come on; you and me together on this!" There was a twisted and misplaced comfort in seeing the tears streaming down her cheeks; to see our minds and hearts sharing this split desire to go through with it.

Standing again, I gestured for her to give me some space. "You take the stool again. I'm kicking."

I took my position on the left so right-handed Kay could swing the stool with all of her strength. I didn't have to lift my leg too high to get in a few good heels; spreading out the existing cracks even more. The two of us were making a lot of progress, but the train was approaching the river fast. "Time it!" Kay shouted. "Together; strike on three!"

Feeling a surge of desperate strength I felt only Paxus could provide, I took a deep breath and started our rhythm. "One, two, *kick!*" Our simultaneous strike instantly turned the whole window into a labyrinth of cracks. "That's it! One more! One, two, *kick!*"

The window finally gave way. Shards of glass shot to the outside, causing the window to catch the heel of my boot. I hopped on my left foot to free myself, falling backwards. The stool lodged into the glass as Kay backed away to keep from getting cut, head hung in heavy panting, catching her breath.

She urged me to be careful as I stood, grabbing the legs of the stool and shaking it about to send shattered glass falling every which way. The train's clattering amplified, mixed in with the whipping of the wind now coming in and the crashing of shards. Getting a firm grip, I raked the stool across the bottom of the broken window, clearing it of remaining glass in order to give us the safe space needed to jump out. Kay grabbed my backpack. "How high of a jump is this, anyway? How deep is the water?"

I swept my hand towards the window. "Throw my stuff out,

now!" As she did so, I looked to the outside. In my head, I counted as my backpack soared through the air. It took only four seconds to fly from the window to the ground. "The bridge is probably no more than a meter or three above the surface of it. It's not even much of a drop, so we won't sink in too deep when we hit the water."

Kay peeked out as well. When she brought her head back in; her eyes meeting mine with a desperate whimper in them. She then turned back to look at the door one last time. After a heavy breath and a shake of her head, she looked back to me and nodded. "Let's go. Yes?"

I looked to the door as well, then to her. My lip quaked, but I answered with what confidence I could muster. "Yeah, let's go."

The moment the refreshment car started going over the bridge, Kay and I climbed through the window. We took each other by the hand, both as a comfort and to steady our balance to avoid slicing our hands on shards of glass, and ejected from the train. It was a short fall, but every centimeter of our descent felt like it stretched on forever. All the way down, I could only recycle my silent apologies to Mika and Dice. Over and over, they repeated as the first hints of regret took hold of my heart. But there was no way to turn this back.

By the time I hit the water, I barely had the energy to swim to the riverbed. Kay helped push me along, but my soul was in as many pieces as the window.

Abandonment.

Impulse.

Cowardice.

And no amount of apology to ultimately justify it.

We had failed. _I_ had failed.

May Paxus damn you, Sydney.

V

It was a truly harrowing experience. Dice and Mika were gone, and Kay and I were left to wallow in defeat underneath the railroad bridge. My thoughts became a never-ending assault on my spirit. Letting Mika slip out of my hands so easily was not an easy thing to accept.

Kay was visibly depressed; drawing in the dirt with a piece of the glass she had found when we hunted for my backpack. She sat by the edge of the river and wrapped herself in my spare blanket. We were keeping our distance from each other since all of our clothes were hanging to dry, leaving us both naked.

There was a lot about the situation I wanted to say, but it was all swimming so actively around my muddled mind. I needed to start talking through everything, but I wasn't sure how tactful it would be to approach a naked woman while barely wearing anything myself. All I could do was admire the scenery. Although it was a welcome alternative to winding up in Exta, I was beginning to wonder if Kay and I would really ride the hours out in silence until our clothes were dry.

This was a good time for me to give the Revolution some thought. The Causes remained the same; loyal to the Producers' rules. Then the rebels came, siding with Al & Jal. Now, Sydney had shown himself again to add a third group to the conflicts. From what Sydney said in his announcement, I could presume the Deserters were under the direct command of the Fifteen.

Sydney…that backstabbing bastard.

He was such an active Cause; such a friendly face. Sure, his actions back at Roy's Inn soured my view of him a little, but had I known he was shifting towards this reprehensible change-of-face, I would never have accepted his invitation in the first place.

How could we have known, though? He was my friend, after all. All the times we spent backing each other up on the forums;

reasoning with the skeptical; setting straight the nay-sayers. Those were good times. Though recalling them made it all-the-more aggravating to accept what he was doing now.

I felt the brush of damp fabric over my shoulder. Kay had thrown my shirt to me. "Could you cover up? Let's talk about this. I think we need to before we go anywhere else."

Without turning to look at her, I unfurled my shirt and set it onto my lap. "Glad we're thinking the same thing. I was expecting we'd be doing this with clothes on, but by all means. Do you have any ideas?"

The tiny hint of confidence in her voice was marred with a quiver. "Being clear on our next step is more important. It's not a time for us to be all nervous about approaching each other. Clothes or not, this is the situation. I think we know each other's boundaries by now, right?" Careful to keep herself properly covered, she eased next to me and sat. I continued facing away until she was settled. "But in answer to your question: no ideas, no. Not yet, anyway."

"Discussing it now is good a plan as any," I replied, now turning my head to catch her eye.

We spent the first few minutes in silence, looking over the river towards the setting sun. The two of us seemed unsure as to who should start until Kay asked, "Did you have *any* idea what he was doing? Any at all?"

It came out fast, almost as a hiss. "I *really* don't want to talk about Sydney right now." I took a big breath of the crisp, summer evening air. I had to stay in control of myself. "But I guess I'm not going to be able to avoid it." I paused and sighed with a deep growl; throwing a nearby stone into the water. "No, I didn't; which is why this feels like...the shittiest thing. I never had a reason to question trusting him."

Kay's reply came out with a sense of sweet caution. "Well, if it makes you feel any better, I think whatever Sydney believes he is going to get out of this, he won't get it. Like, whatever the Fifteen agreed to do for him, *they're* going to stab *him* in the back as soon as they get what they want out of him."

I almost—*almost*—put a smile on my face to hear it. "Sydney *did* say they were 'offered truth.' And I guess the result of the meeting put credence to what you're saying. So, do we let Sydney do his thing? Should we at least warn other Causes?"

"Oh, definitely!" She, too, started pitching stones to the river. "As far as we know, you, me, and everyone on the train are the only people who know about the Deserters. Unless there was a Contact riding, too, there's no way to get the news out. It'll be up to us."

I pointed down the river. "There's a lodge over there. I know we're a little out of town, but maybe we'll find a Contact there. Or the keeper can give us computer access."

She looked to the lodge, then back to me. "Good plan. One step at a time, right?"

"It's all we *can* do right now." I shivered, running my hands through my hair. "But what about Mika and Dice?"

Kay's lips popped to a purse. "I wanted to talk about *them* as much as you wanted to talk about Sydney."

The weight of leaving her heaped on me all at once. My tears shed; voice croaked. "We promised to help and we've failed."

"I wish I could say we could count on Dice—"

"Don't, Kay; please," I interrupted, sharp. "He's her only chance now. Don't put that idea in my head. The two of them have their agreement. And Dice's whole stink about not wanting to be arrested is moot. He's not going to get any more arrested than he is now. One of the few things I can trust right now is he'll stick with her. Coming from me, that's saying a lot."

"Ah-h-h," she realized, "you're right; you're right. Thank you." She pitched another stone. "I feel better about it—at least a little."

"He's pretty clever, too. They'll pick to meet with the Fifteen and come up with something from there. But it looks like the police are going to be the ones looking for Mika's dad now, whether she likes it or not."

Kay responded, smiling, "You mentioned it earlier and it got me thinking. I don't think we're completely off searching, either."

"How so?" I turned my body towards her, intrigued.

She pointed to my gear. "We have the picture with us, right?"

"We do, yes."

The blanket lifted slightly with her shrugging shoulders. "It's a stretch, but the police may come to us looking for the picture. I think it would be a chance for us to get back into the search."

I was nodding wide, finally excited to hear of a way. "And if we're helping the police, we probably avoid the Strip Mines."

"They'd probably force us to denounce the Revolution first. The way I see it, it'll..."

My focus went a bit deaf as all of my attention was brought to my neck and eyes. Kay's gesticulating was creating ripples and small openings in the blanket. Her words were tuned out by an uncanny fit of concentration. *Don't peek! Look to the side; look her in the eyes. Nod. Yes. Blanket. Cover. Paxus—respect; chivalry. Shalynn—purity. Don't even glance. Why now? This is important! Look away and listen. Ooh, a stick! Use that.*

Kay's voice eased back in. "...like the Radio Tower, right?"

I was drawing circles in the dirt with the stick. My brain was trying to fill in the blanks, but nothing was coming up quickly enough. I wound up replying with, "I'd say so, yeah."

"See, there you go! So let's try our best to stay positive, okay?"

That worked!? Thank you, Paxus!

Kay stood, careful to stay covered, and walked to her hanging clothes. "How's your shirt feel? Still damp?"

I ran my hand over it. "Still, yeah." I wanted to stay on subject, though. "I know you said it's a stretch, so I hope you'll excuse me for staying skeptical about the whole situation."

"Don't get me wrong," she replied, louder to cover the distance, "I'm not ultimately banking on it either. But I've learned you and I tend to plan better when we're not rushed and we're in good spirits. In a way, I feel like we may have made a mistake in jumping from the train."

"Now don't say that!" I gently protested, also standing, dangling my shirt in front of me. "It was the right thing to do; it's hard to convince ourselves right now, though. Our heads are a mess, the Revolution is turning into a disaster, and Mika is *still* gone with nothing but a bunch of uncertain factors that have to play out *exactly* the way we need them to in order for her to see her father again."

"Geez, Brigg," she groaned, pulling her shirt off the beams. "Don't make it sound so hopeless. We're both in this, and we both know what we can do in the meanwhile to make sure the Causes can be safe from Sydney's planning. Wetness be damned, let's get dressed, get over to the lodge, and see what we can do about warning the other Causes. One thing at a time, right?"

"Right." I turned to face the river, finally calm and focused. "Go ahead; get dressed. I'll wait."

We were soon on our way up the river. It was getting dark out fast, and we were stumbling through the inconvenience of the new moon's refusal to light the way. Wayward branches, rocks, and small ditches along the trail made it clear this was a path not-too-often travelled. We frequently had to assist each other down the trail, bumping and shuffling all the way. The stars in the clear sky were an awe-inspiring sight, though. Kay and I took a break with about a kilometer or two to go until we would reach the lodge. There was no way we were going to let such a beautiful night pass without stopping to admire it. At the very least, it could take our minds off of our situation for a few minutes.

I was removing my boots to continue airing out my damp

socks. Kay glanced at my bag and said, "You know, you *could* change into fresh socks."

Whipping my socks on my knee, I replied, "My boots are still wet; those will get wet, too."

"Ah, right." She let out a big sigh, curling into a ball, looking up. "At least you *have* the option. My gear is long gone."

I hung the socks on the branches of a small bush within reach. "Did you have anything you really needed besides extra clothes?"

She reached to her side, opening the flap of my backpack. "Nothing that's not in your gear, at least. But now we're out about one-hundred arna."

I grimaced. "Okay, *that* sucks! But don't worry about it. I've got enough for both of us for now."

She closed my bag. "Thanks. I'll pay anything back."

"Don't be ridiculous," I scoffed. "I'm not at home, and you're not my sister. I'm not gonna bug you for it."

Kay faced me. "Oh! You never told me you had a sister."

"And two brothers," I added. "And yeah, life at home isn't really my favorite subject. Come to think of it, I'm not sure why I brought it up."

"Well, I thought we were taking this break to distract ourselves for a bit; talk about something else for a change. Now you have me curious, so feel free to keep going, if you're willing to." Kay cocked her head to the side, patient to listen.

I had to pause. I knew we were trying to lighten things up, but touching on my life at home was a step forward I wasn't sure I was willing to take. After thinking it over for a minute or two, and seeing Kay eager to know more about me, I drew a slow breath through my nose and pushed it out in a loud puff. "Know what; why not?" I mumbled, hesitating only a moment more before obliging her. "My siblings and I don't so much 'get along;' it's more like 'coping.' My dad's a piece of shit. Mom takes her anger at him out on us. Dad takes his anger out on everyone. And we're all stuck in the middle until we're old enough to move out." I was talking tough, but was fighting a lump in my throat.

Her teeth gritted in a frown. "If I may ask: is that why you're out here with the Causes?"

I nodded, reaching for my granola bag. "Asking is fine. And yeah, it's the number-one reason."

"Are your siblings out as Causes, too?"

"They didn't do the Great Walk, but if they decided to go out afterward, I wouldn't know. I haven't contacted home since I left." I offered her a handful. "Frankly, if they're out here, too, it'd probably be for the same reasons."

Again, Kay proceeded with gentle care. "You don't have to go into detail, but have you ever called the Family Support Division?"

Since she asked for no details, I spared her those of the beating I got for having done so. "I did; once. It was about three years ago. Family Support was going to consider doing Safety Separation, but Mom and Dad agreed to take the mediations and classes in order to keep the family together. When the rep asked us kids about it, my siblings were too scared to be moved to Exta and be placed in Matron Care. So nobody went anywhere."

It was common knowledge Safety Separation was only required in the most extreme circumstances. Her new realization to the extent of my issues read clear through her pout and fallen eyes. With friendly tact, though, she didn't push. "Yeah, Matron Care is not ideal, being cooped up in Exta and all."

"Even if it would put my dad on the Assembly Lines, we didn't think Exta was worth it. My parents were okay for a while after taking the courses anyway. Things were smooth up until about this time last year. They're back to their old ways now, though. So I'm done with them. I'm almost eighteen anyway. Leave now; leave later; it's all the same."

I could both hear and feel the anger crawling into my tone. Kay's response of silence only supported the idea I needed to wrangle in my emotions. I took a stick and flung it into the river, trying to calm down, but I needed to get off the subject.

After a cleansing breath, I said, "The other day, you said you have sisters. Do you all get along? What about *your* parents?"

Kay replied immediately, cheerful. "We have our moments, but we treat each other well." She went back to playing with the flap on my backpack. "My sisters look up to me, but I'm a bad example to them sometimes."

"You!? A bad example!?"

"Mostly when it comes to studies. Compared to somebody like Dice, I'm *really* lax on my Interactive Study Grade. I'm only slightly above average; 17 at age 16. So my parents get bent out of shape when my sisters follow my attitude about studies."

"Ah, I get it." I began sliding my socks back on. "So what are your sisters doing since you're out here with the Causes?"

Kay stood and stretched; her voice skewing as she replied. "What else? They're studying hard and behaving themselves, like their big sister asked them to."

I was now lacing up my boots. "I'd figure they'd want to follow you out here."

"Well, they know the definition of 'dangerous.' And they know thirteen and eleven are not exactly the ages you want to be if you're being taken to the Labor Fields." She was already starting to walk ahead. "Also, as you probably guessed: the Slope. I can handle myself. But Shannon, at thirteen, always with her eyes on the boy at the end of our street. He tried to convince her to join us, and I'm sure he would have *loved* to be cozied up in a tent in Gova with her. He had the audacity to approach me on the night of the Great Walk, giving me a dirty look, all like, 'Shannon's not with you?'"

Picking up my backpack, I paced quicker to catch up with her. "You're a good sister, Kay."

My compliment appeared to have deflected off of her mind's

focus on her story. "And I was like, 'No, Derek. Shannon is *not* with me. She's not coming out.' Then, I stuck to him like glue for the first eleven days of the Revolution."

"What happened to him?"

Her voice adopted a clean growl. "Heck if I know. I woke up one morning, and he had already left, along with two other girls we had grouped ourselves with. Little scoundrel. I wasn't the least bit surprised."

I was now walking at her side. "So all of the arguing about the Slope hits pretty close to home, huh?"

"Definitely." Kay started looking down at her feet to watch her footing in the dark. "We're all still young; in our teens; hormones exi—"

My brain kick-started, remembering her exact phrasing from her posts. I recited along with her. "...exist. And revved-up, naive passion is not a good pretense for choosing your life partner."

Kay playfully nudged me. "Save quoting me for the forums."

"Of course," I replied, poking her with my elbow. "It was, like, one of your *best* arguments! I could barely come up with a counter on my own."

She hopped over a small ditch in the path. "It's something I take seriously because I want my sisters to guard themselves. I *have* to set an example for them. I can't tell them not to wander off with the boys if I'm doing exactly that."

My voice swayed with silly sarcasm. "Well, technically—"

"This isn't even *close* to what I mean, Brigg!" Her voice cracked to stern disappointment.

"Yes, yes; you're right." I looked ahead and saw we were almost to the lodge. "Speaking of the situation, let's start figuring out what we're going to post if we can get to a computer tonight."

We started recapping everything between ourselves. It was a shame such a relaxed conversation had to be derailed by having to recycle the realities surrounding our group, as well as the

Revolution. Kay and I knew, however, we were quite possibly the only chance the Causes had of getting any sort of heads-up about Sydney, the Deserters, or anything else the Fifteen may have been scribbling in their playbook.

VI

We followed the river the rest of the way until we reached the lodge. This particular inn, Riverview, was a cozy, log cabin-style building with a nice view complementing its name. Unfortunately, the main office was locked and the overnight stand-in clerk didn't have the key. There was no Contact there either, so computer access was out of the question until morning. Thankfully, we managed to check into their last available room.

"Let's try not to stress too much," I conceded, turning the room key. "The owner will be here by the time we wake up in the morning. It can't be helped."

"I *suppose* you're right," she said through a heavy breath. "Let's not slack in the morning. We still have to figure out where *we* are going from here."

The door was opened. I reached for the light switch. "One thing at a time, right? First thing is sleep."

Kay briefly froze in the doorway, staring at the bed—the only bed in the room. I was a bit taken aback as well, but this was the inn's last room. Kay repeated, "Can't be helped." After a deep breath, she pursed her lips, nodded, and walked towards the bathroom. "I'm getting a *real* shower."

I watched her until the door closed, then tossed my bag off. I knew Kay was less-than-thrilled, so I kept my thoughts to myself to avoid any potential grind of attitudes. With our group split and her gear dozens-if-not-hundreds of kilometers away, she had to have been taking this turn of events harder than she was letting on. "We're gonna be all right, Kay. It's not going to end like this."

I said softly, though I knew she couldn't hear me. This time, however, I felt like I could believe it.

I was trying to keep my head intact, attempting to push aside the thought of Mika falling into Sydney's hands. No matter how many times my mind steered towards looking forward, it kept getting waylaid by the guilty thought: *Was jumping really the right thing to do?*

With a loud, growling groan, I threw my shirt, socks, and boots off and claimed the right half of the spacious, double-wide bed. I snuggled underneath the pale red comforter, turned toward the edge of the bed, and shut my eyes, letting the sound of the running shower lull me.

As tired as I was, there was too much on my mind to go to sleep right away. I tossed a bit, trying to lay on my back, then my stomach, and then to the side. I tried sprawling out and decided it was a bad idea to hog the whole bed. I rotated again, flopping about as my eyes hung half-open. I exhaled, aware of how difficult it was to get comfortable under the circumstances.

After a few more minutes, I heard the shower stop. I figured perhaps it was in my best interest to feign being asleep.

Kay stepped out of the bathroom and without hesitation, ambled over and nudged me. "Hey, Brigg!"

My eyes crept open as I played up my tiredness. "What's up?"

She was succinct. "I don't know where you got the idea I'd share a bed with you, but it isn't going to happen."

My heart became tight and tense. It was too late at night to be putting up with any nonsense. "Too bad," I mumbled. "Looks like you'll be sleeping on the floor then."

Her attitude stepped in. "Excuse me?"

"No!" I interrupted, sitting up in bed, "*You*…excuse *me*! Who paid for this room, again?"

She did not give an answer, meekly clutching the front of her towel. It looked like getting along did not last as long as we wanted it to.

Not expecting her to answer, I continued. "I paid for this room, so I paid to sleep in this bed for the night. The only reason I kept the other half for you is because I figured a comfortable night's rest would do us *both* good. Think about it. We could've been stuck on the train and taken as prisoners. How lucky were we to get this room; this bed?"

Kay pushed her hand into the cushy mattress. "Pretty lucky, yeah." She lowered onto the left half.

"Look," I said, calmer. "I want to share this bed with you as much as you want to share it with me. I'm willing to compromise, though, since we both need decent rest. I'm offering you half of the bed as a courtesy. You can do with it what you want; I'll rest easy tonight knowing I at least offered." I rolled back over, not wanting to say anything else besides, "Goodnight."

Kay delivered a soft, breathy, "Thank you," as she slipped under the covers.

Finding something amiss, I rolled onto my back and turned my head to address her. "Umm...clothes? Pajamas?"

"All my clothes are drying on the line outside of the bathroom window. I don't have my cotton pajamas anymore."

"Here." I sat up, reached down, and took my black shirt from the floor. I handed it to her and looked away. "Try this."

While Kay put it on, she asked, "What about pants?"

"Well, *my* pants are too big for you, I'm sure," I replied.

"Territorial about your pants?"

"Among other things."

Kay stood and wrapped the towel around her waist, then sat back onto the left half of the bed. "I'm decent now."

The mood in the room felt like our time under the railroad bridge. There was a sensitive, walk-on-egg-shells ambience where one was not sure what there was to say next. I decided to keep it neutral and asked her, "Are you comfortable enough?" I had not turned back around yet.

She gave a light relaxed laugh. "It's not exactly as comfortable as my pajamas. This towel is soft, but your shirt is..."

"What?" I rolled over to look. On first sight, my vision was in direct line of Kay's chest. Her full breasts were firmly pressed against the inside of my shirt, which appeared to be a tight fit for her. I spun back to face the wall.

"It's...a little snug." She chuckled with a bit of grunt. "How do you breathe in this thing?"

Unable to purge this now-embedded mental image, I reached down to stealthily adjust myself before I could get too excited. "Are you alright wearing it?" I asked nervously, unable to look directly at her.

"Yeah, I'll be fine." She hummed as I felt her fidget to adjust the shirt. "Are you okay over there?"

I focused my mental efforts to regain control of my body. I was overcome with a light, warm sensation—a sudden desire for sensuality. It coursed through my entire being; pumping hot blood to all the right places. My heartbeat pounded against my eardrums as I tried to make sure my breaths remained steady. I had to shift my focus to something else. "I'm okay, but something has been bothering me for a little while now."

"What's up?"

I breathed in deep and let it out as my mind honed in on a sense of genuine remorse. The arousal flushed from my body and my heart calmed to a crawl. Rolling over onto my back to catch her eye, I said, "Back in Pata, I really *am* sorry for putting my hands on you the way I did. I know we talked earlier about what I went through with my parents, but I can't keep using my past as a shield when I lash out."

She gave me a gentle tap with the back of her hand. "You already apologized."

I shook my head. "I'll be honest; it was as much me being

genuinely sorry, as it was me apologizing to calm Mika. But here and now, with no other influence, I want you to know I am sorry. You have my word: I will *never* strike you again."

Her face flickered with emotion. "I…well…thank you."

My hands slid between the pillow and my head. "I want you to do a favor for me, Kay."

"What is it?"

"If I ever hit you again, I want you to go right to the police. Don't even stop. March right up to them to arrest me."

She snickered under her breath. "That's a bit extreme, don't you think?"

I scowled. "I'm not going to grow up and be like my father. I can't toss people around and not face the consequences."

She slid further under the covers with a soft smile. "Well, you know I was looking out for both myself and Mika. And to be honest, after the fact, I realized how dumb it was to even try that. Not because I got caught, but because it was unfair of me to try and take advantage of the chaos to pull Mika away from you. We were both in the wrong that night. I'm not sure what else to say other than I know I can find it in me to forgive you."

"Really?"

She sat up again, leaning back against the headrest. "Seriously, yes. Both you and I know, though, the apology in and of itself is only half of it. Two weeks ago, I wouldn't've trusted your apology. But since we've met in person, we've become a good team through all of this. We both want the same thing, after all."

"We do." I nodded, tilting my head up to catch her eye again. "I forgive you, too—just like I'll forgive you for having me arrested if I hurt you again."

Her eyes rolled at the thought again. "Come on, Brigg. Are you really serious?"

"Absolutely!" I replied, relaxing my head and closing my eyes. "But save it for if it actually happens. For now, though, let's only concern ourselves with getting a good night's sleep. And considering everything, I'm happy to end the day on this note: forgiveness, and an end to hostilities."

I could feel her slipping back under the covers; her voice was toned down and sleepy "Good attitude. Don't worry. I'm sure we'll be seeing Mika and Dice again." Kay shifted around more before making herself comfortable. She exhaled with a dreamy sigh. "Goodnight, Brigg. See you in the morning."

Through a yawn, I said, "Goodnight, Kay. Let's get some good sleep."

Sleep was coming fast and I could feel myself start to slip away until the tight curves of Kay's figure popped right back to the front of my mind's eye.

Oh Brain, why!?

My charged imagination wandered to the curious fantasy of seeing Kay's chest bare, and what it would feel like to touch her. These provoking thoughts were a relaxing transition from the stresses and self-inflicted burdens wearing me down both mentally and physically.

Brain, I love you, but I hate you. Let me sleep!

But did I really *want* to sleep? The sound of Kay's soft breathing was gradually transitioning into gentle snores. She let out a dreamy moan as she shifted to lie on her back; soon rolling a bit more to face towards me. She was snuggled deep into the covers; completely at peace in rest. I wanted to see if I could get one more glimpse of her figure pressing firmly in my shirt, but she had stopped moving and was completely covered.

I realized something once I had laid there watching her for almost ten minutes. This was a scenario young men my age could only dream about. I was in a bed with a woman with nobody else around—the ultimate treasure of teenage boyhood. Regardless of all the details that went into creating the situation, this was it.

Looking at Kay's restful features, I thought back to the day we met. In such a short span of time, I had gone from being completely alone and aimless to having no shortage of company and a new purpose. Although we had spent the last two, chaotic weeks together and now had a much better understanding of each other; I knew as well as the next person I didn't see Kay as a woman I'd take an interest in. What if, though...

We're in our teens...and hormones exist, I thought. *Is there a possibility she may have been thinking the same thing?*

No way. She made such a stink about even sharing the bed.

Maybe she was feeling me out. Or maybe she really did *want to share the bed and was playing hard-to-get.*

But this is the exact thing Kay was preaching against on the forums. You really think she wants this?

She was going to get into bed in nothing but a towel until I opened my big mouth. Nothing...but...a...freaking...towel!

Yeah, I botched it. Nothing's guaranteed if I try to make a move now.

Make a move on Kay?! Am I out of my mind?!

Come on, I can't lay there and do nothing. It's just us and this bed.

I'm not that hard-up! And Kay is sleeping; it wouldn't be right to wake her up now. Today was draining enough already.

I've never even had a chance to be *hard-up! But thinking about it, it would be best to see if she's really feeling me out. Best way is to feel her out right back—figuratively speaking, of course.*

I slithered my right hand under the covers and reached for my belt buckle. *She saw me in less than my underwear earlier. She probably liked what she saw; maybe that's why she came over to me. And if I'm wrong, I'll tell her I got too warm and couldn't stay asleep.*

This is seriously the old loneliness talking. My lack of experience in this department isn't helping either. Did she really like it enough to not mind seeing it again? Like, what is she really going to do if I take these pants off? I doubt it's like any of the romance novels on the Tome Grid.

My mind filtered through the lens of pure hormones, hijacking Kay's voice to fuel the fire. *'Oh, Brigg! You took them off because were feeling hot? Well, I'm feeling hot, too. Do you mind if I take this off? Better yet, why not all of it…"*

As I unbuckled my belt, Kay shifted, causing me to stop moving entirely. The raunchy fantasy popped to a halt as the potential reality of Kay flipping her lid kicked it away. *You know what? I shouldn't do this here; not now. I'm curious to see how she'd react, but…just…no. This is our first night alone, and it's probably the first of many. It may still be a while before we have any company other than each other. There's plenty of time to see if this was really on her mind.*

Still, I give me ten seconds to reconsider. Ten…nine…

While counting down in my head, I put my belt buckle back together. I placed my hand on my heart, feeling it begin to slow as my arousal and racier thoughts dissipated. Soon, I was calm and able to think about the situation much more clearly; through a mind not muddled by dissipating loneliness and those ever-existent hormones.

There were definitely wants there. But until I had a clear picture of what to do with them, they were going to have to stay back. I laid back and closed my eyes. However, a few forbidden fantasies were still knocking around in my head. Kay's soft, sleepy breathing made it difficult to pull away from this relentlessly amorous mindset.

Doing my best not to jostle the mattress too much, I shifted to lying on my side, facing toward her. I knew I could be content simply watching Kay sleep for what little time I had left to be awake. In doing so, my chest welled in warm gratitude. *Thank Shalynn I'm not alone again.*

And thank you, Kay, for sticking with me.

My heart was calm and at peace, and I finally fell asleep.

Day 81

I

The events of the previous day had exhausted us more than we thought. The two of us wound up sleeping in until well after the sun had risen. I was the first one to awaken. Kay was still out cold, but I was not about to wake her.

Having shifted about in our sleep throughout the night, I ended up on my back and Kay wound up lying on her side with her left arm draped across my bare chest. I took the opportunity to indulge in a long look at how tightly my shirt was fitting her, again fueling fantasies at the sight of her trim, shapely body.

The whole scenario was a well-deserved treat for my red-blooded, teenage self. I was seventeen and most guys my age had all had girlfriends at one point or another, but up until then, I had never been privileged enough to be close to a woman. I decided to make the moment last as long as I could by staying perfectly still; steady, staring, and aroused.

Soon enough, Kay twitched; she was waking up. I closed my eyes and pretended to still be asleep. I felt her move around a bit as she let out the little moan she always would when she woke up in the morning. Her head flopped back down onto her pillow as she whispered, "Brigg…?"

I continued pretending to sleep.

"For somebody who's asleep, your heart sure is beating awfully fast." She took her arm off of my chest and sat up. "You can stop faking now."

I opened my eyes and innocently replied, "Morning, Kay."

She pulled the blanket over to cover herself. Unfortunately, I was not fast enough to realize that my obvious indication of excitement was reading clear from under the front of my trousers. Kay caught a glimpse and covered her eyes with the entire blanket. "Really, Brigg!?" she groaned, deeply embarrassed.

Kay wasted no time in her reactions to my arousal. The shying redhead got up and marched to the bathroom, taking all of the covers off with her. I tried to object by getting her attention, but she clearly did not want to hear it.

With my cheeks and forehead now calling dibs on blood flow, I got out of bed and ambled over to the bathroom door. I gave it a gentle knock. "Kay?"

No answer.

"Come on, Kay! It's not like you saw me naked or anything! What's there to be all embarrassed about?"

Kay opened the door and threw my shirt at me, wordless.

I dared another angle as I put the shirt on. "Come on; it's a natural thing. Men wake up like this!"

She still said nothing. I could hear rustling through the door and recalled her saying she hung her clothes out to dry overnight.

Once she was done, Kay burst through the door, fully-clothed with an embarrassed scowl worn like a new accessory. She strode up and looked intently into my eyes. "I'm giving you one chance to answer this question honestly."

I felt the sincerity of her discontent. It made me hesitant to even answer the question in the first place. "Sure." Honestly, though, I dreaded what she might say next. I could only hope it wouldn't be an odd or awkward accusation.

She muttered in a now-familiar, bitter tone. "How long were you awake before I woke up?"

Truly, time had frozen for me in the bed. I did not know how long I had indulged myself. "Ten minutes...fifteen?"

Kay continued staring into me. Our eyes were locked as I

dreaded her response to my answer. I wanted to say something else to defend myself. Kay and I had buried the hatchet the night before, so my heart was quivering at the thought of our new truce being frayed.

Breaking the silence, Kay gave a unique reply. "You really are sorry," she whispered. "I can see it in your eyes—the same look from last night."

Surprised, I nodded, feeling the urge to explain myself. "Well, I was comfortable; you were still asleep and I didn't want to wake you." I pointed to the clock. "We slept in because we needed it. And you lying across me, it was all..." I petered out, unable to explain what was going through my head.

She exhaled hard, then gently pushed, "All...what?"

Her pecking tone pressured me to spit something—*anything*—out. "New; different." My reply felt like the right direction to go. I tilted into lamenting vocals. "To be honest, I've never been close to a woman before. Like, *ever.*"

"Are you serious?" she asked through a snicker.

I rolled my eyes and twiddled my fingers. "Yeah. I act rowdy with other guys when it's on topic. But in the rare situation I'm alone with a girl, I get really anxious."

"I wouldn't've guessed. You seem so open on the forums."

Scratching the back of my head, I tried to play down my inexperience. "There isn't much to say about it. I've never had time to focus on girls offline."

"I don't see why," she remarked. "Get rid of the temper and I'm sure a girl or five could walk your way."

What—a compliment?! I pulled a mental double-take as her words caught me off-guard. "What makes you say that?"

Kay pointed her finger in my face, opened her mouth and froze. She then turned her gaze aside in coy laughter.

I found it odd such a simple question had stopped her. I smiled and pointed back. "Well? What makes you say that?"

Her hands rose, waving at both sides of her lowered, shaking head. Her smile couldn't break as she turned back towards the bathroom.

I pressed, now playful. "Come on! Don't cop out!"

"Stop!" she giggled, walking faster.

I zipped after her. "You're not getting away!" I managed to catch up to her before she could close the door. "Please, tell me! I'll buy you cookies if you tell me!"

Despite our playfulness, I wanted her to tell me why she felt the way she did about my alleged charm with women. It had never been brought up before, and I was curious to find out Kay's real view on the matter.

"Come on," I pleaded, pulling the door, "let me in there so we can talk about this!"

"Sure thing." Kay complied by releasing the door as I tugged.

With a mighty jerk, the doorknob slipped out of my hand as I fell backwards onto the floor, landing on my hip.

Kay brought the blankets out of the bathroom and threw them in a heaping pile on top of me. A swaggering, mellow tone dripped from her lips, confident and comfortable as I wrestled my way out. "You're handsome and you can be fun to be around. At the same time, you know when to be serious. You never seem to be at a loss for an idea, either. From my experience, you make life more exciting for people around you."

My heart skipped a beat. I stammered into my response. "Y-you really think so?"

Kay was ready to bring me back into reality by adding her own flavor to her uplifting praise. "Yeah, but I only answered so you would buy me cookies!"

Sunk out of my ego trip and amused by her ever-craving sweet tooth, I threw the covers off of me and slouched as I readjusted my position on the floor. "Why did you have to say it like that?"

She gave me a lazy smile and stroked her hair as her eyes met mine. "The answer will cost some freshly-baked cookies."

I cast the covers in her direction with a laugh. "You'll get your cookies. After all, I wouldn't buy for just any girl!" I stood and advanced toward her.

Kay had caught the covers and was rolling them up in a ball. She pushed them into me as though they were the border to her personal space. "Well, what kind of girls do you buy for?"

I snatched the rumpled sheets from her hands and threw them back onto the bed. I could feel my grin stretching wide as I continued pacing toward her. "I like my girls heart-strong, well-intended; firm, but *forgiving*. Green eyes, red hair, and a soft face are big plusses."

Kay held back her smile and took a step away. She deflected my words with harmless sarcasm. "Multiple redheads!? You cad!"

I brushed her comment off with a laugh; reaching out and placing my hand on her shoulder. My confidence spiked in an instant. My heart beat fast and my thoughts raced as I tried to find the right words to say to her. The moment held still as I took full notice of Kay's lithe frame and gentle features. My mind and heart threw the past aside and launched me into thinking our fresh start from the night before was a solid precursor to something more.

Within a moment, my nerves caught up with me. But with the great mood now set, I imagined how far I could go with it. Fantasies from the previous night invaded my next thoughts, actively pushing for me to make them a reality.

Kay's bandaged hand came to meet mine. She gave off a brief, content huff and shyly spoke, "Your hand is really warm."

I chuckled as my simple boy-brain felt to cease functioning under the pressure I was feeling. "Yeah, I get that a lot."

"Your hand is shaking; like you're nervous."

I could not stand the tension anymore. As my eyes took a split-second stroll up and down Kay's body, I took my hand off of her shoulder and placed it to her chin, easing her head toward mine. I stared into her glimmering green eyes as her mouth opened with a peep.

With a slow, deep draw of breath, I whispered, "Are you nervous, too?"

Her face shifted to an entranced stare; our eyes were locked into each other. I *was* nervous; especially due to the fact I was not sure how far I should have been pushing it. *What is this turning into?*

Trying to get back to thinking clearly, I asked, "So, is this what the slippery slo—"

Interrupting, Kay gasped in my face. In a flash, I felt the palm of her hand swiping across my cheek. The sting was wide and hot.

The mood stopped. The joy stopped. Time stopped.

I recoiled from the hit and opened my eyes to see Kay had not moved a muscle since her attack. She was leaned forward with her right arm stretched to her left side. The expression on her face was of uncomprehending disbelief.

I stared into her frightened eyes, trying to collect myself and my thoughts. It was clear I had stepped over a boundary; probably starting to tip down the slope she had always spoken about online. I kept my cool, knowing it would not be wise to be cross with her over the slap.

Kay's breaths were shallow as she set herself onto the floor. She shuddered in her state, unable to speak. I gave her a few moments.

The silence lingered too long for my comfort. "You really are sorry," I said with a forgiving whisper. "I can see it in your eyes."

As if what I had said was a cue to do so, Kay's eyes shook before tears welled up and trickled down her cheeks. "I…I didn't mean to—"

Calm, I assured her, "It's alright. We were having some fun and I must've…" I trailed off into a silent beat. "Look, what do you say we forget about this? I know you well enough to know you had a good enough reason to slap me."

She said nothing and simply cried. She wiped her tears away with the backs of her hands, periodically sobbing. I advanced a few paces in an effort to comfort her. I placed my hand on her head, but she swiped it away. "No!"

"No?"

She lifted both of her hands with her head still sunk. "Just…"

A pause. I waited for her to finish.

Her hands closed into fists and dropped to the floor. "Give me a few minutes alone, okay?"

"Did I—?"

"I need a few minutes to myself."

I nodded, agreeing to leave, and give her the time and space she needed. After entering the hallway, I leaned up against the wall within earshot of the door and listened in case Kay decided to say anything aloud for comfort.

No such comfort was heard.

"She's right," I mumbled, knocking on my forehead and recalling her words from the Radio Tower. "I *am* a bonehead. What possessed me to bring that up?"

I had the unfortunate feeling I had created a new, terribly-awkward tension between us. However, it was only a gut sensation based on the stinging feeling in my left cheek. Part of me wished I had caught myself before making such a thoughtless comment, but the damage had already been done.

II

Kay appeared to let the incident slide. Once she was willing to speak and explain, I felt understood and somewhat validated in my actions. However, while Kay appreciated we were getting more comfortable with one another, the idea of getting *too* friendly too soon felt inappropriate and poorly-timed. I wanted to dig more into her mindset, but I still needed to respect our boundaries, and decided to let it go.

The two of us spoke instead of the more pressing matters as we indulged in free eggs and pancakes in the lobby's cozy corner dining area. The Riverview's owner, a stocky gentleman in his late thirties, overheard some of our conversation. Happy to be of help to some of the "daring Causes," he opened his office computer to us before we even had a chance to ask.

We had everything we needed to say all planned out as I signed into the Cause forum. Kay and I started off by searching the forum to see if anybody else had had an opportunity to spread the word about Sydney. Nothing was there. "So it really is up to us," I said, moving the on-screen pointer to *New Topic*.

Before I could click it, Kay suggested, pointing at the screen. "You've got new private messages, though. Maybe you should check those first."

I glanced up to the inbox icon. "Two messages, huh?" I went up to click it. "Could Sydney be trying to reach out to me?"

The first message popped onto the screen. Kay cupped her hands over her mouth, unable to contain her excitement. "Oh good; it's from Blue!"

My chest got light. I spoke softly as I started reading. "Blue, you have no idea how much we need you right now..."

What's going on Brigg?

I had no idea you were at that bridge in the Pata Sector. Anyway, why are you paired up with Kay? Weren't you two always arguing or something?

In response to your answers to my questions though…

Thanks for the insight on Jalako. Figured she was a she.

Also, I'm sure the missing Producer will show up soon. The whole Revolution is probably going to start getting out of hand with Al & Jal planning on going on the attack.

I see your point about letting the Gray Police handle them.

By the way, I need you to do me a big favor from here on out. Since I'm going to be in contact with you often, I'd like to take the conversation away from the forum's private messaging system. Don't reply to this message; send me your reply through my regular INMail. In addition, stop referring to me as "Blue"; you can call me "Dylan". It's for everyone's safety.

Thanks for the info. If there is anything else I should know about, give me a shout.

-Dylan

Kay tapped my shoulder. "We've gotta tell him what's up!"

I was already zipping to the Reply button, almost immediately forgetting his instructions. Switching to standard INMail, I spoke through a determined grin. "You don't need to tell me *that* twice."

Together, we created a lengthy reply explaining what happened to us on the train. I told him everything I knew about Sydney, the Deserters, and the Fifteen's options for the Causes who were captured. Kay suggested I add the fact Dice and Mika were on the train and physical descriptions of them just in case.

Kay and I re-read the message together before sending it. I let out a disgruntled sigh as I prepared to proceed to my next message. I couldn't quite conjure the strength to proceed further, though. "I don't know what I'm going to do if this other message is from Sydney."

A heavy silence lingered before Kay reached for the mouse. "Want me to do it?"

I looked up and over my shoulder. "Yeah, give me a second." In disgust, I turned the chair to face away from the screen. "If it's from Sydney, leave it be."

"What about Dice and Mika?" I had never heard her ask a question so carefully.

I softly pounded on my leg, unable to come up with a real answer. "Tell me if it's him and if he mentions the others. Otherwise, leave it be."

"All right," she agreed, gentle in tone.

I took a deep breath as I heard the mouse click.

Then, in a blast of shock, Kay shouted. *"It's from BOGEN!"*

I almost fell out of the chair, both at the announcement and the ear-thumping volume it was delivered at. Every bit of stress weighing on me as a result of the Revolution that had been battering my mind was stilled. Bogen, the last standing Producer, was reaching out to us—to *us*! Whatever he felt was the next step, he wanted us to be part of it. The sensations partying in my gut brought me to little more than an excited, hysterical, unfocused mess of cheers, smiles, and aimless pacing. I did everything I could to gain my composure and eased in next to Kay; ready to read. But not before the adrenaline powered out of my throat. "Bogen, you marvelous bastard!"

Dearest Brigg,

I am praying you are all right. Seriously, I went to a chapel and everything.

I've gotten back together with Black. We've been reading on what has happened since the rest of my team was captured by the Fifteen.

I am furious Al & Jal have started a true rebellion. It is not what we called the Causes to do and it is going to get us all into serious trouble. We will be lucky if the Fifteen don't instruct the Gray Police to kill us on sight.

Let me get to the point. I've contacted you specifically since you and your partners appear to be some of the few Causes I can rely on now. I have not made any announcement of my escape public yet and I would like to keep it secret for now. For now, we need to establish a meeting place, regroup, and go from there.

I've escaped the Exta Sector to the south. I'm going to continue southward to Kediel Lake in the Binda Sector. I hope you haven't strayed too far from Fanda and can make it there in a decent amount of time. If you get there before I do, wait up for us.

Black and I are traveling together now. So as soon as you reply to this message I will be able to see it right away. Be sure to include any updates or anything I may need to know about the state of the Revolution. I hope to hear from you.

This isn't over yet.

-Bogen

It was impossible for me to contain myself. All throughout reading Bogen's message, I was dancing in place at the desk. When I was done, I pointed at Bogen's closing line. "See, Kay? It isn't going to end like this."

In the heat of the moment, Kay wrapped her arms around me, still hopping with excitement. I didn't object and reciprocated with one arm around her shoulders as I heard her breathe in a sniffle. "You're damn right, it's not! Come on; let's reply." Her voice frogged up with adrenaline and hope.

We released each other and I sat back down. My fingers wanted to go right to the keyboard, but my brain couldn't even focus on what key to hit first. I pulled my hands back and turned to Kay. "You okay?"

"I'm good, yeah." She caught her breath; her voice smoothed out in calm confidence. "Just...relieved."

"You and me both; like you wouldn't believe." I took my hands to the keyboard, determined to take the first step forward to setting things right.

We spent the next half an hour pouring out our information to him; telling him everything we told Dylan and more. A lot of the message was asking what Bogen planned to do about the whole situation. Informing him of Sydney, we wondered if it would alter whatever Bogen had planned before contacting us.

One thing was for sure: whatever he had planned for the long run, he wanted me and my group in on it. Sure, not having Dice and Mika would probably cause him concern. But maybe we could plan out a way to get them back.

I suddenly got an idea and added instructions for Bogen to contact Dylan to the message, and to see if Dylan would be willing to work alongside us.

Our next destination was in front of us—much sooner than we had expected. But we wound up proceeding into it with an empty and guilty air permeating around us. Simply experiencing being forced into separate paths was still a heavy hit to our morale. We had to keep going, though—for us; for the Causes; and for Mika.

We set out, prepared to meet Bogen and organize to fight back. It was one thing to assume Al & Jal would bring about their own end, but having Sydney blatantly step forward to bring full opposition to the Causes brought the severity of the danger to a whole new level. Soon enough, the only people we would be able to trust would be ourselves and each other.

Episode 6: What it Takes

Our journey to Kediel Lake was a tense and unsettling experience. Throughout the four days it took us to get there, we bore witness to the Revolution's dissipation into disarray and chaos.

During this time, Al & Jal created an official name for their band of rebels: "Zealots."

With Al & Jal orchestrating attacks on various landmarks throughout Eden, their gang and its name became well-known. As their actions escalated in severity, people began wondering how long the Fifteen would stand for it before taking drastic action.

All the while, Bogen, Dylan, and I continued to keep in touch. Although Bogen wanted to stay low for a little while, the news of Sydney and the Deserters prompted him to speak out and issue an alert. The Causes were pleased to see Bogen was back in action to lead the charge against the Fifteen. However, some were not sure if returning to the open was a smart thing for him to do. Now, Al & Jal could set their sights on him when it came to criticizing the actions of the Causes.

At this point, every Cause was aware of Sydney and his intentions. The Causes who still supported the Producers had a lot to say about the Zealots and the Deserters. It went so far; Black herself banned "Al & Jal" and "Doctrine" from even accessing the forum. She also demanded all discussion concerning the Zealots was to go in one single subforum and a subforum for the Deserters likewise. These new developments ate up so much of the Causes' attention; barely any of the rest of the forum was being posted in.

The subforum for the Zealots quickly turned into a recruiting ground for the rebellion. Threads calling for vandalism and ambushing police became hotbeds of debate, name-calling, and threats to each other. The moderators had to swat down any attempts at turning more Causes to violence through the forum. In such a short time, over two-thousand Causes wound up banned from the forum entirely.

The subforum for Deserter discussion wasn't a pretty sight either. Fear, uncertainty, and blame-shifting were turning our once-solid sense of unity and purpose into a disgusting heap of mistrust and regret. Although the Deserter subforum didn't see nearly as much traffic, simply reading the titles of the topics could drag one's heart down enough to give up entirely and go home.

All in all, it did not take long for the once-orderly Revolution to turn into a scene of uncertainty and discord.

One of the worst parts of the whole situation was how the citizens of Eden were reacting. With a newfound reason for the people to be wary of Causes, it became troublesome to find Contacts, clued businesses, or any comfortable place to rest. With the Zealots clouding the Causes' good image, a number of inns stopped serving to Causes altogether. It was unbearably frustrating to know the citizens shifted from helpful to unfriendly in the span of only a few days, all thanks to the actions of the Zealots.

Fortunately for us, Al & Jal failed to realize Vade and the Gray Police were always a step ahead of their rebellion. Naro, as well, stepped up security throughout entertainment hubs in the Fanda and Lucra Sectors. An attempt at trashing the Grand Amphitheatre was squashed within minutes when both Lucra and Gray Police sprang into action. Over thirty Zealots wound up in custody, but captures and arrests only bolstered the Zealots' ire.

Another group of Zealots were found terrorizing neighborhoods in the Doma Sector in order to draw police out. Although fewer Zealots were captured there, Cenia and Vade announced residents were now permitted to fight back against Zealots if police were not present; promising protection through neighborhood watch statutes and self-defense laws.

Despite arrests and other hurdles, it seemed nothing was going to change the Zealots' course. The Causes were going to have to act around the carnage Al & Jal had created.

There was only one point in time Kay and I were able to contribute to the Causes. Even though our own situation was dire enough, the opportunity presented itself and we took it.

The opening happened on our way to Kediel Lake…

Day 84

I

Kay and I diverted our course from the river when we came across another set of train tracks. This section of rail crossed not only the river, but the Doma-Binda border as well. The decision to detour was fueled by the fact we were running low on food. Although I had speared a few fish in our travels, and we plucked some fruits and berries from trees and bushes, we still needed to stock up on supplies in case we wound up in a position where foraging or fishing were out of the question.

I recalled back to the last day I spent alone during the Revolution as I jingled the last twenty-four arna in my hand. I distinctly remembered having had 182 arna in coins the morning of the sixty-third day. "So much for 'self-control and knowledge of my priorities,'" I muttered to myself.

Kay exhaled, fatigued. "What are you bellyaching about now?"

I grunted, knowing I was as irritated as I was about the situation with my supplies. Gripping the coins tightly in my fist, I pointed to my gut. "Trust me: the only aching from this belly is hunger." I put the coins away.

Kay sighed again, appearing to relate. "Right."

I brought my bag out in front of me and sifted through it, hoping to find any food we might have overlooked. The first thing I placed my hand on was the series of glass vials provided by Zoe.

I looked to Kay as she stared at my bag from the corner of her eye. "Still thinking about those?" she asked.

"Yeah." I pulled a vial of red gel from my backpack. "This one especially."

Kay took the gel from me. She pulled the cork from it and smelled the contents. Her face wrinkled into a confused state. "It's like straight rubbing alcohol." Kay paused, pensive, before replacing the cork. "I still don't trust it since it probably came from the Fifteen."

"I wish we could, though." I sighed.

The two of us fell into a silent stroll. I kept digging into my own mind to find something to talk about to pass the time. But everything coming to me involved recycling topics from before. We had shared quite a lot about ourselves. So it was not going to be easy to stay away from deep and personal stuff if it came to talking about something new.

A glance to Kay's bandages put the idea in my head to bring them up. Ever since her outburst at Zoe back at the Delta, it had always remained as the unspoken rule to leave her injuries out of conversations. Since the two of us were now closer, it seemed like I could chance to bring it up.

Before I could ask, Kay had something to say. "I have a confession."

It was good of her to relieve the silence. "What?"

"I hope it won't be a big deal to you. But, the other day, when you showed me your scar and I acted surprised, I really wasn't."

"No?"

She shrugged and chuckled. "Mika told me about it."

I laughed, imagining the scene. "Really? What a little rascal."

Kay seemed thrown off. "You didn't tell her about it in confidence, did you?"

"Nah," I answered, taking the red gel back. "Even if I did, kids her age aren't good at keeping secrets anyway."

Kay smiled; a dreamy reminiscence shone in her eyes. "Yeah."

I saw this as my opening. "Speaking of secrets: I hope you don't mind me asking. It's just you and me, after all. But what is the deal with those bandages?"

Kay stopped and the chipper air surrounding us dissipated in an instant. I turned, waiting for her. Kay's lips were tight as she closed her eyes and hung her head. She reached her right hand across her waist and ran a finger along her dressings.

A shiver clasped my heart as the silence between us grew longer. My mind repeated to itself, *I asked too soon.*

Kay grunted and shook her head hard as if she was trying to shake a bad memory out of it.

I dared to speak. "What's the matter?"

With a jerking sob and a sigh of reluctance, she spoke. "I really *want* to tell you…"

"But?"

Kay did not resume speaking and continued forward.

I remained standing still until Kay was well ahead of me. My eyes stayed on her as the shuddering in my chest subsided. "I seem to be doing *everything* too soon with her," I mumbled under my breath.

I had always felt there was a lot more to Kay's bandages than most would think. I knew when the time came to talk about them; there would be a lot of listening for me to do. I could at least take comfort in the fact she *wanted* to tell me. When she would was up to anyone's guess.

II

The tracks continued on through a residential district in the southern part of Binda. This area was no different from any other housing district. Along its wide dirt roads, blocks of uniform homes were lined up neatly; five meters from the street and three meters apart from each other. A stone walkway stretched from the front of each house to the road with the property's lawn hugging both sides of it.

These residential zones also had shops peppered throughout

them. We kept our eyes open for a convenience store or a café; any place to buy some food. Since we were short on arna, we had to be ready to barter the vials of medicine if it came down to it.

As we passed by a tree, I glanced up to see if it bore any fruit. Among the branches and leaves, I caught sight of a large bird's nest. Shuffling over to prepare climbing, I said, "Looks like this tree's got some eggs for us!"

Harsh and direct, Kay responded. "Um...no!"

I had one foot on the tree trunk; dangling by my arms from the lowest branch. "No?"

Pointing to the nest, she hit me with a disappointed glance. "Momma bird is waiting for her baby birds. Don't do it."

I dropped off the tree. "How is this different from chickens?"

"Chicken eggs are specifically farmed for food. A single farm hen can make a dozen eggs in a couple of days." Kay folded her arms, leaned on her hip, and looked up to the nest. "The eggs in that nest are the only ones the momma bird has. They're her treasure. Leave them be."

I smiled wide and softly pounded over my heart. "Agh! You got me right here! You crushed my appetite for eggs—*not* an easy thing to do!"

Kay relaxed her arms and started walking ahead. "Come on, let's go find a shop."

Continuing through the neighborhood, we had to keep a watchful eye for Gray Police while looking for food. Unfortunately, being new to this section of town, we were going to have to stop and ask for directions.

Before we resorted to asking, however, we decided to follow a few streets at random with the aim of simply stumbling across one. Hopefully, we would be able to buy provisions and get back onto the tracks before being spotted by authorities.

Trying to act casual and remain calm, we navigated the quiet Binda Sector neighborhood. Kay and I stuck close and watched our sides. We could not turn to look behind us for fear of looking suspicious. The way Eden was at the time, it would not take long to run into trouble.

We soon reached an intersection with a small food market on the opposite side of the street. Kay was glancing in all directions. "Everything looks clear," she said.

I looked both ways before attempting to cross. As I stepped away, Kay grabbed my backpack and pulled me back.

"What's going on now?" I asked.

She was trying to hide well behind me. "Look who's coming out of the store!"

We scrambled behind a nearby wooden fence, keeping an eye on the storefront through the cracks between the boards.

A young man dressed in black and sporting lengthy blond hair emerged from the corner store with a wide smile across his face. He was stuffing food into his bag as he turned away, oblivious to our presence, and continued walking.

"It's Albion! I'd recognize his stupid shirt anywhere!"

"What's he doing here? Do you think the other Zealots are with him?"

Before I could answer, Albion looked to the store again. Soon after, two other young men and a youthful girl came out to catch up with him. One of the two males was much taller and more muscular than Albion and the other boy. The girl standing with them was petite, standing the shortest of the four of them. A hooded pink top and shawl draped over her head and shoulders. Tight, brown pants and brown shoes finished her outfit.

"Check out *that* crew!" Kay remarked.

We watched as the four of them conversed.

"They're planning something; another attack?"

Kay seemed confused. "An attack on what? There're no important landmarks for several kilometers around here."

My eyes closed briefly. "You're right," I nodded. "I guess the question now is whether or not we should follow them."

Kay objected. "We still need to buy food!"

I was much more concerned about what Albion was up to. "We can't lose sight of him," I argued. "We can come back for food later. This place isn't going anywhere. But if we let them go, there's a good chance we won't run into them again.

"You're hot about him upstaging you at the Delta."

"You're damn right I am," I admitted. My chest flared and shuddered through a deep breath. "I say we return the favor."

Kay groaned, dousing my poorly-timed fire. "And you expect us to when we are outnumbered...how?"

The blind impulse in me was defeated, but it still didn't shake the fact Albion's crew was behaving in ways far beyond the threshold of suspicious. A rushed pace coupled well with their repeated glances to their sides and behind.

"We have to follow them," I insisted.

Although she knew I was right about the situation at hand, she grumbled about our change of course. "F-o-o-d!"

I chuckled as I took her arm. "Come on. Let's go!"

"F-o-o-d," she persisted, slightly more serious.

We had to be quick, so I gave Kay ten arna, and she dashed into the store for some sweet bread. As she shopped, I continued keeping my eyes on the Zealots. Kay was in and out of the store within a minute, keeping a low profile with a fluffy bun sticking out of her mouth. Her eyes beamed with contentment before turning to check on Albion.

The group of Zealots had a good lead, but was not far enough ahead to lose us. It was easy to tail them, but we still had to proceed cautiously through the neighborhood. My desire to throw off whatever they were planning was more than enough to keep me focused on their path and prepared to act if we needed to. *You're mine now, you little bastard.*

III

Kay and I followed Albion and his entourage all the way back to the train tracks. Once there, we remained hidden behind a tree as we watched the crew of Zealots walk around the vicinity.

We could hear them talking, but could not make out any words. As they conversed, the Zealots gestured to one another, looking all around and pointing to one thing after another.

I whispered, "Come on, Albion. What are you planning here?"

The two of us carefully watched the team of Zealots. The smaller boy had taken one of their bags and was distancing himself from the rest of the group. The girl was discussing something with Albion as the muscular youth rustled through a duffel bag. After a few moments, he pulled out some thick wire and a large wrench.

My eyes went wide. "Whatever they're planning, it's about to go down."

I could see Kay turning her face to me out of the corner of my eye. Once her stare met my profile, she coyly said, "I think you forgot to add: 'Not if I have anything to say about it.'"

"In most cases, you'd be right," I mumbled, turning to meet her gaze. "In this case, though, it's not that easy. We've already established we're outnumbered; gotta play it smart."

Kay sighed. "There you go with the excessive thinking again!"

"Come on," I defended, glancing to her, "you should know me well enough to see I don't discount any possibilities."

"It feels weird. You were on fire to catch Albion, and now you're hesitating."

"*We're* hesitating," I corrected.

"Fair," she replied with a single nod.

We turned back to pay attention to what was happening on the tracks. Unfortunately, the moment I looked out, my eyes met those of Albion's in the distance.

He raised a hand and shouted. "Hold it, everyone!"

The girl asked him, "What's going on, Al? What's wrong?"

His eyes locked onto mine. "We've got company."

Kay peeked over my shoulder. "This is bad, right?"

I quivered. "I don't know yet. He's coming over to us alone."

I realized I had spoken too soon. The girl scurried to catch up to Albion, and the bulky male was making his way toward us from another angle.

"Let's run!" Kay advised.

"Too late to run," I muttered, shaking my head.

Albion's confident voice sounded out, confirming our presence. "Well, well, well; of all the people to find behind a tree."

I rolled my eyes and tried a tough face. "I know, right?"

Albion felt sure of his influence. "Did you track me down to join the rebellion?"

"Ha!" I huffed. "Get serious!"

His arms spread wide with an arrogant tilt in his neck. "Legitimate question, legitimate question." Albion's casual attitude was making me nervous.

Kay whispered in my ear. "Hey, Brigg, muscle boy is going back. You can refrain from soiling yourself."

I turned to her, relieved to hear it. "Funny."

Albion laughed as the girl in the pink shawl approached. "I see the two of you are still getting along. Where are the other two?"

Kay countered with a question of her own, keeping our business private. She pointed to the girl. "Jalako, I presume?"

The young beauty sighed and stamped her foot, reaching out to shake Kay's hand. "I think I've lost track of how many people have presumed wrong!"

Kay apologized. "It's an easy mistake, considering."

"You're telling me!"

Despite the tension, Albion introduced us in a calm and mature manner. "This is Memento. If you remember the name and what she did, I'll give you two arna." Showing he was not just talking, he pulled two arna coins out of his pocket.

Having a decent memory on names, I had the answer. "You helped at the bridge back in Pata."

Albion's brow rose as his smile crept. "I honestly didn't expect you to get it right." He gave the arna to me.

Kay pointed to the larger male. "So Tricky is over there?"

"No," he replied. "Tricky is farther down the tracks."

Even though I knew it was going to open the door to conflict, I said the next thing on my mind. "What's he doing over there?"

Memento interrupted before Albion could answer. "You sure are nosy, aren't you? It's official Zealot business!" Though spoken with an articulate, haughty sneer, the high pitch of her voice caused her words to sound almost musical.

I chuckled. "'Zealot Business'? That's a new one."

Albion turned the nature of the answer around. "If you're so curious, why don't you come see for yourself?"

I folded my arms as Kay gathered our things up to move again. "Letting Causes see what you have planned? Awfully confident, aren't you."

"I figured since there are only two of you and four of us, you can't stop us anyway."

I was unfazed by his sharp comment. "Confident, are we?"

He laughed, pointing to the muscular young man. "Pibs over there could take you down real fast. If you know what's good for you, I recommend you keep your distance and watch the show."

I spaced out for a moment as the images flashed one by one through my head.

A burly youth blocking a door.

The doorknob landing at my feet.

The panicked expression on the young man's face.

And posting on the forums to thank him for aiding the Causes out of the Gateway Inn.

"Pibs…" I whispered.

"What's with him?" Memento asked, nudging me.

Words accompanied the memories. *"Well, this is probably the end of the Revolution for me."*

Deeply concerned, Kay shook me. "Brigg, what's wrong?"

A lot of thoughts raced and created a conclusion I had no time to explain. The next words from my mouth served to shock everybody. "Pibs is a Deserter."

Kay responded, almost in a scream. "What did you say?"

Albion was intrigued. "What's this?"

I broke from my entranced state and began an attempt to explain. I turned to Kay, who would understand my opening statement. "Kay, do you remember what Dice said about Zoe?"

She nodded. "Yeah, she was captured in Pata, and now Sandra has her as an on-foot medic."

Hearing the name of one among the Fifteen, Albion blasted, "*Sandra?!* What are you talking about? What Zoe? What medic?"

I went back to the subject of Pibs. "That isn't important—"

We were interrupted by shouting from farther down the tracks. The outburst had everybody's attention. My first reaction was to run out to the tracks to see what had happened. Albion, Memento, and Kay followed close behind me. My rival demanded. "Are you going to tell me what you're talking about, Brigg?"

Still running off of my presumptions, I replied, "I'll explain later. All you need to know: Pibs is *not* on your side."

"I'll believe it when I see it."

We stepped back onto the tracks and looked in the direction of Tricky and Pibs. "Oh, you can't be serious!" Albion exclaimed.

Not only did we see Tricky flattened out on the ground, but two other figures were standing alongside Pibs. All of the equipment Tricky was using was flung to the side of the tracks. Within seconds, their eyes met with ours across the fifty meters of track separating us. The two men accompanying Pibs stood as tall as he did and were dressed in broad-shouldered gray cloaks.

Albion roared at me, pointing down to the cloaks. "Who are those people?"

I was civil with my response. "I'll have to explain it to you later. Getting away is more important right now!"

Kay jeered, "I think they're after you, Mister Zealot Leader."

Albion huffed. "You'd better have a good explanation."

"Don't look at me," I defended as I turned to start running. "If I hadn't been here, you would've been on your way to the Fifteen's open arms right now."

Albion countered. "Don't even *think* that makes us a team. As long as you're still clinging to the Producers, we're enemies."

"Same here," Memento added.

No matter what we said to each other from that point, the facts remained the same. The objective was to escape now and explain later. Although Pibs and the cloaked men gave chase, it was easy to evade them given the distance between us when we began to escape.

We ran all the way back into the residential area. Once there, we backtracked to the store to hide for a while, as well as gather food supplies. We managed to buy enough food without having to barter the medicine or hit up the Zealots for arna.

A passing thought hit me once the coast was clear. *Why did I even say anything?*

Kay noticed my fallen expression; responding with a glance asking without words. Since Albion was walking in front, I gestured my answer to her: a thumb-point toward Albion; turning the thumb to myself with my other hand puppeting a mouth; ending with a roll of my eyes and a gentle slap to my forehead.

Her mouth wrinkled and eyes relaxed to a lazy gaze of understanding. She nodded with a wide shrug, as if to say, "It is what it is."

It bothered me trying to figure out what possessed me to help

Albion at the time. I rolled with it, though, praying I would not regret it later.

IV

The four of us returned to the river and continued to travel alongside it until dark. All throughout, I told everyone where I had met Pibs before. I recapped the entire story for Albion and Memento while Kay waited to hear what had happened after she escaped the Gateway Inn. Kay knew I was more aware of the finer details from the escape.

With Zoe and Pibs as prime examples, we could determine the Deserters began being assembled as early as the Ordeal of Pata. Although this idea contradicted Sydney's announcement on the train, it was hard to offer any other explanation.

The fact Zoe and Pibs were captured long before the booby-trapped train ride made me believe there were still some kinks in Sydney's new act. As with anything else concerning the Deserters or the Fifteen, I felt some information was being made up or left out simply to confuse and mislead the Causes.

We had a lot to consider about the Ordeal of Pata. From the trap at the hotel, to the unconventional police presence; to the squeeze from Riley and Cenia with the cut train services and curfew; we all, as Causes, saw so much more from our perspective than the general public did. However, even with all of the information between our parties compiled and discussed, some pieces were still not fitting together. The details we were looking for had to have been nestled within whatever transition from Cause to Deserter entailed. Of course, none of us were willing to try and encounter the transition directly.

"Overall, I must admit I'm impressed," Albion complimented, poking at the campfire. "You're the last person I'd expect to be filling me in like this. You're looking for a favor back, are you?"

"Not unless you offer without strings," I replied. "I more or less helped you out of impulse. I said the first thing that came to my mind when I heard his name."

"I was as surprised as you were," Kay added from within our two-tarp shelter.

Albion turned his head to her, grabbing his long hair to keep it away from the fire. "Regardless of surprise, Brigg did everything he needed to in order to pull all of our butts out of trouble." Albion let out a sigh, sounding almost desperate. "It's no wonder the Causes look up to you. You had some balls stepping out there back at the Radio Tower."

I read into his tone. "If you're trying to butter me up to side with you, you're mistaken."

Albion acknowledged my perception through the bark in his reply. "Don't be so high on yourself! You're still stuck on the Producers' ways."

My arms briefly flung upward. "*Somebody* has to be. The Producers encouraged us all to act like adults; display diplomacy, order, *maturity*. Right now, you Zealots are looking like nothing more than petulant children throwing a temper-tantrum because things didn't go the way we expected it to."

He fired back, cranking up his smug sneer. "And the Causes are acting like one-playbook dummies who want to keep trying the same thing over and over, and expecting a different result."

"We could have found another diplomatic angle."

Albion sputtered and stammered in sarcastic, exaggerated disbelief before mocking back. "Were you even *listening* to the radio? Have you been paying *attention*?! There *is no more* 'diplomatic approach!'"

My bursting shout echoed through the trees. "Of course there isn't! You snuffed out those chances with your stupid power trip and these ridiculous Zealot activities! If you keep doing what you're doing, though, the Gray Police and the Deserters will catch up with you. I'm not sticking around to go down with you. Kay and I have more important things to do on top of trying to keep morale high."

He swiped his hand toward me. "Keep your Causes and your morale! All I care about is bringing the truth to light. We chose a new method, and we're sticking to it."

"Oh yeah? Well, for your information: your new 'method' is going to get everybody a one-way ticket to the Labor Fields!"

Memento exited the shelter and continued to speak. "On the contrary, Brigg! In your own words, you said the captured Causes have been turning up as Deserters."

Thinking fast, I batted back. "Yes, the captured *Causes*. I'm not sure what they're doing with the *Zealots* they get their hands on. I see the fields in your future."

"An interesting argument." Albion nodded, tilting his chin.

Kay emerged from the shelter and over to the campfire, sitting next to me.

I calmed as best I could, then continued. "Since you declared the Zealots to lead something more like a rebellion, I'm sure the Fifteen have different plans for your kind."

"Especially with all the ruckus and destruction your party's been carrying out," Kay added.

"Be that as it may," Albion protested, "the Zealots will stay as-is. We'll make the Fifteen talk—"

I cut him off, repeating his words in a ho-hum tone accented with a rolling of my eyes. "...Even if it means turning Eden upside-down to do it. Yeah, we know."

One eyebrow lifted. "Don't get cocky with me! Just because I stole your thunder back at the Delta doesn't mean you have to mock what worked."

Memento supported Albion's comment with a laugh and a pat to his shoulder.

I had to shift the conversation before he could rub it in any more. "Speaking of which, what makes you think your little power trip is going to last much longer?"

"Well, I'm trying to bring the Zealots together in a way to not only increase our numbers, but our unpredictability. I tried back at the tracks this afternoon."

Kay leaned in, meeting Albion's eyes over the crackling fire. "What *were* you trying to do, anyway?"

Albion threw a stick in as Memento excused herself for a moment. "I don't really want to get into it, but thanks for saying something about Pibs before I had a chance to fill him in on the *whole* plan. Let's say simply ransacking landmarks and ganging up on police is not quite having the effects we were hoping for."

I raised my tone to bring out a sense of ridiculousness to his argument. "It's only been six days since the meeting. Did you honestly expect immediate results?"

"Yeah."

"That's absurd!"

He folded his arms, frowning. "Bold claim. Why?"

"If you knew *anything* about the way the Fifteen operate, you would've known better!"

"Oh, so you're the *big expert* on the Fifteen all of a sudden?"

I was back to shouting. "I said no such thing! I meant it's impossible to know what the Fifteen are planning. Our enemies are more 'unpredictable' than your Zealots could ever hope to be. The whole thing with Pibs should've told you the Deserters and the Fifteen are a step ahead of us. Or *you*, at least."

"Then all we have to do is catch up. We need to try more extreme things if we want the Fifteen to stop for even a minute to take us seriously."

"They already *are* taking you seriously! That's why these Deserters even exist in the first place!" It was becoming a chore trying to convince him the Zealots were on the wrong path.

Albion gritted his teeth, fully aware I was making sense.

I continued in a calmer tone, leaning my head forward into my hands. "You need to understand. The Fifteen are extremely meticulous. Everything they do is so carefully planned out; it's as if everything we do is what they expect. It's almost frightening."

"You're intimidated by them?"

A memory from the Radio Tower caught me. The first time I heard the sound of Naro's voice resonated in my head. *"Welcome, Revolutionaries!"*

I nodded, "'Intimidated' is a good word for it."

"Same goes for me," Kay supported.

Memento returned, having heard our last few statements. "I can only imagine what it was like stepping up to Naro."

I lifted my head with my eyes wide as I threw another stick into the fire. "No, you can't. Trust me: there is no feeling like it."

"Can you describe it?" Albion requested.

All eyes were on me as I pieced together a statement to satisfy their ears. "It's like…"

"Yes?"

"It's like you're talking to somebody who you feel could crush you under their little finger. You get this gut feeling anything you say could barrel you into irreversible trouble. The Fifteen have a system where everybody is designated a place in this life, right?"

"Right," Albion mumbled, fixed on my words.

"Well," I resumed, "dealing with Naro was like gambling away our place in Eden's structure, running the risk of turning it into life in the fields. The scariest part about it: knowing he has the power to do it."

Kay shuddered; her lip curling in reviled discomfort.

"So, correct me if I'm wrong," Albion responded.

"With pleasure."

"That's how we should feel about the Fifteen at all times?" he asked, paying careful attention to his phrasing.

I prodded the fire with a broken branch as I repeated his question to myself. It was then I remembered another thing Naro said back at the Radio Tower:

"This...is not going as we had predicted."

Hearing the memory, I felt my argument made more sense. The Fifteen's ability to plan things on a grand scale seemed even more prominent with the recollection of Naro's words.

I sat up and glared into Albion's eyes as I answered him with my greatest sense of conviction. "Yes, we should fear the Fifteen."

Albion laughter burst out as though it were an attack. It startled Memento and Kay, as well as heated my blood enough for my fist to clench. "That's *exactly* what the Fifteen want!" Albion declared.

"This I gotta hear!" Kay grinned.

Albion obliged her, standing up and walking to the shelter. "As long as you continue to fear the Fifteen, the Causes won't be able to get *anywhere* in relation to the truth. What could you possibly plan on doing once you approach the Fifteen again now since talking is even risky?"

"'Pretty please' them into submission?" Memento sneered.

I took my eyes from Albion and stared into Memento's snide expression. "Of course not! We have to take our time creating our *plan*. Whatever we decide to do will have to be put together with an attention to detail rivaling the Fifteen's."

"Is this guy serious?" Albion called back.

Kay stood up to defend me. "You need to knock it off!" She paused and pointed at me. "If it wasn't for this man's thinking, we would not be sitting here around this fire. You'd probably be in Exta, at the Fifteen's feet, groveling, dumbfounded as to where you went wrong."

"You wouldn't've known about Pibs until it was too late!"

Albion returned to the campfire with a bag of nuts. He plucked one out, tossed it into the air, and caught it in his mouth, stalling for a comeback. Memento sighed to cover her partner's turn to speak. "He's still not getting it, Albion."

He gestured with his hand forward, waiting to swallow. "It's all right, Memento. They're right; I'll give them the point."

I smirked. "As I was saying."

"About…?"

"Planning our next moves."

Albion grabbed a small handful of his nuts. "Yes, go on."

To hide our plans to meet with Bogen, I made something up to tide over their curiosity. "I've been thinking about the Deserters and how they're connected to the Fifteen. Since they're working together, I'm figuring the best way to get to the Fifteen at this point is through the Deserters."

"Interesting…" Kay replied, leaning in toward me.

I did not expect Kay's response. "You think so?"

"I think so." Memento agreed.

"You're siding with him?" Kay asked.

"I didn't say that," she corrected. "I'm saying it is a useful idea to commit to memory."

I did not want to reveal I had made it up. However, Memento's unexpected support of the concept made it seem plausible. If one Zealot could agree, then maybe I could get Albion in on the idea. Perhaps, if I could convince them to take action toward the Deserters instead of Eden's landmarks, some order could fall back into place. In order to do so, I had to make the Deserters a more appealing target for Albion.

"Perhaps," I continued, feigning thought, "by organizing your Zealots to focus on the Deserters, maybe you could get information on how to really get under the Fifteen's skin."

He was giving it thought. "It *does* sound nice. But what are *you* going to be doing?"

"Just gonna keep being Causes," I replied. "There's no reason for us or any of our friends to be engaging the Deserters or the Fifteen. We'll be fine with avoiding them."

"Yeah, let's see how long *that* lasts you before you're in cuffs," he snorted.

"I'm not claiming it's safe or foolproof, but Kay and I have our own things to take care of. So as far as the Deserters go, they're all yours; have at 'em."

Albion jumped to the conclusion. "Then it's settled! I'll get some of our side to focus on them. The rest will stick to escalating the rebellion."

I exhaled through my nose, trying to keep from growling.

Albion caught my reaction and jumped on it fast. "Come on, Brigg. Did you honestly think I'd call the Zealots off of Eden's landmarks?"

My lips clenched. I could only lower my head and shake it.

"Looks like a 'yes' to me. Sure of himself," Memento commented. "Bold move."

I shrugged, now aggravated, but hiding it. "Can't blame a guy for trying, right?"

Albion laughed again. "Look, I'll admit, what you said had some merit. I'd recommend you act on your own advice as well."

I groaned, still sullied by my defeat. "Count on it."

Albion walked over and sat next to me. Memento positioned herself next to Kay and put her arm around her. Albion offered me some nuts, but I refused.

"I'll tell you what I'll do for you two," Albion proposed. "Since you've bestowed all of this great information upon us, we're going to play nice tonight. Be warned, though, after we part ways tomorrow, you'd better not cross me again."

"What do you mean?"

Albion glared and raised his finger between our faces. "Again, like I said before: As long as you're clinging to the Producers, we're enemies. Be grateful I'm showing you this much gratitude."

"I don't think 'gratitude' is the word for it," I muttered.

Memento ambled over to the shelter to prepare for sleep as Albion concluded the conversation. "You're tough—I'll grant you that. But you're gonna have to try a lot harder to steer me away."

Reaching deep down for another approach, I found it in me to grip the front of his shirt and pull him toward me. Albion remained relaxed, knowing well he had the upper hand when it came to exchanges of words. We both knew resorting to violence would not change a single word spoken. We would remain correct in our respective places.

Attempting one last time to drill some doubt into his arrogant skull, I murmured through gritted teeth. "I'll tell you for the last time: If you keep this up, I won't have to *try* to stop you. The Fifteen are capable enough to do it without me."

Albion slid his hand up and wrapped it around my fist. A smug grin crept across his face. "Noted."

I released him. "Let's get some rest. We're busy tomorrow."

"With what?" he asked, standing to retire to the shelter.

I grabbed his shoulder as he tried to walk away, turning him back toward me to look him in the eye. "Why would I tell somebody who I know is going to be my enemy tomorrow?"

"Precisely!" He smirked. "You never should. Smart."

As Albion stepped to the shelter, Kay stood, kicking some dirt onto the fire. She came to me, behind my left shoulder and spoke softly into my ear. "I don't like where this is going. I'm not even sure if we can trust him through the night."

"Same here. The only credit I can give him is he *sounded* sincere about it."

"What should we do?" she asked, stepping over to my side.

I tilted my head, quieting my voice a little more. "There's always sleeping in shifts."

"We *both* need rest, though."

"I know," I nodded. "I'm sure you'll be able to sleep easier knowing I'm keeping an eye on you, right?"

She jabbed me in the back and put a sly, sarcastic tone into her voice. "And I trust you'll have your eyes on me at all times while

I'm asleep, like you did the other day."

"Oh, funny!" I took a beat. "True, but funny."

She gave my back another light smack. "You're asking for it!"

Albion hollered from the shelter. "If you two don't shut up and get in here, I'll be changing my mind about this *real* quick!"

I leaned into Kay as we hurried over. "You sleep on the outside. I'll pretend to sleep and wake you up in a few hours."

Kay rapidly nodded with a focused scowl. Her mind was clearly occupied.

We scurried into our sleeping arrangements. Kay was on the far left with me lying next to her. Memento took position to my right and Albion positioned himself on the far right of the shelter. Nobody spoke a word, and the only sound heard was fidgeting and rustling for a comfortable position. It was not long before Albion's grating snore sounded off.

Memento got close to my ear and whispered, "His damn, stupid snore. I hate it!"

Kay gripped my shoulder and turned me to face her. "Got your arms in your sleeping bag? Wouldn't want your arms wandering around at night, right?" Her grin was playful.

I whispered back, matching the attitude. "This coming from the same person whose arm was draped across my chest."

A shine glinted in her eye as she replied. "True. Except there are two things my chest has that yours doesn't. And a stray arm in this close will get you in trouble."

"You don't need to tell me *that* twice!"

"Now you're being a smart-ass."

"Hey, *you're* the one who brought up the subject of boobs!" I had trouble saying my comeback with a straight face as a small chuckle caught in my throat. It quickly amplified to a gruff snort from the back of my nose.

Kay was fighting back her smile. "I was only saying it's easy for your hands to wind up—"

I cut her off, giggling, "On your boobs?"

A plosive laugh burst from Kay's as she tried to contain herself and finish her statement. "…wind up in an inappro—"

"On your boobs!"

Our laughter became louder and much less controllable. Kay tried again. "Inappropriate—"

"Yo-o-our boobs!" I could feel in my gut I was shifting from joking to flirting. This childish tangent rekindled the wants that flowed through me back at the Riverview.

"Grow up, you—!"

"Bo-o-o-o-obs!"

Albion's snore snapped into sarcastic shouting. "*Yes, talking about boobs is the GREATEST way to get to sleep! Best conversation EVER! I should've thought about that MONTHS ago! I could have avoided many-a-sleepless night!*"

Knowing we were not going to stop laughing any time soon, we excused ourselves from the shelter. We picked up our blankets and returned to the still-burning campfire. "We'll go," I said through a snicker.

"Thank you!" Albion growled.

Kay, still trying to regain her composure, replied to him. "We'll come back when it's—"

"Boobs."

The back of Kay's arm swung hard and fast into my gut. "Knock it off or you'll be sleeping out here."

"Fine with me!" Albion declared.

"Fine with us," I responded, still reeling from the blow Kay dealt. I took her hand and led her back to the campfire.

Kay sounded taken aback. "It's fine?"

I hushed through residual giggling as I distanced the two of us from the shelter. "I wanted him to kick us out."

Kay hummed in disapproval. "I don't understand anything you are saying or doing tonight. What are you thinking?"

"Two things," I answered. "First: I'm not going to deal with Albion's snoring. Second: It's better if we sleep from a distance to give the other time to wake up if something goes wrong."

"I see," she nodded. "So all of the teasing about boobs was just a way to bother Albion?"

"At first, no."

"At first?" Kay's eyes met mine as we sat down by the fire. She did not seem to buy into the idea I got us kicked out of the shelter on purpose.

I still felt like I had to keep any evidence of inner desires hidden. I saw no harm, however, in sharing a bit more about myself. "All right, you win. I made it all up. I needed a mindless laugh."

"That's not like you," she said, cock-eyed.

I hung my head, ashamed. The humor died. "Actually, it is."

"Had *me* fooled. Fill me in. What's up?"

"Lowbrow immaturity helps me cope with stress pretty well. I've been keeping it back, afraid of how you'd react. So a more immature outburst has been long overdue for me."

Kay's eyes narrowed. "I'd say I was graceful about it."

"Until you swatted me in the stomach." I patted my gut.

"Right, sorry." Her eyes led aside innocently. "Got something else on your mind—something other than that arrogant jackass?"

"Mika, actually, to be honest." I paused, watching Kay's face hiccup. "I know this isn't the time to be discussing this, but I can't shake the sensation I failed her."

She put her right arm around me and gave my shoulder a gentle squeeze. "You didn't fail her, Brigg. She was a victim of a sneak attack. Nobody could have anticipated Sydney."

A cold fear shot throughout my body, drawing in a deep gasp. The entire conversation with Albion replayed through my mind, causing me to utter on impulse, "That's exactly my point."

"What?"

I lifted my finger to point at the shelter. "It's like I told him: we should fear the Fifteen. We can't anticipate them. You said so, yourself."

Kay's grip tightened on my right shoulder as she rested her head gently on my left. Surely, this was a friendly attempt to calm me down. However, as relaxing as it was, it was going to take a bit more to take my mind off of Mika and Dice.

"Our only hope," I resumed, "is getting Bogen's help and putting the Causes back on track."

Kay's nostrils let out a quick huff. "That's the Brigg I know."

"Meaning…?" I asked, turning to her with a curl in my lip.

She took her head off my shoulder and leaned forward, elbows to her knees. "You said 'hope.' It's a good attitude we need right now. You had it before, but lately it's disappeared under everything going on."

"You're right, you know. I need to get back to focusing on moving forward; back to *overcoming* the obstacles." I turned to face her. My eyes glanced to Kay's lips, causing the lit wick of interest to burn soft and quiet. Although I still had the intention of experimentally pushing the boundaries of our comfort with each other, the timing still felt poor.

I shuddered and then looked to the fire. *Damn, this shyness is an obstacle, too.*

Kay reacted, curious. "Is something wrong? Anything else you need to say?"

I scowled into the crackling flames, thinking hard about how to approach her question. There was still a heavy boding to the air around us. I had to keep from getting down again.

"Anything else to get out of your system?" Kay pressed.

Man, Shalynn must be looking the other way, because purity's about to go out the window! Did that sound like an invitation, or what?! Say something! Do Something!

I turned to her with a smirk, my mind slipping back to

relaxing. "I'm debating between 'Thanks' and 'Boobs.'"

Of the hundreds of thousands of things I could have possibly said...Dumbass!

Kay turned away with a scoff. "You are unbelievea—"

Well, too late now. Might as well..."Boobs."

She tried to keep from smiling. "It's not funny anymore!"

My brow wiggled; mouth curling suggestively. "Then why are you smiling?"

"Because, I—"

"Have boobs?"

Her laugh puffed out. "I'm going to kick your—"

"Boobs?"

Though it was still whispered and suppressed to keep Albion happy, the immaturity of it all brought our spirits back up. Soon enough, the joke got old. But it was just what the doctor ordered.

The two of us decided to stay distant from Albion and Memento. I left my sleeping bag behind in the shelter and placed my blanket on the ground a few meters from the fire. Kay gathered a few more sticks and threw them in. "We'll let it die from here," she suggested, lying down next to me.

"Do you still want to sleep in shifts?"

She was more relaxed than before. "It doesn't matter. If you want to stay awake, you can."

"Maybe for a bit," I sighed, rolling over to face away.

"All right then. I'm going to sleep."

"Sweet dreams, Kay."

As Kay slipped into slumber, I became lost in thought, gazing into the dancing flames.

"Warmth": It was a strange word to be thinking. Again, thoughts of Kay flooded to the front of my mind. It was all I could focus on.

I thought of warmth again—the warmth provided by the campfire. The heat; the popping; the flickering, and the bright orange luminescence created a sensation of physical satisfaction from the cool summer night. I remembered the look on Kay's face when my finger tipped her head up. The mere thought of it made my heart race again.

Emotional warmth—the feeling I truly desired.

I clutched the front of my shirt as my nerves welled up, feeling the urge to be bold with Kay again. Before I knew it, her sleepy breathing was coursing through my focused ears. The breath I had been holding purged itself from my lungs. I shook my head, perceiving futility in the idea of trying to get closer to Kay.

Any way you slice it, she's not going to fall for you. Just keep things the way they are.

Thinking about it more, I knew well my feelings toward Kay were not exactly romantic. Loneliness, inexperience with girls, and curiosities about intimacy had all been plaguing my mind since the day we were separated from the others. Every inkling of teenage manhood coursing through me wanted nothing more than to see those curiosities realized; the inexperience squashed. I wanted to start things up with her, but knew my emotions were not in the right place. The desires were all physical, and although it was obnoxious to admit it to myself, I knew trying to spark intimacy based on physical desire alone was not a wise approach.

As the hours of thought dragged on and the fire died out, my carnal tendencies toward Kay appeared to fade away with it. Perhaps I lost hope. Maybe I accepted the facts. The fear of more than a slap in the face was something to consider, too. With those thoughts weighing heavy on my heart, I nudged Kay awake. It was her turn to keep watch. After she sat up and confirmed her ability to be vigilant, I rolled onto my stomach and went to sleep.

V

That night was the only chance we had to change the course

of the Zealots. There were equal parts success and failure in the attempt. The advance of the Zealots slowed a bit, which to me bore the scent of progress.

There was still a lot for both sides to focus on, though. Amid the commotion the Revolution was causing, a dangerous enemy had begun to lurk. Sydney's Deserters had finally surfaced.

The big problem with them was any one Deserter looked like a Cause or Zealot. Their only goal was to lure revolutionaries to their capture under the guise of a trusting new face. We took what we learned from the incident with Pibs to warn the Causes of the Deserters' tactics, leaving no detail overlooked.

With the Deserters now on the offense, the subforum discussing them exploded with hundreds of new threads. With it came an awful lot of finger-pointing. The Causes blamed the Zealots and vice-versa.

But we knew the truth, and spared no time in presenting it to the forum. I posted news of what I knew of the Deserters' origins, citing Pibs and Zoe as prime examples. I let the Causes know the Fifteen had been creating the Deserter force long before the meeting with the Producers even took place.

The response Kay and I received took our popularity and credibility to an all-time high; the fact we were a couple of forum head-butters now working in tandem notwithstanding. We were praised by many for factual proof neither the Zealots nor the Causes were to blame for the Revolution's latest obstacle. The truth was we were all Causes at the time the Deserters were being compiled. This left both sides to share the blame.

Despite putting an end to the blame-shifting, it was no time to relax. Our mission to meet with Bogen was still our task at hand. While the wave of forum-wide cheers subsided and everyone went back to their business, Kay and I continued on to Kediel Lake as originally planned.

Kediel Lake was isolated from civilization by about three

kilometers in all directions. It was surrounded by tall trees and hilly, verdant terrain—perfect for resting for as long as we needed.

Once we arrived at our destination, we set up a camp. Our shelter wound up being a large, blue tarp slanted from the ground up to a tight length of rope tied to two trees. The front and sides were wide open, giving us a view of the lake.

Not long after setting up our camp, it started to rain. There was something about the smell of warm summer rainfall that invigorated and replenished our spirits. The fragrance of the purest nature drew us out of our little shelter to lie flat on the grass. There, we simply let the rain soak us from head to toe for what felt like hours. I wound up taking a nap, imagining the rainfall was washing every one of my worries away. The pause of relaxation was everything I needed and so much more.

Kay and I didn't say a word to each other the entire time we were lying there. Even long after the rain died and clouds cleared out, the first sound either of us made was the rumbling of hunger. I prepared another spear and, still soaked to the bone, splashed into the lake to catch a fish.

We were settled into our camp, enjoying the tranquil time together. Neither of us would say it, but we both knew this break to regroup and refocus ourselves was going to come to an end once Bogen arrived, and talk of the Revolution would return us to the pressure of our everyday thoughts.

Day 87

I

Kay had become accustomed to sleeping next to me. Although it appeared to bother her when we would wake up in the morning a little too close to each other, she was becoming more graceful about it. That particular morning, however, greeted me with her elbow knocking me square in the chin as she rolled from one side to the other. After accepting her profuse apologies, I shrugged it off as getting what I deserve for putting my hands on her before.

The two of us lazed around in our tiny shelter, each waiting for the other to mention breakfast. All of our other food supplies had been consumed on the trip to the lake. Thankfully, the fish I had been spearing the past couple of days were enough to keep us from starving.

Our stomachs wound up grumbling one right after the other. After a laugh, we knew neither of us was going to complain about fish again for breakfast.

I slipped from underneath the blanket and basked in the cool morning air as it caressed my chest. The sun was barely up and there was fog wisped across the surface of the lake. I cringed at the thought of how cold the water was going to be.

Reaching over to where I had left my spear, I grasped only air. "Did I leave the spear here?"

"I'm pretty sure you did," Kay replied in a half-awake moan.

As Kay rustled out of the shelter, the voice of another female spoke, scaring the living daylights out of us. "Oh, you're awake!"

We jolted to face the voice. Leaning up against the tree

supporting the left side our shelter's rope was a young lady who had been waiting for us to awaken. Her odd sense of style caught my eye. "Who are you?" I asked.

The girl pushed herself away from the tree with her foot and came toward us. "Depends on who *you* are. We can't trust just anybody with the way things are, right? My partner told me not to disclose my name until we find out who you are first."

My heart rattled as numerous possibilities came to me. Her clothes reminded me of the Deserters, and how Zoe was dressed back in the Delta. The girl was sporting a single-strap black top slung over her right shoulder with a black skirt lifted up to her thigh on the right side and down to the knee on the left. She had her elbows and knees protected with cloth covers. A short, white cloak with a flat collar draped over her shoulders. The thumb and index fingers of her black gloves were cut off; the first thing I noticed when she pointed at us. The outfit was indeed unique; a conspicuous contrast to the gentler colors and more practical alterations seen on the clothing of other Causes. I couldn't even spot a single pocket on her clothes.

Although this could have been either Black or Jalako based on appearance alone, I could not haphazardly spit out a name. If this was Jalako, it would be too dangerous for us to cross the other leader of the Zealots.

I asked her, "Where's your partner?"

She pointed with her thumb. "He's in the lake, spearfishing. I hope you don't mind, we borrowed your spear." On cue, we heard a light splash.

Kay kept her eye on the girl as I turned to get a look. The morning fog was enough to shroud the figure standing in the water from identification. I leaned in within whispering distance to Kay. "I'm gonna go see if it's him. Keep an eye on this girl. If she tries anything funny, shout."

I lurched over to the edge of the lake to observe the man

fishing. Though he was facing the other direction, the two notable differences between Bogen and Albion helped me to identify him: hair length and height. There was no mistaking it—Bogen and Black had arrived.

I left Bogen to concentrate on his fishing and walked back to the girls. I nodded to Kay with a smile before addressing the new female. "It's nice to meet you, Black."

The perky, dark-haired woman seemed pleased. "Brigg and Kay, I presume?"

Kay shook her hand. "You presume correctly!"

While shaking our hands, she spoke with stern instruction. "Let me stop you both right here, though. From here on out, call me by 'Tana'. With the Revolution the way it is, the *last* thing we need is for any Zealots or Deserters to be clued in on who I am. We need to take every precaution we can to avoid dealing with people we can't trust."

"Consider it done, Tana." Kay smiled; thumbs up.

A loud, hoot interrupted the introduction. "Sounds like breakfast!" I said through a delighted huff. My stomach replied with another grumble.

Tana laughed as well. "You get used to him being loud."

Hurried, splashing footsteps faded into the sound of grass rustling underneath a running man's feet. Bogen emerged from the fog, excited, holding the spear with both hands. His good mood shone in the sound of his voice when he called to us. "I see more than one other person standing over there!"

Tana called back to him. "Yes, it's Brigg and Kay! It was them the whole time!"

"Excellent." Bogen looked to us. "Since we found you in the middle of the night, we didn't want to wake you up in case you were somebody else."

I sighed, expressing relief. "We thought you were Albion and Jalako. Looking at the way Tana is dressed and all."

"Hey, come on! Don't mistake me for those troublemakers because I'm not wearing white."

Bogen nodded. "She *does* have a point there. At least she's wearing *some* white; her cape."

There was a pause; a precursor to change the subject. Bogen lifted the spear so we could all get a better look at the fish he skewered. The catch had to have been at least fifty centimeters. He sighed with a triumphant air. "This will definitely feed five."

"Five?" I asked, having done the simple math. "Dylan is on his way too, right?"

Bogen regretfully turned aside and inhaled through his teeth. "Actually, quite a bit has happened on our side. Sorry I couldn't explain any further in my message to you. It was risky to even contact you at all when you consider the Fifteen know of the forum. I'm not going to put it past Eliza to peep into peoples' private messages."

I observed the fish weakening at the end of the spear while still speaking to Bogen. "Smart man; makes sense. But again: five people?"

Tana called out to a person we could not see. "We're ready to explain now. Come on out."

Before we saw anyone other than us, Bogen preemptively excused himself. "I'll leave the next part to you three. I'm gonna get to preparing breakfast."

"What's going on?" Kay wondered aloud.

A voice called out from behind our shelter. "A lot. Then again, you would know better than anyone, right?" The owner of the familiar voice revealed himself to be our missing partner.

"Dice!" Kay gasped in great surprise. "Is it really you?"

He came around the shelter and paced himself towards us. "No, it's some other guy who so happens to wear the same exact clothes I do." The sarcasm was genuine in his voice.

She grinned. "Yup—definitely him!" Kay was happy enough

to embrace the surly boy. Dice was as thrown off as I was about her reaction.

While I was also glad to see Dice safe and in one piece, I only had one question on my mind. Between me, Kay, and Dice, we all knew what the question was. I could see the weathered look on his face and determined his information was going to be as difficult to tell me as it would be for me to hear it.

Dice pulled his dice from his pocket. "I've been debating all morning as to how to break the news to you. I know Mika is your number one concern right now."

"Why the dice?" I asked, put off.

In a dark and unfriendly voice, he replied, "I have my own reasons." He jingled the dice in his hands.

Kay backed away from him. Both of us knew something had happened to him. He clearly did not escape the train before it reached Exta. While I felt the need to sympathize for him, I really wanted to know what happened.

I did not hesitate any further and asked him straightforward. "Where's Mika?"

He huffed. "Sydney has her. It didn't shock me he chose to keep her since Mika told me she had met him before."

A memory flashed of Sydney, still Doctrine at the time, consoling Mika at the inn.

Dice gave us a moment to think about what he said as he spat out his wager for his roll. "Less than ten with two numbers even!" He rolled, letting the dice tumble into the grass. The dice came up three, two, and two. He winced in disdain.

His secretive behavior was unnerving. Here, we had a guy who probably knew more than everything we needed to and he was holding it back with whatever game he was trying to play with us. I lost my patience and yelled. "Stop rolling those damn dice and tell us what is going on!"

Tana left us to assist Bogen as a stare-down began between

Dice, Kay, and me.

Dice picked his cubes up off of the ground and kneaded them in his left hand. "I said I had my reasons for resorting to this. But if you really want it straight…" he paused to lift his hand up to his face. His dice were placed in the three spaces between his four main fingertips. "…This better come up all threes."

Not a chance… I thought to myself.

Dice balled up his fist and flung his dice high into the air. As they ascended, he filled me in on his actions. "I know what to hide from you for your own protection. You fail to realize how important you are right now." The dice landed one after the other. Before we looked at them, he had something else to say about the dice. "Actually, you should consider yourself lucky. These dice are what kept me on the side of the Causes."

I could not believe my own ears. "Are you serious?" I hollered. "You rolled your dice for your options in Exta?"

He responded with a grunt before further explaining himself. "Well, they wanted to convert me to a Deserter at first. When Sydney saw Mika and I were friends, he changed his mind and sent me to tell you he has her." We paused then looked at the dice; three, three and five.

"Knew it," I growled.

"I know you pretty well," Dice continued as he scooped them up. "You tend to overanalyze things, yet act off the fly. So I have to watch what I tell you, or we'll *never* have a chance of getting Mika back. I'm sure you'll understand."

I admit to having no idea what he was going on about. All I needed to do was trust Dice would tell us was everything we needed to know; and nothing more.

II

It came as no surprise for Sydney to recognize Mika, but

kidnapping her and setting Dice free to find me was unexpected. What threw me off was the fact Dylan and Bogen had been in contact with Dice, and nobody was able to contact me and Kay to let us know what was going on.

It was true—going back to what Dice was saying about me knowing too many things—if I had known Mika was taken by Sydney sooner, I would have been trying to track down Sydney rather than meet with Bogen as planned.

According to Dice, when Sydney saw Mika arrive on the train, he started looking for me. He even asked her if Kay and I were on the train as well. Not too pleased to see Kay and I escaped, he decided to hatch a plan in order to find me. He would use Mika as bait and Dice as the lure.

Dice's decisive roll then came into play—his decision on how he would present the news to me. His roll was a split decision as to whether he would lure me right into Sydney's hands or stay true to our side and plan Mika's rescue with us. Fortunately for all of us, luck and fate prepared him to assist us in any way he could.

Dice clearly explained what went on after he was released by Sydney to find me. Since he was afraid of how I would react to the news on Mika, he contacted Bogen only on the assumption he was the missing Producer.

Bogen set up Dylan and Dice to meet.

After Dice told Dylan the situation, Dylan ran off to trail Sydney and left Dice to deliver the news. Dice then contacted Bogen again.

Hearing that development, Bogen got Dice to meet with him and Tana. From there, they traveled together to meet with us.

"So Dylan is tracking Sydney, eh?" Kay asked across the campfire, nibbling at her fish.

"Yes," Tana replied. "We've been doing well on keeping updated with him. He's waiting for the opportunity to kidnap her back for us. On the minus side, Dylan says it isn't going to be easy with Sydney and a Gray Police officer around her all day. Fortunately, he says they're treating her well."

"Wow," I nodded. "He must be pretty close to Sydney if he can tell us those details."

Tana nodded as her serious tone appeared to deteriorate. "Mmhmm. I ran into him recently; the day before my fifteenth birthday! He's so brave and daring!"

"You've met him before?"

Tana sweetly sighed with a wide smile on her face. "He's amazing. He's sweet and manly and heroic and smart and—"

"Apparently admired by you!" Kay interrupted with a laugh.

My brow rose. "He must be pretty awesome if he's got space in your heart."

"No!" Bogen grumbled.

"Please do *not* encourage her!" Dice groaned. "I've heard the story once and I do *not* need to hear it again! Save it for later."

After spitting a bone out, I called attention to the situation. "Getting back to the matter, how long do you think it will take Dylan to get her?"

Dice answered. "Since he says Sydney isn't harming her, there's no urgency. From my side, Sydney told me he didn't care how long it took to find you. He wanted me to lead you to him."

I dug further. "I've been meaning to ask why."

He was succinct and serious. "I think Sydney sees you as a threat to the Deserters. After what happened at the Radio Tower and your recent revelation about the Deserters' origins, everyone seems to think you're as influential as Dylan, Al, or any of the Producers. I'm sure he wasn't going to target you first. But with Mika, it makes going after you more convenient."

Bogen had a question for Dice as well. "Who else is Sydney looking to capture?"

Dice picked the meat off of his section of the fish as he murmured. "Most likely you, Bogen. Basically, anybody I listed a moment ago is top priority of Sydney and the Gray Police."

Kay sounded suspicious. "You seem to know a lot about what's going on here."

Dice had his defense ready. "I want you to know these are all conclusions I've drawn for myself. Everything I said may not be entirely accurate, but it makes the most sense."

Everyone nodded in agreement to Dice's disclaimer.

Uncertainty for the future ambushed my thoughts. Sydney had his sights set on me—and Mika was paying the price for it. I knew it would only be a matter of time before Sydney would send me a message saying: "I'm here, come get the girl."

Distress encroached on my quickening heart. On one side, Kay and Dice knew more than anyone how I would feel if anything happened to Mika. On the other side, Bogen and Tana were counting on me to keep the Causes rallied. I was once again experiencing the feeling of having far too much expected of me.

Tana interrupted my thoughts, ticking away on her laptop. "Brigg, Kay, you two have a lot of fans out there."

"Yeah?" I looked up to see she was accessing the forums.

Tana clarified her statement. "There are four—no—six topics asking where you, Kay, Dice, and 'the little girl' are. Some of those topics are rumors. I'll get rid of them."

I turned up an open, general question. "Would it be a good idea to let the Causes know what's going on?"

Bogen answered strategically. "With Al & Jal still out there with the other Zealots, I don't think it's a good idea to draw attention to ourselves."

With everything going on, it didn't seem quite right to lay low. Nevertheless, we were going to have to trust Bogen's judgment. "Then what do we do from here?" I pressed.

With Bogen's mouth occupied with fish, Tana answered for him. "We need to wait until we hear from Dylan. He's waiting for the right moment to get Mika back for us. We're probably dead in the water if we try to get Mika back ourselves."

"Dylan must really know what he's doing, huh?" Kay was smiling, hoping to get Tana to talk more about him.

Bogen caught Kay's intention and jumped to answer. "Yes, he does!" He then pointed to Kay. "Stop that!"

Tana's wide grin and dreamy eyes shifted back to a countenance of business as she turned her laptop towards us. "Until we hear from him, here is a map of Eden's train system."

"What good is this to us?" Dice had enough curiosity in his tone to cover the thoughts of everyone else.

Tana pointed to a large train station northeast of our location and explained. "We can wait around this area here. Once we hear from Dylan, we'll know where we have to travel next, right? Well, if we have to hop a train to reach where he is, it will save us time if we are already near one."

Her foresight eased my mind, but it couldn't stop me from being at least a little skeptical. "Considering what happened the *last* time we got on a train, is going by train really a good idea?"

Tana pointed out the six train routes exiting the station she marked. "As you can see, only two of the tracks head out west in the direction of Exta and the other four don't. We won't get on any trains headed toward Exta. Simple."

I tried not to be overwhelmed. "Then, we wait for Dylan."

III

We sat quietly for a time as our breakfast disappeared into all of our stomachs. The sound of Tana tapping away on her laptop was the only noise between the five of us. We were keeping to our own thoughts and taking time to think about the road ahead of us.

I was uncomfortable knowing Sydney was looking to flush me out from amongst the other Causes. It made the future cloudy and intimidating to approach. My heart was tight and my head was in a fog of confusion.

Regardless of the fear, everything seemed to be in order, barring a few minor details. Thankfully, we were certain of our next objective. Also, Dylan was taking it upon himself to do the hardest part for us. All in all, we had nothing to worry about besides being where we needed to be at the right time.

Bogen excused himself and sauntered over to the edge of the lake. He seemed to have had a lot on his mind. "What's with him all of a sudden?" I asked Tana.

"Like I said," she replied, "once you know him long enough, you get used to some of the things he does."

"Think he's coming up with a backup plan?"

Tana sighed, "I wouldn't put it past him."

After a few minutes to himself, Bogen invited us to join him by the lake's edge. "Hey guys, come over here and check this out."

We all looked at each other with puzzled faces. Intrigued by his hardy tone, we proceeded over to him.

We stood in a side-by-side line a mere meter from the water. Looking far out over the lake and taking in the scenery, I was once again reminded of my time spent in the Gova Sector. The sounds of Kediel Lake's lush surrounding greenery rustling in the breeze soothed my shattered nerves.

Bogen drew a deep breath before asking the rest of us, "What do you see here?"

Dice responded, "Do you want the obvious answer, or is it something else?"

Bogen scratched the tuft of hair on his chin. "Look down at the lake and you'll see what I'm talking about."

Our focus shifted to the lake at our feet. Since the fog had parted and the sun was shining, a clear reflection was rippling across the surface of the water. "Do you see it yet?" Bogen asked with a coaxing grin.

"I see us," Kay replied. "What about it?"

"Let me ask you all: How many of you still think Hatcher is out there somewhere?"

My answer came without hesitation. "I think he is. But I still feel there's a chance the Fifteen got a hold of him."

Dice then said, "I'm thinking since the Fifteen didn't mention him, he may be hiding or lost with no Contact."

"For this long?" Kay contested. "Nobody has heard from him in about two months. How does any Cause go two months without seeing a Contact?"

Bogen called us all to order, leaving Kay's question to linger unanswered. "What I'm getting at by asking about Hatcher is…" he paused to gather his words.

I took the liberty of finishing his statement. "You wanted to see if we still believed he would show, right?"

"Something like that," he answered, still in thought.

Always the pessimist, Dice asked, "What good is it to think he's out there?"

"Please hear me out on this," Bogen insisted. "All of the other Producers felt Hatcher would arrive in time for the meeting. All the while, we maintained the rules we set to keep Eden peaceful while still expressing our protest." His tone of voice changed to anticipating inquiry. "Now, do the three of you feel as if you've been holding on to those rules?"

I snickered at the question. "Do you think I would've gone to the Radio Tower if I wasn't sticking to the Producers' rules?"

"I'll admit," Kay began, "I only followed Brigg to the Radio Tower for my own reasons. It happened to be for the greater good. As for the rules, I've been doing my best to stick to my own thing while keeping things peaceful."

Dice patted his pocket, allowing his dice to rattle inside. "I haven't broken any rules yet. I've just been lucky."

Bogen laughed. "Well, as long as you think Hatcher is out there, and you're still willing to stay true to the Producer's rules, I think I'll make you all Honorary Producers."

My heart lightened; my breath stilled. This great honor being presented to us was as uplifting as it was unexpected. "Really?"

Kay was pleased as well. "Honorary Producers?"

"Can you do that?" Dice asked.

Bogen emphasized, "It won't be any different than when I chose to start the meeting without Hatcher. Hatcher even said each Producer could act on his or her own; they shouldn't feel the need to hang onto his every word."

Dice hung his head, fixing his gaze on the reflection in the lake. "Honorary Producers." He kneaded the dice in his hand as he repeated the phrase.

Bogen continued. "Let me level with you. The Causes have to stay together and they need somebody out there to continue encouraging them to do so. But I can't do it alone. The capture of the other Producers has demoralized the Causes enough to where Al & Jal…well, you know."

I looked to him, once again taken by the sincerity in his voice.

Bogen exhaled and furrowed his brow. "My point is: Al & Jal have brought the Causes to divide themselves amidst the chaos the Fifteen and Sydney have created. I feel we should make it our goal to bring them back together. Once we do, we can approach the Fifteen from another angle. Another diplomatic meeting is out of the question, though."

"What angle do we have, then?" Dice turned to look at him.

Bogen caught Dice's eye, but gave the answer to all of us. "I was hoping the five of us could figure it out together."

Tana and Kay gasped; Dice glowed with an impressed expression. I, too, felt the impact of Bogen's heartfelt proposal. His way with words had the title of "Honorary Producer" sounding much better than it did at first.

I looked Bogen in the eye and nodded. With little holding me back, I simply said, "I'm in."

Kay smiled, reminiscing as she spoke. "I wanted nothing to do with either Brigg or Dice when I first met them. But I guess it doesn't matter now. The Causes and the Revolution have to be put back on the right track. Count me in."

Tana took the floor next. "Even though Contacts aren't supposed to involve themselves in the affairs of the Causes, you guys are going to have a difficult time without me. I'm in too."

We all looked at Dice, who was still thinking it over. He stood and stared into the lake as he shuffled his dice in his hand. "I can't go this alone and there's nobody else who I can trust. At the same time, I'll warn you, I can't be depended on to be totally cooperative. Will that be a problem?"

Bogen grinned. "We'll talk it out if it comes along."

Dice chuckled, catching Bogen's eye again. He brought his dice up to his face, once again holding each one between each of his fingers as if it were a pose only he could pull off. With a crooked smirk and a gleam in his eye, he announced a wager. "A number between three and eighteen."

My bursting laugh came natural. "We don't stand a chance!"

He threw his dice behind him and waited a moment. Without even turning to look at them, he declared, "I guess I'm in."

Bogen took a deep, relieved breath and thanked us for understanding his position. He was grateful for our acceptance of his offer. In summation to our initiation into the Producers, he had one last thing for us to do. "Look down into the lake again and tell me what you see *now*."

As instructed, we looked again, this time a little harder. Kay spoke first in a manner of guessing. "The future?"

Puzzled by her answer, I looked at her. "Bold words, yes?"

"Bold," Bogen declared. "But she's close. We are the hope of Eden," he replied with a whimsical sigh. "The five of us—plus Mika and Dylan—are the hope of Eden."

My spirit was lifted to a point where I could not help but stare at the reflection on the surface of the lake. Hearing we were the hope of Eden filled me with more confidence than I felt I could handle. I was awash with the sensation we were unstoppable, and the days of the Fifteen's grip would end soon.

Kediel Lake became a place of pride and vanity as the five of us posed in the reflection on the water. We laughed and joked, trying to create a portrait of what five people who declared themselves as the hope of Eden would look like.

The five of us took a long look at ourselves before breaking the pose and taking a seat in the grass. Reassured of our purpose to Eden, we returned to planning our next move.

Of the whole list of priorities we could think of, Albion, Jalako, and Sydney had to be taken care of first.

Sydney had Mika, and was waiting for me to come get her. I hoped and prayed Dylan would be able to retrieve her. However, it would have been foolish to not prepare myself in the event something was to happen to him. I figured since Sydney already resorted to kidnapping, he would not be too hesitant to try other means to lure me out. His band of Deserters served to complicate things as well, since it left us without the ability to trust anybody we did not already know.

None of us were sure what to do about Al & Jal. The Zealots were getting more out of control as each attack took place. They committed themselves to making an example of the Fifteen's refusal to our demands. While the Gray Police were still onto them, resistance against the Zealots only served to anger them further. As a result, Al & Jal were gaining influence at a problematic rate. We had to find another way to slow them down, if not stop them entirely.

IV

The five of us tried to stick to wooded areas and stay out of the view of the public. When we had to cross through developed areas, we kept our eyes open for any Gray Police. Once again, travel had become a tense and taxing endeavor.

Bogen shared with us his unfortunate opinion of the existing panel of Producers being a lost cause. The people with whom he spent so much time planning being captured at the Revolution's most critical moment was deeply upsetting to him. He felt his decision to go on without Hatcher was the worst one he had ever made. Now, seven young people no different than himself were probably suffering because of his haste.

The rest of us tried to cheer Bogen up about the whole Hatcher decision. We told him nobody could have predicted what would happen without Hatcher. To lift his spirits, we told him how the Causes in the Delta were reacting to his speech to the Fifteen over the radio. We let him know every Cause out there felt going on without Hatcher was the right thing to do at the time. Bogen was no guiltier on the decision than anyone else who agreed to it.

Dice had a unique angle to look at it from. He stated we should get used to overwhelming consequences for our actions. Declaring ourselves as the Hope of Eden was a broad undertaking. If we were to hold ourselves to the title we accepted, we had to be prepared to accept anything ahead of us.

It was a dark and uncomfortable realization, but every word of it was true.

Day 89

I

We were about half a day's walk away from the next train station when the anticipated message from Dylan finally arrived.

Dear Bogen and Company,

It was quite a task, but I finally managed to get Mika away from Sydney. Don't kill me, but she's injured. She busted her left arm and leg pretty good when she tripped during the escape from the farmhouse. But she is conscious and in one piece.

If "farmhouse" caught your attention, I guess you know where we are. I don't know why, but Sydney carted Mika to the Terra Sector.

Yes, the Terra Sector.

I have no idea what his intentions are, but it really pissed me off I've had to follow him to practically the middle of nowhere!

Mika and I are hiding out in the basement of another farmhouse. The owner knows we are Causes and is only helping us because Mika is injured. He wants us out of here as soon as she can walk without help.

If you are worried about coming to get her, feel free to know we're pretty far from where she was held. Sydney had her in house B19. After I retrieved her, I carried her all the way to house D24. That, boys and girls, is a long walk! My muscles need time to rest as well.

I'm going to see if I can reason with the owner of this house to let us stay until you arrive. Until then, you should have no fear coming by train since the Exta Sector is in the opposite direction from Terra. Tana is a smart girl. She'll have your way mapped out in no time.

I'll be waiting for you all.

-Dylan

There were sighs and exhalations of relief all round. As for me, I was unbearably overjoyed by this news. The guilt that had been quietly crushing my spirits was easing away, allowing my soul to once again breathe. My mind was clear and ready to hop on board with planning our next step.

Even though we would take the train as planned, the Terra Sector would still take a long time to travel to. Since traffic into Terra was usually non-existent bar supply trains and transported prisoners, only two rails went into the sector. The rail going through the north border of Terra was for people, while the rail from the west sent supplies to and from the farmhouses in the sector. The north rail was our best way in.

Tana pulled up two maps from the Interactive Network. The first was of the train system in Eden and the second was a map of the Terra Sector's House Grid. She explained the course while pointing the whole thing out.

The only way to access the rail to Terra was to first travel all the way north into the Lucra Sector, where the one of the rails to Terra began. Once there, we would head to the nearest farmhouse. According to the grid map, C28 was the closest house to both one of the train stops and the meeting place.

The trip was going to take a couple of days. After ironing out a few more details, we continued forward. From that point on, our only concerns were to avoid the Gray Police and keep updated on Al & Jal's antics. Hopefully, things would not get too out of hand while we ventured to meet with Mika and Dylan.

II

We arrived at East Binda Station at 5:00 pm. It was a busy evening, but the ticket lines were moving smoothly. Uniformed station staff was dutifully cleaning the corridors, causing everyone to pace themselves on and around the wet floors. The fragrance of soap and cleaning agents broke through the less-desirable musk of summer sweat lingering around the crowds.

Our vigilance was unsurpassable as we anticipated a Gray Police officer around every corner. Skulking about the station and darting our eyes about appeared suspicious to the few citizens who noticed us. Nobody said anything, though, perhaps because of fear generated by the actions of the Zealots. We were nervous anyway because the scene could change in the blink of an eye.

After we obtained our tickets, we saw an encounter with Gray Police was close at hand. Bogen was the first to notice them and ordered us to wait.

Two officers were pacing along the platform for the northbound train, both with their nightsticks at the ready. With stony expressions and sure postures, they were clearly waiting to engage anyone who would step onto the platform. The one on the right looked younger and more athletic while the one on the left appeared bulky, toned, and more seasoned in his duties.

Minutes passed as we thought of a plan. Surely, our unconventional appearance would be a dead giveaway we were Causes. Knowing looks would be the key to our discovery was vital to the care we had to take in boarding the train. What complicated things the most was the fact we were carrying most of our possessions with us, indicating we were living out of our backpacks as most Causes were.

Dice gave an idea. "We need one of us to go over there and see how they react to anyone getting onto the platform."

"Only one of us?" Kay asked.

Bogen added, "We need to ease up on the 'Cause look.'"

Kay found fault in the idea. "How can we without leaving all of our stuff behind?"

The words thoughtlessly fell out. "*You* don't need to worry about *your* stuff, remember?"

Her face snapped to a solid glare as Bogen continued to push his version of the plan. "That could work to our advantage."

"What do you mean?" Kay wondered, breaking her stare.

"Of the five of us," he mumbled, "You—Kay—look the least like a Cause right now. You look like a teenage girl recovering from a twisted wrist and a sprained ankle. We can use your look and Brigg's quickness with words in a combination to test the officers' reactions."

"Ooh," I grumbled, grimacing. "Give me a moment; gotta psych myself up."

Bogen pointed at himself and Dice. "The two of us look a little more suspicious, and Dice has his gear, too. This robe I wear isn't for decoration, either." He shook a little bit, letting his belongings jingle around to demonstrate his point.

I took a look at Dice and could somewhat see what Bogen was talking about. But at least Dice's appearance would be a bit easier to fix up to make the idea of him being an average citizen more believable. Bogen's clattering robe would get him noticed as a Cause from a kilometer away, and Tana being dressed mostly in black made her look more like one of the Zealots.

Bogen explained his suggested instructions. "You'll have to empty your pockets into your bag and leave it here with us. Take only your coin purse and your tickets. We need to see if they'll stop *anyone*, or only stop people who look like Causes. Either way, it will help us gauge how to get past them."

I emptied my pockets of all of my small traveling items. My hands and fingers were snagging on my clothes in uncoordinated stiffness as I asked, "What should we say to them?"

"Make something up," Bogen shrugged. He then turned to Kay. "Make sure you limp. It might drum up some sympathy."

Kay confirmed her role, but issued a warning. "If you see us run, try to keep up."

After many deep breaths, we calmed down and prepared to face the Gray Police. Kay started off with an improvised-yet-believable limp—noticeable, yet not over-exaggerated.

As we made our way up the platform, I became short of breath and nervous. I decided to try and interact with Kay rather than engage the police head-on. However, without taking the time to think of my words, I blurted out the first thing that came to mind. "Are you sure you're going to be okay, babe?"

She shot me a nasty look. "Babe!?"

I gritted my teeth. "Sorry, getting into character."

Both of the officers looked at us as we proceeded toward them. The slender guard nodded to the other then continued to pace and patrol. The other officer called out to us in a deep and intimidating bellow. "Can I help you?"

Okay, they're probably checking everyone.

I concentrated on keeping my anxious fit from displaying on my face. "Yes, you can." I paused and noticed there were two trains ready for boarding, to the left and right. "My girlfriend and I are headed up to the Lucra Sector to hit up the Gaming Coliseum. Which of these trains is the northbound one?"

The mustachioed officer pointed to the train on the left while fixing a look at Kay. He pointed at her with his nightstick. "What happened to her?"

"Her?" I was frozen, stuck for an answer.

Kay slapped me on the back of the head. "This genius here backed into me and sent me down a flight of stairs. This little trip is only a fraction of his apology."

Good one, Kay.

The officer chuckled in a reminiscent fashion. "Well, your

train is over there." He pointed again. "Have fun."

"Sure thing," I said with a smile that probably looked as awkward as I felt.

After the officer turned away from us to regroup with his partner, I told Kay to get on the train. Now, I had to figure out a way to get the others past the Gray Police.

When I turned back to the platform entrance, I almost jumped out of my skin at the sight of Dice. He was out in the open and strutting toward the northbound train. Before I could panic, I calmed upon noticing his collar was down, he was not wearing his visor, and looked as though he even took the care to smooth out his hair with his fingers in an attempt to look less unkempt.

Sure enough, the same burly officer called to Dice. "Can I help you, young man?"

I watched the scene unfold as my heart sank into my stomach.

Dice showed no fear in being approached. "Yes, sir?"

"Where are you headed?" The officer had his hand on his holster as he was eyeing him over.

Dice replied to him. "I've got my bags packed and I'm ready for some fun over in Lucra."

His words reached out to me. I joined in the conversation while pretending Dice was a stranger. "You're going there, too!?"

He turned to me, having caught onto my act. "You bet! I even have my lucky dice and everything ready to roll." He then pointed to the train. "I take it that's the northbound?"

"It certainly is!" I declared; acting excited. "You can sit with me and my girlfriend. She's cute; redhead; bandages; you can't miss her."

"Sounds good."

The Gray Policeman showed no sign of suspicion and allowed Dice onto the train with no dispute. Now, all I needed was an excuse to regroup with Bogen and Tana.

After a quick thought, out came a plausible excuse. "I'll be right back. I'm going to go use the restroom here at the station before the train departs."

The younger officer looked to the clock and said, "Better hurry, then. This train leaves in six minutes."

I nodded as I saw Dice vanish into the northbound train. I then dashed away from the platform.

"I can't believe Dice did that!" Tana exclaimed.

"Me neither," I huffed, still trying to catch my breath.

Bogen, having heard the officer's declaration of a time limit, was focused on getting onto the train. "Any way you slice it, in the eyes of those guards, we might as well have 'Cause' written across our foreheads." He looked me in the eye with his point up front. "You're going to have to distract them."

"How do you suppose I do that?"

"I don't know how you should do it; you're the creative one! The only thing I can think of is to scream 'rebels!' really loud and hope both of those guys come running."

I took Bogen's blithering into my brain, combined it with our encounter with Albion, and formed a plan. We would only have one shot, and it required perfect timing and a little bit of luck. All I had to do was await the final boarding call, which would occur two minutes before departure.

We waited, shaking with uncertainty.

When the boarding call came, I put on my best panic face and ran back onto the platform. "Officers! Rebels!"

The two policemen had my undivided attention. "Where!?" the older one asked, urgent and demanding.

"I heard them in the bathroom! They're plotting to do something to the eastbound train!"

My false claim caught their ire. "The eastbound is headed for Fanda's Grand Station."

The athletic one pressed. "How many were there?"

"It sounded like there were four or five of them. I only heard their voices. I don't think they realized anyone else was in there. They left for the eastbound platform before I ran back here!"

They looked to each other with a sense of urgency and mild panic. "Let's go."

The Gray Police left the platform to track down the imaginary rebels. Once they were out of sight, I ran over to retrieve Bogen, Tana, and the rest of our things.

Bogen beamed with delight as we scurried aboard the train. "That's the kind of genius I will always expect from you!"

"Well," I replied, "Don't keep the bar set *too* high on me. Not to say I'll disappoint you, but I'm not perfect."

He shot me a thumbs-up. "Keep it up. We need quick thinking like yours."

We rejoined Kay and Dice and situated ourselves in a semicircle booth. After placing our bags and items in the rack overhead, we flopped into our seats and let the sounds of the train departing lift our anxieties away. "I was on pins and needles the *entire* time!" I announced in one loud exhalation.

"Nice going, stranger." Dice snickered.

Still winding down from the nerves, I followed his joke and lazily put my hand out to him. "It's nice to meet you. I'm Dartmouth; call me 'Brigg.'"

Dice laughed, shaking my hand. "I'm Charles; call me 'Dice.'" He laughed even harder. "Your girlfriend is lovely!"

Tana was laughing along with it. "Maybe I should post a little announcement on the forum!"

"Hey, no filler topics!" Bogen responded, playful, pointing at her with both index fingers.

She wiggled her head in jocular defiance. "I'm admin; I do what I want!"

I wanted to laugh and play along with it, but I wasn't quite sure how Kay felt about the unexpected upgrade in our friendship. She glared at me as she spoke through a playful, sassy pout. "Call me 'babe' again and *you'll* be going down that flight of stairs."

III

Tana was seated in the middle of the booth, hammering away on her laptop. Dice and Bogen were hovering over her shoulders, invested in watching her bang her administrative gavel throughout the Cause Forum. This left me with Kay to enjoy the sunset through the window.

Kay sighed with a lilt in her breath. "It's been awhile since we've actually been able to enjoy something like this." She said it quietly enough to where I almost couldn't hear her over the clattering of the train.

"We?" I asked.

Kay shrugged. "Well, you know, we've been focusing on all of the commotion lately."

My head bobbed with lips in a suppressed pout.

"You've been spending a lot of time thinking lately."

I fogged my window with a long, loud sigh. "I'm really worried about Mika."

"Don't, Brigg," she said. "Dylan has her now. Although, I'd rather have her here with us instead of her going back and forth with people she's only acquainted with, at least she's with someone we can trust."

I exhaled, accepting her position. "I know; you're right." I reached up into one of the front pockets of my bag and pulled out the piece of canvas with the picture of Mika's father on it. I looked down at the drawing for a few moments before slipping it into one of my side pant pockets.

Kay nudged my foot with hers. "Don't sweat it, Brigg. We're going to find him, and Mika won't get dragged away from us again, I'm sure."

"I gave the kid my word; I'm gonna stick to it. Once she's

back with us, I'm not letting her leave my sight again." I made sure to have her eye contact. "Thank you, Kay, for staying with me through all of this. I don't think I could have managed to get back to this point without your help."

Her face flicked with off-guard delight. "I'm not sure what I did exactly…"

I reclined and slung my head across the back of my seat, fixing my eyes to the ceiling. "Trust me when I say you helped keep me on the right path." My voice faded to a mumble as everything around me slipped away in a glossy sheet of beige. The thought of the length of our trip took over my body and dragged it into a lazy slump. The only thing I could process was rest.

For once in a long while, I did not feel like being bothered. It was the first time since the sixty-third day of the Revolution I reverted to the old mindset of self-concern. Deep down, though, I hoped nobody would take my inclinations to ignore them personally. I was simply looking forward to some well-deserved rest. I emptied my mind.

Through allowing the sounds to lull me to sleep, there was one thing I heard that was impossible to let pass. It was the last thing I remembered hearing after shutting my eyes.

Kay's voice…saying the one thing I had never expected her to say so sincerely:

"I trust you."

Day 90

I

The next time I opened my eyes, it was 1:43 am. It was silent and the only light was coming from dim blue bulbs and the moon. I was the only one awake.

I stood and looked around the car. The five of us were the only occupants. Looking at the others, I could not help but smile. Each of them had claimed their own spot in the car to sleep in. The sight of our team sprawled about like we owned the place brought an unexpected feeling of humor to me. "We are the hope of Eden!" I whispered to myself, withholding laughter.

I noticed Tana was using Bogen's robe as a blanket, and got an idea. I retrieved my spare blanket from my bag.

Kay had fallen asleep curved along the semicircle booth. I placed my blanket over her. She shifted in her sleep as I did so. "Thanks," I whispered, "I'm glad I can trust you, too."

There was not a whole lot to do by myself. Alone, I realized the same sensations I experienced in the early days of the Revolution were not all they were cracked up to be. I remembered the peaceful, relaxing, and carefree time; the taste for adventure. But none of that seemed to matter anymore. Those concepts did not have the same effect as they did at first.

I caught my reflection in the window and stared at it for a little while as I thought long and hard about how far I had come. Considering everything, I could not have asked for anything different to have happened to me. Although there had been a lot of hardship and anxiety, I was happy to have the attention and the company of people I could trust; proud to be standing on that train with a mission and people I could call friends.

I amused myself by trying a variety of heroic poses to pass the time. In doing so, I thought back to Kediel Lake when Bogen had us examine our reflections. The phrase "Hope of Eden" whisked its way through my mind again. I took a serious look into those three words.

I spoke to my own reflection. "We are only the Hope of Eden because we've chosen a path. It is a path of resistance; defiance. This path bears a million forks and not a single sign. Every move we make and every choice we decide on will have consequences all of Eden will see and hear. But when the time comes to put it all on the line to free Eden from the Fifteen's grasp, we need to prepare ourselves. When the dust settles and the parties disperse, the truth will be revealed. From those hidden truths, we can start a new era of prosperity and growth. That's how this Revolution must end. And we have what it takes to make it happen."

After speaking, I stopped and continued to lock eyes with myself. Although I felt funny having said it only to myself, I felt relieved and reassured the Causes were doing right.

Being one of the Producers put me just as in charge of things as Bogen was from the beginning. Therefore, it would only be a matter of time before I would be helping lead the Causes down the right path. With the five of us working together as the new band of Producers, I found a new confidence things would turn back to our favor.

After one last, hard look at myself, I returned to my seat. Tana's laptop was within reach, so I accessed the forums.

First, I checked for any private messages. There was no new word from Dylan—or any new messages.

Next, I looked for any new information concerning the Zealots or the Deserters. The only thing new was somebody allegedly seeing Jalako. Within the next few posts, though, his claim was dismissed since the user defined Jalako as a "he."

I sighed and began poking around the latest hot topics.

After all the effort spent boosting my confidence, one glance at the hot topics was all I needed to send my spirits back to the bottom floor. On impulse, I shouted in disbelief, "What is this!?"

Bogen sprang to his feet so fast I could swear he thought Gray Police were on the scene. "What's going on? What happened?"

I could not speak. All I could do was stare at the screen, reading the same phrase over and over as if I was trying to believe it was not there.

"Did you find something new?" he asked as the others slogged into consciousness.

I nodded, almost frozen. I lifted my finger and pointed, keeping it there until everybody was over my shoulders to see.

Sure enough, it was all real. Smack in the middle of the hot topics were the eight words we could have never imagined reading all in the same sentence:

"Bogen and Brigg are traitors to every Cause!"

Making matters worse, the author of the topic was none other than the mystery woman herself: Jalako.

"I thought you banned Al & Jal!" I said to Tana.

She defended herself. "I banned the username 'Al & Jal.' They must also have their names separate from each other as well as their combined alias. A terrible oversight on my part; I'll be sure to ban their names too."

"Please do!"

Bogen opened the topic and scanned it up and down. "From the looks of things, the fact Jalako wrote this will draw more attention to it than any other topic."

We read the original post by her. It was an extensive and detailed post with strong arguments to back up her claims.

In short, Jalako stated, since the Producers were captured and

Hatcher never showed up, it was the Causes' duty to organize a different method for the Revolution. Albion proposed rebellion after the broadcast of the meeting, and the Causes accepted it. Jalako claimed the Causes were thereafter dead and the Zealots were the new force behind the Revolution.

She went on to sling mud at Bogen. Jalako charged him with plotting to stop the Zealots and bring the Revolution to an end without change. She alleged he was trying to regain his influence and start the Causes back at square one. This, Jalako argued, would destroy everything the Revolution was and anybody who was captured by the Fifteen would have lost their free will in vain.

A lot of my past posts were marked when Jalako started to take her sights on me. The reason she targeted me in the first place was because Bogen called out my name over the radio. She claimed I was in cahoots with Bogen's exaggerated intentions, and I should be ignored or be turned in to the Gray Police.

The rest of her post was her ranting of not knowing who the rest of "their little friends" were. Regardless, Jalako put it out there for the Causes to be careful of them too. Of course, she was referring to Tana, Kay, and Dice. Unfortunately for Mika and Dylan, they would later be added to her allegations as well.

"Fortunately," Bogen sighed, "there are only fourteen replies."

"Knowing how the forum is, fourteen replies is fourteen too many," Tana replied with dread in her voice.

Kay added to Tana's pessimism. "This topic can spread by word of mouth at this point."

"Everyone, let's stay calm," Bogen coaxed. "This is something I'm sure Tana can easily take care of."

Tana's hands quivered as she took the laptop back from me. "He's right. All I have to do is delete the topic, and then ban Albion and Jalako. Simple."

We left her to take care of the offending remarks as Dice shared his opinion. "This is obviously a scare tactic. They're trying to generate more uncertainty among the Causes while we are out of the public eye. I'd bet twenty arna Naro is probably having a field day with his daily newscasts since the Zealots are out causing mischief. Channel Three is probably running on 24/7 propaganda, and Al & Jal could be leap-frogging off Naro's pressure to attack us. Just a theory, though."

Bogen had drawn a finger to point at Dice, brow furrowed and ready to speak.

Dice's face hiccupped as he caught something in his words. "Mind you, this *does not* mean you should regret saving the Radio Tower in the first place."

I had to keep us on topic. "So you're saying Al & Jal are taking advantage of our mission to retrieve Mika?"

"No; their timing is just wildly convenient," he said. "We've been absent from the forums for the past few days. The last thing any of us posted was Bogen reinforcing the Producers' way. Any business we've had on the forums has been private messages."

Tana agreed. "We've not been posting while feeling out the situation and focusing on Mika."

Bogen had a solid reply. "You're right, Tana, but it's not like we're dawdling. There's a lot to get done and we still need time to do it. Jalako's playing her cards first."

Tana grumbled. "And with this post alone, we can tell her hand is on fire."

I flopped back into my seat and grunted. "It looks like we're all guilty of 'oversights' today."

A few moments passed before Tana growled with dread. "Guys, I think we have a problem here!"

"What's the matter?" I asked.

"I can't delete the topic—or *anything!*"

"Impossible!" Bogen shouted. "You're an administrator. You *made* the damn forum! You should be able to!"

"I've looked everywhere," Tana wailed in panic. "The option

to delete content has disappeared."

"How could that happen?"

"Eliza has to be limiting my access in some way. I don't know the extent, though." She shrugged with a vile frown. "I *did* manage to ban Albion and Jalako, though."

Through a grumbly breath, I dropped my forehead to rest in my trembling hands. "That's one headache out of the way."

"Check the list of administrators!" Bogen ordered.

"On it!"

After a couple of clicks and keyboard strokes, there was a pause. Seconds later, Tana covered her mouth with her hands as her eyes grew wide.

"That doesn't look good," Kay hesitantly responded.

Bogen was the only one with some semblance of a grin on his face. "I was right, wasn't I? Jalako's name's on there?"

"Worse."

Bogen's brow hung low. "How…?"

Wordless Tana turned the laptop to face us. To our surprise and horror, three new administrators had appeared on the list: Deserter A, Deserter B, and Deserter C.

"Screen-cap and post a warning, now!" Bogen barked, and then wasted no time in fixing his stress and ire towards me. "Brigg, I'm sorry, man, but your slip at the Radio Tower keeps coming back to piss me off!"

I exhaled with deep regret. "Yes, I know; I'm sorry!"

"What can we do about it?" Kay inquired, hoping to shift the conversation to something productive.

"Since Eliza is able to manipulate the forums, we may have to make another one."

"Making a new one would take some time," Tana announced. "I don't think we have the luxury of spare time at this point."

"Did you post the warning?"

She nodded. "Yes."

I took a few deep breaths. "Good. Hopefully, the Causes will act on this news—"

Tana suddenly screamed. "No!"

"What now?" Bogen growled in frustration.

"My warning was deleted!"

All of us were silent for a few minutes as we took in what it all meant. Eliza had the entire Cause forum compromised. Thinking into it, having Eliza control the forum was significantly worse than having it wiped from the Network. This was clearly another one of the Fifteen's attempts at breaking down the Causes. Once again, the Deserters were on the front lines, under the direct command of Eliza this time.

"This is a nightmare!" Tana sobbed.

"We're screwed!" Kay added. "The Causes won't be able to keep up with the Fifteen if we have a panel of Deserters as administrators."

"Ironic." Dice hummed.

I turned to him. "How can you be so casual right now?"

"The forum that brought the Causes together is going to be the one to break them up. How can you not find it ironic?" Something about his pained eyes and the weak shrug of his shoulders made it seem like he was remorseful for being thoughtlessly smug at the worst possible time.

Despite my observation, his words still brought a swelling to my chest. "Shut up!"

Dice raised an eyebrow, reaching into his left pocket for his dice. "Your hostility tempts me so." He pulled his dice out in front of his face, one between each finger as usual.

"Dice!" Kay scolded. "Stop it."

Ignoring her, he continued with a wager. "Total will be even!"

The dice rolled to the floor. The total came up as seven: two threes and a one.

"Ooh," Dice grunted, "you're lucky. I *really* wanted to finish what I had to say. I'm not a cheater, though."

Staying on the main concern, Kay opened up a suggestion. "I'd hate to say it, but we may have to tell the Causes to abandon the forum. As long as Eliza has a set of Deserters in on it, it'll be impossible to plan a move against the Fifteen."

Bogen's robe lifted high behind him as he spun to address Kay. "Sounds like it would be exactly what they want us to do. Why else would they make it so blatantly obvious the three new admins are Deserters?"

"Chalk one up for Bogen!" Dice remarked. "Good call."

It seemed all too familiar to me. "This is what I warned Albion about. Instead of wiping the forum, they've created a plan to put us right where they want us."

"It's like the creation of the Deserters," Kay commented.

"Correct!" I said. "Consider how long ago I said the name 'Cause' to Naro."

Bogen thought back. "It was about…"

Kay had the answer. "It was three weeks ago…almost."

"Three weeks," I repeated. "It took the Fifteen *three weeks* to act on how to use my leak against us." I let my words linger in the air for a second before passing my next thought. "I have a feeling the Fifteen know *every* move we can make from here."

Dice took the floor. "So if we abandon the forums, the Fifteen have us divided with no medium for communication. If we make a new forum, the Fifteen follow us. And if we keep using the same forum, the Fifteen will be ahead of us at every turn by knowing every move the Causes will make."

It was a heart-wrenching sensation to hear every one of our immediate options could be stifled by the Fifteen's careful planning. "Each possibility is covered. They got us," I grumbled.

Bogen growled, "Then we'll have to go with the least painful option." He called for Tana's attention.

She looked to him. "Yes?"

The usually-energetic youth appeared torn. "Start sending private messages to some of the other Causes. Let them know what's going on and tell them to stop accessing the forums. We're going to abandon it."

I gasped at the news. "What about Hatcher?"

Bogen was quick with his answer. "If he ever *does* post again, I'm sure the Deserters will delete the post, like they did with Tana's warning."

"I'm also going to have to tell all of the Contacts they're out of a job," Tana said.

"What are we going to do about Jalako's post?" I asked.

"There's nothing we can do about it," Bogen hissed. "Let's hope the Causes see through her arguments."

Dice suggested, "It wouldn't hurt to read the replies."

I exhaled. "It might, but why not?"

We read what few replies had already hit the topic. It was uplifting to see a couple of Causes still siding with us. However, those who agreed with Jalako dismissed those people as lost and confused about what was best for Eden.

Reading the thread helped us to finally see the true separation of the Causes. Going through the replies was like watching the structure the Producers built falling apart in our own hands.

"The forum is now a total loss," Bogen muttered.

"To make matters worse," Dice added, pushing his glasses up, "we won't know what this will do to the Causes around Eden until we get Mika back and return to civilization."

"Right," I agreed. "The only people we can trust now are each other, Dylan, and Mika."

I felt Kay's hand rest on my shoulder. "Yeah, let's try to keep our head in the game. We can't let this bring us down." She opened my pocket, took Mika's picture out, and handed it to me.

It took me several minutes to calm down and get my thoughts back on track. I repeated to myself in barely audible whispers,

"Mika and Dylan come first. This is the path."

I stood and paced around the car, collecting my thoughts. The post from Jalako and the forum takeover were an overwhelming combination to press through. It was going to take a clear head to get any leverage against the Fifteen.

At one point, I stood alone at the end of the car opposite the others. I took a moment to greet my reflection one more time. I looked into my own eyes and mustered a confident smirk. Once again, I spoke to myself. "Stay strong, Causes. They have our answers." I smiled and nodded at how right it all sounded.

"This is the path we've chosen...

...and we have what it takes to see it through to the end."

Episode 7: End of the Road

Traitor.

The word passed through my thoughts every minute. The five of us were distraught by the feeling there was no end in sight for the Causes' hard times. With the latest move by the Fifteen fresh in our minds, we had no choice but to abandon the Cause Forum.

There was no telling what the future held for us. The only thing we were certain of was our mission to retrieve Mika from the Terra Sector and team up with Dylan. From there, the only thing to make matters worse for our party was to encounter complications during our switch in Lucra.

Surprisingly, there were no Gray Police in sight and the station itself was effortless to navigate. It was the only sigh of relief I could breathe through the turmoil taking place otherwise.

We took solace in the fact we were physically distant from hostile forces on all sides. It gave us the space we needed to decide for ourselves when it was safe to approach the front of the Revolution again. With Dylan on our side and Mika back in our hands, we would find ourselves in a better position to re-establish our influence. Until then, our focus was Mika, Dylan, and nobody else. We would worry about Jalako, the Revolution, and the Fifteen later.

We did our best to stay relaxed as we made our approach to the Terra Sector.

Day 91

I

We were on our trip to Terra on the Land's End Rail. The stretch of railroad's name derives from it being the closest rail to Eden's outer wall. The tracks run as one huge curve and remain an equidistant twenty-five kilometers from the border of the Zica Sector; and a total of forty kilometers from Eden's outer wall. This was as close as anybody could get to Zica and still feel safe.

The five of us found ourselves engrossed in a conversation about the borders beyond our reach. Talking about it with the others was a good way to get my mind off of everything for a while. Soon enough, we were throwing the conversation in all sorts of directions. It soon became apparent we were avoiding topics of anything Revolution-related. The long trip became grounds to completely forget our worries. We even chose not to check the forum again until we arrived in Terra.

In time, we came upon a section of Land's End Rail passing through the Gova Sector. Memories raced back to me of the last day I had spent alone. Gazing upon the forests and fields had me look back to those days I spent surviving in it.

Without looking directly to her, I posed a question to Kay, "I was wondering, why were you on the train the day we met?"

She stared at me for a moment as if she would have never expected such a question from me. "The group I was traveling with had abandoned me. So, I chose to take a ride through the Gova Sector to blow off steam and clear my head. Why?"

"Curious, really," I said. "Any idea why?"

She raised an eyebrow and copped an attitude. "Well, if the way we 'got along' the day we met was an indication—"

I raised both of my hands. "Say no more, say no more!"

Kay's voice became sarcastic with her upcoming rhetorical response. "Any other questions?"

I answered her anyway. "Not really. I was remembering how it all started for us."

Bogen seemed curious. "You camped in Gova, too?"

I answered by going back over the events of the sixty-third day of the Revolution. It spiraled into everyone sharing stories of the Revolution's early days. It was an enlightening conversation, allowing us to learn more about each other and how we handled situations. My stories were not nearly as useful since I had spent the first sixty-two days of the Revolution by myself. Any tips on teamwork were better off left to everybody else.

Kay had a lot to say since her original motivation was to help protect the women taking part in the Revolution. Our arguments before the Great Walk only served to fuel her self-acclaimed role as the protector of young ladies across Eden. Her time in the early days of the Revolution was spent keeping a wary eye on the men who accompanied women; making sure they behaved themselves.

Tana and Bogen had quite the story too. The two of them spent almost the entire Revolution together. However, there was only one point in time when the two were separate due to a train boarding incident. During that mishap Tana met Dylan in person. Tana was quick to point it out.

Everyone seemed to be open about their tales except for Dice. Unfortunately, Dice's input made me a little uneasy about what his true motives were. I remembered him mentioning an agenda he had. When I paired that up to the other things he was saying then, it made me skeptical of the amount of loyalty he would show us.

What he said before accepting the Honorary Producer title felt like a warning, but I was not about to drag everybody's mood down by putting Dice in the hot seat about it. I let it go for the time being and chose not to be surprised if he were to dismiss himself again.

II

After a long, relaxing trip, we finally arrived in the Terra Sector at 8:30 pm. A cloudy sky and a vast plain greeted us as we stepped off the train. Stations in the Terra Sector were only small, unmanned platforms for entry and exit. Thus, even upon our arrival, the five of us were the only people in sight of each other.

Twilight was fading fast into darkness.

According to Tana, our destination, farmhouse D24, was about thirty-five kilometers west-southwest of the train platform. Unfortunately, that put a lengthy trek ahead of us. Our chances of reaching D24 before we collapsed from exhaustion seemed slim.

Kay issued a complaint. "It's a shame it's so cloudy tonight. We'd have a great view of the stars out here."

I was prompted to look up and observe the overcast sky. Gusts of wind howled past us as clusters of clouds traveled along. The grass and plants surrounding the road rustled about, creating a cacophonic sound both soothing and eerie.

Unsettled, the five of us chose to stick close, prepared to run if the need came about.

In the far distance, we spotted a windmill churning; a windmill generating power to the nearest farmhouse, C28. "I have an idea," Bogen announced. We should see what we can do about staying the night in any of the houses we see on the way."

Dice appeared to see the potential in Bogen's suggestion. "If we can stay, great; if not, we press on."

A bolt of lightning streaked across the sky, closely followed by another. Dice jumped up, yelped, and dashed far ahead of us.

All of us ran to keep up with him. Kay found Dice's behavior unlikely and amusing. "Dice? Afraid of lightning?"

I smiled with her. "It would seem so."

"He's the last person I'd expect to be afraid of anything," Tana added.

"Look," Bogen interrupted. "We can tease him about it later. Let's see if we can get indoors for now."

"Sounds good to me!" I chuckled, anticipating roasting Dice.

Exhausted from running the rest of the way, we had to pace ourselves up the porch stairs of the quaint little farmhouse.

The house was built like any other housing unit in Eden. The only difference was the power being generated by wind rather than sun panels or water turbines. It was plain, painted white, and had no second floor.

"Man," I said, "for belonging to farmers, these houses sure don't look special to me."

Dice spoke hushed, "Remember: most farmers are also Labor Field prisoners."

Tana had a different focus. "I'm going to contact Dylan and tell him we're in Terra."

"Yes, tell him," Bogen said with a grin. "As for me…" He approached the door, took a deep breath, and knocked.

Tana sat on a chair on the porch as the rest of us watched the door, awaiting an answer. We could hear footsteps coming from the other side. I held my breath in hopes of being welcomed without any trouble.

Bogen took a step back as the door creaked open. The eye of a young girl peeked through to examine us. The girl was surprised to see five strangers at her door. "Can I help you?"

Bogen was lost for words. He was expecting someone much older. "One moment…" Bogen pulled us all into a huddle.

Before he could say anything to us, the girl opened the door further and poked her head out. "Are you rev'lutionaries?"

We all stood still, counting on Bogen to cover the inquiries.

As he turned to answer, she cut him off. "You look like it."

The little girl opened the door the rest of the way and stepped onto the porch in a slow and wary fashion. All the red-headed tyke was wearing was a long, white children's nightgown and a pair of worn, gray slippers.

Bogen exhaled, figuring nothing was going to get past this new face. He answered her honestly. "Yes, we are revolutionaries."

The girl paced around the porch, keeping her eyes fixed on us and her arms to her sides, keeping her distance. Gentle glances of curiosity paired with a subtle twitch in her foot, as if she were ready to sprint back inside and lock the door in seconds. "I've heard of the rev'lutionaries, but never seen any. Are you all lost?"

Bogen took a few steps toward her and began to speak. But the child was not inclined to trust us. We failed to notice she was holding a long knife in her left hand, which she had been keeping close to her side. She brandished it. "Stay back!"

All of us backed away with our hands raised. Tana, thinking quickly, pulled up evidence of our agenda from her laptop.

Bogen stammered the situation from our cowering position on the porch. It took a few moments, but the girl was receptive.

Tana stepped forward with her laptop screen loaded with maps and messages from the past several days. "See, this is what brought us here." Tana stepped out to the young stranger with the screen facing out. The two girls sat down in the middle of the porch, and Tana walked her through the bare bones of our story; not divulging too much.

Kay was under the impression that getting the young girl to warm up to us was a mission best left to the ladies. She walked over and spoke with her. "What's your name?"

The little one answered without taking her eyes off of the laptop screen. "Amanda."

"Are you alone here, Amanda?"

"Well, my mommy took the carriage to go get food for the

house. I'm worried. She's been gone for two days now."

Tana went on to ask, "What about your dad?"

"My daddy left a couple of hours ago. He went to his friend's house, house B27. He said I'm in charge until he gets home."

Kay and Tana continued to take turns coaxing Amanda into trusting us. To nobody's surprise, Amanda was instructed by her father not to invite anybody into the house. Before she could turn us away, though, it began to rain. Having heard enough about our situation, Amanda did not have the heart to leave us out in the storm. She went against her father's instructions and invited us into her home.

III

We tried to take up as little space as possible as we made ourselves at home in C28. Amanda gave us the living room to use as our base of operations.

The room was modestly furnished with three flower-motif chairs and a big, mauve sofa. It remained adequately lit by two wall-mounted lamps on both sides of the brick fireplace. The beige carpet was firm, but a little old with a single stain near the side of the table in the center of the room.

Amanda took a liking to Kay and Tana. The girls wasted no time stepping into the kitchen to fix a meal. All of us understood how deprived we had been of a home-cooked dinner. Kay and Tana fought their own exhaustion for everybody's enjoyment.

As for the men, we were busy making sure Dylan and Mika were still in position for retrieval. Everything regarding their situation was as we left it. According to Dylan, Mika was still having complications walking. Thankfully, the owner of the farmhouse was being sympathetic. Dylan and Mika were trying everything in their power not to wear out their welcome.

We kept our reply to Dylan's latest message simple: "See you tomorrow at D24."

Kay called out from the kitchen. "I hope you guys don't mind, but Amanda isn't allowed to cook any of the meat in the house!"

The three of us groaned as our dreams of savoring a slab of beef were washed away by the unmistakable scent of vegetables. Dice sneered in jest. "Woman! You best be cookin' me a steak if you know what's good for you!"

My jaw dropped and I laughed. "He did *not* say that!"

Kay fired back, "You'd best be grateful I'm cookin' at all!"

Bogen patted Dice on the back as his giggling came under control. "I like this guy! He's funny!"

Dice smirked, his eyes focused on the laptop. "Only when I feel like it, trust me." He turned to a serious note. "I'm going to check on…*the* topic."

"You mean Jalako's drivel?" I grunted in spite.

"Yeah." It was muttered with apology dripping from his tone.

Frustrated, I stood from the sofa and took a seat on one of the chairs at the window. "I don't really want to think about her right now. But if there's anything important, let me know."

"Sure thing, we got'chya." Bogen sighed.

I thought of the next day's itinerary. In doing so, I caught something none of us had thought of. I felt it would be senseless to have all five of us go to D24. Since Dylan was already imposing on another man's house, I was sure the last thing the man would want was too much added company.

The thoughts also presented me with an opportunity for some time to myself, as well. I could already smell the open plains and fresh air of the Terra Sector. I could already hear the birds chirping and the gentle breeze, uninterrupted by chatter of fear and discord.

It was too appealing to pass up. "Hey guys," I said, "how about I make the trip by myself tomorrow?"

"Oh, no you don't!" Tana objected. "I've been waiting to see

Dylan again. I'm going there whether you like it or not."

Kay countered, too. "Why would you go alone?"

I kept my motive to relax hidden. "What's the point of all of us going there when we're going to come back here, and then double back to the train anyway? Plus, the guy living in D24 probably isn't gonna like his house crowded with too many people. If it's only me and Dylan—"

Tana cut me off. "And me!"

"And Tana, we can take turns carrying Mika back starting from the moment we get there."

Bogen replied, "Then I'll go with Tana."

Dice argued, "Actually, I'm not sure if Mika would be comfortable with you. Out of all of us, Brigg has known Mika the longest. Although it's not by much, I still have a point, right?"

"Maybe." Bogen did not seem convinced.

Dice pressed. "The only time you met Mika was back at the Radio Tower. You didn't stay long afterward. I wouldn't be too sure about what kind of impression you left on her."

Nodding and considering Dice's point, Bogen directed his glance to me. "I'm not really seeing any reason we can't do it Brigg's way, then. Anyone?"

"I've got nothing," said Kay as she prepared plates. "I don't mind taking the time to relax as long as we're not imposing."

Amanda replied while grabbing flatware. "You're not. It was getting boring here by myself. And I want to hear about the Revolution some more."

"Trust me, kid," Dice said, reclining. "We've got stories."

Bogen announced with comfort. "It's settled then. Tana, it's going to be you and Brigg tomorrow, okay?"

"All right!" she squeaked.

Kay added, "The rest of us will stay here and watch over Amanda. Hopefully, her parents aren't in a rush to get home. We're not looking for any trouble, you know?"

The last few details were put into place over our dinner of string beans and herb mashed potatoes. The plan was set up and everything looked good to go. I was going to travel to D24 the next day, rain or shine, so Tana prepared accordingly to accommodate her laptop.

With a long walk ahead of us, Tana and I turned in early on the sofa, resting our heads on the armrests. The others stayed up for a little while longer since they were under no obligation to join us on the trip to D24.

Tomorrow was going to be a big day for all of us as it would complete our team. Combined, the seven of us would get the Causes back on the right track.

Day 92

I

The afternoon sky was still filled with clouds as Tana and I continued our walk across the Terra Sector's open fields. Although Tana was brimming with energy at the thought of Dylan, my good spirits were fueled by thoughts of retrieving Mika.

Kay, Dice, and Bogen were on my mind as well. It did not feel right traveling without them even though my decision to do so was voluntary. Sure, I was going to rest for a little while once we reached the other house, but I had every intention of returning to the others by the end of the day. The peaceful image of the three of them resting up was foremost in my thoughts as Tana and I babbled back and forth to each other about nothing in particular.

The friendly, mindless banter between us was interrupted as another windmill became visible. Rhythmic galloping was closing in on us, accented by the light squeak of a rusty wheel. It was not coming from only behind us, though. The noise grew louder and seemed to be coming from several directions at once.

Within moments, and without giving us a second to run, three horse-coaches had surrounded us. Two Gray Police officers emerged from each coach and stood at attention.

Tana and I took a back-to-back position and prepared to defend ourselves. "How did Gray Police find us all the way out here?" Tana asked.

"Your guess is as good as mine," I replied, defeated.

After a pause, I heard a voice familiar to me. "You know, Brigg, you look helpless standing there like that. I figured the big hero you are would be more confident. I'm disappointed."

There was no mistaking it. Even though Dylan managed to get Mika away from him, Doctrine—*Sydney*—stayed in the Terra Sector and waited for me to show up. Clad in a broad-shouldered gray cloak and sporting a new, near-bald haircut, he revealed himself from the coach nearest to me. He took slow, methodical steps toward us. His posture and garb were an intimidating display, forcing me to keep my focus fixed on him.

Unfortunately, the Gray Police took advantage of my lack of attention to Tana. Her shriek pierced the air and shook my nerves. I turned for a split-second to see her being dragged away before turning back to keep my eyes on Sydney.

After Tana was restrained and taken into a coach, the action stopped for a brief moment. The Gray Police were eyeing me up as if they were all going to dogpile me the second I moved. My eyes darted in every direction. Panic and fear crept into my heart, gradually replacing any hope.

The only thing I could think of was to feign accepting defeat and play it by ear from there. I exhaled, stood straight, and decided it was time to use what I knew about him against him. Sydney liked to win arguments and liked to gloat. In some ways, he was like Dice, except Sydney usually agreed with me. If I could bait him into talking too much, it could give me space to think of the next step. "If you're going to capture me, save everyone's time by sparing the melodrama and do it."

"An important moment like this deserves a little flair don't you think so?" Sydney's mocking confidence was infuriating enough to dispel my fears. I clung to the anger, feeling deep within that I would need to unleash it soon.

To stall, I asked, "How did you find me all the way out here?"

"If there was any one thing I knew about you—" he explained, taking a few more slow steps toward me, "—it was Mika's safety being your biggest priority. I don't know why; maybe Kay's right, huh? You can admit it if she is."

My eyes flicked left and right, flashing glances at the surrounding officers. "I told her I'd help find her dad. It's as much about her safety as it is my word."

"Right, right. We're all trying to make good on our deals and promises made."

"'We?' What promises have *you* made to anyone?"

He pointed to me with a relaxed arm. "The deal I made to flush you out. And I gotta thank Mika because she made it *really* easy!" The teeth he flashed in his vile, haughty smirk looked temptingly punchable.

His words felt like an invitation, so I took it. "Threatening a lost, young girl because you can't get the job done yourself? Classy; a pinnacle of chivalry, you are! Paxus smiles upon you!"

He was so caught up in what he had to say to me, his massive display of ego turned my remark into little more than useless noise. "When I saw Mika get off the train, it was like time froze. The perfect little pawn. I knew she was the key to luring you out into the open." He spread his arms wide, presenting the Terra Sector to me. "You can't get more out in the open than this, eh?"

I dreaded what intentions lurked beyond this conversation. "That's why you brought her all the way to Terra?"

"Oh, there's more to it."

I scoffed. "Obviously."

Sydney circled me like a vulture. "I have to hand it to you, Brigg. Not only did you come here exactly as I planned, but you also brought me the Producers' personal Contact." A dark chuckle pushed out in a huff. "Are you really the traitor everyone has been saying you are?"

His question was like a punch in the heart. Kay, Dice, and Bogen were now on their own with no Contact. In haste for a comeback, I spit out, "I'm no traitor; you are! I'd have braved Zica with 'Doctrine.' But not you; not who you are now."

"Wrong!" The might behind his voice echoed across the

plains. "Try harder! It won't take much for Jalako to convince the Causes you 'delivered' her to me. It's a twist we can effortlessly work to our favor."

"How do you know about that!? Tana banned you from the forums!" Right after saying it, I rolled my eyes, remembering all-too late the power Sydney had been mingling around.

His raised his tone, arrogantly gloating. "Uh, hello! Last time I checked, I was working with the Fifteen. Do we forget Eliza can do *anything* with the Interactive Network?"

My teeth bared as the extent of Sydney's betrayal hit me. He was using his knowledge of the Cause with power backed by the Fifteen. With Sydney this many steps ahead, it was as though all of my efforts toward the Revolution were turning out to be in vain. The only thing I could do now was to keep him talking. If by some miracle I managed to escape capture, I would leave a little bit wiser as to how Sydney and the Deserters were operating.

"Remind me, Brigg." He spoke with a wry curl in his lip. "Did I ever tell you where I'm from?"

"Could you tell me how that's even *remotely* relevant to what you're doing right now?"

With a pompous pout and narrowly-spread arms, he leaned back slightly and replied, "You'd find it pretty damn relevant if I told you I'm from South 7, Lucra, right?"

The words themselves knocked the wind out of me the moment they left his lips. "So...the Great Walk..."

"I've been playing this role since Day Zero, Brigg. I can't be a traitor to the Causes if I never actually was one in the first place." His palms turned up, and he caught my eye with a proud smile. "The ambush on South 7, Lucra was neither a mishap nor a coincidence. The Causes wanted a peaceful protest, but I had a better idea. And ratting out the Causes of my district is what got my foot in the door. Guess my 'anonymous tip' isn't so anonymous now. Oh, well!"

"You *did* NOT!" The blood boiling within me surged me toward him, but the Gray Police matched my steps.

"Oh, I very much *did*! The only thing I didn't tell them about was the Forum, just in case I lost favor with Biktor and had to curry it back up."

With fingernails digging into palms, my clenched fists struggled to restrain themselves from knocking Sydney's jaw off of his face.

He snuck a quick glance at my fists and curled his lip. "In my time working with Biktor I've learned a lot. Having this knowledge makes me understand why we have to bring an end to the Revolution. For Eden's sake, the Causes cannot succeed."

"What's that have to do with me!?"

"Simple," he smirked. "You're the hope of the Revolution. Your name is one on every Cause's lips. Despite Jalako's recent accusations, you still have followers and respect. You have principles, and you're willing to take risks for them. The Causes are happy to see you and Bogen are still out and about. It gives them hope, but hope needs to die if we want any chance at restoring Eden to normal."

Sydney mentioning me being "hope" made me think of the rest of the gang. I had to shift my approach to the situation to keep Sydney from tracking down the others. Taking another glance to the surrounding police, I knew there could be no more stalling. I had to move this forward while keeping his focus solely on me. Getting under his skin seemed like the right thing to speed this up and keep his attention. It was time to piss him off.

I took a deep breath and tried to channel Dice at his most condescending. "All right then," I exhaled. "Like I said: cut the damn drama and take me in. You won your petty victory, but you're still flapping your jaw. Let's get a move on!"

As I was barking at him, he merely stood there, waggling a finger and shaking his head; lips pursed with clear and confident attitude. "I'm afraid you've got the wrong idea." He then turned his head up to the Gray Police and signaled to them. They all piled into the horse-coaches. Within a few moments, the coaches departed. Tana was taken away and the Gray Police were gone.

All that was left was me and Sydney, standing fifteen meters apart from each other. The sounds of the horses galloping and the faint squeak of the carriage wheel grew softer until the gusts of wind and the light patter of rain overtook them.

Sydney and I stood alone in silence.

II

I could feel my hands trembling, shaken by the discomforting hostility spewing from Sydney's unwavering posture. "I—"

"You don't understand," he interrupted. "That's a line of yours all too familiar to me. You didn't understand at the Gateway, and you don't understand now." In an unexpected move, he lowered onto the grass. He stretched his legs out and leaned back onto his elbows, looking inappropriately relaxed. "I came here expecting you to not understand my position anyway."

The look on my face had to have been one of unparalleled confusion. It felt like a mind game to see Sydney go from the sinister Deserter leader he had become back to the Sydney I always knew as Doctrine.

I took a few paces closer to him. He did not move.

I took a few more steps. He continued to be still.

After I took one more step, he looked up and spoke through a slight frown, nearly choking on the words, "Have you ever wanted something so badly you'd give up anything for it?"

I backed up three steps. "What are you talking about?"

Without missing a beat, he replied. "Knowledge."

It intrigued me. "Knowledge? What kind of knowledge?"

"The only knowledge that matters," he replied. "It's the same knowledge that started this Revolution. I want to know why the Fifteen do what they do."

Knowing the mood between us had changed, I sat on the grass. His motives and position came to clarity: he initially mingled online with the Causes to learn the "whys" of Eden and the Fifteen; he deserted them in the beginning for the same goal. I stayed silent, my way of telling Sydney I would be patient and wait for him to organize his words.

"I've been given an offer," he began explaining. "An offer by the Fifteen; an assignment to stop the Revolution by breaking the Causes down from the inside out. As you can see, my methods have been effective so far. We're to the point where Deserters could outnumber the remaining Causes eventually."

"I gathered as much." I growled, expressing frustration about the Deserters as a whole. "So, what happens when you complete this assignment?"

A sinister grin washed away his previously sullen expression. "I will become a member of the Fifteen. You understand, right? They'll read me in when I join them. Then I can change things for the better on the inside." There was almost a desperate plea, like he wanted validation; confirmation he was on the right path.

My mind went blank at that terrifying thought. The Fifteen were pulling out all the stops to end the Revolution without revealing the truths the Causes sought. They had gone as far as to offer a position of power and control in exchange for the dispatching of the Causes.

Sydney had been given an opportunity to be important. To have the truth we all sought, and the authority and rank to do something with it. Judging by his words and expression, he was desperate for it. He was not going to let this chance pass him by.

I felt a raindrop tap me on the head as I asked, "So, why did you send the police away? Why are we here alone?"

Sydney looked to the sky and answered. "I'm not sure if I'm

ready for it. Being a member of the Fifteen would require me to do a lot of things I don't agree with. Biktor's role as a member of the Fifteen is a pretty loaded position. Nobody with any sense of a solid conscience would seek to take his seat. The power and knowledge, however...are far too tempting to turn away from. So I'm at a bit of an impasse; especially considering the things he's tasked me with today and in the coming weeks."

"Like what?"

He spread his arms out again. His face became overshadowed with humane remorse. "Like this—where we are right now and what we're about to do."

"Do?" I was getting annoyed with the cryptic talk. "Can you stop dodging it and tell me what is going—"

Sydney interrupted, slamming his fists into the ground. "I was sent by Biktor to kill you, damn it!" He lowered his head and repeated softer. "Brigg, no, Dartmouth...I have to kill you."

I crawled backwards to distance myself. A familiar mix of fear and anger charged me with adrenaline.

He raised his head to look at me. "Once we get rid of the Causes, we'll only have to focus on ridding Eden of the Zealots. The citizens of Eden never saw reason to bring harm to the Causes following the Producers' rules. But with the passive Causes out of the picture, we can turn the Gray Police loose to take care of the Zealots as they see fit. This will bring about the end of the Revolution and will open the door to restoring peace and order." He drew his finger to point at me. "You, Dartmouth, are one of the keys; one of the few who are keeping the Causes united. You're still that hope. Please understand: the Revolution needs to end, man! Eden won't be able to handle it if the Causes win."

The shiver in his voice was of distinct urgency. He had already made that point, but the way he was relaying it now brought dread and curiosity forward. "Okay, Sydney. You've gotta tell me why."

His head swayed with frantic shaking. "No way. It's

information entrusted to me. If I'm going to be a member of the Fifteen, the secrets stay with me."

I had a feeling it wasn't going to be easy. Conceding to his position, I got back to the topic of his mission. "So, how do you plan on doing this?"

Sydney stood as I followed to my feet. There we were again, standing about fifteen meters apart. "I'm getting a little sentimental, but don't let it fool you," he warned. "I have every intention of ending your life here in this field. The only thing you can count on now is that I'm giving you a fighting chance."

I had the briefest flash of my father taunting me to fight back. "That doesn't make sense! Why even give me a chance?"

He tugged at his gloves, then pulled off and discarded them. "This is where my fate is decided. If I kill you, I get to become something greater. If you kill me, then I won't be around when the carnage sends Eden into total ruin, nor will I live with the guilt of ending more lives after yours." His voice cracked as if he had lost all composure. "I'll be honest, man: I hate this. I really hate this. I want this spot, but had no idea what it would cost me."

I had to try one more time. "Are you sure you have to do this? Is there really no other way?"

"Biktor won't accept my failure today. I'm already on thin ice for hiding the Forum from him. This is how he wants me to prove my loyalty." He removed his cloak and a strong gust of wind sent it flapping away. The rain picked up, making the grass slick, and moistening the dirt to mud.

Sydney's clothing was a show of preparedness. His sleeveless shirt appeared to be padded and his black pants were snug to avoid being grabbed by the leg. Most telling were his heavy, thick-soled boots. The thought of being kicked by his monstrous footwear was enough to tell me I wanted this fight on the ground. "I'm sorry our loyalty to each other had to end this way, Dartmouth. This is it, man. One of us leaves here alive. I'll take it either way and accept my fate!"

I had seen this sick sort of psych-up before: it was dad, talking himself into taking things out on me and my siblings. The difference was that Sydney only had about ten kilograms on me.

Sydney hunched down for a moment then dashed straight at me. He loaded up for a big swinging punch. I was quick enough against such a poorly-broadcast attack. I dodged to my left and hooked his elbow with my arm. Spinning around and behind him, I shoved my elbow into his back while kicking the back of his knee. He fell forward onto his hands and knees.

I hunched down behind him, balled my fist, and hammered it into his temple. With that strike, something inside me snapped. Clearly, home life conditioned my ability to take a beating, as well as dish one back. I had a lot to work out.

Kay's accusations.

Dice's insolent taunts.

All the times in the past where I felt alone and abandoned.

All the humiliations my father visited on me for as long as I could remember.

Mostly, critically, the betrayal of a friend. Not only to me but to everything we believed in together.

These thoughts were as much fuel as it was distraction. While I was dwelling on them, Sydney threw an elbow to cover-up from my fists. His padded shirt cushioned a blow I attempted on his kidney. I tried to flatten him to the ground by punching his arms, nearly cracking the bones in my left hand on a metal plate near his elbow. All it did was anger me more. He rolled off another temple shot, getting his knee between my legs to shove me away.

The rain trickled from my hair, with a drop crawling right into my ear. It caused my entire head to twitch as reflex tried to shake it out. My eyes stayed fixed on Sydney, trying not to allow that moment to create an opportunity for him. I was backpedaling while shaking my head to the side, but Sydney sprang to his feet and advanced with fervor.

My heart jumped to alert. Ignoring the discomfort in my ear, I dashed into him again; he stopped and braced for me. I tackled him, but he stayed active on the ground. What few punches I could land through his rolling and dodging met with the ground behind his head or the padding along his forearms. I was not doing much damage to him, and my whole torso tingled as if to tell me of the energy I was wasting in my fury.

Sydney managed to get his knees to his chest, and used his legs to push me off again. I was tired, and slower to stand this time. The rain started getting heavier, and I was gasping for air. I pulled my hair back and patted it down, then swiped my hands down my face to refresh my view of the field.

I noticed the weather was giving Sydney more of an advantage than I had thought. My eyes were forced shut as bursts of strong winds blasted my face with raindrops. I tried to circle around him to get the wind out of my face, but he matched my steps with the seemingly-infinite space behind him.

"I told you I was prepared." He pointed toward the sky. "Didn't expect rain, though." He put one leg farther in front of the other, presenting himself as a smaller target. His hands were up and ready to cover his face. "Don't blink now." He took careful, deliberate steps toward me as my stance mirrored his.

Sydney was fighting like a true athlete, while I appeared more like some stoned-out hack at a jayda lounge, desperately clinging to a purpose. He had a bit more muscle and the damn protective gear, but I had a wider reach and had clearly been in more fights. I knew, though, the most important comparison was the one we could not physically see. Sydney had the promise of prestige and knowledge. I, however, feared for the life and safety of my friends and the Causes. And for me, this fight was not only for my life, but I had to prove to myself I was not as weak as my father had made me believe.

As Sydney drew near, I blinked and swiped the rain off my eyes. He rushed in to attack, but I took a wide, half-blind sidestep and swung at his face, knowing full-well he was going to use those damn pads on his forearms to block them. Sure enough, my fists slammed right into the padding. I squinted through the rain, waiting for the right opening. As Sydney prepared to swing back, I struck him with a full-strength right hook. I was too quick for him to block this time, and my fist smashed right into his jaw, whipping his head sideways. His eyes wandered aimlessly.

This was the opening. I reached deep within to find every thought and emotion that could add fire to my fists. I thundered into him, throwing a flurry of hooks, crosses, body shots, and uppercuts. As his face started to bleed, it felt disturbingly good; right, even! My soul broke free in a raging, otherworldly cry as my arms hooked and swung with complete impunity.

Sydney stumbled away and shouted in a gasp as he flopped to the ground. "I'm sorry!"

An apology? At this time? It ripped my mind into an inappropriate moment of pause to my violent outburst.

Although I was breathing hard, dripping with rain, and near total-exhaustion, I was standing over Sydney like my father over me, and *I liked it.* With it, though, I felt nothing in my entire life had ever been more draining. I took the opportunity to finally circle him and put the wind to my back.

"I'm sorry," he repeated as he flung a clop of mud in my face. "I can't let you win."

The mud was thick enough to knock my head back. It splattered sloppily, nestling around my eyes with some going up my nose. My rage instantly drained, swelling into fear as I had no idea what Sydney could do while I staggered around, blinded.

My fear was realized as I felt his hands clench around the back of my neck. In the next instant, he drove his knee hard into my gut. Still blinded, I wrapped my arms around his leg and drove my head into his chest. We went down again, with me on top.

"This is the kind of fight I expected from you, Dartmouth. I mean, you don't know when to give up right?" I was out of breath, still too busy clearing mud from my eyes to reply to his pointless banter. He used the opportunity to grab my left arm with both his hands and twist. In order to stop the pain he was inflicting on my elbow, I was forced to roll. He anticipated and followed to reverse our positions.

Now he was on top. However, he was between my legs. In this position, it was easier to squirm around to rob his punches of power, and the rain made it easier to clear the mud from my face. Sydney's bulk and quick perception made him much more formidable. I could only imagine what it would have been like if Sydney had had any decent fighting experience behind his actions and motives.

After a few glancing blows, he kipped himself back and stood. I was able to get an eye open to see his right fist balled up and reared back. Sydney's left hand was spread wide, coming straight for my neck as he came down for his attack.

Aligning my hand, I managed to intertwine my fingers into his left hand and give it a clear, savage twist. The bones were snapping as Sydney yelped. His right hand still got a good shot to my head. I managed a smile through the risky trade-off.

He howled horribly as he jumped back off of me. I stood, spitting out blood. With one more wipe away from my eyes, my vision was restored enough to feel safe. Looking over my bedraggled opponent, I saw the matching black eyes. My left hand pulsed with the splintery twitch of broken fingers. Sydney, however, appeared a lot more broken and a bit more wobbly.

"I've gotta keep at it," I muttered through my labored breathing, shaking the water out of my heavy hair. My feet planted and I dashed forward again. Sydney sprawled his body out in an effort to stop me. I could tell by his stance that tackling him would put me at a disadvantage. In a flash of some of my quickest thinking, I lowered my head upon approach and brought it up hard into a head-butt below his jaw. His mouth slammed shut with a crack, and his body flopped down powerless as though the blow had killed him outright.

Sydney rolled over onto his back, and then stopped moving. His chest throbbed up and down as he heaved through his exhaustion. This was the moment in which I could end him. All it would take was a nice, hard pressure to his throat, and hold it until his breathing would stop.

I paced towards his head, my hands and fingers spreading in preparation; drops of rain streaming from my fingertips. As my feet fell next to Sydney's head, I thought about Mika, Kay, Bogen, and even Dice. They knew I had a temper, but would they accept me as a killer? Even in this situation? Could I accept myself after this? Could I justify it, throwing in my past as a scapegoat?

Was it in me? Could I *really* end another person's life?

I crouched down, easing my hands toward Sydney.

Closer; my fingertips were touching the sides of his neck.

My thumbs pushed in. His body pulsed.

As I pushed harder, a memory of my father strangling me until I blacked out punched through. I recalled the terror; the writhing; the clenched teeth; the fight for one more breath. *I'm really doing this! I'm going to survive! I'm really going to kill him!*

Looking at Sydney's straining face, the thought repeated. Not with fury or victory, but with disgust and panic. *By Paxus, I'm really going to kill him! Stop!*

My arms flew up, instantly releasing his throat. The warmth of tears contrasted with the cold rain on my cheeks. As my throat ejected a jabbering wail, my trembling hands groped the air, gathering raindrops. I let out a distressed shriek as my hands clasped my skull. *I almost did it. I was really gonna do it. I need to stop; I need to breathe. Paxus, Shalynn, Delta, help me!*

I thought back to my time at Kediel Lake; how relaxed and carefree I felt as I let the rain soothe my cares away. Desperately, I wished I could feel it all over again. A harsh rumble of thunder taunted me, telling how oh-so-far away I was from any such calm.

Beaten, exhausted, and praying for reprieve, I wished with every fiber of my being I could once again lie in the grass and quiet my soul. The downpour had a coaxing caress to it, almost compelling me to tilt to my side and rest.

However, I was still coming down from the mental static that whispered of the various justifications for killing Sydney. If I stayed there any longer for any reason, one of us was going to die. I could not stand the thought of either of us winding up on the belt of the Spirit Furnace. Betrayal notwithstanding, he was still a young man with plenty of life ahead of him. It simply wasn't in me to finish the job.

I could not do it; I would not do it. I stood from my crouch, turned around, and walked away.

I got less than a few meters when Sydney called after me. "You know, Dartmouth, there *were* regrets." In total disbelief the tough bastard was still conscious, I spun back to catch his eye. He stayed flat on his back, looking straight up into the sky. His mouth fountained a spray of blood as he coughed his next sentence. "All the lies I had to tell you, friend."

I tiptoed forward. His head turned to the side.

"Back in Pata, everything was falling together. Biktor gave me the jayda; I gave it to Roy. Vade got more clues into the underground porn ring." His voice shuddered and shook through his weakly-flapping lips. "*Everything* was perfect, and you, Kay, and Mika were totally clueless.

"Me being at the Gateway was no fluke either; it was all arranged. The Pata police left after Biktor came to pick me up. The only thing that wasn't planned was when I started to grow a conscience again."

His confession rocked me; disturbed me. For a brief second, I was once again trying to figure out who it was I was fighting.

"I'm glad I warned you back at the Gateway, Brigg. It gave me one last chance to redeem myself. However, it took too long for your role in my plan to come to fruition."

"Will you shut up!?" I hollered, pulling my hair back again. "I don't care. You screwed up! All right, I get it!"

Sydney said nothing more. He wiggled his hand in a gesture that demanded a response. I had nothing to lose from hearing him out, feeling his confession might help later. I threw the motion to speak back to him. "What plan?"

"You were next," he responded. "You were the next person on my list to bring to the Fifteen and convert to our side. I wanted to do it by gaining your trust in real life; not only on the forums. I thought I could gradually convince you to come to our side. That was why I invited you to Roy's. You were in the right place at the right time when I set out to find my next target."

"What made you change your mind?"

He turned his head to the other side, spitting out another mouthful of thick blood. "Deep down, I couldn't help but feel like I should be helping the Causes. I did what I did for the guarantee of obtaining the knowledge the Fifteen possess. I was searching for the truth, but I chose the wrong path. Now, I'm here on the ground, in this field, ready to die by the hand of the man I wanted as a partner."

Thunder rumbled as the rain lightened up for a moment. I took a couple more steps forward, not quite trusting he did not have one last trick.

"Now," Sydney continued, "the only chance to end my walk down this road is here and now. Come on, Dartmouth. You can't leave me here alive. I lost. If I live after losing here, the role I'll play for the Fifteen will kill me slowly, and I'd rather die fast; now, if possible, by your hand. We were friends. So do this last favor for me: do *not* let me leave the Terra Sector alive."

It was not in me to give him this satisfaction; he could live with his consequences. I started to walk away again when he wailed out, crying, screaming something to stop me cold: "If you don't kill me *right now*, they will send me to kill Mika! I *swear* to *Paxus* they will!"

I was ready to be the better man until that moment. I was tired from beating him and being beaten in turn, having become a walking series of cuts, bruises, and contusions. I had to dig deep to find the energy to turn around and confront him one more time. This was it; my limit.

While I was still processing the threat to Mika and what it could mean for the others, Sydney rolled over and struggled to his feet. Despite declaring defeat, he appeared poised to engage me one last time. The two of us were unsteady on our feet. So as we neared each other again, the fancy footwork we started off on was nowhere to be seen. Sydney spoke loud and sure. "As soon as the Fifteen realize who her father is, she's as good as dead anyway."

My advance halted immediately, causing me to slip on the wet grass. "Wait, she told you?"

As my brain was blanked from this startling news, I watched unresponsive, staggering to stand upright, as Sydney produced a small knife from a compartment in the sole of his boot. As his answer, he thrust the blade toward my chest, aiming for my heart.

The sting of the slice dealt an unreal burn across my entire left side. The knife slid astray after coming into contact with my vest, preventing it from embedding into my flesh, but tearing it along the way. On sheer reflex and impulse, my right fist hurdled forward at an uncontrolled speed and smashed Sydney square in the throat. In the same instant, I could feel the warmth of blood dripping down.

Sydney wriggled, writhed, and struggled to breathe. He was tapping himself on the stomach and pounding on the ground, desperate for a gasp of air. I picked his knife up out of the grass and threw it as far as I could with what strength I had left. I heaved out a cough of blood and fell to one knee, then to my side, trying to apply pressure to the bleeding slice.

I removed my vest with the intention of tying it around my torso to keep pressure on the cut. The slice through left front pocket caught on my thumb, tearing the pocket off, and spilling its contents onto the wet grass: A piece of parchment, folded, with two one-arna coins wrapped inside it. The parchment, too, was sliced all the way through until it reached the coins; one now-dented, the other one slashed.

As I unfolded the parchment, my face wrinkled and my eyes welled. The half-drawn picture of me was staring back at myself, my own blood staining the left side of the page. Looking down at the coins, I cried, "Looks like I used them for something special, Mika. You did good."

Glancing to Sydney, I saw he had caught his breath but was still collapsed to the ground, trying to get information from him at this point would have been met with a killing blow. I could not chance it. I had to relax and put pressure on my cut.

The caress of the downpour was not enough to ease any of the pain I was feeling. My breaths were short and heavy, and my body broke into a bitter chill. Rain and sweat crept across my open wounds, stinging my nerves. When my head felt light and vision blurred, I fought with all my heart and soul to stay conscious.

But it was not enough.

I mumbled with what breath I could muster. "I guess I'm really going to die here. I'm sorry, gang. I tried. I really tried.

"Stay safe. Mika, find him. And do it quick. You couldn't tell me, but tell _them_, please!"

Vision…

Thought…

Breath…

Everything…

…it all slipped away.

And my world faded to black.

Day ??

I

A gentle, feminine voice called to me. "Dartmouth…"

Is that…Shalynn?

Again, like a song. "Dartmouth~"

All was dark. I was terrified to even open my eyes and barely had the strength to respond. It even hurt to breathe.

The same soothing voice called again. "Brigg…"

My skin was touched with a cloth. The salve on it caused a stinging sensation. My face twitched as a weak groan involuntarily sounded from my throat.

"You know," the voice continued, "Sandra will be pleased to know you're alive."

Alive? Who…?

I heard footsteps as a smooth, casual male voice penetrated the silence. "Let's try opening a window." The sound of curtains being swept to the side rattled within the room, and the light from the sun beamed through the window. All of this helped me to realize somehow, some way, I was still alive. I had survived the battle with Sydney.

I scrunched my face before opening my eyes to see the source of the soft lady's voice. Before I could speak, the young woman giggled. "Remember me? It's me, Zoe. Month of May."

"Zoe…" After a few blinks, the man who entered the room came into view. My eyes grew wide when I first saw him.

His outfit was an easy window to his identity. It did not take any more than the denim pants and matching short-sleeve denim jacket—an all-blue ensemble—to deduce it was Dylan.

His face bore dark, foreboding features; narrow eyes, and his face seemed to exude a sense of self-righteousness. The back of his hair was in a long, thin ponytail while the rest of his hair remained short. My previous mental image of the man faded.

I was excited to see him nevertheless. I wanted to sit up, but Zoe insisted against it. Dylan spoke to me. "Save your energy," he recommended. "Sydney did a good job of beating the piss out of you. You've been out for the past several days. We were afraid you weren't going to wake up."

I spoke one word. "Mika…"

"Bogen and the others have her. She is in good hands now."

I tried to sit up again, but Zoe forced me back down. "Don't move!" she ordered. "You might aggravate your injuries."

There was a lot I wanted to say to Dylan. So I mustered as few words as I could to relay my message. "Tana… caught…"

"Actually," Dylan replied, turning his eyes aside, "there's something you need to know." He paused and looked to me before calling out to the other room. "Tana!"

Tana's voice called back, "Yes, Dylan?"

The breath was ripped from my lungs. There was no way Dylan could have rescued her as well. "How?!"

"Boy, have I got a story to tell *you!*" He laughed with a crooked grin. "I've gotta say you really impress me, Brigg. I seriously didn't expect you to win; I was hoping Sydney would live. Since that's not the case, I have to change my plans up a little bit. Won't be easy, but I can make it work."

My heart grew cold; my very soul was stunned.

Dylan continued, remorselessly casual. "I found it odd Sydney decided not to use these." He took a pair of gloves from his pocket; the gloves Sydney removed before our fight. Dylan dropped them on my leg, allowing me to feel their weight as they sounded a metallic clink. "But he used the knife. I'm surprised.

Tell me, Brigg, was he *that* conflicted about killing you?"

I looked to Zoe, then to Tana and Dylan again; completely stuck for how to respond.

He picked the gloves back up and tossed them to the corner of the room. "Still not getting it? Sydney give you brain damage?"

I closed my eyes and turned my head to the side. "So *you* weren't really a Cause either, were you? Or you 'had a better idea' like Sydney did?"

"We can start there. At least I sense you'll understand me."

I flexed a burning scowl. "Well, it's not hard to understand you stabbed us all in the back!" I turned eyes to Tana. "And *you?* Really? How long were you acting to us; the whole time?"

Her only response was a lowered head, gently gritted teeth, and a long glance to the side oozing with guilt.

"Don't be too hard on her, Brigg. She's standing here because she gets what I'm trying to get done. I've got my own way of ending the Revolution so everyone can be happy. The Causes will get their truths, the Fifteen will keep their balance, and the people worried about the God-Spirits' favor can be at ease. Everything'll work out in the end." He shifted to correct himself. "Sure, since Sydney is dead now we have to take a little detour. But that's not going to stop us. Right, Tana?"

Tana answered with guilt in her voice. "Right."

Dylan caught my eye again. "I'm sorry I had to resort to this. Mika's a good kid, and I want her to find her dad. But I can't get on the Fifteen's good side without tying a few knots in the Revolution." He lifted Tana's laptop carrier and patted it twice. "Publicly posting you've killed Sydney has started quite the stir!"

"You lie!" I challenged. "Tana sent a warning to the forums. The Causes have probably abandoned it by now."

"Now, now," Dylan responded, "let's not be stupid. Take a second to remember where Tana is standing. Then try to tell yourself she *really* sent those warnings."

As the truth came to light, my heart raced inside of my chest. Dylan's guiltless rambling and disturbing news allowed despair and rage to completely cloud out rational thought. Against Zoe's advice, I tried to spring from the bed. Unfortunately, my wrists and ankles were shackled.

"You should consider yourself lucky," Dylan euphemized. "You're strapped to a bed. Sydney, however, choked to death on blood and teeth." His attitude was unflinching.

Dylan laughed and thrust my covers off. I gazed at my battered body before turning an eye to him. "Dylan—"

Cocky, he cut me off. "—is going to take really good care of his bargaining chip: you. If you thought the Revolution was out of hand before, you ain't seen nothin' yet! I'll be replacing Sydney and taking lead of the Deserters until I figure out which group I should get rid of first."

I roared with what grams of strength I had in me. "You're insane! Tana, how can you side with him?"

Tana tried to justify her actions in a timid explanation. "I…I understand what Dylan wants to do. What he says is possible. We can find out what is going on with the Fifteen and still—"

I shouted at the top of my voice, "You betrayed *all of us*! Do you have…any…" I stopped as my head started to feel airy.

Dylan consoled her in a warm embrace. "It's all right. As long as you feel we can do this together, there's nothing to worry about. It'll all work out; just like I said it would."

Tana was frozen; her usually-cheerful features now sullied by a state of apology and confusion. She responded to Dylan with little more than a weak hum in her throat. Dylan then kissed her on the forehead and sent her back to the other room.

Dylan brought his attention back to me as Zoe put some of my dressings back in place. "I'll have you know: the only reason your friends are still out there is because I don't think it is fair Mika was never a Cause in the first place. We can't have an innocent kid like her getting wrapped up in the affairs of the Revolution any more than she already is. And while it was good of you and your friends to help her, Sydney and I had to flush you out to stay on good terms with the Fifteen. Sorry it had to turn out this way, but we had to save face."

Empathy towards Mika's situation wasn't what I was expecting from him. "Where is Mika now?"

"I sent her back to your friends at C28. They're probably no longer in Terra at this point. Mika needs to find her dad, but I can't have my hand in the search if it involves helping you and your crew directly. We definitely can't have the Fifteen clued in on who you guys are looking for."

"Wait," I insisted, recalling some of my last thoughts before my blackout. "Sydney said he knew who Mika's father is. Did she tell you, too?"

Finally, something I said gave Dylan a time to pause. Before long, he answered while tapping his forehead. "She did. But it's staying up here. All I can say is: she was right to keep it hidden. That little girl has quite the quest ahead of her. Trust me."

Rage and curiosity formed a strange brew in my gut. "Come on, man; tell me. You've captured me; I'm stuck here. What could it hurt your plan to tell me now?"

"Plenty," he scoffed. "I'm not taking my chances. Give it time; you'll find out. But you're not getting it from me."

Zoe put the cover back over me and excused herself. "I'll go get your bathing water ready, Dartmouth."

"Take your time; he's not going anywhere." He watched Zoe exit the room before excusing himself with one last tidbit. "We'll be transporting you to Exta in a couple of days. All you have to do is sit back and watch the party. Your role in the Revolution now changes at our decision. You might as well enjoy it, though; Zoe's about to give you a full-body sponge bath...you lucky boy, you!" He left, chuckling at his cleverness.

Now alone, I knew it was the end of the Revolution for me. I did not know how it happened, but I survived being a victim of Sydney's destiny. However, being beaten from head to toe was the least of my problems. I was a prisoner, unsure of where I was. I had no idea what Dylan had in store for me. But from what I could discern, he was a man with his own kind of mission.

It appalled and terrified me to see Dylan trying to play the Revolution from both sides. I couldn't even wrap my head around his logic; the idea this was the only way he could get everybody what they wanted. He was taking a tremendous risk with potential to cause everybody a great deal of hardship.

I realized a lot had been going on behind me. Becoming such an important face in the events of the Revolution was my greatest accomplishment and the most important addend of my downfall.

It felt like the enemies of the Causes were not going to stop at Albion, Jalako, Dylan, Tana, the Gray Police, and the Fifteen. There had to have been more out there who would go to greater lengths to end the Revolution for either side.

One thing was certain. Bogen, Kay, Dice, and Mika were in serious danger; especially without Tana on their side. The only thing positive was Dylan's sincerity in announcing Mika's position. I was a bit baffled by Dylan's compassion for her situation. But I was glad it worked to our favor for the time being.

As Zoe returned to the room with the bathing supplies, I saw it as my opportunity for some answers. She took the cover back off me and prepared to wash me down. "I hope you don't mind," she said, almost hesitant, "but I started applying the red gel to your scar."

Stuck where I was, I was forced to throw out my previous mistrust of the salve. Jangling my shackles, I replied, "Well, from what I can see, I'm relegated to following doctors' orders for now. All things considered, I appreciate it."

Zoe nodded as she sloshed a cushy green sponge in the bucket of soapy water. She eased it across my skin, softly speaking. "Dylan is going to present you to the Fifteen. I'm not sure what they'll do with you since you helped Naro in Fanda."

I shook my head, slow and careful. "I doubt they'll show any compassion."

"They may ship you out to the Labor Fields once you recover from your injuries. But there's a lot they can do with you since the Causes still look up to you."

"What happened to you? How did you end up like this?"

"Well," she grinned, lifting my arm to scrub under it, "as you assumed correctly the last time we met, I *was* captured back in the Pata Sector. When I was brought before the Fifteen, Sandra chose me and two other girls to be medics for the Causes. She says her job, as well as ours, is to heal, not to judge."

"So," I wondered, "that would make you a Deserter, right?"

Zoe answered without hesitation. "Yes, it would. The Fifteen have been doing a fantastic job with the captured Causes."

"Is that so?"

She sounded inappropriately excited about the fact she was a Deserter. "Of course." She then shrugged, taking my point of view into concern. "Sure, Sydney was taken under Biktor's wing and well…you know."

My brow rose. "Makes sense…"

"If you remember the broadcast of the meeting, you may recall Sandra saying something about injuries among the Causes being far too much for her to handle."

"Yes, I remember."

"She appointed some of the captured Causes to take care of them." She rinsed and wrung the sponge, then applied it to my chest. "I was here on standby because Sandra knew of Dylan's plan to set you up to fight Sydney. I was sent to care for the survivor: you. Of course, it could have been Sydney. It was a shame how he had to die. Morie was standing by as well to take care of the body of the defeated."

"I had no idea I messed his teeth up so badly."

Zoe comforted the guilt on my mind with her next statement. "Well, Dylan is out there telling everybody you killed Sydney. I believe that isn't the case. Sydney's death was an accident brought on by injuries you inflicted on him, but you didn't inflict an out-and-out killing blow."

I smiled for the first time since I woke up. "Good to know." I took a deep breath and flinched. Expanding my chest had caused me a great deal of pain. As it spread through my body, I recalled many of the strikes Sydney had landed against me, but couldn't tell if I had broken ribs, swollen kidneys, or any other internal injuries. The only clear thing was there was no telling how long it would take me to heal.

Zoe comforted me, situating my pillow and coaxing me to speak no further. "Relax until we get you over to Exta. I have a feeling you're not done with the Revolution yet."

I heeded her instructions, laid back, and shut my eyes, allowing her soothing caresses to wipe my body clean. I tried to calm down and convince myself I would be able to figure something out once I arrived in Exta. Whatever the Fifteen would offer me or do to me, I knew I would have to keep my eyes open for any chance to turn the tide to my favor. Until then, I had to suck it up and come to terms with what had transpired.

I was on my own in the hands of the enemy. With a sense of dire hopelessness, I shed a single tear and quietly apologized to Mika and the others. Considering what I learned about my teammates in the time I knew them, I smiled knowing Mika was in the best of care. Bogen, Kay, and Dice were the best company for her. I huffed in pained amusement, thinking about how it took *this* to finally separate me from Kay. It was a shame, though, as she had finally grown to trust me.

I was praying my friends would not fall victim to the guises and trickery of Dylan and the Deserters. It saddened me to know the danger of the Revolution was now going to be escalated by whatever Dylan had planned. Reflecting on what had happened to me, I feared for the lives of anybody taking part in the Revolution.

Fighting tears, my heart left Mika to the care of the others and accepted this as my fate. There was nothing I could do for the others now. It was up to them to finish what I had started.

Epilogue

Day 92

III – Kay

Bogen called me, breaking my train of thought. "Kay! You've been staring out of the window for the past half an hour!"

I jerked at the sudden sound, having been distracted with my worry for Brigg and Tana. With the way things were at the time, we could not afford to lose any people on our side. Tana's skills with computers and Brigg's quick, analytical thinking were too important to be lost.

Dice laughed in response to Bogen; being inappropriately cheerful under the circumstances. "Maybe it is like you said."

Bogen cocked his eye to him. "How do you mean?"

Dice sauntered over to me with his chin high. "Her concern brings to question what was going on while we were separated."

Although nobody in our group bothered me more than he did, I felt no need to feed into his heckling. I dignified his comment. "We managed to reconcile our differences."

Bogen took a rowdy shot at my reply. "With or without physical contact?"

The two boys yukked it up as if they had been waiting for Brigg to leave to turn their sights on my time alone with him. Knowing what Bogen was implying made it much less funny to me, though.

I remained calm. "If you count the one time I had to slap him in the face, then it would be *with* contact."

"Haha, brilliant!" he merrily roared.

If I had not known any better, I would have assumed Dice and Bogen were trying to use jokes and laughter to ease the tension of the wait. I would have felt the need to join in the antics, had it not been at my own expense.

Little Amanda approached. "What's so funny?"

Since the men appeared to be in a mindset slightly too mature for a nine-year-old, I said, "It's nothing you need to worry about."

"Until you're older." Still chuckling, Dice glanced up to Bogen. There was an uncharacteristic shimmer in his eyes; a familiar one to me; an expression longing for praise I had seen all-too-often on the faces of my sisters. I never thought I would see Dice seeking approval from anybody, but his face clearly read, "How was that; good?"

It was far from me to even consider what the two of them ever talked about in private. My mind was too occupied to have the boys' rowdy comments crowding out what was relevant. I tilted my head in focused disappointment. "Really, Dice!?"

Bogen responded to him, encouraged by my reaction, and put a wrap on any raucous mindsets. "It might've been a bit too far."

Defeated, he leaned into the chair's backrest, relaxed. "Yeah, probably."

The mood in the farmhouse had become a mix of emotions. While we were all nervous about our friends, each of us was expressing our concern in different fashions.

I breathed deep and rolled my eyes upon a realization: Brigg's tendency to overanalyze things had rubbed off on me. It was comforting in a way, yet a tricky thing to accept. It seemed every time I tried to divert my attention, my mind kept reverting back to thoughts of Brigg's safety and what was going on out in the fields of Terra. Soon, the time he and I spent alone invaded my mind.

I sat back at the window and reminisced…

"If you count the one time I had to slap him in the face…"

The one time I had to slap him…

"Are you nervous too…?"

My heart shook as I recalled hearing those words. My hand clenched as I set it on top of my leg. I sighed loudly as I massaged my forehead. "Why did you say *those exact* words, Brigg?" I muttered, wishing he could hear me.

My view of the Terra Sector's open plain was obstructed by the frightening sight of a horse-coach. It drew the breath from me as I scrambled away from the window.

Bogen saw it as well. "We've got company!"

The door to the coach opened to reveal two Gray Police officers. Dice spoke up. "This is the part where we hide, right?"

"It all depends…" Bogen replied.

"On what?"

"If there's anybody else with them." He continued with an observation. "The officers are talking to somebody in the coach."

We waited and watched. Sure enough, one more figure, a young girl in a black dress, stepped out into the rain.

I gasped loud on sight. "It's Mika!"

"No way!" Bogen shouted, coming closer to the window.

Dice was thrown as well but spoke calmly. "What's this all about? And what happened to her clothes?"

"I don't know," I answered. "Maybe Sydney tried to make her a Deserter!"

"Poor kid…" Bogen sighed.

Through the rainfall, Mika hurried to the front door and knocked on it in frenzy. "Something's *definitely* wrong," I growled.

Dice ran to the door. "The police are dropping her off here."

I peeked to the window to see the coach leaving.

Infuriated, Bogen stormed over to the front door with Dice. I followed close behind.

Dice let Mika in. The rushed girl was panting with tears rolling down her face. "Guys…help!"

Bogen was not in the mood for any hesitation. "I thought you were injured? What is going on here?"

Mika answered in a panicked wail of several concise facts. "Dylan tricked all of us! He teamed up with Sydney! Brigg is in trouble! Sydney's gonna kill him!"

"Wait," growled Bogen. "Dylan?!"

She rapidly nodded. "He said he's a Deserter now! What's going on?! Nothing makes sense!"

As Bogen's face distorted in fury, Mika's news slithered into my ear and shot directly to my heart. A sensation of true fear shook my body as the many angles of the predicament tangled themselves in my brain.

A state of shock spread across all of us as Mika continued filling us in through desperate sobs. "Brigg is probably fighting off Sydney right now. I don't know where they are. It was all out in the middle of a field."

Without another second passing, Bogen dashed out the front door. "Let's go! If we head toward D24, we might run into them!"

"On foot!?" I asked, hurried.

Amanda chimed in, knowing this was an emergency. "We have two bicycles on the side of the house. You can use them."

"Thank you," I said. I then turned to Mika to give her a hug and comfort her.

Mika's grip around me was disturbingly soft. Every sniffle and sob from the rattled young girl felt like a pin driving into my chest. "Please, help him," she cried.

I stroked her soaked, blonde hair. "Don't worry, Mika. Everything will be all right."

Deep down, I knew it was a lie. I dreaded to dwell on the thought of Brigg not living to see another day.

Without any further delay, and despite the pouring rain, Bogen and I hopped on the bicycles and pedaled as fast as we could in the direction of D24. "Dartmouth," I mumbled, "if you die today, I swear I will find you out in the Great Beyond and kick your ass! You're not going to leave us hanging here like this and get away with it. You hear me?"

Amidst the countless raindrops trickling down my face, the fresh warmth of a lone tear streamed along. With the panic and fear residing in my heart, I knew that day would be the one to change my views, my hopes, and my life.

Kay will be the next to share her experiences with you in

Wanderlust Seasons: Book Two

Autumn of Fates

www.ingramcontent.com/pod-product-compliance
Lightning Source LLC
Chambersburg PA
CBHW030831110726
47900CB00006B/1841